FIRESTORM
THE SWORD OF LIGHT
BOOK II

AARON HODGES

Edited by Genevieve Lerner
Proofread by Sara Houston
Illustration by Christian Bentulan
Map by Michael Hodges

ABOUT THE AUTHOR

Aaron Hodges was born in 1989 in the small town of Whakatane, New Zealand. He studied for five years at the University of Auckland, completing a Bachelors of Science in Biology and Geography, and a Masters of Environmental Engineering. After working as an environmental consultant for two years, he grew tired of office work and decided to quit his job in 2014 and see the world. One year later, he published his first novel - Stormwielder.

FOLLOW AARON HODGES...

And receive TWO FREE novels and a short story!

https://aaronhodgesauthor.com/newsletter

ALSO BY AARON HODGES

The Sword of Light

Book 1: Stormwielder

Book 2: Firestorm

Book 3: Soul Blade

The Legend of the Gods

Book 1: Oathbreaker

Book 2: Shield of Winter

Book 3: Dawn of War

The Knights of Alana

Book 1: Daughter of Fate

Book 2: Queen of Vengeance

Book 3: Crown of Chaos

The Evolution Gene

Book 1: Reborn

Book 2: Havoc

Book 3: Carnage

Descendants of the Fall

Book 1: Warbringer

Book 2: Wrath of the Forgotten

Book 3: Age of Gods

Book 4: Dreams of Fury

The Alfurian Chronicles

Book 1: Defiant

Book 2: Guardian

Book 3: Conquest

The Swords of Heaven and Hell

Book 1: Darkstrider

The Four Circles

Book 1: Help! My Wizard Mentor Had A Heart Attack And Now
I'm Being Chased By A Horde Of Giant Spiders!

The Untamed Isles

The Path Awakens

FOREWORD

Thank you to everyone I met on the road who encouraged me to continue my writing journey (as well as my actual adventure through Central and South America). I know I would never have completed Firestorm in time without the support of some wonderful people along the way.

I hope you enjoy the finished product!

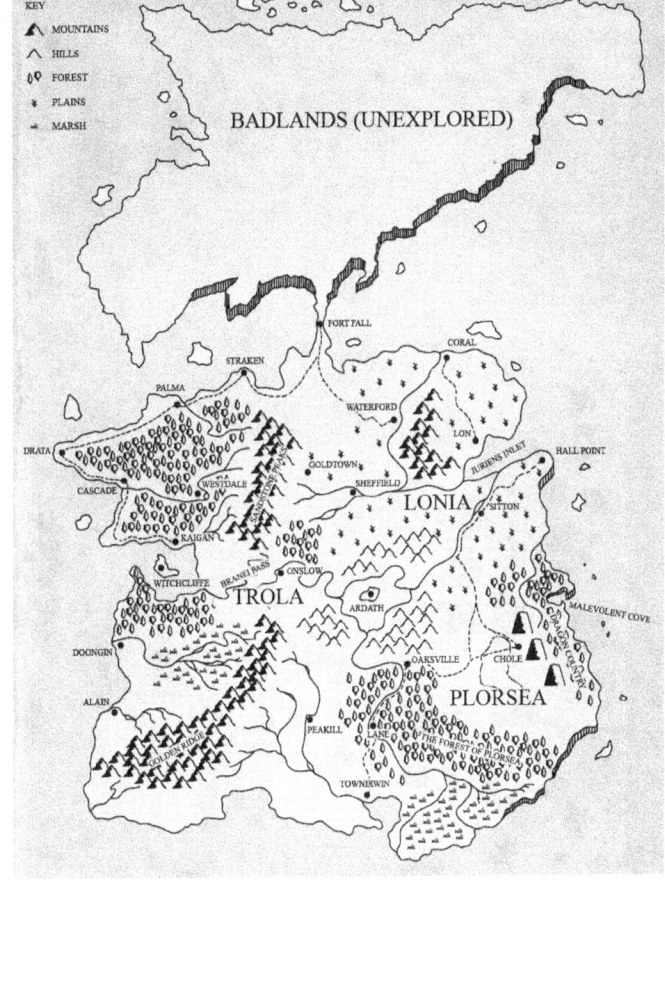

KEY

- MOUNTAINS
- HILLS
- FOREST
- PLAINS
- MARSH

BADLANDS (UNEXPLORED)

FORT FALL

STRAKEN

CORAL

PALMA

WATERFORD

LON

DRATA

GOLDTOWN

HALL POINT

CASCADE

WESTDALE

SHEFFIELD

LONIA

JURIENS INLET

SITTON

KAIGAN

WITCHCLIFFE

BRANFI PASS

ONSLOW

TROLA

ARDATH

MALEVOLENT COVE

DOONGIN

OAKSVILLE

CHOLE

PLORSEA

ALAIN

GOLDEN RIDGE

PEAKILL

LANE

THE FOREST OF PLORSEA

TOWNIRWIN

Home is where your heart is.
And there's no place like home.

PROLOGUE

They appeared as the first glow of the morning sun touched the horizon. Great wings thumped the cool air, golden scales glittering in the dawn's light; one, two, six, a dozen. Bursts of flame licked the treetops as the beasts circled, great eyes staring down at them. Wind whipped about the cove, catching in their golden wings.

Below, the surf roared and waves rushed up onto the black sands. The tang of salt stung the air as a fine mist of sea spray settled on their clothes. A breath of wind whistled through the trees of the coast, carrying with it the bite of winter. Beyond the breakers, the sea raged on hidden reefs. Dark cliffs towered overhead, casting the cove in shadow.

Eric sat on the cool sand watching the dragons, his chest tight with dread. He knew what they were here for, what they wanted. The body of Nerissa lay nearby; her golden scales dull with death. The dragon's bravery had saved them all, her crimson flames driving off the demon. But Nerissa's defiance had come at a price. Now her kin had come to claim their own.

He prayed that was all they sought.

His companions sat close, watching the display in grim silence. Inken was beside him, her arm resting gently against his back. Reaching down he squeezed her hand, drawing strength from her presence. She glanced at him with her hazel eyes, scarlet hair shining even in the shade. Tears and burns marked her clothing, but beneath her skin was whole; healed by the Goddess Antonia.

On either side of them rested Michael and Caelin, the doctor and the soldier. Caelin sat with his legs folded, muscles rippling as he tensed, ready to spring. A short sword lay across his lap, his fingers lingering on the hilt. The sword did not belong to him, but to Eric's teacher, Alastair.

Eric's eyes slid out over the water, memories of the night before returning. His chest clenched tight, but he kept the tears from his eyes. Alastair was at peace now—the same could not be said for the rest of them.

Michael also sat with his legs crossed, but he held only a small pack stuffed with what remained of his medical supplies. Little good they had done Alastair. At least they had kept Eric alive long enough to be healed by Antonia's magic. He would never forget how the doctor's strength and skill had helped bring him through the darkness. Michael stared up at the circling dragons, his short-cropped hair and beard betraying nothing of the ordeals of the last two days.

A roar came from overhead, returning Eric's attention to the sky. A dragon dropped from formation and descended towards them. Swallowing his fears, Eric pulled himself to his feet. His companions followed suit, fingers hovering close to weapons. His hand lingered in Inken's. She gave it a squeeze and flashed him a smile.

The ground shook as the beast thumped onto the beach. The wings beat a final time, sending a cloud of sand billowing out around it. Eric raised a hand against the onslaught and struggled to keep the dragon in sight. Air hissed as its mouth opened to reveal rows of glittering teeth. The stench of rotten fish billowed across the beach, followed by a wave of heat.

Who are you who trespass here? The voice reverberated through Eric's mind. The dragon towered over them, its bulk covering the black-sanded beach.

Eric's knees trembled, but through his fear he remembered Caelin's actions from the day before. Forcing his limbs to obey, Eric bowed to the dragon. There could be no mistakes here; one swipe of those claws could slice him in two.

Straightening, he looked the dragon in the eye. "Greetings, dragon. This is Inken, a bounty hunter from Chole. These are Caelin, sergeant of the Plorsean army, and the doctor Michael. My name is Eric. I am apprentice to the Magicker, Alastair," he paused. "Or I was, until he was killed last night by a traitor. May I ask, what is your name, dragon?"

He did not mention the fifth member of their party—Enala, the girl they had come all this way to find. She still sat catatonic amongst the trees behind them, unresponsive to the world around her.

My name is Enduran, and you are not welcome here, the dragon's nostrils widened as it sniffed the air. Its eyes scanned the beach until they settled on the body of Balistor, still lying where he had fallen. *The blood of our sister is on your hands.*

Caelin stepped forward. "No, Enduran. It is on the hands of that traitor. He was an agent of Archon—he tried to kill us all. I…stopped him, though he had been my companion for many weeks. We are not your enemy."

It was you who brought him here, brought him into our midst. His

3

actions fall on your shoulders, a growl rumbled from deep in Enduran's chest. Eric braced himself, expecting flames to follow. *But you speak the truth—it was your blade that felled the slayer.*

The dragon shifted on the beach, its claws digging great grooves into the sand. Its tail flicked out, shattering a spire of rock that stood amidst the dunes. It growled again. *Enough blood has been spilt on our land. My people will not be responsible for anymore. We will give you the day to leave our lands. Come nightfall, we will put our sister to rest. Her body, and all who remain on this beach, will be cleansed by dragon fire.*

Eric swallowed. "But we will not survive Dragon Country alone. We have no horses, no supplies. We are trapped on this beach."

Flames licked from between the dragon's lips. Eric shrank backwards, holding his breath.

There is a Lonian fishing vessel nearby. I shall tell the sailors of your presence. It is up to them whether they wish to rescue you. Either way, we will not wait. With that the wings beat again, sending sand flying across the beach.

Eric raised his arm again and squinted through the sandstorm, watching Enduran rise into the sky. As he drew above the height of the cliffs the other dragons joined him, their wings carrying them out across the ocean.

Eric watched them go and then turned to his companions. "What now?"

Caelin smiled. "We wait. And pray the dragons don't send the Lonians fleeing halfway across the ocean."

"They're not exactly known as a timid bunch," Inken countered. "I'd say our chances are good." She moved up the beach to where their scant possessions lay scattered.

Eric followed her, his boots sinking into the coarse sand. "Fishermen, or Lonians?" he asked.

"Both," Inken laughed. "Although I was referring to the Lonians. Gods' know, they held the Trolans to a standstill during the Great Wars."

"Although unlike the Trolans, they've settled down a little since those days," Caelin replied as they sat in a circle.

Eric spared a look at the bundle of rags lying nearby, where Enala still lay inert. She had not moved nor said a single word since the night before, when Balistor had killed the dragon she rode. Whatever bond had been shared between dragon and girl, its loss had tipped Enala over the edge.

A muffled sob came from the pile of cloth. Michael moved across and sat beside her. He began to speak, but Eric could not make out the words.

He shook his head. Enala was a problem for another day, once they had escaped this deadly land. He glanced at the ocean, straining to make out the tell-tale sails of a ship, but the horizon remained empty.

"They're likely to be some distance away," Inken said, noticing the direction of his gaze. "The Lonians fish right down the east coast, but they stay well clear of these waters. The reefs are treacherous for the deeper hulls of their fishing vessels."

Eric nodded, but a rumble from his stomach gave away his impatience.

Caelin laughed. "I know, we're all hungry. But there's not much we can do about that for now." He eyed Inken. "Unless a certain bounty hunter thinks there could be game nearby?"

Inken gave a short smile. "Believe me, if there was, I wouldn't be lazing around here." She glanced at Eric. "Even if I'm hesitant to leave. No, I haven't seen a single bird or rabbit in the trees since we arrived. For whatever reason, dragons or demon or curse, the forest around this cove is empty."

Caelin sighed. "That is a shame," he said. "Still, I'm sure we can survive a few more hours. A fishing ship is bound to have plenty of food on board."

"If they come," Eric interjected.

"They'll come," Caelin grinned. "I have every faith in our Lonian neighbours."

The captain glared down at the company, lips twisted in a frown. A thick black beard matted his face, giving him a fierceness that would send lesser men scurrying. He folded his arms, the short sleeves revealing bulging muscles criss-crossed by old red scars. Even standing below them on the beach, he towered over the four companions.

Behind him, the dingy crunched on the sand as a wave rocked it. His crew milled around the vessel, eying their captain nervously.

Caelin had taken the initiative, offering the sailors a tale about their being Plorsean ambassadors who had come to treat with the Gold Dragons. Eric couldn't help but think it was a poor lie, given the dead dragon lying on the shore. Not to mention Balistor's body, which everyone seemed intent to ignore.

"Enough!" the captain finally cut across Caelin. "I've heard enough. Never in my life have I heard such a tall tale."

Caelin's face turned scarlet. Eric guessed the sergeant

did not have a great amount of experience lying, and getting caught in one clearly left him uncomfortable.

He opened his mouth to reply, but the captain spoke again. "I don't know what the five of you are really doing here, but I don't really care." He waved a hand. "From what I've seen, I want no part of it. I don't need this kind of trouble on my ship." He turned to leave.

"Wait!" Eric shouted.

He stepped after the sailors, reaching out to halt the captain's departure. The crew drew their swords and advanced on him, faces darkening at the perceived threat.

Eric raised his empty hands. "Wait, wait! You're right, Caelin was lying," he paused as the captain turned. He shot Eric an impatient scowl and raised an eyebrow.

"Thank you. Like I said, Caelin lied, but I swear there is good reason. We are emissaries for the Goddess Antonia, it is on her behalf that we are here."

The black eyes of the captain locked on Eric's. "Oh? And what did the Goddess want with a rugged bunch of no goods such as yourselves?"

Eric glanced at his companions, seeing them as the sailors must. Antonia had healed their injuries, but the past days had reduced their clothing to an assortment of burnt and bloodied rags. He swallowed. Only the truth would convince here—no other tale could explain their presence.

He looked at the big man, studying him closely. "You seem like a trustworthy man, captain, but our purpose is a great secret. We cannot risk word spreading. I will tell you, and you alone, if you swear to secrecy."

The captain laughed. "Bold, aren't you? Why should I swear to anything? I could leave you here to die, for all I care."

"Hear me out. You will understand the need when I have finished," Eric met his gaze, and held it.

The captain's face darkened. He gave a sharp nod. "You have five minutes to convince me. You alone. Come." He waved at the twisted trees.

Eric nodded and followed the captain up the beach. His men made to protest, but their voices fell on deaf ears. The captain obviously felt Eric was small enough not to warrant caution.

Eric couldn't help but smile at the captain's error.

Even so, his heart quickened as they entered the trees. Silently he debated how much he would need to tell. This man would accept nothing but the truth, but *too* much truth could also prove dangerous here. Anyone involved with their quest risked the wrath of Archon; he could not risk alienating the man through fear.

The darkness beneath the trees drew them deeper into the forest, until finally the captain turned and glared down at him. "Your time starts now."

Eric ran a hand through his hair, trying to decide where to start. "How much do you know of the Sword of Light?"

The captain blinked. "The Sword? How does this have anything to do with that Trolan trinket?"

"*Everything*. That trinket and the power of the Gods are the only things keeping Archon banished in the Wasteland."

A shudder shook the captain at the mention of the Dark Magicker's name. "So the legends say. Others claim Archon is long dead."

"He isn't. His influence is everywhere now. He has been waiting…waiting for a seed he planted decades ago to take root." Eric took a breath to calm himself. "When the Gods and King Thomas unleashed the spell to banish Archon from our lands, Archon cast a curse of his own. He bound the spell to Thomas and his bloodline. Over the generations it has slowly stripped the magic from the Trolan royalty. The same magic they need to wield the Sword of Light."

The captain's hand drifted unconsciously towards his sword hilt. There was fear in his eyes. "What are you saying?"

Eric stared back. "That the magic of the Sword no longer protects the Three Nations. Archon is already preparing to invade. Yesterday, we were attacked by one of his demons; his first probe of our defences."

"You killed it?"

"No, the dragon drove it off. That was before we were betrayed by our companion Balistor, another of Archon's servants, who slew the dragon and my mentor, Alastair. Antonia is hunting the demon now—it won't survive her wrath."

The captain shook his head. "This can't be true. What you're saying…what you're saying means the end of everything…"

"I am telling the truth," Eric paused to let his words sink in, "but there is still hope. King Thomas had a sister, one who was never affected by the curse. Alastair tracked down her ancestors, but Archon's minions got to them first. Only one survived—Enala. Yesterday, we finally found her."

The big man blinked. "You mean the girl on the beach? The blond that's gone mad?"

Eric bowed his head and sighed. They would have to deal with Enala's state of mind eventually, but right now they had more pressing concerns. "Yes, that is Enala. And believe it or not, she is our last hope. Archon has hunted her across Plorsea, and it has almost driven her insane. But Antonia believes she will recover. It is our job to make sure she has the chance to do so."

Silence fell as the captain weighed up his words. This time Eric did not back down. He only had one chance to convince this man to help them. He would not fail.

Finally the captain gave a sharp nod. "Okay, Eric. I'm not sure I believe you, but such a tale deserves the benefit of the doubt. It would be a bold lie indeed to tell such a story. We are heading for the Lonian capital. I will take you that far. After that, you're on your own." He held out his hand. "The name's Loris."

Eric gave a grim smile. "Thank you, Loris. You won't regret this."

Loris shook his head. "Somehow, I doubt that."

———

THE BOW OF THE SHIP ROSE SHARPLY INTO THE SWELL AND then crashed back down the other side. Wooden boards creaked as water rushed over the side to swamp the deck. Sailors walked through the water, shouting at men who dangled overhead. Wind cracked in the sails, driving them through the unbroken waters. The sun shone high above, its heat beating upon the exposed deck. The stench of fish seeped from the cargo hold below.

Eric's stomach lurched with each rise and fall of the ship. He had never been at sea before, but he had heard of seasickness. He stumbled across the deck, grabbing for the railing, and lost the battle to keep the meagre contents of his stomach down.

Laughter came from above. He looked up in time to see a sailor dropping from the rigging. A grin split his bearded face as he joined Eric at the railings.

"It helps if you don't look at the ship," he said, pointing to the distant coastline. "Keep your eyes on the horizon.

That way when the ship moves, the eyes and body both tell your mind the same story. If you look at the deck, it tricks your eyes into thinking you're stationary, even though your body can feel the ship lurching about."

Eric's head spun and he could hardly make sense of the sailor's words, but he managed to look out at the rocky coastline. Even from a distance, the jagged cliffs towered over their little vessel. Scraggly trees grew from the rock faces, their crooked branches reaching out like fingers. Behind them, the ocean stretched to the horizon. He was glad they would not be venturing that way; the great expanse of water filled him with a dread he could not shake.

A white bird with grey wings cawed from the sky, landing in the ship's rigging. He tried to ignore it. Following the sailor's advice, his stomach had already begun to settle, so he risked a glance at the sailor. He realised they must be almost the same age—around eighteen. "How long have you worked at sea?"

The man leaned back against the railings, arms outstretched as he stared up at the sails. "Most of my life, but I only joined the captain a year ago. Before that I worked as a dingy rower in Lon. Where are your friends, our other unexpected cargo?"

"Sleeping." The others were making the most of the opportunity, but Eric's sickness had been much worse inside the tiny cabin. "What happens with the sickness when you close your eyes?"

"That works too sometimes, but makes it difficult to get any work done," the sailor laughed, then glanced around. "Speaking of which, I'd better get back to my post before the captain sees me slacking. Nice to meet you." He crossed to the mast and climbed back into the rigging.

Shaking his head, Eric moved away from the railing,

looking for a good place to sit. It was time to test his magic. He had not reached for it since he'd been stabbed. Shuddering, he remembered the pain of the *Soul Blade* piercing his stomach, the demon's cackle in his ear. If not for Antonia's magic, he would be dead.

He spotted a pile of crates stacked against the cabin and started towards them, stumbling as the vessel shifted beneath him. Righting himself against the mast, he stepped more cautiously until he could climb atop the nearest create. There he crossed his legs, leaned against the crate behind him, and closed his eyes.

Eric drew a deep breath in preparation. Sadness clenched his heart as he remembered the last time he had meditated. The company had been whole then, Alastair still alive to guide him. Now he was alone. The thought terrified him.

Drawing another breath, he allowed his thoughts to drift on the gentle ebb of his conscious. He focused on each inhale and exhale, allowing all other sensation to drift away. In out, in out. The air hissed from his mouth as he blew out, his chest swelling with each inhalation.

Sound began to fade away. The lapping of water against wood, the flapping of the sails, even the shouts of the sailors drifted from his consciousness, leaving him alone in the silence of his mind.

His thoughts proved harder to tame. The last few days had been hell. The night before last was a blur, a convoluted mosaic of flames and darkness and flashing red scales as the dragon chased them through the forest. If not for Inken, he would have perished.

The thought of her set his heart racing in his chest. Images of their time spent in the glow of the night clearing flashed by: the hot steam, the luminescent ferns, the splashing of water as they tumbled in the water. Shaking his head, he smiled and let those images fade as well.

Memories of Alastair he could not so easily let go. Even now he could see the old man's emerald eyes, the edges crinkled in amusement. He had been Eric's mentor, his saviour and friend. His death remained carved in his mind: Balistor, poised over Alastair's unconscious body, the sword flashing in the sunlight, plunging down, down, down.

Tears burned in Eric's eyes, but he fought to let the image go, if just for a moment.

In out, in out.

Then only memory of Enala remained; of the brave girl sitting atop the gold dragon, their last hope. Then Enala mad, rocking in the sand, catatonic. She still had not eaten, would barely drink. If it kept up, their last hope would perish without any assistance from Archon and his minions.

Finally, the last of his thoughts drifted away and Eric found himself falling into the familiar calm of his inner mind. A blue light flickered in the distance. The glow seemed cool and calming, but he knew from experience it had a darker edge. Magic had a mind of its own, a will to be free. But he was strong now, strong enough to control it.

Moving towards the distant spark, the light grew until it became a great lake of magic, stretched out before his consciousness. Lightning flashed across its surface, rising from the depths like a serpent. The blue glow warmed his soul.

Eric stretched out a phantom hand and watched a thread of power rise in response. It drifted towards him, wrapping gently around his wrist. His mind tingled as the power filtered through him, but he did not release it. He would need every drop in the coming weeks if they were to see Enala safely to the Sword of Light. The enemy facing them was legion, and without Alastair and Balistor he was now the last Magicker in their small fellowship. The power radiating from his magic gave him reassurance though, where for so long it had been a source of fear.

Beside him a door slammed and he felt a hand back on the ship grab him. Eric's concentration snapped as someone shook him.

"Eric, stop! What are you doing?" he heard Inken yell.

Eric's eyes snapped open. He looked around in shock, finding Inken standing over him. Her face was twisted in panic, her eyes wide with fear. Rain poured down around them, drenching her scarlet hair. With a start, Eric realised he was soaked to the skin.

The ship pitched violently, almost toppling Eric from the crate. Inken stumbled and fell against him. He caught her before the rolling of the ship sent her tumbling. The wind howled through the rigging above, tearing at the sail. The sailors shouted over the gale, terror in their voices as they struggled with the sails. Storm clouds blackened the sky, while sheets of rain and hail lashed the deck.

They toppled from the crate as the ship lurched again. Eric struggled to stand, reaching for his power. His mind reeled with shock—he hadn't released his magic, had he?

"I don't think this is me!" he shouted, grasping for Inken's hand.

"What? How is that possible?"

Lightning crashed. Eric winced, instinct driving him down into his magic. Power flooded his mind. He opened his eyes and saw a bolt flashing towards the mast. He raised a hand and gripped it with his magic, hurling it into the raging sea. Thunder clapped as it struck. Boiling water geysered into the air and crashed over the railings. It swept towards them.

Inken tackled him backwards into the cabin. Breath exploded from his chest as they tumbled from the water's path. Eric gasped, struggling to sit up, already searching out the next flash of lightning. Panic swamped him, stifling his concentration. His magic began to slip from his grasp. They could not afford that.

Eric closed his eyes and sank back into the abyss. He wrapped the magic threads in an iron grip and opened his spirit eyes. The storm raged around them, pulling his phantom body skywards. The air crackled with the energy of the Sky element, but he worked on instinct now—and desperation.

Threads of magic stretched out from him, forming hooks of blue light to grasp the surging wind and rain. Gritting his teeth, Eric unleashed a surge of energy, pushing them back from the ship.

Almost instantly, the air stilled and the sails sagged in their rigging. The violent crashing of the waves faded, leaving the ship to settle back into a gentle rocking. The scent of rain was strong in their nostrils.

Eric drew in a breath of relief.

Then a surge of energy burnt through his mind—and the storm returned with renewed fury. The mast groaned, cracks appearing in the thick wood.

Eric stared in disbelief. It was not possible. His magic remained embedded in the storm that had struck them, holding it back from the ship. But this wind and rain had appeared from nowhere, as if summoned by some unnatural force. That was impossible—the first thing Alastair taught him was that Magickers could manipulate the Light, the Sky and the Earth, but they could not create.

Only the Gods could do that.

A sudden force struck Eric, hurling his soul back into his body. Gasping, he opened his eyes, searching for the words.

"*Where is she?*" A voice boomed over the roar of the storm.

Eric stood in the doorway of the cabin and watched in terror as a figure materialised on the bow of the ship. Wind and rain swirled around him. Thunder crackled as lightning struck the ship, the shock wave knocking sailors from their feet. Energy rippled along the figure's condensing arms and shoulders, gathering in his outstretched fist. The figure seemed to coalesce from the Sky itself, until a man stood on the deck, pure rage etched across his face.

Hair as white as snow hung down to the man's shoulders. His ice blue eyes glared at Eric, dark patches hanging beneath them. Lines of stress marked his forehead, but his face was clean shaven. He wore clothes similar to the sailors —a loose blue tunic and black pants.

Eric knew him from the vision Antonia had once shown him.

Lightning crackled around the man as he took a step. "*Where. Is. She?*"

The sky turned white as lightning flashed, casting long shadows across the deck. It raced towards Eric, crackling as it went.

Panic and fear fought within him, but instinct took hold. He reached out with his magic, with his hands, to catch it. The lightning flared as it struck. Thunder clapped and a shock ran through his body.

The force of the blast threw Eric backwards into the wall of the cabin. His head crashed against the wood, sending a jolt of pain down his spine. His ears rang and his head spun. He tasted metal on his tongue, then burning.

"*Tell me where she is, now!*"

Suddenly the man stood over him, seeming to tower higher even than the mast of the ship. Lightning crackled again. He held a fist above Eric, energy dancing along his skin.

Eric stared up at the Storm God, fear making his heart thud in his chest. "Who, Jurrien?" he croaked.

"My sister, Antonia. *Where is she?*"

Eric struggled to understand his words. He wiped the streaming rain from his face. His body shook with pain. "Antonia? What do you mean?"

The God sucked in an angry breath. "She is gone. I can no longer sense her, feel her anywhere. But the taint of her magic is on you. You were with her, not long ago. *What has happened?*"

Eric shook his head. "She left. She wanted to hunt down the demon Archon sent to kill Enala."

"*What?* One of Archon's demons is *here?*" he swore. "How could she be so *foolish?* Going after it alone, in her state!"

"She seemed okay in the cove," Eric croaked.

Jurrien's icy eyes bored into Eric, his teeth grinding as he clenched his jaw. "She was exhausted. We barely held off Archon's last attack, and then she runs off babbling about *Alastair* and *Eric* and *Enala*. How she summoned the energy to heal the lot of you I do not know. But to then go chasing a demon…" he covered his face with his hands and turned away.

"Alastair is dead," Eric whispered. Jurrien had known his mentor as well.

Jurrien shook his head. "The old man was going to bite off more than he could chew sooner or later," he spoke the words with venom. "But I never thought he'd bring Antonia down with him."

Eric struggled to his feet. "Alastair had nothing to do with this, whatever *this* is!" he argued. "The demon was *your* responsibility, yours as well as Antonia's. It should never have stepped foot in Plorsea in the first place."

The Storm God advanced until only an inch separated them. He towered over Eric, his muscular stature no less intimidating for his silver hair. Eric looked into his eyes and saw the depth of power and wisdom there. He found himself remembering his first encounter with Antonia, the light-hearted Goddess of the Earth. The fight went from him as he realised the meaning behind Jurrien's words.

"Are you saying she's gone?"

The God's eyes softened. His shoulders slumped. "I don't know. This has never happened before. I can always sense her, even those rare times when we sleep. But now— nothing. I need to find out what has happened." He waved a hand as he spoke.

The wind ceased with a sharp snap. The sails slumped and the rocking of the ship slowed, released from the violent grasp of the waves. The crackle of lightning around Jurrien died away, until he seemed just an ordinary man.

A man weighed down by worry, teetering on the brink of defeat.

The last God standing.

Eric prayed it was not so. "She was with us last at Malevolent Cove. She headed into Dragon Country on the trail of the demon."

Jurrien nodded. "I will follow her path. I just hope I am wrong." He turned and walked to the railings. With a grunt he levered himself over the side. A gust of wind caught him as he fell, propelling him into the sky.

Eric released his breath and looked around the ship. Jurrien's appearance had left the wooden boards at the prow burnt and blackened, and a part of the sail had torn loose in the wind. The rigging hung in a tattered mess. Crates and supplies lay strewn across the deck, broken free by the raging waves and wind. Several barrels bobbed in the ocean around them, slowly drifting away. The creak of straining wood came from the mast.

His companions stood nearby, their clothes wet, faces bedraggled. They stared at him in shock, but one by one moved to stand with him. Inken placed a reassuring arm around his waist, while Caelin grasped his shoulder and gave it a squeeze. Michael only nodded. There was no sign of Enala. Together they looked across the deck to where Captain Loris stood amongst his spoiled supplies.

Slowly the crew gathered around Loris, voices whispering as they glanced in their direction. Eric recognised the look on their faces all too well—the mixture of terror and rage. Blame would soon follow, and—if they did not put the mutinous glances to rest—violence. He sought out the young sailor he had spoken to earlier. His heart sank when he found the man and saw the hate in his eyes.

But for once his magic had not been responsible for the havoc. He did not intend to suffer the consequences of the Storm Gods anger.

Eric took a step forward. The captain opened his mouth to stop him, a purple vein popping on his forehead. Eric spoke over the top of him.

"Well, I hope you all enjoyed your first meeting with Jurrien, the God of Lonia. He's not much for introductions, apparently."

His words had the desired effect. A shiver went through the crew and the captain's words died in his throat. These were Lonian sailors after all; they named Jurrien their God. Eric had never been to Lonia, so he was not sure how the people generally regarded the Storm God, but he doubted they were likely to argue with someone on speaking terms with him. Even if his conversation with Jurrien had largely revolved around dire threats on the God's part.

At last the captain drew in a breath. "What are you all standing around for?" he bellowed. "Back to work! I want this ship ready to sail within the hour." He banged his fist against the mast to emphasise his words.

Loris walked towards the rear of the ship to take over from the helmsman. He glanced at them as he swept passed. "Guess your tale had some truth to it after all. Just wish I'd been wrong about the trouble." The glare in his eyes could have melted iron.

As he passed, the others turned to stare at Eric.

"What's happened?" They asked in unison.

———

JURRIEN SLUMPED AGAINST THE TREE, A DARK WEIGHT crashing against his soul. Around him, the forest was silent, dead. All colour had leached from the trees, leaving the woods grey and lifeless. Not a single creature stirred. Birds and squirrels lay in silent death on the leafy ground, their tiny bodies twisted in agony. A rotten stench spread throughout the clearing. The taint of dark magic hung thick in the air.

A single tear ran down Jurrien's cheek. He let it fall, unable to believe, to comprehend what his eyes told him. Antonia lay amidst the fallen animals, eyes closed. Her auburn hair spread out around her head, her tiny lips parted slightly, as though she still breathed. She could have been sleeping, if not for the blood staining her sky-blue dress. The blood had seeped out around her, soaking into the earth that had borne her.

A groan rattled from Jurrien's throat. His fists clenched on empty air. He closed his eyes, opened them again, but the image did not change. His soul reached out for his sister, for some last trace of her.

Nothing. She was dead, gone.

He was alone.

And Archon was coming.

Inken rested her head against the wooden crate and looked down at Eric. She smiled fondly as she watched him sleep. His head was nestled in her lap, a few wild tufts of dark brown hair covering his eyes. His chest rose and fell in a steady rhythm, interrupted every few breaths by a muffled groan. The brief fight with Jurrien had clearly cost him more than he'd let on.

She reached down and wiped a streak of soot from his cheek, then brushed the hair from his face. A gentle warmth filled her heart. Just yesterday he had teetered on the brink of death. She had come close to losing him forever. Then Antonia had come, had saved him.

Now not a day later, Antonia's brother had almost reversed that blessing. Inken could not believe Jurrien had attacked them. With empty ocean all around, far from any spies or demons, Inken had allowed herself to relax—and the Storm God had taken her by surprise.

Now she realised the darkness could find them at any time. She would not be caught unawares again. Her bow lay within easy reach, her sabre strapped to her side. If they were attacked, she would be ready.

Across the deck she could see Caelin arguing with the captain. She knew it would take every ounce of diplomacy the young sergeant possessed to cool the man's temper. Even then, it might not be enough. Eric's words may have averted a mutiny, but Inken could sense the crew's anger, festering just beneath the surface. They feared the power they had witnessed. The captain's command could only do so much to stop that fear from bubbling over.

It would be a long two days before they reached Lon.

Inken's hand brushed the hilt of her sword. Its leather grip felt reassuring, although hostility from the crew did not worry her. She was confident Caelin and herself could handle them if it came to it. After facing demons and Magickers, Inken would almost cherish a fair fight.

It was the aftermath she worried about. Even if they defeated the sailors, they would be left stranded at sea. None of their fellowship knew how to sail a dingy, let alone a ship.

Behind her, silence blanketed the cabin. Inken sighed. Its only occupant was the girl, Enala. She had yet to speak a single word. It was past time that changed. They had to reach her, bring her back from the brink of whatever crevice she teetered on.

Inken gave a wry smile. The men did not have a clue about how to go about the task. It seemed bringing Enala back to the world of sanity was up to her. It would be easier now. Before, in the cove, the fear of Eric's death had weighed on her mind.

She sat there a few minutes more, enjoying the warmth and closeness of Eric's body. How the young man had wormed his way into her heart remained a mystery, but she was not about to let him go now. The ship offered little privacy for a couple—the crew slept in hammocks beneath the deck while their company squeezed into the small cabin with the captain—so she had to savour every little moment.

Finally, she lifted Eric's head from her lap and tucked a rolled-up jerkin underneath him for a pillow.

Eric stirred, his blue eyes flickering. "Where are you going?" he murmured.

Inken leaned down and kissed him, lingering as their tongues met. It was a while before she pulled away. "I want to check on Enala. You get some sleep. We need you well rested."

Eric yawned and nodded, closing his eyes again.

Inken grinned and stood, climbing down from the crate and walking back to the cabin door. Pulling it open, she made her way into the darkness within. A single candle provided the only source of light in the small room, and it took a second for her eyes to adjust. A desk was crammed into the rear corner, making way for the sleeping rolls they'd squeezed into the cabin. A single bed took up the other wall.

Enala lay curled up on the bed, covers drawn around her head, so that only a few tuffs of blond hair showed. The covers shook as the door swung closed, and a half-choked sob came from the dark. It was the only noise the girl had made for two days.

Inken sat herself on the end of the bed. The pile of blankets grew still, so Inken scooted backwards across the mattress until she could lean against the wall. Pulling her knees up to her chest, she sat in the darkness, contemplating what to say.

What *could* she say to this girl? In less than two weeks, Enala had witnessed the brutal murder of her parents, the death of a friend, and the loss of the dragon she rode.

Never mind the revelation that the ancient evil known as Archon was hunting her, wanted her dead.

It was too much for anyone to take, let alone a seventeen-year-old girl. Inken doubted she had the strength to cope any better—she would be in the same position as Enala if their positions were reversed.

Even so, Enala had to know she was not alone anymore. For Inken herself, the search for Enala had never been about the Sword of Light, but a girl who needed protection from evil. She had to convince Enala that, though they were strangers, they cared about her. She had to convince the girl to trust them.

Inken released a long breath as she realised she had no idea where to start. She chuckled, and decided not to mention to the others that she was as clueless as them. Still, she had to try *something*.

So closing her eyes, Inken began to talk.

She began with the trivial, the mundane. She spoke of the white mare she had purchased just a few short weeks before, and how absurd she'd felt riding such a conspicuous animal. A bounty hunter riding a white horse would be the talk of the town—not an ideal situation for a profession requiring subtly. She spoke of her debt back in Chole, the cost of her equipment, her old friends and what they must think of her now, after she'd betrayed them to rescue Eric and the others.

Then Inken spoke of her childhood, of the time her mother finally decided she'd had enough. Cold to the end, the woman had walked away without looking back. Not a kiss or a hug goodbye for the five-year-old she left behind, just a wave and a door slammed in Inken's face.

From then on it had been just Inken and her father.

And things had only grown worse. Her father was a

notorious drunk, and with her mother gone, his attention soon turned to Inken. He often returned drunk in the early afternoon, unleashing strings of profanities which quickly disintegrated into screaming fits; the kind that shook the walls and led to knocks on the door from neighbours. In his drunken rage, the man blamed Inken for everything from her mother's desertion, to their poverty.

Inken had learned to keep her mouth shut in those early years. Eventually the neighbours stopped knocking.

For years she'd suffered his insults, his curses and threats. She had grown thick skinned, deaf to all but the worst of his accusations.

But on the first day he'd hit her, the ten-year-old Inken had walked out the door and never looked back.

Hot tears spilt from Inken's eyes and ran down her face. In all her years, she had never told a soul about her past. She had always thought of it as just that—her past, nobody's business but her own. She could not imagine what made her speak of it now. Not even Eric knew the story of her parents.

She heard a rustling come from the other end of the bed and tried not to look. She glimpsed movement from the corner of her eye, and then Enala was curling up beside her, lips still pursed tight. The young girl pulled the covers up around them and leaned her head against Inken's shoulder.

Inken stretched out her arm and wrapped it around the girl. They sat in silence for a while, each contemplating the various horrors which were their lives. Inken had lived on the streets for most of her teenage years, but she did not regret the decision to leave. She smiled to herself, thinking of the convoluted path she'd taken to become a bounty hunter.

But that was a story for another day.

"We may not seem like much, Enala, but we're all here for you," she whispered.

Enala wriggled closer. "How do you know?"

"They're like me. Eric, Caelin, Michael, they're good people. They want to help you, help everyone in the Three Nations. You can trust them."

Inken caught a flash of blue eyes in the darkness. "I hope so." She heard Enala's soft voice.

"You can," Inken repeated, then. "Are you hungry?"

For the first time Enala met her eyes. "Bloody starving," she said, flashing a hesitant smile.

Inken laughed. "I'll be right back."

———

"WHAT'S GOING ON HERE?" CAELIN LOOKED UP AS MICHAEL interrupted his argument with the captain.

Captain Loris scowled at the doctor. "None of your business."

Caelin raised an eyebrow. "None of his business? I think the good doctor would be just as upset as the rest of us were you to abandon us on some deserted beach."

"What do you expect me to do?" the captain snapped. "The crew are an inch from mutiny. God or no, that *thing* almost sank us. And he was clearly not fond of the bunch of you. The men are *scared*."

"I don't think he's coming back," Michael put in. "He was looking for his sister, Antonia, and I can assure you we don't have the Goddess of the Earth tucked up our sleeves." He waved at the wide sleeves of his coat with a smile.

"That's all well and good, but the crew don't know what's going on. And from what I've heard, the less we tell them about the whole affair, the better." His jaw tightened as he clenched his teeth. "They won't stand for this. This is your fight. I cannot risk the lives of my crew for your affairs. We are only simple fishermen."

Michael spread his hands. "And I am only a priest. Caelin is only a soldier. We are all *only* something, but this fight goes beyond who and what we are. It doesn't matter to Archon; to him we are just souls waiting to be enslaved."

Caelin glanced at the resolve on the doctor's face. Michael's words warmed his heart, gave him hope.

But the captain wasn't having any of it. His brow drew into a scowl. "Archon or no, it's *you* who are a threat to our lives just now. Won't matter a jot whether Archon comes or not if we're at the bottom of the ocean."

Anger swamped Caelin. He swore. "If you abandon us in the middle of nowhere, you risk the lives of everyone in the Three Nations," he growled, then drew in a breath. "This is your chance to be more than *just* fisherman, to make a difference in this world."

"And what about our world? Who will pay our wages if we lose our cargo? Who will feed our wives and family if the ship sinks?"

Caelin wanted to shake the man. Michael interrupted before he got the chance. "We understand your concern, Loris, and the concerns of your men. I assure you, you will be safe. Jurrien will not return, nor any other vengeful spirit. And if it's money that concerns you, then perhaps we could come to an arrangement?"

"What?" Caelin and Loris asked in unison.

The captain glanced at Caelin and then continued. "What sort of payment? A priest's blessing is all well and good, but it doesn't pay the bills."

Michael smiled. "The temples of the God's are not rich,

but I am sure they have a few spare funds to reward the ship that provided us safe passage to Lon."

Caelin swallowed, wondering whether Michael was bluffing. If so, this was one man he did not want to play poker with.

The captain grunted. "And what about *our* safe passage? It would have to be a hefty sum to convince my men to continue with this business."

Michael grinned. "Gold is a strong motivator, I believe."

Straightening his shoulders, Michael began to negotiate with the captain what they considered a 'reasonable' price for their passage. Caelin could only shake his head in wonder. He had not seen this side of Michael before. Until now the doctor had been withdrawn, and Caelin had assumed him to be a fearful and timid man.

Now he found himself reappraising that first assessment first assessment. With his priestly upbringing, Michael might never be a fighter, but there was clearly more to the man than the green robe of his order.

Ten minutes later Caelin joined Michael at the railing, their passage to Lon assured. At least for now. They stood in silence for a while, staring out at the jagged coastline. A gull skimmed the waves, its high-pitched caw carrying across the water.

Caelin glanced at Michael. "That was well done," he hesitated. "Is it true though, will the temple in Lon really pay?"

Michael smiled, running a hand through his greying hair. "I think so."

Caelin laughed, but Michael continued. "It's at least standard practice for the Earth Temples to have a stock of gold available to aid those doing Antonia's work. I can only assume the Sky Temples would be the same," he laughed himself. "Perhaps they even have a store to cover damages when the Storm God loses his temper."

Caelin chuckled. "I hope that was not a common occurrence."

Michael's face darkened. "I doubt it. Whatever is happening with Antonia, it must be serious. For Jurrien to lose control like that…I mean, his temper does have a reputation, but even so…"

Caelin glanced at the burnt timber at the bow of the ship. "Agreed."

Silence fell again. A sadness came over Michael's face. "I've been thinking; it might be best if I were to stay in Lon."

"What?" Caelin glanced at the doctor. "Why?"

"I don't know what part I can play in the coming battle. I am not a fighter," Michael echoed Caelin's earlier thoughts. "I do not want to hold you back. Elynbrigge asked me to join you, but I don't know–"

"The choice is up to you, Michael," Caelin interrupted, "but I believe we all have a place in this company. You may not have magic, but you are a doctor, and a diplomat, apparently. There is no telling when we might need your skills. We need more than fighters on this quest."

Michael drew in a breath and nodded. "I will think on it."

They both looked up as the door to the cabin opened. Inken appeared, smiling in the afternoon sunshine. She moved across to join them.

"They'll take us as far as Lon, but it's going to cost the Sky temple an eye and a leg."

"That's good news," Inken's smile widened. "I have some news of my own. Enala is hungry."

They gaped at her. Inken laughed at their shock. "Do

you think these sailors could be convinced to part with some supplies?"

Caelin grinned, feeling a little of the weight shift from his soul. Finally, some good news. With Alastair's death and Antonia's disappearance, it had begun to feel as though things were spinning out of control. If Enala recovered, they would at least have one thread of hope to cling too.

"For the amount of gold we've promised, she can have a feast if she wants." Caelin spun and marched towards the captain.

A cry from the rigging stopped him in his tracks.

"Man overboard!"

———

THE TREE BRANCH ROSE BENEATH GABRIEL AS THE WAVE swept past, carrying him high into the air. He looked around, desperate for a glimpse of land, but the ocean stretched out in all directions. Swells rolled across the dark blue water, whitewash breaking at their tips. Sea spray misted the air, cutting off sight of the horizon.

The soft lapping of water against his log rocked him towards sleep. He struggled to hang on, just a little bit longer, but his strength had long since faded. Only minutes separated him from the dark depths of the ocean now. Soon he would slip beneath the waves, never to be seen again.

Gabriel swallowed, his mouth paper dry from the long hours in the salty water. He prayed his sacrifice had distracted the dragon long enough for Enala to escape. Otherwise, his death would mean nothing.

A shiver racked his body as he remembered the beast; the gaping jaws, the teeth and crackling of flames as the dragon hurtled towards him. The deafening snap of its wings, the roar that sent prickles of terror running down his spine.

Knowing he had no chance on the surface, Gabriel had released his rotten branch and dived deep into the river. The current whirled him around, dragging his helpless body deeper as the dragon's bulk smashed into the water. A talon tore at his coat, ripping the skin beneath, and then the river had carried him from reach.

Lungs exploding, Gabriel clawed his way to the surface. In the muddy waters he struggled to tell the difference between up and down, and panic threatened to overwhelm him. Then his head burst into the sunlight.

He drew in one ragged breath before the current pulled him back under. The power of the river sent him tumbling head over heels. A rock struck his thigh, then knee, then shoulder. Gabriel screamed, air gushing in bubbles from his mouth. He kicked out, desperate to reclaim the surface.

The next time he broke free he grasped at the water, struggling to stay afloat. He glanced around, searching the sky for sign of the red dragon. A roar came from the distance, but he could see nothing through the canopy of branches overhanging the water.

The trees on either side of the river rushed past as the current grew faster. He struggled against its pull, fighting to reach the far shore, but there was no making headway against the river's might. At last, gasping for breath, he rolled onto his back and let the current take him.

Branches flashed past overhead, sunlight glinting between them. Golden leaves hung from the trees, breaking lose and tumbling down with each gust of wind. The freezing water spoke of winter's fast approach. With it would come the freeze, and months of hardship for the people of the land. At least it rarely snowed in Oaksville.

Oaksville, the name rang in his mind, carrying with it the image of a man standing before a raging forge, hammer in hand.

My father, he realised with crystal certainty.

He saw himself then, standing at his father's side, arms up to their elbows in thick leather gloves. Heat washed over him, bringing with it the ring of a hammer on iron bars, the roar of the bellows as they worked the forge.

As he drifted down the river, one by one his memories returned to him. His proposal to his fiancée, the day the old soldier had given his father a sword. The horror of the storm, of finding all he had loved destroyed, his family dead. His fiancée's last painful breaths. The agony washed over him anew, pulling him into the darkness.

The demon.

He remembered the demon and its wolf, his slow decent into madness. His heart twisted with a brand-new pain as he saw his murder of the guardsman at the gates of Chole. Guilt swept through him. He was no better than the two he had hunted.

Then he stood outside Enala's house, and he knew what came there. The discovery of her murdered parents, and the girl herself hiding in the basement. The fight with the terrified Enala, then their battle with the demon wolf. The flight from Chole, the days of trekking through the wilderness, all the way to the Onyx River.

And there, the red dragon.

By the time he returned from his memories the trees had vanished. Cliffs rose on either side of the river, funnelling the waters through a narrow gorge. The current picked up speed, leaving him battling to keep his head above the water. A heavy object knocked into him. He fumbled at the log, gasping as he pulled himself atop it.

Collapsing onto the sodden wood, he clung to its broken branches, overcome by the cold and exhaustion. The water turned white as it raced over hidden rocks. The log rocked as it bounced off unseen objects. Gabriel lay shivering, the cool wind providing little relief from the icy waters. He battled to stay conscious.

He could not remember when the log had finally left the river and drifted out to sea. The cliffs had continued all the way to the coast, hemming in the raging river. Eventually Gabriel had fallen into a kind of half-sleep, his arms still clutching at the log while his mind drifted.

Then the sky had widened as the rocky cliffs gave way to...nothing. When Gabriel raised his head to look around, he found himself drifting on the ocean, the cliffs of the shoreline already growing smaller.

Cold and exhausted, there was little he could do but watch as the current carried him farther out to sea.

How long he had drifted, Gabriel could not say. More than a day, for night had come at least once. But whether it was one or two or three, he could not recall. His mind was awash, his head throbbing. He ground his knuckles into his temples, willing the pain of the migraine away. His tongue rasped across his parched mouth, every sense screaming out for water.

Shivering, he held on.

His mind drifted and his grasp on the log loosened. Tears formed in his eyes, but he would not give in. This was not his time to die—not yet.

No, it is not, a chill voice sent fear through his soul. *There are still things for you to do.*

Gabriel cracked open his eyes, dread seeping into his heart.

A dark figure hovered over the water, staring down at

him. Cold seeped from the ethereal body, a ghostly wind that spoke of death. Black spirits raced about the spectre, covering it in a deathly cloak. It towered over his helpless body.

Gabriel closed his eyes. There was no mistaking it; this was the same entity which had come to him in the forest.

"What do you want, demon?" he croaked.

To help you, the spectre whispered, *as I once did before.*

"Go to hell, foul demon," Gabriel spat. "I will die before I take your help again."

And die you will. A chill ran down Gabriel's spine as its voice echoed in his head. *Soon you will slip beneath the dark waters.*

"So be it," Gabriel grated.

I can save you, Gabriel. You know I ask nothing in return.

Gabriel would have laughed if he'd had the strength. He knew now the demon lied, that its aid would cost his soul and more. He had sworn to Enala he would never allow himself to be drawn in by evil again. If that meant his death...

You do not wish to die. Honey laced the demon's voice. *Take my hand, Gabriel, and live.*

Gabriel looked up and saw the demon's outstretched hand. Purple veins lined the pale skin, and long white nails grew from its fingertips. He shuddered as it reached for him, his only lifeline in this grim ocean.

Temptation rose within Gabriel, temptation for the warm lure of life. If he took the offered hand, he would survive this nightmare. He could begin a new life, a better life. All he had to do was say yes.

He stared at the demon, watching the spirits roaming over its spectral form. A chill determination filled him, the temptation turning to dust. Death itself clothed this being; how could life come from such a creature?

Gabriel summoned the last of his strength. "No!" he shouted.

And the demon vanished.

A splash came from nearby. Gabriel looked up, his mind still reeling from the encounter. His vision blurred in and out of focus, but through the cloud he saw a ship surging towards him. Its prow cut through the waves and overhead men swung through the rigging like spiders. Its sails billowed out, filled by the ocean breeze.

Gabriel opened his mouth and tried to shout. The call came out as a croak, the wind catching it and whisking it away. He groaned and struggled to pull himself farther out of the water. Raising one hand he began to wave, praying they would see him. In desperation, he called again.

The ship drew level with him. Gabriel gritted his teeth in frustration, despair rising to swamp the fickle hope.

"Man overboard!" The cry carried across the water.

Eric paced across the empty hall. His footsteps echoed from the stone walls as he wove between marble pillars. The massive columns stretched high above to where the ceiling should have been; but here there was no roof to protect against the elements. The stars glittered overhead, staring down into the silent hall.

Midnight approached, and Eric doubted anyone else would be visiting the Sky temple at this time of night. Reaching the far wall he spun on his heel and began his third lap. It had taken two days and a night to reach Lon, during which time he had barely slept an hour.

Gabriel remained unconscious, but Eric knew it could not last. Michael said he was exhausted, dehydrated from his time in the ocean. But soon he would wake, and Eric would have to face the man who had hunted him halfway across the Three Nations. There would be a reckoning.

Questions spun through Eric's mind, each more difficult than the last. How had Gabriel survived the attack by the Baronians? How had he followed them across Plorsea, all the way to Dragon Country? And how had he found Enala, and rescued her from Chole?

Eric swung a fist at a column as he passed. He immediately regretted the reflex as pain shot up his arm.

Closing his eyes, Eric shrieked into the night. "Alastair, where are you? *I need you!*"

The wind caught Eric's words and swept them into the sky. He was alone now; Alastair was gone and there would be no bringing him back.

He had told the old man of his fear; that Gabriel was the one person he could not face. How could he, when Gabriel embodied the very crimes for which he sought redemption. How could Eric defend himself against a man from whom he had taken everything?

Eric's magic had destroyed Oaksville, had robbed Gabriel of his life and his family. Now the man had returned from the grave to haunt him, to remind Eric there was nothing he could do to balance out the evil he'd brought to Oaksville.

Eric sank to his knees, guilt weighing on his soul. What could he say to the man? That it had been an accident? That every action he had taken since was to make up for the horror he had wrought?

It would not matter, could not. Eric had seen the hatred in Gabriel's eyes when they'd last met; only revenge could quench that rage.

Inken had tried to reassure him on the ship, but there was nothing she or anyone else could say to make this right. When they arrived at the temple, he had held her tight, giving his silent thanks for her support. But he knew in his heart he would have to face this alone, that this was his battle to fight.

He excused himself after dinner and wandered out into

the night. The ship had dropped them on the temple's private wharf, ensuring Lon's citizens did not notice their arrival. The sailors had been happy to see the backs of them, some even cheering as the company carried Gabriel ashore. The captain accompanied them for as long as it took to claim his payment.

Fortunately the Sky priests had been happy with the price Michael negotiated. Jurrien had apparently called on them before their arrival, and warned of their approach. A group of priests had met them as they disembarked and led them to an empty dormitory usually reserved for apprentices.

The temple grounds consisted of the massive hall and a collection of smaller buildings and living quarters. After leaving the others, Eric had picked his way through the adjoining buildings until he reached the great hall.

Looking around, Eric imagined it during the day, when people flocked here seeking guidance from the Sky priests. He needed guidance now more than ever, but he doubted it was the kind the priests could offer. And from what he'd seen of Jurrien, the God did not seem to share his sister's approachable manner.

Reaching the centre of the hall, Eric stopped and sucked in a breath. Pacing would get him nowhere. Exhaustion had frazzled his mind. Thoughts bounced around his head like a broken wagon wheel, lost and confused. He needed to concentrate, to focus on the larger problems at hand. He could do nothing to change the current situation, at least not until Gabriel woke.

Letting out a long sigh, Eric sank to the ground and crossed his legs. Closing his eyes, he began to meditate. Alastair had taught him the technique as a way of controlling his emotions and learning self-control. Eric needed those skills now more than ever. His thoughts were chasing themselves around his mind in a self-destructive loop, always returning to the awful dread of the confrontation to come.

He breathed in again, seeking the calm centre amidst the storm. Thoughts assailed him, but as each rose he fought to let them go, to set them aside, if only for a moment. Turmoil crashed against him and exhaustion rolled through him like the ocean tide. He needed sleep, desperately. He had to break this cycle of anxiety.

Eric sank deeper, thoughts drifting back over the last few days. The confrontation with Jurrien loomed, but he pushed it aside. Still, he felt a pang of curiosity from the thought, from something Jurrien had done. As he left, the Storm God had leapt from the deck of the ship, where the wind had caught him and propelled him into the air.

Jurrien had *flown*.

Eric possessed the same magic as the God, and while he did not have the power to create, he *could* manipulate the winds as Jurrien had done. Could he also fly?

He smiled then, another memory leaping to mind. In Chole, Caelin had thrown him from a second story window and in his fear Eric's magic had summoned the wind to catch him. For a few seconds, he'd hovered several feet above the ground.

Sinking into his magic, Eric released his tethers to the physical realm and sent his spirit soaring. Silently, he sent feelers up into the clouds, seeking the great gusts which formed where land met ocean. Working his magic, he wound threads of power around the howling gales.

Grimacing, he syphoned his power into the threads, and drew them down, gathering the winds together as they came. The gusts fought him, pushing against the bonds holding them. Energy surged through his mind as he poured more magic into the fray, binding the air pockets tighter. With the city so close, he could not afford to allow such powerful gales to escape his grasp. The last thing he wanted was to start tearing the roofs off buildings.

Back in his body, he shivered as the first pocket of wind reached him. The gale whipped around his seated form, tearing at his clothes and hair, carrying the icy chill of the air currents high above the city. Shivers ran down his spine, but he smiled, happy to have come this far.

Turning inwards, he focused, pulling the wind in tighter and tighter knots. The gusts grew stronger, striking with a force that threatened to knock him flat. Clenching his fists, he pushed the pockets of air down to the paving. His feet grew numb as the icy wind wrapped about his legs, but now the rest of him remained warm.

With a shock, he felt the pressure push him upwards, lifting him from the cool tiles. He opened his eyes and gasped at the sight of several inches now separating his feet from the ground.

The magic slipped from his control, and the wind erupted outwards, whistling across the empty hall and upwards into the sky. He fell to the ground with an undignified thump.

Eric grinned, worries forgotten. His heart pounded hard in this chest as he clapped his hands in excitement. This was something new, something useful. But he needed practice. Closing his eyes, he tried again.

———

LON GLOWED IN THE DARKNESS, LIT BY THE LIGHT OF A thousand torches. The capital of Lonia spread out beneath him, the central hub of the farming nation. Rooftops glistened in the moonlight, each holding a family, a handful of souls asleep to the world. To the east the calm waters of the harbour lapped at the seawall, the nation's ships rocking at anchor. The walls of the citadel rose to the south, towering over the city.

Eric swallowed hard, staring down at the lights far below. The air jerked and he dropped several feet. Sweat dripped down his forehead, only to be whipped away by the swirling air. Goosebumps pricked his arms and a shiver ran through him. Within, his mind was in freefall, his vision spinning at the distance below him.

His fear of heights had come crashing back.

Stupid, stupid, stupid, the word danced about his head.

It had all been going fine. It had taken hours, but he had finally managed to keep himself aloft without losing control of the winds. He'd spent another hour floating around the great hall, then the temple grounds, lifting himself higher and higher as his confidence grew.

He had not noticed the fear at first, had not recognised the familiar tingle as it crept into his mind. Even as he soared higher, Eric reassured himself, convinced the wind would catch him if he fell. After all, it was the fall he feared, rather than the height itself. Nevertheless, the terror had trickled into his consciousness, slowly eroding his control. His movements grew jerky and erratic, and his panic began in earnest.

It was not until he tried to halt his ascent that he realised the magic had latched onto his fear, using it to take over. Now he rose faster than ever, as sudden judders threw him about each time the magic slipped. Terror rose in this throat, feeding strength to the winds. They twisted about him, converging from all around.

Eric sucked in a breath, wrestling for control. Within, the magic stalked his mind, a wolf in the darkness. He drew back, fear robbing him of strength. He could not face the beast now, suspended hundreds of feet in open air. If he lost, things would become far worse. Alastair was no longer here to protect him. There would be no coming back if the magic took control again. To lose would be to unleash his magic on Lon.

The winds swirled, gathering force and growing stronger. The cold sent shivers through Eric's unprotected body, his thin clothing woefully inadequate. His teeth chattered as the wind sucked the last warmth from his skin. Eric wrapped his arms tight around his chest and looked down, stomach roiling from the height.

He watched with horror as the wind swirled faster. He could feel the pressure building, a tornado forming high above the city, with Eric at its centre. If he did not act soon the destruction would be unimaginable.

Summoning his courage, Eric reached again for his magic. At his touch the power surged, and the winds holding him ceased, sending Eric into free fall. He spun through the air, hurtling towards the city, and all thought of control vanished.

When they caught him again, Eric could barely find the strength to breathe.

The tornado howled, drawing in the surrounding clouds, dampening the air. Tears ran down Eric's face. He could not let this happen, not again. He could feel the magic flooding from him, a free flow drawing in more and more of the Sky element. The air above the city darkened, the black tail of the tornado stretching down. Soon it would reach the city, and chaos would rein unchecked.

He could not let that happen.

With a scream he reached inside, wrenching at the magic within. The wolf rose before him, swamping his conscious, its blue glow shining with an angry rage. He felt no comfort from the magic now, no gentle pool of energy to draw on. The wolf towered over him, his magic come to life, fed by his fear.

Eric drew on every ounce of courage remaining to him, determined to defeat the wild beast. The wolf growled and came closer. With every step it took, it grew. Its teeth glinted with the blue of his magic, jaws dripping bloody malice.

He shrank back in despair. As he turned to flee, Alastair's words from long ago raced through his mind. *Master your fear. That is the magic's only weapon against you. If you do not fear it, your magic cannot harm you.*

Eric swallowed, turning back to the beast. He remembered the terror he'd felt after the desert, the fear of his magic had threatened to overwhelm him. Knowing the risks, he had faced that fear and vanquished it. In doing so, he had returned the rains to Chole.

Now he must do the same, or his wild magic would destroy the city below. He could not allow that to happen.

He faced the beast, reaching out to grasp the glow of its fur. Fear sent a tremor through his knees, but he squashed it down, baring his teeth at the beast before him. They stood facing one another, locked in a silent battle of wills.

Then Eric blinked, and watched as the wolf started to shrink. It growled and took a step towards him, raising hairs on his neck, but he stood strong. He knew he had won. The winds still buffeted him, throwing him about the sky, but the fear no longer crippled him.

Taking a firmer hold of his magic, he sent its tendrils out to bind the wolf. It screamed and leapt for him, but the magic grasped it tight, locking it in place. Eric smiled, and drew the beast back down within him, until it vanished into the glowing pool of light.

The air still raged about him. He reached out again with his magic, confident now he could halt the whirling twister. Gritting his teeth, he tore apart the binds holding the winds together. The swirling ceased as air erupted outwards into empty sky.

"*You fool!*" The air shook with the power in the voice, and then a dark body hurtled from the sky.

Eric caught a glimpse of white hair and a face twisted with rage before Jurrien smashed into him. The breath whooshed from his lungs and he found himself suddenly in free fall, careering through the clouds towards the ground below.

As he reached for his magic, a fist crashed into his face.

"*Don't!*" Jurrien snapped, his hands digging into Eric's shirt.

Their plummet towards the earth ceased with a violent jerk. The wind reformed around them, controlled now by Jurrien. He looked up at the God, his face lit by the light of the city below. Fear tingled down Eric's spine as he saw the anger there.

When they reached the ground Jurrien tossed Eric to the grass. Before he could recover, the Storm God grasped Eric by the collar and wrenched him to his feet. Jurrien pulled him close, leaving Eric no choice but to look into those icy blue eyes.

"How could you be so reckless?" Jurrien hissed. "Did Alastair teach you *nothing?*"

"I...I don't know," Eric stuttered. Tears came to his eyes.

"All I know is Alastair is gone. He's dead, and I...I'm lost." He waved his hand at the sky. "The magic...it just took control."

A tremor of rage swept through Jurrien. He tossed Eric back to the ground. Thunder clapped as Eric rolled and came to his feet.

"You are no Magicker. You do not even deserve the title of apprentice. If it was in my power, I would strip the magic from you here and now. I do not care what my sister thought of you. You are as likely to kill us all as save us!"

Eric shivered with cold and fear. "I had control of it, there at the end." His voice shook, but he stood his ground. "I may be a novice, but I will not let history repeat itself."

Jurrien turned his back, fingers raking his hair. "I cannot afford this...these distractions." He spun. "Antonia is dead. I am the only one left to stand against Archon."

The breath caught in Eric's throat. "No," he choked. "How can that be possible?"

"She was weakened by our battle with Archon. The demon took her by surprise. And it used the *Soul Blade* to do the foul deed, which means it now has her powers. It must be found, and quickly, before it collects any other magic."

"How could you not have told us?" Rage grew from Eric's sorrow. "Where have you been?"

"I have been everywhere: alerting King Fraser and King Jonathan to the threat, the council of Lonia too. Mustering our armies, spreading the word. Archon is coming, and the Three Nations must stand together if we are to have any chance of stopping him." He shook his head. "Even then, I do not believe it will be enough. Even with the Sword of Light, without Antonia we would lack the power to stop him." He clenched his fists. Lightning crackled along his arm.

"Where is the demon now?" Eric asked.

"I have Magickers hunting it. They will signal me when it reappears, though they will not have the power to stop it. If it collects any more magic, it may be beyond even my powers. Last signs showed it heading north into Lonia, towards us."

"It is coming here?"

Jurrien scowled. "How should I know what it will do next? Perhaps it is trying to return to its master. Perhaps it is hunting the last of the Sword wielders. Or perhaps it is coming for me. I do not know. There is too much to consider."

"What can we do to help?"

Jurrien laughed, the sound harsh and mocking. "Help? *Help?* You could start by leaving my city be," he fell silent, and Eric thought he might finish with that. When Jurrien continued his tone was sombre. "Your priority must be getting Enala to the Sword. It lies in Kalgan, a long way from here. Archon's agents will be looking for her now."

"The best path to take would be a ship up the river to Ardath. From there you will have to continue on foot through the Branei pass into Trola, and then down the coast to Kalgan. It will take weeks. I only hope we have the strength to hold Archon back that long."

"When can we leave?"

Jurrien exhaled sharply. "It will take a few days to organise. My priests will take care of it. I must leave, there is much to be done." He turned and walked into the night.

Eric opened his mouth to wish him farewell, but the God vanished before he could speak the words. Shaking his head, Eric sank to his knees. Exhaustion rose in his chest, sucking the strength from his limbs. His stomach twisted. He hung his head, taking a deep breath. He needed to return to the dormitory and sleep. Only then would he have the energy to take in everything Jurrien had said.

Footsteps came from nearby. Eric looked up in time to see a figure emerge from the shadows. A familiar voice greeted him.

"So, we meet again."

4

Gabriel woke in darkness, the last dredges of a nightmare clinging to him. Panic gripped his mind and sent him tumbling from the bed. Climbing to his feet, he stumbled across the unfamiliar room, fumbling for an exit as he struck a wall. He cursed as his elbow caught on a doorknob, and then slipped silently through the unlocked door.

Outside he hurried down an empty corridor, trying doors until he found one leading outside. Slipping into the night, he started across the grass, the dew cold on his bare feet.

Wind whipped at him and he heard a crash from overhead. Looking up, he froze, fear gripping his heart. The lanterns of the city lit the sky above, revealing black clouds spinning inexorably towards a whirling centre.

Gabriel took an involuntary step backwards. He gaped, unable to comprehend the vision. Light flickered across the underbellies of the clouds, and it seemed he looked into a portal to hell itself. The wind on the ground picked up as the tail of the twister grew closer.

Then another crash came, followed by the flicker of lightning, and the swirling ceased. The clouds drifted to a stop and the wind died away, returning the night to tranquil silence.

Gabriel stared as two figures tumbled from the sky, plummeting towards the grounds on which he stood. As they approached they slowed, finally landing close to where Gabriel waited. They did not appear to have seen him.

Taking a breath, Gabriel continued through the night, creeping towards where the two had landed. He shivered in the cool; even without the wind, winter was not far away, and the clothes he wore were thin, not made for the outdoors. A dull ache throbbed at the back of his skull and his knees shook, but he did not care.

Gabriel could hardly believe he lived. He had been just minutes away from sinking beneath the waves when the ship appeared.

It seemed someone, or something, was still looking out for him.

The faces of his rescuers had appeared only as blurs to his sunburnt eyes, but as he turned a corner and saw the two figures standing on the grass, he knew who they had been.

Gabriel stared at the young man, the same one he'd hunted halfway across Plorsea. He could hardly believe it. There he was, the demon boy who had burned Oaksville to the ground, who had murdered Gabriel's family and left him for dead.

He felt the familiar anger well up within him, the hate that had driven him so far. He watched as the older man turned away, vanishing into the night. Taking a breath, Gabriel walked into the light.

"So, we meet again."

The young man looked up, and Gabriel saw with surprise the lines of exhaustion stretching from his eyes. "Gabriel," he paused. "You're awake."

His words confirmed Gabriel's suspicions. "So it was you who rescued me at sea." He stared. "*Why?*"

"Because we could not leave you there to die. That is not who I am."

"We? Who else is with you?"

The young man smiled. "There are five of us, though you know only one—Enala."

Gabriel started, the name echoing through his mind. *Enala?*

He shook his head, anger catching light. "You have Enala? What have you done with her?" He took a step closer.

The young man rolled his eyes and raised his hands in surrender. "We have done nothing with her. In fact, she saved our lives back in Dragon Country. And then we saved hers. We are protecting her against forces you cannot begin to understand."

"Oh really? And why should I believe a word you say, *demon*. Who are you? What do you want?"

Eric scowled. "My name is Eric, and I am no *demon*. I am a Magicker—or at least I have been for the last few weeks," he looked away, his voice dropping to barely a whisper. "Before Oaksville, before Alastair, I did not know what I was—only that I was cursed."

Gabriel watched the young man, his anger mounting. "What are you saying? That Oaksville was not you? That it was some accident?"

Eric met Gabriel's gaze, the lightning blue eyes piercing him. "I am sorry, Gabriel. There is nothing I can do to make it right, but I had no control of my magic then, no way to stop the forces that descended on Oaksville." He sucked in a gulp of winter air. "But I have spent every moment since then trying to atone."

Tears welled in Gabriel's eyes as he listened to Eric's words. He could hear the pain in his voice, the regret. But he could not bring himself to believe the words, to believe it had all been a mistake. Everything he had sacrificed, it could not have been for nothing. He had sold his soul, had committed *murder,* all to bring justice for his family.

"My parents, my fiancée." His voice shook. "They are dead because of you."

Eric hung his head. "Yes."

Only a few feet separated the two now. Gabriel reached out and grabbed Eric by the shirt. His eyes widened as Gabriel lifted him into the air and shook him. "*They're dead!*"

Eric kicked out, striking Gabriel hard between the legs. Gabriel choked and tossed him to the ground. He stumbled back and glared at Eric.

Eric climbed to his feet, sadness on his face. "I cannot change the past, Gabriel, but I will do everything in my power to make the future better."

Gabriel answered with a cold laugh. He waved at the sky. "And that? Was that you making the future better?"

Eric paled. "Yes, it was me. I lost control, for a while. But I stopped it." He brushed dirt from his arm. "I am not perfect, but as I told Jurrien, I will never allow what happened in Oaksville to happen again."

A chill spread through Gabriel's stomach. "Jurrien?"

"Yes, the Storm God is not a fan of me either. But we

have bigger dangers to consider now, other threats to face. Even here, Enala is not safe from the ones who hunt her."

"What do you mean?" Shaking his head, Gabriel looked around, realising he had no idea where they were. "Where are we? Who is hunting Enala?"

"We are in Lon. And Enala is being hunted by Archon. He wants her dead, Gabriel, and if he succeeds the rest of us will quickly follow."

Gabriel stared, his head spinning. "*What?*"

Eric grimaced and began to talk. Gabriel could only stare as Eric told him of Enala's lineage, and the curse that had been placed on the Trolan king's bloodline. His head throbbed and his heart quickened with fear. He sank to the ground as he listened to Eric's tale of the events which had unfolded since he'd separated from Enala.

Swallowing hard, Gabriel tried to process what Eric was saying. He thought back to the cool, collected young woman he had fled with from Chole. Devastated by the loss of her family, she had nevertheless shown a steely courage in the face of her pursuers. She had been as at home in the jungles of Plorsea as in the dusty streets of Chole.

But the last hope of the Three Nations? It cannot be true. The thought whispered through Gabriel's mind.

"Archon's minions will not give up. If they succeed, the Three Nations will fall before Archon's magic. Jurrien has asked us to protect her at all costs, to take her to the Trolan capital. Until she picks up the Sword of Light, she is in terrible danger."

Gabriel swallowed, eyes fixed on Eric. There had to be more to this, something missing from the story. He would not, could not trust Eric.

"Where is she?"

"This way," Eric strode past and back towards the building Gabriel had woken in.

Gabriel followed, lost deep in his thoughts.

They entered the dormitory through a small set of doors in the front and found themselves in a modest entranceway. This was a different door from which Gabriel had fled. He looked around as they wiped their feet on the rug, taking in the bare stone walls and simple wooden floors. Beyond the entrance way he glimpsed an interior lounge furnished with couches and a table.

Eric picked his way through the lounge. Gabriel followed, the path lit by a fire burning low in its grate on the far wall. Eric did not look back, and Gabriel guessed he did not care much whether Gabriel followed or not. He moved slowly though, shoulders slumped in exhaustion.

Gabriel's own energy was quickly fading, his body still shattered from the time adrift. His mouth felt dry and his head pounded with a headache. It would take some days yet before he made a full recovery.

Together they made their way through a door at the end of the room and into a corridor Gabriel recognised. Eric strode down its length, glancing at the doors on their left until he reached the one he wanted. Reaching up, he tapped on the door. They waited.

Shifting on his feet, Gabriel glanced up and down the hallway, suddenly nervous. How would Enala react to seeing him again, after thinking him dead? Only a few days had passed since the river, but to Gabriel it felt a lifetime. The world had changed while he drifted at sea, and his mind was still racing to catch up.

Eric reached up to knock again, but the door creaked open and a woman leaned out. Red hair hung across her face and she looked as though she'd just woken from a deep sleep, but she smiled when she saw Eric. She reached out and embraced him, then noticed Gabriel standing in the shadows. Her smile faded.

She stepped back and stared at him. "You must be Gabriel." It was not a question. "Glad to see you are awake."

Gabriel nodded. "Who are you?"

The woman hesitated and then held out her hand. "My name is Inken. You must be here to see Enala."

"Yes, is she awake?"

Another face appeared behind Inken. Dark rings hung below her eyes and her blond hair was unkempt, but her sapphire eyes brightened when she saw him. "Gabriel." Her voice exploded into the corridor as she launched herself at him.

Gabriel laughed as she knocked him back a few steps. He held her tight against his chest, relief flooding him. He had never expected to see her again, not once the dragon attacked and the current dragged him under. To find her here, alive and well, was a miracle.

He heard Eric clear his throat and glanced up. "You two obviously have some catching up to do. We'll talk in the morning." He glanced at Inken. "Shall we find someplace else to rest?"

Inken laughed and leaned across to kiss him. "Let's."

They moved away down the corridor, leaving the two of them alone. Enala drew him into the room. Inside he found four wooden bunk beds and little else. Only two of the beds had been slept in, the ruffled covers suggesting Enala and Inken preferred the bottom bunks. Heavy curtains hung over the window at the end of the room. A thin sliver of moonlight shone through a slit between them, providing a touch of light.

Enala moved across to her bed and sat down. Gabriel followed suit, lowering himself onto the bed Inken had occupied. He looked across at her, just able to make out her smile in the darkness.

"I can't believe you're here," she whispered. She reached across the space between the beds and grasped his hand.

Gabriel smiled in return. "I can hardly believe it either. How did we get to Lon?"

Enala shrugged. "It's a long story," she said, shivering, and he saw the glint of tears in her eyes. "This was just where the ship was heading."

Gabriel hesitated. "Eric...he told me some of what happened. About your dragon?"

A sob cut the air. Before she could reply Gabriel moved to sit beside her. He pulled her into a hug, offering his silent comfort.

So at least part of Eric's story was true.

"Her name was Nerissa," Enala spoke at last. "She found me not long after I lost you, as I knew she would. I have known her since I was a child, when my family used to bring me to Dragon Country. I always thought nothing could hurt me so long as I was with her. I thought..." her voice broke. "I thought she could protect me."

Enala trembled in his arms. He held her tight, lost for words. He knew next to nothing about this girl, had only known her a few days. But during their time together they had become friends, comrades in arms against the unknown force pursuing them.

At last, Enala broke away. She glanced at Gabriel. "You remember now, don't you? What happened to you before the demon."

Gabriel took a deep, trembling breath. "Yes." Slowly, he

recounted his story, starting with the storm that had destroyed Oaksville. He did not hold back, made no attempt to cast himself in a better light. He had done so much wrong, made so many mistakes he could hardly bear to recall them. But after all she had been through, Enala deserved the truth.

When at last he finished, he drew in a deep breath and looked Enala in the eyes. "We cannot trust these people, Enala."

———

"Doesn't say much, does he?" Inken commented, lying on the bed beside Eric.

Eric smiled and pulled her closer, brushing a strand of hair from her face. "He had plenty to say earlier."

Inken smiled back, her skin tingling where Eric's fingers touched. "And?"

She felt a shiver run through Eric. "I said what I could. I don't think it made a difference," he hesitated. "I'm glad he's alive though, that I could apologise. I know it cannot make up for what happened, but maybe now I have a chance to show him who I really am, that I'm trying to put things right."

"I hope so too." She flashed him a sly smile. "Although I couldn't help but notice some strange goings on in the sky when I looked out the window earlier."

Eric groaned and Inken leaned across to kiss him. "What happened?"

"I wanted to try something, to copy what Jurrien did when he leapt off the ship."

"And?"

"It worked, but I pushed too far, too fast. The magic

took me well above my limits, and I lost control." Inken heard the venom in his voice.

She smiled. "Stop being so hard on yourself, Eric. You took control again before anything happened, that's what matters."

Eric gave a sour laugh. "Small victory that," he paused. "I didn't really have time to think about it. Jurrien showed up again. He had a lot to say about me and my magic."

Inken's heart gave a lurch. She suddenly found herself wishing she had followed Eric earlier.

"Ouch." Eric flinched away and Inken realised her nails had dug into his arm.

She released him. "Sorry, Eric. I do not like Jurrien; he is not like his sister. He is shrouded in anger, where Antonia is a calming force."

"Was," Eric's voice cracked. "Antonia was...he found her in the forest. The demon killed her. She's...she's gone."

Inken stared, unable to speak. She felt hot tears in her eyes but made no effort to wipe them away. A sound rumbled up from her chest, a half-warped sob that she abruptly cut off. She shook her head. "No," she choked. "How could that happen?"

"I don't know," Eric's voice broke again. "But we have to go on, for her. It's up to us now, to ensure Enala gets to the Sword in time. Maybe it will be enough. Jurrien is preparing the Three Nations for war and hunting down the demon."

Silence fell then, the weight of responsibility settling around them like a lead weight. With Antonia gone, the likelihood any of them would survive the coming war seemed non-existent. Last time it had taken the powers of all three Gods to overcome Archon. With only Jurrien and the Sword of Light, could they even hold their own?

"We have to try," Inken whispered.

"I know. We can't give up. I won't rest until we finish the quest Alastair and Antonia started."

Inken pulled him close again, leaning over to kiss him. Their lips met, fierce and hard. She held him tight, desperate to feel the life within him. He had come so close to death on the beach. Just thinking of the danger to come filled her with fear—not for herself, but for the reckless young man she loved. Eric told the truth; he would not run from the peril they faced—he would rather die.

Inken feared it may come to that.

Unbidden, hot tears ran down her cheek. Sobbing, she broke away from Eric, turning her face to hide the tears.

He heard her grief anyway. She felt his hand reach up to stroke her hair. Closing her eyes, Inken took a deep breath to calm herself.

"It's going to be okay, Inken."

Inken felt a wild, insane laughter bubbling within her. She held it back. They both knew the lie in Eric's words. If even the Goddess of the Earth could fall to Archon, what chance did mortals have? Even if by some miracle they managed to defeat Archon, how many of them would survive the battle? How many souls would perish? Who of their company would live to see the dawn of a new peace?

It would be so easy to turn now and run, to find some hole in which the dark tendrils of the north would not find them. But she knew they could not. There was too much at stake, and if Archon conquered, the darkness would find them wherever they hid.

No, there was no choice but to fight.

Slowly the sobs subsided as she regained her composure. They lay there in silence, each lost in their own thoughts. Here in Jurrien's temple she felt safe, even if she now counted the Storm God amongst her adversaries. The darkness felt almost comforting with Eric beside her, as if it could hide them from the world without. But she knew it could not last, that morning would soon bring the light of day. If they remained, Archon would find them.

Only one option offered them hope. Get Enala to the Sword of Light, before all hell broke loose.

Inken closed her eyes and breathed in Eric's familiar scent. Whatever the future may bring, they still had this moment, right here, right now.

She resolved not to waste it.

✿ 5 ✿

"Y̶ou lied to me," Enala stood in the entrance to the lounge, arms folded across her chest.

They had been talking before she entered, but they broke off now, staring up at the two of them in the doorway. Silence settled like autumn leaves as Enala looked around the room, eyes lingering on each of them. Inken, Eric, Caelin, and Michael; she knew their names, though she had not spoken to half of them.

She and Gabriel had stayed up half the night talking. He had told her of the past he now remembered, of the storm which had destroyed Oaksville and killed his family. At first she had not believed him when he claimed Eric had brought the storm. She may not have spoken to the young man, but she could not believe he was a killer. But Gabriel was insistent, unwavering in his belief.

Now Enala wanted answers. Inken had said she could trust them, that they cared about her. But if Gabriel was right...

Eric shifted in his seat, looking like he was about to

speak, but Inken beat him to it. "No, we didn't. I know you trust Gabriel, that he saved your life in Chole. But there is more than one side to this story."

Enala glanced at Gabriel. He stood staring at Eric, his face blank, unreadable.

She looked back to Inken. "Tell me then."

Inken nodded. She glanced at the others. "Enala and I are going for a walk. Don't eat all the food," Enala caught the warning glance Inken shot Caelin as she stood.

Caelin raised his hands in surrender. "Don't look at me. I was thinking I'd get some exercise before breakfast anyway," he looked at the others. "Perhaps Gabriel and Eric will join me. You too, Michael, if you're interested?"

Enala picked her way across the room and joined Inken as she walked out into the cool morning air.

"I'm quite alright thank you, Caelin," she caught Michael's words as the door swung shut behind her.

Inken led the way across the grass and into the gardens surrounding the temple grounds. White frost crunched beneath their boots as they made their way through an archway hung with winter roses. Mist billowed from their mouths with every breath, but the sun had just peeked over the rooftops of the nearest buildings. As its rays reached them, warmth spread through Enala's limbs. The rich scent of roses hung in the air.

"I first met Eric and Alastair in the desert of Chole. I was dying; my horse had fled and I was unarmed and badly injured. If Eric had not spotted me, I would be dead," they left the grass and stepped onto a gravel path leading through the gardens.

"What does that prove? That he has a soft spot for you?"

Inken scowled and Enala felt her cheeks grow hot. "Perhaps you'll let me finish before you begin flinging accusations. There is far more to this story than Gabriel knows. Eric has never meant to hurt anyone with his power; he did not even know he possessed magic before Alastair found him in Oaksville."

"What do you mean?"

"Before Oaksville, Eric spent the better part of two years wandering the wilderness, afraid to return to civilisation for fear of what he thought of as his curse. He did not know it was magic, only that there was some power within him he could not control. But finally, he could no longer bear the isolation. He went to Oaksville to begin a new life, but within an hour of entering the town he was attacked by slavers," Inken spoke in a soft voice.

"When an emerging Magicker has not been properly trained, their magic is tied to their emotions. It is unleashed when they are overwhelmed. When Eric was attacked, his fear and anger took control, and his magic lashed out to protect him."

"What do you mean?"

Inken stopped, gravel crunching beneath her boots. The thorns of a nearby rose caught in Enala's coat as she turned to meet Inken's gaze. "Eric had no choice in what happened, not once attacked. He had every reason to fear for his life, to feel enraged at the men attacking him. He could not direct how his magic responded to those emotions, not without training."

Enala looked away, remembering her horror as she hid in the basement, while men murdered her parents upstairs. The anger had almost driven her to madness. She thought of Eric, unarmed and at the mercy of such thugs. Then she felt a pang of horror as she imagined the helplessness he must have felt once the power was unleashed. To know it was his doing, but being powerless to cease the destruction.

Tears sprang to her eyes. "Does Gabriel know this?"

Inken shook her head. "So far, he has not been too receptive to any explanation.

"Can you blame him?"

"No, of course not. But he is not the only one to have lost those he loves," she paused, choosing her next words carefully. "Eric's parents were the first victims of his wild magic."

Enala's heart twisted in pain. She opened her mouth, but found no words.

Inken nodded, a sad smile on her lips. "You, Gabriel and Eric have much in common. Like it or not, you are linked by tragedy, and will continue, I hope, to fight together on the side of good," she paused. "You should also know; Eric is determined to put right the debt he feels for Oaksville. That is why he used his magic to bring the rain back to Chole."

Enala gaped. "What?"

"That was when I knew he was not the demon everyone thought him, and when I decided I wanted to get to know him better," Inken winked.

Enala stared, lost again for words. Eric may have cursed Gabriel's town to ruin, but he had saved Chole, her city. How could anyone weigh the two deeds against one another, as great and as awful as they were?

Yet Enala could feel the truth in Inken's words, that Eric had never meant to harm Oaksville, that he'd had no control over what happened there.

"I'll try to talk to Gabriel," Enala finally offered. "But I don't know if he will listen. The two of them might have to work it out themselves."

Accident or not, Eric's magic had still caused the death of Gabriel's family. Whatever the circumstances, Enala could not blame him for hating the young man. But perhaps the truth might at least open a dialogue between them.

"Agreed," Inken smiled. "I think us girls had best stay out of this one."

Enala shot back a sly look. "You really love him, don't you?"

She saw Inken's cheeks redden, and laughed. Inken wagged a finger back at her. "That is none of your business, miss. You don't see me asking about what's between yourself and Gabriel!"

Enala felt her own cheeks warm. She opened her eyes wide. "Whatever are you talking about?" she asked. "We're friends, we slept in separate beds and everything."

Inken laughed. "I'll bet," she sniped, but let the subject drop.

They rounded the corner of a building and found themselves at the end of the garden. In the distance the dormitory's shale roof gleamed in the morning sun. The far-off ring of steel blades carried to their ears. Beside her, Inken straightened and reached for her sabre. Enala edged closer to the woman.

She searched the grassy lawns ahead, her eyes picking out two figures battling in front of the dormitory. They both stopped dead as they recognised the fighters. Gabriel and Eric were locked in furious combat, swords slashing at one another as they stumbled on the icy grass.

Inken moved first, her long legs eating up the distance. Enala trotted after her, reaching out to grab her shoulder. "Wait," she said, pointing.

Inken tore herself free, but glanced towards where Enala pointed.

Caelin stood nearby, arms folded as he watched the two with an amused grin. Enala could practically hear Inken's teeth grinding as she switched directions and headed for the sergeant.

Enala could not help but grin. "Like you said, Inken. Maybe they can work it out themselves."

———

ERIC RUBBED HIS HANDS AGAINST HIS ARMS, STRUGGLING TO warm himself. A shiver ran down his back as the wind whipped past. "What are we doing?" he asked through chattering teeth.

Caelin stood with hands on his hips. "Jurrien paid me a visit this morning. Apparently you need another way to protect yourself, Eric," he turned to Gabriel. "And I'm sure you could use blowing off a little steam."

Eric glanced at Gabriel, heart sinking at the mention of Jurrien. The sun shone across the nearby rooftops, but they stood in the shade, the frost still thick at their feet. Eric already missed the gentle warmth of the fire burning in the lounge. The sky shone with the bright blue of morning, without a hint of cloud.

Caelin tossed a long bundle of cloth to the ground in front of them. It rattled as it struck, unravelling to reveal a collection of swords.

"These are practice blades. They're lead weighted, but the edges and tips have been blunted, so you shouldn't be able to damage each other too much."

As he spoke, he drew his own sword and beckoned Eric closer. Eric moved across to him, but stepped back as Caelin flicked the sword into the air and caught it by the blade.

He held it out to Eric. "First though, this is yours, Eric. It saved my life in Malevolent Cove, but I know Alastair would have wanted you to have it. Make him proud."

Heart pounding in his chest, Eric reached out and gripped the hilt. The worn leather felt warm and the short sword light in his hand. It shone in the morning sun, revealing the faint traces of runes etched in the metal. Eric looked closer, but could not make out the writing. He guessed it must be something to do with the spell on the blade, which protected its user from magic.

Remembering himself, he grinned up at Caelin. "Thank you, Caelin. I will."

"What did you want with me?" Gabriel asked.

Caelin's eyes turned on Gabriel. "I thought you might enjoy being Eric's sparring partner."

Eric made to object, but Gabriel beat him too it. "Why would I want to help *him?*"

Caelin met Gabriel's stare. Eric looked from one to another. "Maybe because we saved you, pulled you from the ocean waters rather than leave you to drown. Or because we rescued Enala, when you had failed her," Caelin paused, a sly look in his eyes. "Or perhaps you'd just like the chance to land a few blows on the boy."

Gabriel glared at Caelin, then shrugged his shoulders and approached the pile of weapons. Retrieving a practice blade, he stepped in front of Eric. "Well, let's see what you're made of then."

Eric scowled back. Gritting his teeth, he stepped around Gabriel and found a practice blade of his own. Lifting the heavy weapon, he laid Alastair's blade by the pile of swords. As he turned to face Gabriel, he drew in a deep breath of cool air. Bracing himself, he walked across the grass and squared off against his foe.

Caelin clapped. "Good! Now, before you begin, let me show you a few things about fighting with the sword," he picked up a blade for himself and moved between them.

"The first thing a good swordsman needs to learn is how to stand in a fight. A true fighter will use any number of stances in a fight to overcome his opponent. Different stances allow you to move in and out of attacking range while maintaining your balance, and without overexposing yourself to an attack. I'm going to show you one or two, and hope that'll be enough for now."

He moved his feet so they were shoulder width apart and facing forward, with the right about a foot in front of the left. "This is called a forward stance. It doesn't matter which foot is in the front, so each time you move you can step straight into this stance. It gives a fighter a solid, balanced base to launch and defend against attacks."

Eric moved his feet to mimic Caelin's, feeling awkward with the heavy blade in hand. He followed the soldier's movements as he drilled them in the basics of thrusts, parries and blocks. Eric immediately began tripping over his own feet as he struggled to obey Caelin's instructions. His body ached from the brief scuffle the night before, and within his magic felt drained and weak.

He watched Gabriel swinging the practice blade to match Caelin's movements, a bored smile on his face. His large shoulders wielded the blade with ease, although his movements were slow and somewhat clumsy. Still, Eric could not help but think the power in his swing would leave a nasty bruise.

"Okay, that should be enough for now. How about the two of you show me what you can do," Caelin stepped back and folded his arms. "The practice blades may be dulled, but you will still need to be careful," he gave them each a hard stare. "Blows to the head are off-limits."

Gabriel grinned and raised his blade in mock salute. "It's about time," he crouched low and crept towards Eric.

Eric wiped sweat from his brow and took a firmer grim of his sword. He kept the tip pointing at Gabriel the way Caelin had shown them, and slid into the forwards stance. After half an hour of practice, it almost felt comfortable. Pushing down his fear, he summoned an arrogance he did not feel, and waved Gabriel forward. "Come on then, let's see what you've got."

Gabriel grinned, and charged.

Eric held his ground until the last moment, and then ducked beneath Gabriel's wild swing. He leapt backwards as Gabriel attempted to reverse the cut, lashing out with his own blade to counterattack. The blow went wide, but Gabriel still flinched backwards in surprise.

They eyed each other. Eric smiled, masking his nerves, and motioned Gabriel forward again. The larger man scowled and edged his way to the left. Eric followed him, careful to keep his stance tight. His eyes narrowed as he searched for an opening. He held his sword low, ready to strike when Gabriel moved into range.

Gabriel struck again, more cautious now, aware he could not simply beat his way through Eric's guard. He slid forward, swinging his blade at Eric's side in an awkward cut. Eric danced backwards to avoid the blow, then leapt to the attack. His sword snaked out, biting at Gabriel's thigh.

Stumbling backwards, Gabriel swore and fixed Eric with a glare. Eric did not attempt to pursue his larger opponent, guessing it would be foolish to come within range of Gabriel's blade. Instead he dropped into a crouch, and waited.

Gabriel bared his teeth. "What, are you afraid?" he spat.

Eric only smiled, refusing to let Gabriel get under his skin.

With a scream, Gabriel charged across the open ground.

Eric backtracked, raising his sword to fend off a wild blow. Their blades met with a dull ring and the blade vibrated in Eric's hand. Pain lanced down his arm as he blocked again. Gabriel was not holding back any longer; each blow carried the full force of his strength.

Ducking beneath a wicked swing, Eric leapt back out of Gabriel's reach. He brushed a hand through his hair, already feeling the heat of exertion burning off the morning chill. Gabriel paused to do the same, a grin on his face. He was enjoying this.

The break did not last long. Gabriel brought his sword about and returned to the attack. Eric swung to counter, but his feet slipped on the damp grass and his sword went wide. Pain lanced from his side as Gabriel's weapon struck his hip. Swearing, Eric kicked out, catching Gabriel on the knee. They both stumbled backwards.

Gabriel's grin widened. "There's more where that came from."

Eric did not waste energy replying. He panted heavily, breath fogging the crisp air, the exertions of the night already catching up to him.

This is exhausting! Eric now had a new respect for Caelin's endurance. He had watched the sergeant take on three men at once while hardly breaking a sweat.

The ache in his hip throbbed in time with the beat of his heart. Cursing his clumsiness, Eric allowed his anger to take hold. He gripped the practice blade tighter, and leapt to the attack.

Gabriel's eyes widened. He raised his sword in a clumsy block, but Eric's sword slipped beneath and struck him in the stomach. Gabriel staggered backwards, wheezing as he fought for breath. Eric stepped back, allowing him to recover.

When he did, Gabriel leapt at him with a roar. Eric stood his ground, fighting to hold his own as Gabriel unleashed a string of blows. His arm shook with each clash. He began to retreat, ducking and dodging, while making the occasional attack of his own. Several times Gabriel's blade snuck through, biting at Eric's flesh. Within minutes his arms and body stung from the kiss of Gabriel's sword.

Gabriel kept on, seeming to gain strength with every blow. Swearing, Eric fought on, his strength waning rapidly. His boots grew heavier, his weary legs unable to move with the same speed as earlier. He struggled to keep his blade moving, to jump from the path of Gabriel's blows. He all but gave up counterattacking.

His foe's grin widened with each swing. It seemed adrenaline now more than countered whatever fatigue he felt from his time adrift.

At least, even exhausted, Eric still moved faster than his opponent. He found himself studying Gabriel's movements, watching for the first clench of muscle or flicker in his eyes to reveal his next attack. Gabriel's bulk made him slow and his inexperience provided more than enough warning for Eric to avoid most of his blows.

Not all of them though, Eric winced as Gabriel's blade bounced from his own and smashed against his elbow. Arm numb, Eric backed away.

Sensing blood, Gabriel pressed the attack.

Eric swore, feet carrying him to safety as Gabriel's blade glanced from his shoulder. He lashed out to cover his retreat.

Gabriel knocked the blow aside, contempt on his face. "Not so tough without your magic, are you?" he mocked.

"Least I'm not a bumbling buffoon like you," Eric snapped back, pain driving his anger.

Gabriel only grinned, and struck again. Eric raised his sword but Gabriel knocked it aside, his shoulder driving into Eric's chest. The force of the collision knocked the wind from his lungs, sending Eric tumbling across the ground. The sword spun from his grip, landing a few feet from where he lay.

Gabriel laughed and raised his sword over Eric's head.

Dimly, Eric heard Caelin shouting something. His ears rang, making Caelin's voice seem distant and frail. He summoned the last of his strength and threw himself from the path of Gabriel's blade. A soft thud came from behind him as mud sprayed the air.

Gabriel wrenched his blade free of the earth and came after him. Eric gasped for breath, unable to summon the strength to move. The sword appeared overhead, already descending towards his head.

Eric raised an arm over his face in a feeble attempt to protect himself.

Metal shrieked on metal as another blade blocked the blow.

"Enough," Enala growled. "If you want a real contest, you'll fight me."

———

Enala studied Gabriel and Eric as they fought, wincing each time the heavy blades found flesh. Gabriel's bulk clearly gave him the edge, but both would have some nasty bruises come tomorrow. She herself was used to the harsh sting of practice blades; her parents had taught her from a young age how to fight. It was a pleasant change to see someone else suffering.

The two young men appeared almost equally incompetent, but she could see Gabriel slowly gaining the advantage. His strength and reach drove Eric backwards, and despite his speed, Enala could see Eric beginning to fade.

She could also see the rage masked behind Gabriel's eyes, that he would not stop should Eric fall. Moving away from Inken, she walked to the bundle of blades beside Caelin. Retrieving one, she crossed the field to where the fight was drawing to an end.

As Eric fell she leapt forward, her sword flicking out to catch Gabriel's blow. Her own anger caught light in her chest, rising from the depths of her pain. With everything they faced, how could these two still be fighting one another? A dark tide was sweeping towards them, and their only chance of survival was to stand together.

"Enough," she growled. "If you want a real contest, you'll fight me," it was all she could do to hold back her rage.

"What are you doing?" Gabriel snapped. "You know what he did!"

"I do—you don't. You don't have the whole story, so enough of this nonsense. If you had listened to anyone, you would know what truly happened. These people helped me, saved me. Some of them gave their lives for me. And the fight is not done yet. So if you want a piece of Eric, you'll have to go through me."

"Get out of my way, Enala. I don't want to hurt you."

Enala laughed and swiped out with her sword. The blade rapped across Gabriel's knuckles. He swore and dropped his weapon.

"Pick it up, and show me what you're made of."

Gabriel growled and swept up his blade. He made a few weak swings, clearly expecting the blows to knock the sword from Enala's hands. Enala swept them aside with contempt, and then slashed out with her own weapon. Gabriel yelped as it connected with his elbow. The sword slipped from his numb fingers.

"Pick it up," she nodded to the blade.

Five minutes later Gabriel sat on his knees, gasping for breath and cradling his right arm. Purple marks spotted his skin where bruises had already begun to swell. His sword lay discarded on the ground nearby. He looked up at Enala, hurt in his eyes.

Enala stared down, anger still boiling within. It raged against her restraint, screaming for her to teach Gabriel a lesson. He had almost killed Eric, almost struck him down while he lay unarmed and helpless. What good would that have done any of them? Inexperienced or not, Eric was the only Magicker their little company had left.

She grated her teeth, fingers clenched around the pommel of her sword. The blade trembled in her hand. Pressure swelled in her chest, her frustration bubbling within.

Then she took a deep breath, and it vanished.

Enala stood, panting softly. She felt a slight sheen of sweat on her forehead, but otherwise she showed little sign of exertion. Despite Gabriel's strength and her small size, the blacksmith had not been hard to tame. Gabriel might be brave, but his skill with a sword left a lot to be desired.

Turning, Enala walked back to where Caelin and Inken stood watching and tossed her blade back onto the pile.

"Who trained you to fight like that?" Caelin asked.

Enala shrugged. "My parents. They taught me how to fight when I was young," she glanced at them. "Perhaps they knew more about all this than they let on."

"Maybe," Caelin eyed her closely. "We have a few days here in Lon before the ship can set sail. If you're interested,

I'm sure Inken or myself would be happy to have you as a sparring partner. The Gods know those two aren't up to it," he nodded to where Eric and Gabriel still sat nursing their bruises.

Eric laughed as he stood. "Agreed. Gabriel was bad enough," he held out his hand. "Thank you."

Enala shook her head. "No, thank you," she looked around. "Thank you all. I had no idea what you went through to find me. If not for you, I don't think I would be alive right now. That Balistor, he would have found me, one way or another. I am sorry for how I've acted," she stepped up and hugged Eric.

"You're welcome," Eric smiled back as they drew apart.

They turned at the sound of Gabriel climbing to his feet. Enala's heart sank as he stared at her, his face twisted with emotion. He clenched his fists and closed his eyes. He opened his mouth to speak, and then closed it again. Spinning on his heel, he stalked from the field.

Enala glanced at the others. "I'll talk to him."

🌺 6 🌺

Gabriel looked up as the door to his room opened. Before he could object, Enala slipped into the dormitory, eyes downcast. She clenched her fists, sucked in a breath, and then crossed to sit on the bunk opposite him.

Neither of them spoke. They sat quietly in the dark, the silence stretching out into an unbearable tension. Gabriel gritted his teeth, the bruises to his body and pride feeding his anger. He made to speak, and then thought better of it. With a stubborn grunt, he rolled over on the bed, turning his back to Enala.

"I'm sorry," he heard her whisper. "I lost my temper. There is so much happening here, Gabriel. So much to take in," her voice cracked.

Hearing the sorrow, the loneliness in her voice, Gabriel took a breath and turned back to her. "You betrayed me."

Anger flashed in Enala's eyes, burning away the tears. She took a deep, shuddering breath, and shook her head. "No, I was not betraying you. I was stopping you from doing something stupid, something you would regret."

Gabriel sat up on the bed, staring hard at Enala. "I would not regret killing him," he struggled to contain his anger. "It is all that has kept me going since I left Oaksville."

"Yes," Enala replied. "Hate is a strong force. But it is also an evil one—it has already driven you to make awful choices, to commit murder. Or do I need to remind you what you told me last night?"

Gabriel saw again the dying guard in Chole, choking in his own blood. He looked away, unable to face the fire in Enala's eyes. "No, you don't need to remind me," he took a breath and looked back. "But Eric is no innocent. He killed my family, you know this!"

"Do I? Do you? Have you given even a moment to consider everything may not have been as it seemed in Oaksville?"

"You mean that it was an accident?" he shook his head. "I don't believe it."

"Don't, or won't?" Enala asked.

Gabriel bared his teeth. "Both!" he snapped, and made to stand.

Enala was on her feet first. She shoved him backwards onto the bed, landing on top of him and pinning him flat. "You will listen to what I have to say!" she grated through clenched teeth. "Then you can go or stay, it is up to you."

Looking into her crystal blue eyes, Gabriel almost thought he saw their colour change, tainted red by the fire of her rage. He swallowed and nodded.

Enala's expression softened. She released him and retreated to her bunk. "I hope you will stay though, Gabriel," she sucked in a mouthful of air and blew out. "I need you."

Warmth flooded Gabriel's chest, filling him with an urge

to go to her, to hold her tight. He pushed it down, determined to keep the anger in his voice. "Speak."

Hurt spread across Enala's face and her eyes hardened. "Very well then," slowly, she began to repeat Eric's story, of the first emergence of his wild magic.

Gabriel listened in shock as Enala explained Eric had lost his own parents that first night, and had then spent almost two years in self-imposed banishment, haunting the backroads of rural Plorsea. He struggled to block out Enala's words as she spoke of Eric's decision to begin a new life in the town of Oaksville, and her account of the slavers who had accosted him within an hour of entering the town.

He knew what was coming next, and try as he might, he heard the truth in Enala's words.

By the time Enala finished, Gabriel was quietly sobbing to himself, torn again by the loss of his parents, his fiancée's death.

Could it all have been an accident? He questioned himself. *Could this all have been for nothing?*

"Are you okay?" Enala whispered, reaching out a comforting hand.

"Leave me!" Gabriel batted away her arm. "Get out, leave me!"

Enala drew back, her eyes watering. She gave a curt nod and stood. Making her way to the door, she turned back at the last minute. "I'm sorry, Gabriel," she murmured.

Then she was gone.

———

ENALA TWIRLED THE PRACTICE BLADE IN HER HANDS, TAKING measure of its weight. It was heavier than the weapon she'd used over the last couple of days, and much heavier than the real sword Caelin had presented her with earlier.

She smiled; its weight would be perfect for building a little more strength and speed into her strikes. Across from her, Inken grinned back.

The older woman moved to position herself in the centre of the practice field. Enala squared off against her, as she had for the last two days. So far they had kept to light sparring, but even then Enala had been hard pressed to hold her own. Inken's reputation as a bounty hunter was obviously hard earned. She provided a much better challenge than Gabriel, and today Inken promised there would be no holding back. It would provide a good distraction from Gabriel's continued absence.

"Try not to hurt each other too much," Caelin joked from nearby.

"Wouldn't dream of it," Enala replied.

Inken laughed. "Confident aren't we?" she motioned Enala forward. "Show me what you've got then."

Enala shifted her feet and leapt, swinging her blade low at Inken's elbow. Inken stepped back, bringing her own sword down to counter. Enala dodged to the side, reversing her swing to catch Inken's blade on her own. Steel rang as the two separated.

Inken brushed hair from her face. "Very good."

Without warning Inken struck out, her practice blade sweeping towards Enala's head. Heart pounding, Enala blocked high, wincing at the force of the blow. Then Inken's foot swept up to strike her in the chest. The kick sent Enala crashing to the ground.

Enala gasped but refused to stay down. She rolled backwards, coming to her feet in a single movement before Inken could follow up her attack.

"Dirty move," Enala commented.

"No such thing in a fight to the death," Inken replied.

They clashed again, blades ringing as they circled one another. Enala soon realised the truth of Inken's words. The bounty hunter treated her blade as just one tool in her arsenal– she was just as likely to lash out with hand or foot as she was her sword. This was a new brand of combat for Enala. Her parents had taught her to fight, but they had never taught her to fight dirty.

Fortunately for her, Enala was a quick learner. After half an hour she began to adjust to Inken's sudden attacks, learning how to avoid the fists and feet lashing at her. Finally, when she thought she might have a grasp of Inken's unorthodox style, she launched a counter of her own.

Ducking beneath Inken's swing, Enala lashed out with her foot, driving the bounty hunter backwards. Bringing up her sword, she feinted low. Inken's blade leapt to meet it, but Enala pulled back and spun on her heel, reversing her sword's cut. The blow bounced off Inken's shoulder.

Inken cursed, pulling back, but Enala did not cease her attack. She pressed on, her sword slashing in a series of brutal swipes. Several times her weapon came within a hair's breath of contact, but Inken was no longer playing around. Lines of concentration were etched across her face, her eyes coolly studying Enala's every movement. The air rang with the clash of metal.

Then Inken calmly swiped her blade aside and lurched forwards. Caught off-guard by the sudden counter, Enala walked straight into Inken's head-butt.

Pain lanced from her nose, forcing her back a step. She stumbled, tripping over her own feet and toppling to the ground.

Enala gasped, tasting blood on her tongue. Rage surged

through her, a burning in her chest that screamed for vengeance. It built inside, heat spreading through her limbs until all she could see was red. Fists clenched, a low growl echoed from her throat. The sword hilt felt hot in her hand. The tension grew, building until it seemed she must explode.

"Okay, I think that's enough for today," Caelin interrupted, stepping between them.

Enala blinked, and the heat vanished. She looked up as Inken offered her a hand.

"Sorry about that, Enala. I got a little carried away."

Enala nodded, wiping her arm across her face. Blood ran from her nose. Wincing, she took Inken's hand.

Michael joined them and handed her a towel. "Here, this will help with the blood," he leaned in for a closer inspection, reaching up with gentle fingers to test it. "Doesn't look like she broke it. Just a little nose bleed. Keep your head down and don't worry about messing up the towel. It should stop shortly."

"Thank you, Michael," she glanced across at Eric. "Let that be a lesson to you, Eric. Never mess with your girlfriend."

Eric grinned back. "Don't worry, I figured that one out pretty quickly. Just last week she shot a Red Dragon through both eyes."

Enala blinked, unsure whether Eric was joking. Then again, after the fight she'd just had, she wouldn't put anything past the bounty hunter. The woman was tough.

"Eric," they all swung round at Gabriel's voice. Enala's heart sank. She had hardly seen him for two days, since she had tried to explain what Inken had told her. What he wanted now, she could only guess.

"Eric," Gabriel said again. "Could we speak? In private?"

Eric looked from Inken to Enala, and then back to Gabriel. He frowned, uncertainty on his face, and then nodded. Gabriel waved a hand at the dormitory and the two moved off towards the building.

"To be a fly on the wall for that conversation," Caelin muttered.

———

GABRIEL'S HEART THUDDED IN HIS CHEST AS HE LED ERIC across the field. His mouth felt dry, his tongue parched even though he'd just drunk water. His knees shook and a sick feeling twisted his stomach. He could hear Eric behind him, sense the young man's nerves as he followed Gabriel into the dormitory.

Closing his eyes, Gabriel struggled to summon his courage. *Who knew an apology could be so hard?*

He hadn't wanted to listen, hadn't wanted to believe what Eric had told him. But he could not ignore Enala, not after everything they'd been through. It had been her courage, her innocence that freed him from the demon's grip. If not for her, who knew what monster he would have become.

Even if she was too late, he thought. He looked at his hands, remembering the blood of the innocent man he had killed. *Who am I to judge, I am no better.*

He looked up at Eric, standing across the room from him. This was the one he had hunted all this time, had sworn vengeance on. Even now, a part of him wanted to lash out, to drive a sword through Eric's chest and watch the life drain from his eyes. As he had watched his fiancée's life drain away.

But he could not, not now.

He breathed out a long sigh. "I'm sorry," he whispered.

Eric blinked. "What?"

"Enala told me everything. About Oaksville, about your magic, about why it was unleashed. She told me everything you have done since, everything you and your friends did to help her."

"And you believed her?" Eric walked across and slumped onto one of the couches, a look of disbelief in his eyes.

Gabriel shrugged. "I must. Enala brought me back to the light, freed me from a demon's spell. I owe her. If she believes your story, so must I."

Eric closed his eyes, and then looked up to meet Gabriel's stare. "I am truly sorry for your family, Gabriel. If I could go back…"

Gabriel raised his hand to silence him. A tremor ran through him as he fought down his grief, his anger. "I won't pretend this is easy. I won't pretend I can forgive you. But I am sorry for attacking you, for hunting you. And I should not have tried to kill you while we sparred," he took a deep, shuddering breath. "I don't know if I trust you, but I do know I am tired of hate and anger. So, let there be peace between us," he offered his hand.

Eric hesitated, staring at the offered hand. Gabriel could not blame his mistrust; in truth he had spent the last few days debating whether to offer Eric his hand, or a dagger. But he spoke the truth now; the hate must end. He could not live his life beneath the shadow of the past.

Finally Eric gave a cautious smile and took his hand. "Okay, truce it is."

A long silence stretched out. Gabriel coughed, struggling to find the words. Then he shrugged. "Well, shall we go practice with those swords?"

Eric laughed. "Don't think it'll be so easy this time. I'm ready for you now," he waved towards the door, clearly doing his best to hide his nerves.

Gabriel smiled as Eric opened the door and let in a fresh blast of icy air. Outside the sky had opened up, and rain now bucketed down, leaving water pooling across the grassy fields. The wind caught the door and threw it back against the wall before Eric could catch it. Thunder rumbled in the distance.

Inken and Enala had just walked up the steps and quickly ducked inside. Caelin still stood in the rain, arms folded, eyes catching theirs. He beckoned.

Gabriel's heart sank as he looked out at the rain. He stepped out the door, allowing the cool water to run down his face. His hair and clothes were instantly drenched.

Gabriel shivered as he followed Eric to where Caelin waited, already regretting his apology. Or at least the timing of it.

"Good luck," he heard Inken call from the doorway.

"Think I'll need it?" Eric shouted back over the rain.

"Most definitely," she called. Laughing, she and Enala disappeared into the house.

"That doesn't bode well," Eric observed, glancing at Gabriel.

When they reached Caelin, the sergeant wasted no time tossing them each a practice sword. "If you two are done making up, perhaps today you can learn to work together. It's time I showed you how a real swordsman fights," he waved a practice blade of his own. "Touch me if you can."

"What?" Gabriel asked.

In response Caelin leapt forward, sword sweeping out at Gabriel's weapon. The blow knocked the blade from his loose fingers and sent it tumbling. Gabriel flinched back as Caelin rapped him lightly on the arm.

"You will both work together to fight me. Let's see what the two of you can do," Caelin grinned.

Gabriel gritted his teeth, glancing at Eric as he retrieved his sword. Eric gave a quick nod and then looked back to Caelin. It seemed the young man was willing to test their fragile new trust.

Raising his sword, Eric edged sideways away from Gabriel. Realising Eric was trying to divide Caelin's attention, Gabriel moved in the opposite direction. Together they attempted to encircle their foe.

Caelin grinned. "Very good. Let's see just how fast you can move," he stepped forward, blade slicing towards Eric.

As Eric jumped back, Gabriel sprang to the attack. Eric's sword rose to block Caelin's blow as Gabriel stabbed out with his own weapon, aiming for Caelin's exposed back. Caelin's sword slid through Eric's guard and struck his arm, then the soldier was spinning on his heel, sword already raised to parry Gabriel's blow.

Gabriel's blade rang as their weapons met, then pain shot from his shoulder as Caelin's sword slid up to sting him.

Next thing Gabriel knew, he was toppling to the muddy ground, tripped by a blow from Caelin's foot. He swore as water soaked through his cloak and touched his skin. Shivering, he climbed back to his feet, mud dripping from his clothes. Eric moved to his side and shot him a glance.

"Together?" he whispered.

Gabriel nodded and they launched themselves at the sergeant. Eric's blade found only empty air, but the ring of steel and shock down Gabriel's arm told him his had at least connected. Reversing his weapon, he stabbed for Caelin's side, even as Eric struck again.

Caelin spun in place and Gabriel's thrust swept past. His fist swung out, connecting with Gabriel's head to send him reeling backwards. He kept his feet this time, but his vision spun and blurred around the edges. He backed away, shaking his head to clear it.

Across the muddy grass, Eric fought on, lashing out with wild swings at their wily foe. Caelin slipped past each attack like an eel through water, his sword licking out every so often to parry a blow which came too close. The grin he wore told them both he was enjoying this far too much.

Gabriel took a tighter grip of his sword and threw himself back into the battle, determined to wipe the smile off Caelin's face. They attacked together, swords flashing as the rain poured down around them. They swung at Caelin's face, his legs, his arms, anywhere they could.

Not once did their blades touch skin.

To his left Gabriel saw the frustration building on Eric's face. His own anger bubbled towards the surface. Then Eric lurched forward, blade raised high. Grinning Caelin moved to block, just as Eric dove forward, ducking beneath Caelin's attack and coming up within the sergeant's guard. He raised his sword to strike.

Caelin's knee rose up to smash Eric in the face. The younger man reared backwards, sword dropping from his limp fingers. He swayed, head lolling to either side, and then toppled to the ground.

———

ERIC'S VISION SPUN AS CAELIN'S BLOW STAGGERED HIM. PAIN lanced through his head as he dropped to his knees. He swayed, a sudden weakness spreading down his body. He glanced up at Caelin, opened his mouth to speak.

Then darkness rose to swallow him.

But he was not alone there.

Eric shuddered as another presence slithered into his mind. The foreign touch sent a tremor down to the foundations of his consciousness. Shadowy fingers rose around his thoughts, dark claws slicing into him.

"Hello, Eric," *the voice sounded triumphant, ecstatic.*

Eric shivered. It knew his name. He could feel the dark tendrils digging deeper, searching out his secrets, seeking to claim them.

Eric shrank back, reaching out for...what? Memory escaped him, slipping through his fingers like water. How could he fight such a force?

The image of Enala mounted atop her dragon drifted through his thoughts.

"Ahhh, so that is her, the hunted one," dread sank deep into Eric's soul. It knew!

"Where are you taking her?"

Eric fought against the shadow's grip. Pain twisted its way through his being as the claws dug deeper. Slowly, visions of the coming journey slid from his conscious, and the outline of a ship began to take form.

Still he struggled, clinging to the slightest distraction, to a mystery within his conversation with Jurrien. Why had he spoken to the God? What had happened that night? Jurrien had come, stopped him, hated him.

For what?

Magic!

Lightning crackled as the spell broke, memory of his magic bubbling up within. Blue fire raced through his thoughts, lightning in the darkness. Gritting his teeth, he turned it on the intruder.

A blast of white light lit the confines of his mind. He heard a dark, angry cackle, and then silence resumed.

"Eric, are you okay? Caelin asked.

Eric cracked open his eyes, groaning as the light set his

skull afire. Like a dream, memory of his internal battle quickly faded away, vanishing from his thoughts.

"What happened?"

Caelin offered a hand. "You pulled a bold move, but made the mistake of placing your head in range of my knee."

The contents of Eric's stomach threatened to come up as he took Caelin's hand. "What?" he mumbled.

Caelin placed a steadying hand on his shoulder. "While in a fight, it's almost always a terrible idea to lower your head. It makes a very tempting target."

Eric nodded, holding back another groan. His stomach swirled again but he fought it down. Mud soaked his clothes, and he wanted nothing more than to be dry again. Swallowing the nausea, he looked around for this sword. His legs shook when he tried to take a step.

Caelin laughed. "I think that's enough for today, you've both taken quite the beating. Anymore and Inken might just kill me. Come on, let's get out of this rain."

They made their way to the dormitory and pushed open the wooden doors. As they crossed the threshold a wave of warm air swept over them. Eric closed his eyes in relief, already feeling halfway better. Looking inside he spotted Inken and Enala sitting on the couches in quiet conversation, each holding a steaming mug. A fire blazed in the hearth, casting a warm red glow across the lounge. The scent of roasting meat wafted over from somewhere deeper in the building.

Inken frowned when she saw Eric. She rose and made her way over. "That looks like a nasty bump."

Eric raised a hand to his forehead, wincing as his fingers brushed across the bruise. "Blame Caelin."

He grinned as Caelin shot him a glare.

The look Inken shot back was far worse. "Oh I will," she growled, taking Eric's shoulder. "For now though, let's find you some clean clothes."

"I can look after myself you know," Eric attempted to take his own weight and stumbled sideways into the wall. The room began to spin.

"Oh really?" Inken raised her eyebrow.

Eric fought back a laugh. "I guess you could help, just this once."

Inken smiled and took his arm again. Together they made it up the hall and into their bedroom, where he struggled into a clean set of clothes. When they returned to the living room they found everyone already seated and dry, each with a glass of the steaming red liquid.

"What are you drinking?" Eric asked.

"It's mulled wine," Enala answered. "Apparently somewhat of a Lonian specialty. Warms the stomach on cold winter days like this," she picked up an empty mug from the coffee table and poured more wine. "Here, try it."

Eric took the offered glass and sank onto the spare couch. As Inken joined him he took a sip of the wine. The rich red was coupled with the spice of cloves and cinnamon, and when he swallowed warmth flowed down his chest. He took another sip.

"I have some herbs that could help with the pain, Eric," Michael offered. "Or some ice might help," he tossed a bag across the room.

"Thanks, Michael," Eric placed the icy bag against his forehead. "The wine and ice will do for now."

He looked around the room at his friends. Michael and Caelin sat opposite him, while Gabriel had taken the seat beside Enala. Inken leaned into him and sipped from her own mug. They all looked worn out from the day's exertions. Through the clouded glass window behind Enala, he saw darkness had fallen outside. They would need to light the lamps soon.

"You must be the only one who won't be hurting tonight, Michael," Eric offered.

"Agreed," Enala groaned. "I'll be staying on Inken's good side from now on."

Inken laughed. "You did pretty well yourself. You almost had me a few times. Whoever trained you was very good."

"I don't know, I could have used a few more rounds myself," Caelin teased.

Gabriel scowled and muttered under his breath. Eric could only agree—they hadn't even come close to touching the sergeant.

"Don't worry, Caelin," there was ice in Inken's voice. "I wouldn't mind switching sparring partner's tomorrow."

Caelin didn't even have the good grace to look abashed. He shot Inken a grin, but Eric guessed it wouldn't last long tomorrow. If anyone could beat the wily soldier, it was Inken. If not in a fair fight, certainly in an unfair one.

"Do we know when the ship leaves yet?" Michael asked. "Has anyone heard from Jurrien or the priests? It's been a few days."

Caelin shook his head. "Silence. All they've said is to stay on the temple grounds. They don't want anyone to know we're here, in case Archon's servants get wind of us. The fewer who know about Enala, the better."

Eric looked around the room, a thought dancing just out of reach. The others turned to him, waiting for him to speak, but the memory eluded him. He shook his head, and immediately regretted the action as the pain returned.

"Makes sense," Gabriel continued Caelin's train of

thought, then. "So, does anyone know what there is for dinner?"

Michael grinned. "Well, as luck would have it I used my time somewhat productively today. I rummaged around the priest's storage shed, and actually managed to find the ingredients to put together a decent meat pie. It should be ready right about now," he rose and made his way into the adjoining kitchen.

As he opened the copper stove door, steam billowed out and the aroma of roasting meat became overwhelming. The steam rolled into the lounge, rising to the ceiling where it began to dissipate. Caelin followed him into the kitchen and took out plates and cutlery. Before long they were each presented with large slices of meat pie. Thick gravy and chunks of mushrooms overflowed from the pastry onto the porcelain plates, mixing with the steamed vegetables.

"Another Lonian delicacy. Once upon a time the shepherds here began making use of their tougher leftover meats by baking it inside the pastry of a pie, along with various spices. Today they've become a staple here, and most just use regular meat. I learnt the recipe during my apprenticeship," Michael offered.

Eric's stomach growled. He couldn't even remember what he'd had for lunch, but it was well past time for a hot meal. He grabbed his knife and fork, glancing around to ensure everyone had a plate of their own.

As he raised the first chunk of meat and pastry to his mouth the front door burst open and crashed into the wall. Eric leapt from his seat, his food tumbling to the ground. Outside lightning flashed, casting strange shadows across the lounge. He saw Caelin fumbling for his sword, felt Inken rising beside him. He was reaching for his magic when he realised who had invaded the quiet of their gathering.

Jurrien strode into the room, his footsteps slow and measured, but his face alive with power. The door slammed shut behind him.

"The ship is ready," he announced. "You leave at dawn."

❧ 7 ❦

E ric sat on the deck of the ship and watched the trees on the river bank slide past. Branches stretched out towards them, long limbs mirrored in the water beneath. But here the Hall river was wide and its current slow, leaving long yards between themselves and the banks. Below the oars rose and fell in quick succession, crewed by the mariners Jurrien had sent. With each heave the ship surged forward, carrying them up the river towards the distant lake city of Ardath.

Birds swooped past, chasing the insects which swarmed about the ship, biting wherever they found flesh. Eric slapped another and felt a satisfying squelch as the mosquito died. Flicking it over the side, he wished the birds well on their hunt.

The forest on either side of the river appeared dense, but he knew from their maps that the farmlands of Lonia lay just beyond the treeline. The farmers here cultivated the forest along the riverbanks to keep their cattle from the swift currents. The trees also served to keep the waters clean of the runoff from their livestock. They had travelled well into the Lonian floodplains now, where pasture flourished and cows ran in great herds, but the river remained a deep, clear blue.

They had left Lon three days ago. On the first day the ship made its way across Jurrien's Inlet, and the following morning had started up the Hall river. Now they were drawing close to Sitton—the port city marking the halfway point along the river.

So far, their progress had felt unbearably slow, the minutes whittling away like hours. Restless nerves plagued Eric, and he knew the others were just as eager to reach the end of their quest. But Kalgan remained a distant prospect —first they must reach Sitton, then Ardath, before making their way on foot through the mountains into the nation of Trola. There, if all went to plan, they would find the Sword of Light.

The weak winds didn't help, but Jurrien had warned not to use magic to speed along their journey. Fellow Magickers could sense when someone released powerful magic, and they did not want to broadcast their passage to Archon's minions.

The boredom made matters worse. Other than some limited training with Caelin, they had little to do but sit and stew over the struggles to come. Eric rubbed a bruise on his leg, another of Caelin's lessons—to never stop moving in a fight. His whole body ached as though it had been put through a meat grinder, but at least his skills were finally improving. Caelin praised his speed and reflexes, but Eric had yet to develop the intuition needed for an actual sword fight.

Eric used the quiet to meditate, practicing his control and ability to draw on his power. He kept his magic suppressed, but he hoped the practice would still prove valuable.

He ran his fingers over the hilt of his sword. Its weight felt awkward on his belt, but he now wore it at all times. He felt a sense of pride, that he might be worthy of carrying Alastair's blade, the same weapon his mentor had wielded in the war against Archon. He hoped he might one day live up to that legacy.

"Still nursing your bruises?" Caelin joined Eric at the rails.

"Just a few," Eric gave a sour reply. "Actually, I was thinking how much more enjoyable sailing on a river is. No seasickness, no raging Gods, no vengeful castaways to collect."

Caelin laughed. "We're not there yet, although we'll sleep in Sitton tonight. We'll collect some supplies and enjoy some solid ground beneath our feet, then press on first thing in the morning."

"Thank the Gods, I'm going crazy on this ship," he glanced at the sun. Noon had long since passed and the days were steadily growing shorter with winter's approach. "Will we arrive before dark?"

"If all goes well."

Eric laughed. "And when does that ever happen?"

Nevertheless, a few hours later the evening sun found them pulling into the sleepy port of Sitton. Wooden docks stretched out into the river to greet them, empty but for a few barges and the odd fishing rig. The city spread out from the docks and up into the foothills of the river. The nearest buildings looked old and showed signs of wear, while the white roof tiles of those behind gleamed red in the dying sun.

Eric stretched his neck, taking in the city. It appeared to

rise from the river itself, old stone walls hedging the water-front revealing the settlement's violent past. Sitton had not been spared the wars which had once torn the land apart. But new buildings now rose above the old, spreading up the hill above the city. Great spires of marble and domes of shimmering metal stood amidst the stone houses, revealing the wealth of trade passing daily through Sitton.

Their ship drifted up to the docks where men waited with ropes to pull them closer. As they drew alongside their own sailors leapt across the gap and began helping those ashore. They tossed ropes to those remaining on the ship and pulled the vessel tight against the wharf. Eric could not help but be impressed by the speed with which they accomplished the task.

Inken joined him as he moved to where the sailors were lowering a plank down to the docks, allowing the less nimble passengers to disembark. She swung up onto the railings beside him. "Not going to jump?" she asked as she leapt to the wharf.

Eric raised an eyebrow, feeling no desire to take a spill into the river. Turning he strode along the deck and wandered across the plank, much to Inken's amusement.

"Sorry," she offered. "I just couldn't wait to be ashore. I've never spent so much time on the water. It almost makes me miss that damn white horse I bought back in Chole," Inken whispered in a conspirational tone.

Eric smiled. Earlier he'd had the same thought about his horse, Briar. It'd taken him a week to get used to riding, but he had almost enjoyed it after that. The ship might move faster, but it was boring, offering little to do but sleep and watch the riverbanks.

They followed Caelin down the dock. They knew which inn the crew would be staying in, but they had no desire to wait for the mariners to gather their gear. Fresh beds and dry land beckoned.

As they wound their way through the thin crowd of people around the docks, Inken tucked her arm under his. "It feels good to have solid ground beneath my feet again," she whispered in his ear. "I was going crazy, cramped up on that ship."

Eric waved away a fly and smiled. "Me too. I didn't realise Jurrien would be sending quite so many marines—I felt like a sardine packed in a barrel."

Inken squeezed his arm. "I miss you," she looked around. "I think they will be okay without us for an hour. The marines are right behind us. How about we go explore a little. It would be nice to have some time to ourselves while we're ashore."

Eric's hand drifted to the pommel of Alastair's blade as his eyes scanned the crowd. There was a calm air to the way people moved here, a peace missing from other towns and cities he'd visited. He nodded to Inken. "You know the way to the inn?"

"I heard the captain giving Caelin the directions. Now come on!" she tugged at his arm. Smiling, Eric allowed her to pull him into the crowd and into one of the side streets leading farther up the hill.

"Have you been here before?" Eric asked.

"No, but I've heard about the place. The temple here is said to be quite unique. Since the river marks the border between Lonia and Plorsea, the temple is dedicated to both Antonia and Jurrien."

Two storied buildings lined the street, but through the gaps overhead they made out the spire of a temple. Inken took his hand and they made their way towards it. The buildings closed in around them, growing larger as they climbed the hill. The dirt roads close to the port soon gave way to bricked streets, worn smooth by the passage of wagon wheels.

Eventually the afternoon crowds heading to and from the markets gave way as they entered into quieter streets. Eric wrapped his arm around Inken's waist and exhaled with relief. After spending two years in the wilderness, crowds still unnerved him. Even without the usual bustling rush of larger cities.

The temple surprised them when they finally stumbled across it. The overlapping walls of the surrounding buildings hid the towering spire as they drew near, forcing them to circle the spot where they guessed it must be. Knowing its general direction, they persisted until they reached the tiny street in which it hid.

The temple's sheer marble walls stretched across one side of the street, the rich stone streaked by faults of blue and green. Where the architects had found such a variety of marble, Eric could only guess. The spire stretched high into the sky, vines of ivy clinging from the enamels. As they approached a bell high in the tower started to ring. Its shrill clang echoed loudly in the street.

They made their way to the entrance, where the oaken gates stood open.

Inken glanced at Eric. "Do you think they know about Antonia? That she's gone?"

"I don't know. But either way, we better not say anything. We don't want to draw attention to ourselves."

Inken smiled, nodding to their swords and her bow. "We might be a little too well-armed for that. I'm not sure many citizens take a casual stroll to a temple with this sort of weaponry."

Eric glanced down at his own blade. "Would be nice if we didn't need them."

He felt Inken's hand on his head and looked up. "One day, Eric. Remember what we said, we will get through this. Don't lose sight of what we're fighting for, don't lose hope. We will finish this quest of Alastair's and find peace again. Then you can put up that sword, and live your own life."

Eric leaned across and kissed her. As their tongues met a shiver ran across his skin. His heart beat faster as he pulled her hard against him. Her fingers curled in his hair and he felt a pinch as she bit his lip. When they separated the taste of cinnamon lingered on his tongue.

"Are the two of you in the right place?" a man in sky blue robes asked, emerging from a doorway.

His face was lined and his eyes careworn, but he wore an amused smile. He carried a walking staff of oak, which he leaned on heavily as he approached them.

Inken's cheeks reddened and Eric felt his own grow warm. "Sorry, sir," he offered. "It's been a long and crowded ride up the river."

The priest waved a hand. "Not at all. We are used to couples passing through, and seeking some quiet with each other. We do not judge—that is not the way of the Gods," he smiled. "So what brings two young lovers to the Temple of the Earth and Sky."

"We heard It was the place to visit in Sitton," Inken offered. "Although we really just needed to get away from the rest of our company for a time."

"Understandable. I remember my youth all too well. Welcome, anyway. You will find all the peace you could want in the courtyard," he turned and waved for them to follow.

They made their way down a short corridor and back

out into the lengthening shadows. There they found themselves in the midst of a tamed jungle. Vines grew up the walls and hung from dense trees. The last calls of the evening chorus faded away as they walked between the trees. The scent of azalea flowers and chamomile drifted in the air. Chimes hung from the branches, ringing in the afternoon breeze. Lanterns lined the marble walls, the strange flames within casting a flickering blue light beneath the trees, as though lightning flashed overhead.

The priest bowed and disappeared back through the doorway, leaving them alone in the strange courtyard.

Eric smiled, the glow of the lanterns bringing back memories of their night at the hot springs in Dragon Country. It could not have been much more than a week ago, but already it seemed a lifetime. The trials they'd suffered since had strengthened the bond between them more than he could ever have imagined.

"What life would you want to live, Inken, when this is finished?"

Inken lifted her bow off her shoulder and held it in her hands. "I don't know. This used to matter to me, this life on the road, the thrill of hunting down criminals, testing my skill against theirs. But I don't know any more, not after this, after doing something so much more meaningful. Now…" she shook her head, returning the bow to her shoulder. "I think it would be nice to try something new," she smiled, "maybe something less life threatening."

"Like fishing?"

Inken chuckled, nodding her head in amusement. "Like fishing."

They sat together in silence for a while, watching a red finch hop its way along a nearby branch to its nest in the tree trunk. Quiet settled over the courtyard like a mist, blocking out the world outside, the worries of tomorrow. They sat there, relishing the quiet, the chance just to be with each other. Eric felt his heart swell, fed by the warmth of Inken at his side, and knew he loved this girl more than anything else in this world.

He had finally found peace.

Somehow, he knew it could not last.

A dim rumble carried from outside. Dread swept through Eric, washing away the peace. The sound swelled, as though whatever caused it was growing larger.

Or coming closer.

The rumble erupted into a roar as the ground started to shake.

They leapt from the bench and stumbled as the tiles shifted beneath them. Eric clutched at Inken, desperate to keep his feet as the earthquake shook the world. The walls of the courtyard groaned, cracks racing through the marble. He glimpsed the spire through the treetops, swaying in the dying sunlight.

Eric could sense the magic in the quake, the power surging through the air, boiling the ground with a force unlike any he had felt before. He could almost touch it, almost taste its metallic tang.

This nightmare could have only one source.

Terrified, they held each other and waited for the world to end.

With a sound like air being sucked from the room, the shaking ceased. But the groans continued, the buildings around them straining beneath their own weight. The cracks in the walls widened, spreading around the courtyard.

The priest reappeared in the doorway. "You must get

out of here, now. The temple, the tower, it won't survive another one."

Eric and Inken swept up their belongings and sprinted for the doorway. They ducked into the corridor after the priest, desperate to make the street outside. Dust trickled from the ceiling and tiny pebbles bounced onto the cobbled floor. A mosaic of spider webbed factures criss-crossed the walls. The old man moved quickly now, fear adding speed to his limp. The clack clacking of his staff echoed loudly in the dark corridor.

As they emerged into the street they were greeted by the blood red light of sunset. Eric turned to Inken. "It's him. Thomas, the demon, whatever it is. I could feel the magic in the air, like Antonia's, but *tainted*, dark."

"The demon?" Inken pressed her hand to his chest. They both remembered all too well what had happened the last time they'd met it. "It's here?"

Eric nodded, his hand clutched around his sword. "Yes, or close. That was no natural earthquake. Its power, it could only have been caused by God magic."

Inken knelt and strung her bow. "We have to find the others," straightening, she looked down the street.

Pandemonium had engulfed the city around them. People poured from the surrounding buildings, mingling on the road in horror and confusion. Nearby several buildings had collapsed, sending bricks tumbling into the street. Eric glimpsed an arm amidst the rubble and quickly looked away.

But there was no avoiding the chaos. Everywhere he looked, people stumbled through the broken bricks and mortar, dust coating their clothing as they pleaded for help. Others had already begun to pick their way through the debris, pulling survivors from the broken buildings.

Closing his eyes, Eric struggled to think. The desperate cries of the villagers assailed him, begging for help. Swallowing his guilt, he closed his heart to them. They could not stop to help these people; they had to find Enala, had to get her to safety. They did not have the power to stop the demon—with Antonia's power, only Jurrien stood a chance against it.

"The inn is this way," Inken started to pick her way through the rubble, glancing back at Eric.

Eric nodded and they began to run. His mind raced and the world seemed to slow. As they dodged through the wreckage, he glimpsed the horror on the faces of the villagers, the blood streaming down their faces, heard the boom as another building crumpled.

How did the demon find us? The question raced through his mind. Or was it just here by coincidence?

Either way, Enala was in grave danger. They had to find her, now.

Together they leapt over the broken bricks in the street and ducked beneath shattered walls. People ran in every direction, hindering their headlong rush through the city.

Another rumble came from the distance but they did not stop. Shoulders tensed with expectation, they ran on.

A sharp crack came from ahead. Eric glanced up and saw a wave rippling through the very earth, tearing the bricked road to pieces as it rolled towards them. The street rose up beneath them and tossed them from their feet. Nearby buildings seemed to crumble at the seams as the earth shook them to pieces.

A sharp crack came from behind them. Eric looked back in time to see the tower of the temple topple into the street. Metal shrieked on stone as the bell struck the ground. Dust billowed out in all directions, spilling into the surrounding streets.

Eric coughed, holding his shirt across his face. But the quake had passed, and he struggled to stand.

Dark laughter echoed from the crumpled buildings. Eric spun, eyes searching the clouds of dust, seeking the source. But the sound came from all around, chasing the people through the ruins of the city, bringing fresh terror to the populace.

Ice slid through Eric's veins. He looked across as Inken grabbed his hand.

"*Run!*"

𝕤 8 𝕤

"I'm glad you came," Caelin slapped Michael's back as he joined him at the bar.

Michael grinned. "Didn't think you could handle all these young folk without me?" he slid a draft of ale across to the soldier with a laugh.

Caelin shook his head. He would never admit it, but there was some truth to Michael's words. "No, no, I just figured we would need a doctor around if I'm going to continue beating them every day."

Michael took a swig from his mug. "You're pressing them hard."

The mood turned sombre. "Ay, I am. Enala is tough, far tougher than I expected. And Eric has his magic. But we have seen ourselves that neither is always enough. They need to be prepared for anything. I won't always be there to protect them."

"You're a good man, Caelin. So long as we have men like you around to fight the good fight, men like me will continue to hope."

Caelin grimaced. "You sell yourself short, Michael. If not for your skill, Eric would have bled to death on that beach before Antonia had any hope of healing him. And it was your quick thinking that got us to Lon in the first place," he paused. "How are you, now...you know, with Antonia gone?"

Michael shrugged, face hidden in his mug. "I cannot believe she is gone, not for good. Once Jurrien destroys that demon, he will free her from the *Soul Blade* and restore her to life. I have faith things will work out."

Shaking his head, Caelin glanced at the older man. "I am glad we have you, Michael. For myself, I'm finding it harder and harder to hold out hope. Enala is strong, but can she truly wield the Sword? And without Antonia, will that even matter?" he swallowed another mouthful of the cool ale. "But as you say, we must have faith. Jurrien will come through."

"He will. And I am glad I came too. I don't know if I could have stayed in Lon, not knowing your fates. Thank you for convincing me."

Caelin gave him another slap on the back. "My pleasure," as he stood a rumble came from the floor.

Then the ground began to shake.

Caelin stumbled as cracks spread through the wooden floor boards. Struggling to keep his feet, he grabbed for the bar as Michael toppled from his stool. The other patrons screamed, lurching from their tables towards the doorway. Burning lanterns fell from their brackets and shattered on the floor.

Instinct screamed for Caelin to follow the townsfolk outside, but Gabriel and Enala were asleep upstairs. If the building went up in flames, they would be trapped, and their quest would all be for naught.

As the shaking subsided he turned to the nearest lantern, where oily flames were already licking at the varnished wood. Pulling off his cloak he beat at the flames, attempting to smother them.

"Michael, get the others! We have to get out of this building," he cried.

Michael pulled himself to his feet and raced for the stairs.

The flames caught at Caelin's cloak and heat washed over his face. He tossed it to the ground, spinning in search of a better weapon against the fire. A whoosh came from across the room as the blaze raced up the curtains. Then the bartender was there, dousing it with a bucket of water.

Caelin looked across the counter and glimpsed a barrel of water sitting at the back. Grabbing a bucket from beside the door, he raced to join the bartender. Water hissed as it struck the flames. Steam and smoke billowed across the room, but within a few minutes they had the blaze under control.

Michael appeared at the top of the stairwell leading Gabriel and Enala. They carried a bag over each shoulder and their swords strapped at their waists. Each wore a grim expression of terror.

"This cannot be coincidence," Michael coughed through the smoke. "This has to be Earth magic. The demon has found us."

"How?" Gabriel asked. "No one but Jurrien and his priests knew we were travelling up the river. Could it not just have been an earthquake, no more than that?"

"Either way, we had better get out of this building," Enala observed. "I've never felt one like that, but we used to have earthquakes in Chole. There are usually aftershocks.

Every so often buildings would collapse, so it's best to move outside while you have the chance."

Caelin nodded. "Okay, let's get out of here," he moved for the door. The innkeeper, satisfied his property was at least safe from the flames, had already fled.

Moving through the swinging doors, Caelin found the streets outside the inn empty. He looked around, surprised, and glimpsed the innkeeper disappearing round the corner at the top of the hill. The others followed him outside as he turned to look downhill towards the port.

He took a step backwards, fear sending a chill right down to his toes.

A dark forest now blocked the road, black trunks towering above the buildings. Vines wrapped around the trees and slivered like snakes through the branches. The grey leaves whistled with the wind, dagger-like twigs stretching out towards them. Thorns stabbed from every surface of the vegetation. Not a hint of life came from the dark forest.

Caelin saw the trees were marked by faces, their mouths open, twisted in pain. He watched as new vegetation sprang from the ground, the forest advancing towards them. He shuddered, dread gripping his very soul. There was no mistaking what they faced now.

The demon had arrived.

"We need to get to the ship," Michael whispered beside him.

"I know. That's in our way," he nodded towards the dark forest.

"Then we cut our way through," Gabriel insisted.

"No," Caelin glanced around, "nothing that goes in there is coming out alive."

"Can we go around then?"

"I doubt it," Enala's face had paled, but she remained resolute. "The demon cannot know exactly where we are, or we'd be dead already. It is just making sure we can't get to the river."

The rumbling came again, followed by a second quake. This time the earth itself rippled. The power of its movement knocked them from their feet. They crouched on the bricked road, eyes squeezed shut, and endured.

When the shaking stopped, little remained of the city around them. Fortunately, the buildings in this area of Sitton were made of wood, so most had collapsed inwards on themselves rather than toppling into the street. But flames were already taking light in the ruins, the smouldering remains of fireplaces and lanterns catching amidst the fresh kindling. Smoke drifted in the air.

Then the laughter began; a bleak, evil sound that sucked the hope from their souls and the strength from their limbs. It echoed around the city, bouncing from the ruins to encircle them.

"Come on, we have to try," Caelin fought against the laughter's pull, hauling himself to his feet.

The others stood with him.

"Where do we −?" the crackle of thunder interrupted Gabriel.

They turned together to look at the forest. A bolt of lightning fell from the sky, disappearing somewhere amidst the blackened trees and leaving a white streak in Caelin's vision. He stared, breath held, waiting.

"Eric?" Michael whispered.

———

THE LAUGHTER CHASED THEM THROUGH THE CRUMBLING streets, haunting their footsteps like the ghosts of the past, driving them on. Eric felt a pain in his chest, an icy fist clenching hard around where the *Soul Blade* had pierced him. It grew stronger as they approached the inn.

When they turned the final corner they slammed to a halt, shocked to find a murky forest stretching across their path. Faces of terror stared out from the trunks of the trees, red eyes alive with pain. Thorny vines waved at them, reaching out, *alive*, searching for prey. The forest itself stood dead, no birds or animals in sight, a perverted mirror of the temple courtyard.

"The inn is on the other side, I think," Inken murmured. "What do we do?"

"Not far now," Eric whispered back, already moving, instinct taking over.

He reached out with his magic, summoning the power of a distant storm cloud. Thunder crashed and lightning flashed from the sky to strike his outstretched arm. A blue arc of energy took shape in his hand. With a scream of rage, he pointed it at the forest.

Blue fire leapt from his fingers, burning its way through the dark apparitions. A strange, eerie scream sounded as the lightning touched the trees. The red vanished from the haunted eyes as the electric glow bathed them, and the vines curled back to wither and die. In seconds he had burnt a path through the evil forest.

Eric grabbed Inken's hand. "Let's go!"

They sprinted down the path as the lightning continued to burn its way closer to the inn. Vines and branches reached for them, thorny fingers grasping at their hair and clothes. Inken drew her sword and struck back without breaking stride, wild swings keeping the dark limbs at bay.

Seconds later they burst through the other side of the forest, into the last light of the dying sun.

Except burning buildings now lit the city streets. By their light they saw their four companions, eyes wide, mouths open in astonishment. Inken and Eric raced towards them, eager to put distance between themselves and the twisted trees.

"About time you two showed up," Caelin wore an anxious smile. "We were getting worried."

"Sorry, we didn't expect company here in Sitton. The demon is coming; we have to go. We can't fight it."

"Agreed," Caelin pointed behind them. "Think you can blast your way back out, Eric?"

Eric turned, cursing to see the path had already closed.

"Stay back," he moved closer to the forest, gathering more lightning to him. The air crackled as the power danced in his hands, raising hairs on his arms. Pointing his finger, he unleashed the pent up force. The trees of the forest again gave way, burnt to ash.

They moved quickly, shepherding Enala between them, Caelin bringing up the rear. They struck at the vines with their blades, ducking through the tangled assault. Only Michael was unarmed, although Eric had yet to draw his blade. Lightning crackled in his palm; that was all he needed.

Halfway through the trees, a scream came from behind Eric. He spun, hand raised to strike, but a vine shot from the thicket and wrapped itself about his wrist. He gasped as thorns bit deep into his skin. Before he could react the vine gave a jolt, and began to drag him towards the darkness beneath the trees. In horror he glimpsed one of the faces in the trees waiting for him, its eyes now warped with hunger, the dark mouth opening wide to reveal its twisted teeth.

He fought against the vine's pull, digging in his heels as he searched for help. But the others were also trapped, engulfed in a fury of whirling green. Two vines wrapped about Enala, dragging her towards the thicket as Inken struggled to cut herself free and reach the younger girl. Only Caelin held his own, his sword a far more dangerous viper than those assailing him.

Eric gritted his teeth. He could not use the lightning to aid his friends in fear of hurting them, but he could free himself. Blood gushed down his arm where the thorns pierced him and the gaping mouth was growing steadily closer, but he had no intention of feeding it. As another vine shot towards him, he closed his eyes and willed the lightning outwards. A flash of blue burned through his eyelids to the crash of thunder.

Opening his eyes, he found nothing but scorched earth and ash. Nodding in satisfaction, he drew Alastair's blade and leapt to Enala's aid. The sword flicked out, slicing through the vine holding her sword arm. Free again to swing her weapon, Enala cut away her other bindings and leapt back to the safety of the path. The others joined them, staring out at the writhing wall of vegetation.

"What now?" Michael shouted.

"Now, the game is over," a rasping voice came from the shadows.

A figure stepped into the light, black cloak billowing about him as the vines drew back. He held a sword clenched in one hand, a dark green glow seeping from the blade like blood. Beneath his cloak Eric glimpsed the pommel of a second sword. A pale hand reached up to pull back the hood, revealing the face of the old King Thomas. His demon black eyes stared across at them, their empty horror sending a chill to Eric's stomach.

Thomas, the demon, whatever he was now, began to laugh. "You did not think you could really escape, did you? That I would not find you? Archon's minions are everywhere, his dark tendrils seeping into the minds of your people. Without the Gods to protect you, there is nowhere in the Three Nations you can hide, *Enala*."

A chill swept through Eric as the demon spoke Enala's name. *How does he know her?* A memory rose, just out of reach, and then faded into the darkness.

Caelin stepped forward, waving them back. "Run, get Enala out of here. I will try to hold it," he turned to the demon. "You will not have her, *demon*."

The demon laughed, Thomas' face twisting beyond recognition. "You think you can stop me, *mortal?* You think I could not kill any one of you in an instant?" It twirled the *Soul Blade*. "I do not even need Antonia's magic, you are nothing before my power."

Caelin spat, waving his sword. "I hear you were a great fighter once, one who did not need to use magic as a crutch in his battles. Are you too much a coward to fight me?"

"A coward? No," the demon loomed over Caelin. "But I am no fool either. You will not distract me, mortal," he raised a hand and swung. An invisible force gripped Caelin by the shoulders and hurled him back into the others.

The laughter came again, curling around them, stealing their courage.

Eric stood against it, lightning crackling in his palm. "Leave now, demon."

The demon stared down at him. "So we meet again, Magicker. Your power was most exquisite. A shame I could not keep it," it's head twisted. "Perhaps this time," it disappeared with a blink.

Time stood still for Eric. He tried to move, to throw

himself aside, but his feet seemed stuck, frozen in place. He knew what would come next, could almost feel the deathly touch of the *Soul Blade*. The breath whooshed from his lungs as he watched his companions, saw the horror on their faces.

Except Michael's. Somehow the doctor was already moving, his shoulder crashing into Eric, smashing him from his feet. Eric tumbled backwards, eyes locked on Michael's, his fear turning to dread.

Michael stared back, and smiled.

His eyes widened as the *Soul Blade* pierced his heart, but the smile did not falter. The black metal tore through his chest, the demon's cackle ringing from the trees. A gurgling cough came from the doctor's throat. Then the demon pulled back its blade, and sent Michael toppling to the ground beside him. Tears ran down Eric's cheeks as the light faded from his friend's eyes.

"*No!*" he turned on the demon, lightning surging through his body. Without thought, he unleashed it on the creature.

The bolt struck Thomas' body and hurled him backwards into the thicket. Eric climbed to his feet, energy crackling in his fists, but the demon had vanished.

Its voice echoed from all around. "Another foolish mortal," it whispered. "Giving away his life for yours. But then, what use is a priest without his God, I wonder? Perhaps he simply wished to join her," the cackle came again.

Anger surged within Eric. He made no effort to control it, feeling the power building inside him, the raw energies of his wild magic. Ruin had already come to this city; his magic could not make things worse now. The demon had to be stopped.

The magic rushed from him, summoning the elements of the Sky, binding them together in a conflagration of wind and hail and lightning.

The rage washed all thought from Eric's mind, leaving only the single, burning desire to destroy Archon's dark servant.

When the demon stepped back into the light, he unleashed his magic. The very air shook at its coming. With a crash it struck the demon, light flashing and wind gusting as it hurled the dark thing backwards. An explosion rang out, a blast of wind knocking them flat.

Eric rolled across the ground, struggling to force his magic back into its cage, to protect his comrades from its wrath. He braced himself against the wind, squinting through the dust. Smoke hung where the demon had stood. The blast had blown Michael's body clear. He lay face down, unmoving, blood pooling around him.

The smoke began to clear, drifting away with the dying gusts of wind.

The soft cackle of the demon echoed through the forest.

9

Inken nocked an arrow, spinning to search the woods for the laughter's source. A shiver ran through her soul, but she refused to bend. The bowstring twanged as she loosed into the smoke still drifting in the street. Before the arrow vanished she had already nocked another.

"Caelin, Gabriel, get Enala out of here!" she yelled.

She spared a glance for Michael, a lump catching in her throat as she took in the pool of blood surrounding him. He lay motionless, his bag discarded, medicines scattered across the broken road. She fought back tears; there would be time later to grieve. Or so she prayed.

Caelin grabbed Enala and they retreated down the burnt path. Eric stepped up beside Inken, lightning still crackling in his hands. The sight raised hackles on her neck —she doubted she'd ever become used to it. But just now Eric's magic offered their only chance of holding their own. They had learned in Malevolent Cove just how ineffective mortal weapons were against this foe.

Stones cracked as the demon stepped from the shadows,

arms raised. Before they could react, the ground shook, throwing them from their feet. A crack split the earth, racing towards them, and Inken reached desperately for Eric's hand. But the fissure tore between them, ripping them apart, and she found only empty air.

Inken struggled to her feet, gripping her bow tight as the ground continued to shift. Across the chasm now separating them, she watched Eric fighting for his life, the deadly vines all around. Lightning flashed, but it no longer seemed so effective. The vines wrapped about his torso, thorns tearing into flesh.

Then there was no more time to think about Eric. The demon stood before her, sword raised, and it was all she could do throw herself backwards. The razor edged blade swept past her eyes, slicing through a stray wisp of hair. She already knew her sword was useless against this foe. She could only hope to distract it long enough for the others to get free.

"Why do you resist? You cannot hope to defeat me. Do you really think you can save her, that I would allow her to escape?" the demon waved a hand.

Inken risked a glance back. Lead settled in the pit of her stomach. The forest had already claimed her comrades, trapping their arms and legs in the thorny thicket. Blood ran down the dark tendrils, the monstrous tree trunks standing in wait, mouths stretched wide.

Tears brimmed in Inken's eyes as her strength evaporated. She sank to her knees and stared up at the demon, grief blurring her vision.

"Good girl. You know when you are finished. I will enjoy watching the girl die, after what her *dragon* did to me," the demon growled the last words.

"Pity the beast did not finish the job," a voice boomed

from overhead.

Inken's heart surged as Jurrien plummeted from the sky, energy crackling around him. Blue fire fell with him, it's almost tender touch burning through the black forest. Her companions regained their freedom as the vines holding them crumbled to nothing. They stood in a daze, staring at the Storm God, blood running from their limbs.

"You did not think you could fool me forever, did you *Thomas?*" the God growled, his voice crackling with power.

The demon king laughed. "Ah Jurrien, I was wondering when you would arrive. Late as usual, my old friend. Although I admit, I had been hoping to take care of our companions here before you arrived. I'm sure they will wait though."

"No, this ends here, *Thomas*. I should have guessed the magic had taken you long ago. I should have hunted you down then, put you out of your misery. But no longer," Jurrien pointed a finger. "Your suffering ends today, old friend."

The demon drew the second *Soul Blade* and waved it at Jurrien. "This one's for you, old man. Archon forged them himself," he held up the first blade, staring into its sickly green glow. "He was very pleased to see how well they worked. Your sister put up quite the fight."

Jurrien's face darkened. Inken backed away as the air crackled. A dull pain shot through her skull and her ears popped as the air pressure plummeted. Storm clouds took shape and began to circle Jurrien. Lightning lit the black clouds and wind howled through the trees. Inken braced herself against the tiny hurricane as the very earth shook with its power.

In the eye of the storm, Jurrien released his pent up fury, screaming as he threw out his hands. A ball of lightning gathered between them. Jurrien drew back an arm, and hurled it at his foe.

The demon was already moving, retreating into what shelter remained of its dark forest. But Jurrien would not be deterred. He wrenched his hands apart and the ball exploded outwards. A rain of lightning tore apart the forest, burning the trees to dust. The dark powers of the earth retreated before the Storm God's rage.

Jurrien stalked into the smoking remains, the hurricane still swirling about him. His ice blue eyes searched the ruin, seeking the demon.

But his foe was not defeated yet. The earth beneath Jurrien tore open, revealing a vast gulf stretching down to a red glow far below. The God dropped several feet before the wind caught him and propelled him upwards.

Inken stumbled as the earth shook. With a roar the pit snapped closed, entombing Jurrien in solid rock.

Panic gripped Inken. Then a blue light pierced the broken cobbles, streaming up into the night. A bright flash forced her to look away. A groan came from the ground, then a boom. When she turned back a crater marked the street, and Jurrien now hovered several feet above the ground. A purple bruise marked his face, but he scowled down at the demon, undeterred.

The demon raised a sword in mock salute. "You are a wily foe. At least you put up more of a fight than your sister."

Vines burst from the street, ensnaring the God's legs. The demon leapt as they dragged Jurrien lower, the *Soul Blade* aimed for his chest. A spear of lightning materialised in Jurrien's hand, sweeping down to block the blow. Swinging it further, he burned himself free and spun in the air. Roaring in defiance, he hurled the spear at the demon.

Sparks erupted outwards as the spear struck home. The full power of the God's rage hurled the demon backwards, sending it bouncing across the rubble. Thunder rumbled as another spear of energy appeared in Jurrien's hand. As he hurled it the demon rolled, and the lightning scorched only bare earth.

Jurrien dropped to the ground, wind swirling in his frost white hair.

Inken turned and stumbled back towards her companions, thunder ringing in her ears. Together they retreated from the fight, the flashes of lightning crashing around them, the fallout from the battle coming dangerously close to killing them all.

Twenty feet further down the pockmarked road, they drew to a stop, hedged in by the last trees of the demon's forest. Eric drew Inken into an embrace before they faced the others. Despite the Storm God's efforts, the demon still seemed unstoppable. And its forest, decimated as it was, still surrounded them.

"What do we do?" Caelin shouted over the shriek of the battle.

"There's nothing we can do for him. This is his fight," Eric replied. "The lightning I control is nothing to that creature, only Jurrien seems to have the power to harm it."

"We have to get out of here," Gabriel spoke up, casting a nervous glance at the two titans. "Just in case things don't go our way."

"Can you burn another path?" Inken asked.

Eric shook his head. "I've already tried. The vines are growing resistant, and regenerating themselves faster than I can cut my way through. The demon does not want us going anywhere."

Inken hesitated, an idea coming to her. It was dangerous, but it might be their only way out. "What if we fly?" she asked.

Eric paled. "I've only tried that a couple of times since it went wrong in Lon. Jurrien warned me…"

"I think Jurrien has other things on his mind right now," Enala offered.

Inken eyed the Storm God. The battle had closed to weapons now, *Soul Blade* against Jurrien's spear of lightning. Jurrien looked hard pressed to hold the demon at bay, its dark blade coming closer and closer. Sweat dripped from his brow and Inken wondered how much energy the Storm God had already spent.

Eric ran a hand through his sweat-soaked hair. "Okay, maybe. Let me see," he closed his eyes, forehead creased in concentration.

The forest began to sway in the rising air currents. Then the roar of the wind arrived, drowning out the clashing blades. It tore at Inken's hair, flicking leaves and stones at their faces as a vortex gathered around them.

A shiver ran down Inken's neck as the pressure lifted her half a foot off the ground. Her arms windmilled, struggling to keep her upright, and her heart beat hard in her chest. But the wind pushed all around her, keeping her stable.

But there she stayed, hovering only two feet from the earth. A minute passed, then another. Sweat beaded Eric's forehead, until at last he released his breath and they dropped gently back to the ground. She looked at Eric, heart sinking.

"There's too many of us," his voice was a whisper. "I can't concentrate the wind enough to carry us all."

Inken closed her eyes, fighting back tears. She summoned the image of the temple courtyard, drawing strength from the few quiet moments they had stolen together. She knew what they had to do, but it took all her courage to speak the words. "Then you have to take her. You have to take Enala, and leave the rest of us behind. She's all that matters now."

"No," Inken did not miss the tremor in Eric's voice. "I won't leave you," he shook his head, looking around the circle. "Any of you."

Inken reached out and grasped his shoulders. She kissed him, and drew back. "You have too, Eric. You have to get her as far from here as possible."

"We can't just leave you here," Enala interrupted. "We can't abandon you!"

"You can, and you will," Caelin stepped in. "Inken's right, your life must be our priority. If you die, we are as good as dead anyway," he turned to Eric. "Do it, Eric."

Inken nodded. "You can do it, Eric. You must."

He looked into her eyes for a long moment. She saw the pain there, the uncertainty. But they both knew this was their only option. It had to be done. They could only pray Jurrien would emerge victorious.

Finally, Eric closed his eyes, forehead scrunched with lines of worry. "Okay. Come on, Enala. Let's see if this works."

Enala stepped up beside him and the wind gathered again. This time the currents did not buffer Inken or the others. They watched from without the whirling tempest as Enala's hair whipped in the air, the red lock caught beneath her ear.

Inken's eyes fixed on Eric's. His face grew grim and her own heart twisted with despair. She struggled to keep it from her face though, lest Eric turn back. Instead she blew him a kiss.

This time it did not take long for Eric's magic to work.

The two lifted from the ground, rising higher and higher into the air. Enala gripped Eric's hand, holding them together as they drifted over the forest towards the river.

Inken stretched up on her toes to watch them go. She raised a hand above her head in farewell, and saw Eric and Enala do the same. Then they were gone, vanishing over the distant rooftops, and all she felt was the pain of loss. Tears came unbidden to her eyes, but she fought them off. She took a great, shuddering breath, struggling for composure.

Fists clenched, she turned to the others. "Now what?"

———

JURRIEN GRITTED HIS TEETH AND TOOK A STEP BACK. Exhaustion crept through his soul and a dull ache throbbed in the muscles of his back. Blood ran down his arms and chest from a dozen small cuts. The kiss of the *Soul Blade* stung, sucking at his life force. Lightning crackled in his hand, the pain feeding his anger.

Thomas stood across from him, the same sly smile on his face. *It is not Thomas*, he reminded himself. The man who had been Thomas was long gone. Sadly, the old king's proficiency with the blade had not been lost with him. Jurrien would not win this battle of blades, but so far the demon had evaded each of his attacks.

"Take all the time you need, Jurrien. The *Soul Blade* will wait," again the soft cackle.

Jurrien scowled back, reaching deep for the strength he needed. He heard the silent cries of his people from all around, the pleading of the townsfolk suffering the wrath of this monster's magic.

"Are you ready to die, demon?" he growled.

Thomas swung the *Soul Blade* in a lazy ark and yawned.

"I'll admit, Jurrien, I do enjoy the contest. Not many have held their own against me. Of all Archon's warriors, I am the greatest. His champion, as Alastair once was to me," he shook his head. "I am disappointed the old Magicker did not meet his end at my hand. Alastair deserved better than a death to one so low as Balistor."

Jurrien closed his eyes, the demon's words drowning in the sea of misery echoing from his people.

I cannot let my sister's magic be perverted like this, the thought spurred him on.

He launched himself at Thomas, lightning arcing from his arms.

Thomas threw himself to the side, and his magic burned a path deep into the cursed forest. The *Soul Blade* flashed out, striking for Jurrien's throat. He raised his spear, thunder crashing as the blades met. Then Thomas' foot rose to smash Jurrien in the chest, forcing him back. He brought his spear up to block the next blow, but still felt the lick of the cursed steel on his cheek.

Cold spread from the wound and Jurrien sensed another trickle of power sucked from his soul. This could not go on; his magic bleeding away drop by drop. He spun on his foot, summoning the wind to blast the demon. Thomas hurtled backwards through the air before a vine reached out to catch him.

Magic surged as Jurrien spun the currents into a vortex, attempting to launch Thomas into the sky, away from the source of his power. If he could pin him in the sky, the demon could not avoid a killing blow.

But more vines shot out and wrapped themselves about Thomas, pinning him to the earth. The ground beneath Jurrien split open once more, heat billowing up from the flames far below. He drew the wind back to himself and rose into the sky, feeling the whoosh of air as the crevice snapped shut below him

"Nice try, old friend," Thomas growled.

Jurrien threw a bolt of lightning in response. He was tired of talking to the creature wearing his friend's body.

Thomas vanished and Jurrien threw himself to the side, already familiar with the demon's trick. The hiss of the *Soul Blade* as it sliced past raised hackles on his neck, but his hands were already moving to strike back. He heard a satisfying crackle as his spear found flesh.

Twisting, he attacked again, but Thomas had already retreated out of range.

"You will pay for that," Thomas growled, anger twisting his face beyond all recognition. Even the voice had lost all resemblance to Thomas'. "I grow tired of this game, Jurrien. It is time it ended."

Jurrien shivered. The demon's cloak billowed out, growing until it seemed darkness itself clothed the fiend. The earth shook and Jurrien quickly summoned the wind to lift him to safety.

Before he could rise five feet, a vine tore from the dirt to wrap itself about his wrist. He growled as thorns bit deep into his mortal flesh. Before he could swing the spear another snatched at him, and another and another, as a mass of cruel tendrils blackened out the sky. He struggled within the thicket as the thorns tore through his defences.

Concentrating, he drew lightning from the air, magic flooding from his body. His skin crackled with energy, burning away the vines. Relief swept through Jurrien as they fell away like spent tinder.

Then fresh panic surged as he felt the piercing sting of their return. He opened his mouth to cry out, but a thorny tendril wrapped about his head, cutting off his scream.

Jurrien struggled to control his dread. The familiar magic of his sister surged around him, usually so soothing but tainted now by darkness. His own power coursed within, battling with the dark forces, drawing energy from the air itself to burn at his earthly entrapments. Yet his body remained imprisoned, the godly strength of the vines threatening to tear him apart.

But that was not how the demon wished for him to die.

"Do you see now, Jurrien? Do you see how weak you really are; how much stronger your sister was? Gentle, sweet Antonia. Always the light-hearted one, the beacon of hope. But this power of hers, it can level cities. How she must suffer, locked away in the blade, knowing the death her magic now brings."

The demon appeared through the thicket, the darkness around it merging with the forest Antonia's magic had brought forth. The pale face looked up at him, blank eyes showing no hint of life.

"But your power, your power will be welcome too."

Jurrien wanted to curse the creature, but the vines choked the response from him. He reached again for his power, to summon all his strength and strike him down. With shock he found only a tiny pool remaining. The rest had withered, trickling away with each drop of his blood, spent in the battle to free himself. There was maybe enough for one last attack, but he knew now it would be futile.

"Relax, Jurrien, you must relax. It will not be so bad. You will have a blade all to yourself, see?" It held up a *Soul Blade*, the steel still black, empty. The demon grinned. "Now your sister, she fought it. The process did not go well for her."

Rage boiled up within Jurrien. He shrieked against the gag, teeth tearing at the vine. He tried to swing his arms, to kick out with his legs, anything to free himself. But his struggles were futile, the vines refusing to budge an inch. There was no escape this time, not for himself at least.

Closing his eyes, Jurrien opened his spirit mind and soared into the sky, seeking the fellowship. Elation rose in his soul as he saw Enala and Eric had already fled. Following the scent of Eric's magic, he found them racing across the farmlands to the south.

Jurrien reached out with his mind to Eric. *I am done, Eric. Do not turn back!*

His message sent, he turned back to the city. There he found the others still trapped by the forest, helpless before the demon's magic. A shiver went through Jurrien's soul. They had given everything for this quest. He must give them a chance to run. He had magic left for that, at least.

Summoning the final reserves of his strength, Jurrien sent lightning rippling through the forest beside the company. Such an easy task, yet exhaustion swept through him as the last drop of his magic trickled away.

As the energy burnt its way through the nightmarish trees, Jurrien plummeted back to his body.

He gasped as pain exploded from his chest. A cool black tide swept into his body, seeking out his soul. In despair he reached for his magic, desperate to resist, but found only emptiness.

No! he screamed in the confines of his mind.

Then Jurrien slumped against the black blade piercing his heart.

And the Storm God's soul went screaming into the *Soul Blade.*

10

"What do we do now?" Enala shouted over the howling wind.

"I don't know," Eric called back, fighting to keep the despair from his voice. Jurrien's final words rang in his mind. "We were meant to head for Ardath, but I don't think I can take us that far."

Eric could sense his pool of magic shrinking; keeping them airborne was sapping his strength at a shocking rate. But at least they were making good time. They had already travelled over a league upriver, although it was difficult to tell for sure in the darkness. The stars glittered overhead, but the half-moon failed to cast enough light to illuminate more than the dim reflection of water below. It was eerie, flying through the night, unable to see where they might end up. At least Eric could not tell how high they were; somehow that seemed to have kept his fear at bay.

"It may have been a trick," Enala suggested. He had told her of Jurrien's message.

Eric shook his head. "No, I don't think so. If it was the

demon, it would have told us to turn back. No, Jurrien is gone," he closed his eyes, his heart twisting as he thought of Inken and the others. He should not have left them, should have found a way to save them all. But there was no turning back now. "We're on our own now."

"They may have escaped, Eric," there was strength in Enala's voice, enough to almost give him hope.

Tears spilt from Eric's eyes. Angrily he wiped them away. "I don't see how; if Jurrien could not even save himself."

How could you have left them? The question raced through his head, haunting him.

Clenching his fists, Eric forced it to the back of his mind. He had to focus, think of what to do next. They had to assume the demon now had Jurrien's magic. That meant it could wield the God powers of the Earth and Sky. No one could stand against such forces. Their only chance was to put as much distance between themselves and the demon as possible.

"If it has Jurrien's power, will it be able to fly now?" Enala asked.

A chill swept through Eric. "Maybe. Let's just pray it first has to learn how to use the Sky magic. That could be why it hasn't shown its face until now; it had to master Antonia's powers first."

Enala nodded. "That makes sense. But when it does, it will head this way. It knows we have to go to Kalgan; the Sword is there. Do you think we can outrun it, once it learns to wield the Sky magic?"

"No," Eric's power was still fading fast. The God magic would not have the same limitations. "In fact, I don't think I can carry us much further."

"How long can you last?"

"Maybe another hour, no more than that," Eric shrugged. "We won't get as far as Ardath."

He caught the glimpse of water away to their right and altered course to keep with the river. So long as they followed it, they would eventually arrive in the lake city of Ardath, capital of Plorsea. But if the demon knew their plans, it would be on their trail within hours. Even without mastery of the Sky, intuition told Eric it would catch them long before they reached the city.

Eric coaxed a little more magic into the winds, driving them faster. Emotion swirled in his chest, fear and sorrow battling within. He closed his eyes, seeing again Michael's face as he pushed Eric from the path of the blade. The short smile of farewell. He had sacrificed himself to save Eric, and who knew whether the others had followed him.

I left them to die.

Eric glanced up at a squeeze from Enala's hand. "It was their choice, Eric. Whatever happens, we have to honour them, Michael and the others. We will make it to Kalgan, and turn the Sword against that demon and whatever other creatures Archon sends," Enala drew a deep, shuddering breath. "We will not let their deaths be in vain."

Tears blurred Eric's eyes again, but in the darkness he no longer cared. "Okay," he whispered, the winds whipping the word away.

"So do we go to Ardath?" Enala asked.

Eric swallowed, thinking hard. "No," he replied. "The demon must know we would head that way. If it can fly now, it would overtake us within hours."

"Then where? We have to get to Kalgan and the Sword, and Ardath guards the only passage through the mountains for leagues around. What other choice do we have?"

Frowning, Eric searched for an answer. A chill iced his

heart as the answer came to him. There was another way to Kalgan, one that did not pass through the mountains. Antonia had shown him the way, in the vision of Alastair and Thomas fighting during Archon's war. There was a secret passage to Kalgan, one guarded by a creature which might prove more dangerous than the demon behind them.

"We must go to Chole," Eric whispered.

"What?" Enala shouted back, confusion sweeping across her face. "Chole is in the wrong direction!"

"Exactly. The demon will never guess to look for us there."

"But the Sword of Light is in Kalgan."

Eric nodded. "I know. But there is an ancient passage between the two cities, a magical path called The Way. Unfortunately, as far as I know, only two people have used it in the last five hundred years and lived."

Enala fell silent. Finally, she turned to him. "Who were they?"

"Alastair and Thomas."

Enala gave a grim nod. "Okay, we go to Chole."

Eric's sense of dread grew. Silently, he reached for the winds and directed them away from the river. The image of the skeleton's grin as it attacked Alastair appeared in his mind's eye. He fought down his fear, but in truth he did not hold out much hope for their new plan. His mentor had only survived through sheer luck. What chance did they have?

But then, they didn't stand a chance against the demon either.

Eric closed his eyes and sent a desperate prayer to whatever entity remained that Inken and the others had survived. Every inch of his being screamed for him to turn back, but he kept on, jaw locked, neck straining, hands clenched so hard his fingernails bit into his palms. There was no choice, they had to keep going.

They flew on for another hour, then a second as Eric strained every mile he could get from his magic. Below they caught glimpses of open farmland in the dim moonlight. Patches of forest flashed by, and the odd stream, but otherwise they saw little. They held each other close, shivering as the wind drew the heat from their bodies.

Eric felt his concentration waning with his fading strength. His eyes drooped, the chill creeping through his body. Finally he could go no further, and they drifted lower in the sky. With the trickle of magic remaining, he directed them towards the ground in a downwards spiral.

He could see no roads or buildings, only the gently rolling hills of northern Plorsea and a flock of sheep huddled together in the pasture. A few looked up at their approach, and then returned to their slumber. Apparently two humans falling from the sky did not bother them overly much.

Despite his best efforts, they were still moving too fast when they hit the ground. Their feet went out from under them, a final gust of wind sending them rolling across the dry grass. Eric bit back a curse as his shoulder struck a rock buried in the field. When they finally came to a stop, he was thankful just to be in one piece.

They lay there a while then, taking stock of their bruises and checking for broken bones. Eric took a deep breath, savouring the grassy scent of the field. Nearby several sheep finally climbed to their feet and trotted away, their angry grunts loud in the night's silence. Exhaustion washed through Eric's body as his muscles began to ache. The flight had pushed him too far; he had spent some of his own life-force to bolster his magic. Now he would suffer the after-effects.

"Are you okay?" Enala asked as she stood.

Eric took stock of his body, the twinging pain already spreading to his arms. Soon they would start to cramp and seize. Then the real pain would begin. If he was lucky he might still be able to move. Either way, they needed to find shelter before he was completely immobilised. He pushed himself to his feet, his injured shoulder shrieking in protest.

"For now. But we had better get out of the open. Who knows what's out here."

"Easier said than done. It's pitch black, we have no torches, and all I could see as we landed was farmland," she glanced at the stars. "From what I can tell, Chole is in that direction," she pointed to where he guessed was south.

"That's a start. We should probably avoid the roads anyway," he took a step down the hill. His leg crumpled as pain tore into his calf. He would have fallen if Enala had not caught him.

"I don't think you'll be going anywhere in this condition," Enala observed.

Eric ran a hand through his hair. "We don't have much choice; we need to find shelter."

Enala shook her head, forehead creased with worry. "I don't know much about magic, but you don't look good, Eric. You're pale as a ghost. And we're not going to get far in the dark anyway. It must be almost midnight," she looked around. "At least we seem to be on the leeward side of the hill here. There doesn't seem to be much wind."

"Where did you learn so much about the outdoors?" Eric glanced at the younger girl. Blond hair hung across her face and her copper lock had caught on her nose.

Enala made a face. "My parents, remember. They taught me how to survive."

"Okay, so what do we do? We didn't exactly have time to grab supplies before we left."

"No, and you're in no condition to go anywhere. It's going to be a rough night. But you rest, I'll see if I can find some wood for a fire."

"Is that a good idea? The demon might not be far behind."

"If it is, I don't think it'll need a fire to find us. But if our plan worked, it shouldn't be anywhere near us. We should be safe here, I hope."

Raising his hands in surrender, Eric sank back to the grass. "You win. But I lived in the wilderness too, remember. There are other things out here, dangerous creatures and people. A fire might attract them."

"Maybe, but there are others it will keep at bay," she laughed suddenly. "And I'm *cold*," the laughter overtook her then, her whole body shaking as she bent in two, hysterical tears running down her face.

Eric couldn't help but laugh himself; a painful, hopeless laughter rising up from the gulf inside him. Michael was dead, another friend lost to the darkness. And Jurrien had followed, the last God standing against Archon's power, and their companions had probably gone with him. They were alone, fleeing for their lives from a mad, unstoppable demon.

And here they were, worrying about thieves and the wildlife.

Finally the laughter subsided. Eric wiped his eyes, offering Enala a gentle pat on the back. "Okay, good plan. Let's at least be *warm*."

Enala took a deep breath, cooling her last bout of

laughter, and straightened. She wore a small smile, reflecting the self-directed mirth. With a wink she made her way into the darkness and disappeared around the bend in the hill.

Lying back, Eric tried not to second guess the decision. Worry gnawed at his conscience; whatever Enala said, he should not have let her wander off alone. If she was lost…

"Okay, sleepyhead. We have fire."

Eric snapped awake, shocked he'd drifted off to sleep. The exhaustion had crept up on him, stealing him away the second he closed his eyes.

Enala sat across from him, smiling happily in the light of the small fire. She held her hands out to the blaze, her grin growing. A pile of wood and kindling lay beside her.

Stretching, Eric tried to hide his surprise. "How did you light it?" he asked.

"It wasn't hard. An old trick I learned when I was young. If you're lucky, I'll show you one day. We were just fortunate I found a dead tree with plenty of firewood."

"Another time," Eric nodded. Holding his hands out to the flames, he let the warmth seep into his frozen joints. The cold had crept into his bones while he slept. A sharp pain lanced through his body as he moved. He tried to stifle a groan, and failed.

Enala moved across to sit beside him. "Are you okay?"

"Nothing a bit of sleep and food won't fix," he paused. "We don't have any food, do we?" His stomach rumbled.

"Afraid not. It was too dark to look properly; in the morning we might be able to find berries or something. Oh, and the firewood will probably only last an hour or so. Enjoy it while it lasts."

Eric groaned and lay back again, trying to rest his aching body. He closed his eyes, the light of the fire flickering across his eyelids. Its heat provided some scant comfort against the night's chill. At least the hill sheltered them from the cursed wind. He'd had more than enough after their flight.

Eric flinched when he felt Enala's body lie down next to him. Instinctively, he reached out an arm and drew her closer. It would be a long night; they would need each other's body heat to keep out the cold. They held each other close, silent, eyes closed, and listened to the chirping of the crickets and the crackle of the fire.

Before long Eric felt himself drifting back towards sleep. This time he made no effort to resist…

Eric's eyes shot open. He stared up at the stars, feeling the cold wash over him. He had no idea how long he had slept, but he sensed the fire was cold and dead. There was only Enala's warmth beside him now.

He frowned, exhaustion threatening to pull him back down into sleep. What had woken him? The growl of an animal? The wind? Or the muffled whisper of a footstep?

Fog clouded his mind, the lure of sleep reassuring him they were safe. But something had woken him. Groaning, he tore himself from the clutches of sleep and sat up.

The sound of movement came from nearby. Eric struggled to his feet, alert now but his aching body refusing to obey.

He looked up in time to see the club descend. He opened his mouth to cry out, then pain exploded through his skull, and he fell back into darkness.

———

"Go!" Inken screamed.

There was no time to stand there in shock. Just a

moment before a bolt of lightning had erupted from thin air to dance amongst the forest in front of them. The rotten stench of burning meat and wood reached them as the trees burnt, clearing a path to safety. For a precious second Inken stood shocked, searching for Eric, expecting the young Magicker to drop from the sky.

Then, with a sick sense of dread, Inken realised this was Jurrien's final gift to them.

"Go!" Inken screamed again and sprang forward. She raced into the gap left by the lightning, not stopping to check if Gabriel or Caelin followed. They could not afford to hesitate now. The demon remained preoccupied with Jurrien, but that might not last long. They needed to get as far away as possible, while they still could.

As she ran, Inken glanced at the writhing mass surrounding them. Already the blackened shoots were beginning to regenerate, shooting from the earth to chase them down the narrow alley. She picked up the pace. Fear bordering on panic drove her onwards, concern for her companions coming a distant second.

The path before them narrowed as the vines reached for them. But the end was close, the walls of a broken building beckoning through the unnatural forest.

They burst from the last of the trees, vines tearing at their skin as they made their escape. Inken lashed out with her blade to free herself and pressed on. Their respite would not last long, not if they remained in Sitton. Ahead the street sloped down towards the river. The ship was their only chance.

She glanced back to check on Gabriel and Caelin. They nodded back, their faces strained and haggard. Inken guessed hers did not look much better. They jogged down the street, dodging through the ruined buildings and rubble littering their path. Any faster and they would break an ankle in the darkness. If not for the burning buildings, their pace would have been even slower.

As they neared the waterfront, a flash of light lit the sky behind them. They looked back in time to see a blue glow erupt from where Jurrien and the demon had fought. A rumble of thunder followed, then a blast of wind struck them, forcing them to their knees.

As quickly as it had appeared, the conflagration vanished, and a deathly silence fell over the company. No one spoke. They knew what had just happened.

Jurrien, God of the Sky, was dead.

They were alone now, the only ones left to stand against the darkness.

Inken swallowed hard and picked up the pace. The ship could not be much further, but with every step she expected the laughter to begin anew, as the demon came for them. She glanced back over her shoulder, searching for the first sign of pursuit. She prayed to whatever force of good remaining that Eric and Enala were a long way from here by now.

A surge of relief swept through her as they turned a corner and found the river waiting for them. Their ship still bobbed on the water, alone now in the docks, the other vessels long since fled. The contingent of marines they'd left behind stood guard at the dock, faces grim. Terrified villagers packed the railings of their vessels, eyes glancing up at the city.

The marines parted as they approached, the captain offering Caelin a salute.

"Sir, everyone but your party is aboard. I don't know what's happening up there, but we took as many villagers on board as we could and then closed the dock," the man hesitated, eyes drifting up to where the light had appeared. "Where are the others?"

Caelin shook his head. "Dead or gone. There's no time to discuss things now. Get the ship ready to depart. We have to be gone five minutes ago."

"Already done, sir," the captain announced as they boarded. "Everybody hold on! Throw ropes, we're underway!"

Men leapt to obey the captain's command, as eager as anyone to leave the doomed city. Ropes were cut and oars shipped as they pushed off the dock. Minutes later the ship was surging up the river, the frantic beat of the oars driving them onwards at a rapid pace.

Inken could not tear her eyes from the broken city. Flames lit the shattered buildings and the thick smoke rising from the once beautiful city blacked out the stars. She could see little chance of survival for any soul remaining within its walls.

As the ship raced around the first bend in the river, the burning city slowly disappeared from view.

Closing her eyes, Inken let the first tears begin to fall.

———

THOMAS CLOSED HIS EYES, FEELING THE NEW POWER coursing through him. It twisted with the dark magic that now ruled his mortal body, joining with the green tendrils of Earth magic. This was a wild force, this Sky element, a power he had never wielded before. It fought him, surged against his will, fighting for freedom.

The demon inside grinned at the challenge. Antonia's power had come easily; as a mortal he had possessed Earth magic for decades. Yet the Sky was different: unwieldy, demanding, struggling for control. It would take time to master.

Ah, but when he did.

Thomas lifted his face to the sky, breathing in the destruction. His tongue darted out, tasting the ash of his conquest. Closing his eyes, he savoured the screams of the dying echoing up from the city. The destruction was almost complete. As was his mission.

He frowned then, sensing an absence. His quarry had escaped, the girl fleeing with the boy who wielded Sky magic of his own. And Jurrien had saved the others.

Shaking his head, Thomas dismissed them. The mortals were of no consequence. The other two though, he would hunt them to the ends of the earth.

He smiled. It would not come to that. No one remained to stand against Archon's magic now. The Three Nations lay open before his master's power. His taint would spread, and those who grew tired of the yoke of the Gods would rise up against their rulers. This time, there would be no resistance, no Gods to unite the people against his master's crusade.

And whispers of the two he hunted would spread. They could not go undetected for long. Word of their passage would soon reach the ears of Archon's servants.

But of course, he knew where they must go anyway. The kingdom of Trola lay far to the west. In its capital, the Sword of Light waited for its rightful wielder. The Sword was their only hope now, the only God power remaining to protect the Three Nations. They would claim it if they could.

Thomas grinned. But not if he claimed it first. He began to march through the ruins of Sitton, following the taint of magic the boy had left behind. It was already fading, and soon all sign of their passage would vanish. It did not matter. He would wait for them in Kalgan.

He glanced at the night's sky. The boy and Jurrien could fly. A useful skill, even if the dark magic already allowed him to travel faster than any mortal. He would need to discover the secret to their flight. With the strength of the Storm God's magic, he had no doubt he could outpace the boy.

Thomas laughed, basking in the power of the two *Soul Blades*. A surge of joy throbbed in his veins as he reached for Antonia's power. He felt the dim shriek of her soul as he tapped into its destructive force. A tremor raced out from him, buckling the earth in one final wave of destruction. With a roar and a whoosh of dust, the last of Sitton toppled to the ground.

Thomas walked from the ruin, into darkness.

❧ 11 ❧

Enala wriggled on the hard floor, struggling to find a more comfortable position. The task was almost impossible with the wagon lurching through every pothole in the rutted road. The rope tying her hands behind her back also didn't help, or the dirty rag that had been shoved in her mouth. She winced as the wheels struck a rock, tossing her into the air. Canvas sides covered the rear of the wagon, leaving her blind to the world outside.

Eric lay across from her, unconscious. His breath was laboured and a purple bruise marked his forehead. Sweat beaded his brow, while grass stains covered his clothes. He groaned as the wagon bounced again, but still did not wake.

His warning call had woken her, but before she could even draw her sword rough hands had grabbed her and thrown her to the ground. There had been at least six, too many for her to fight alone. She had been overpowered in seconds, then stripped of her sword and dagger. Then they had then been lugged overland for hours in the darkness, finally arriving at a faint track where a wagon waited.

Sunlight had begun to seep through the canvas cloth hours ago, and Eric still showed no sign of stirring. Enala pulled at her bonds again, hoping to stretch the rope enough to free herself. The coarse threads cut into her wrists, refusing to yield. It seemed their only hope was if Eric could regain the strength to summon his magic.

That's if he wakes at all, a cynical voice whispered in her head. She shook herself, forcing her mind to other thoughts. There had to be another way out.

The banging of the wagon wheels lessened as their pace slowed. When they drew to a stop she shifted herself to watch the flap at the back. She fixed a scowl on her face, wishing she wasn't gagged so she could curse whoever entered. Anger boiled up within, surging through her veins. Her heart thudded and pressure built in her chest, a white hot heat begging to be released.

Enala clenched her fists, fighting the anger. She could not afford to be reckless.

Stones rattled outside as boots approached the rear of the wagon. A shadow appeared against the canvas, then the flaps were drawn aside and a woman carrying a bucket pulled herself into sight. Her grey eyes surveyed them as she brushed short black hair from her face. She wore the long pants and leather jerkin of a man, both stained a deep black. A scar stretched from her jaw down to the collar of her shirt.

The woman paid no attention to Enala. Instead she hoisted the bucket with two hands and poured it over Eric, a wicked grin fixed on her freckled face.

"*Arghhh!*" Eric screamed and seemed to rise into the air. He gasped as he tripped over his bonds, tumbling face first to the floor. He shrieked again, the whites of his eyes showing as he looked around in panic.

"Good, you're awake," the woman ignored the string of curses which followed, "the chief wants to meet you."

She reached back and pulled the cover across. Sunlight streamed in before a large man stepped up to block it out. Enala swallowed as he stepped into the wagon, already reassessing her first impression. The man wasn't large, he was huge; towering over them in the confined space. He had to bend just to stop his broad shoulders from touching the roof. Thick leather armour covered his barrel-like chest, painted black in a match of the woman's clothing. His hair had been pulled back in a ponytail, which draped over his shoulder and a matted beard covered his face. He wore a great two-handed sword strapped to his back.

His black eyes stared down at them. Enala shivered as they lingered on her, seeing the naked greed there, the black soul of a man used to having whatever he wanted.

"What have we here?" the man boomed. "I expected only the Magicker."

"They were together when we found them, Thaster. I thought you might like to talk to both."

The man nodded. He waved at Eric. "And he is secure?"

The woman grinned. "Absolutely. He used too much of his power anyway, he'll be no problem to control."

"Good, I don't want any trouble from him," the man turned back to them. "I am Thaster, chief of this Baronian tribe. You are my captives. If you are lucky, we will find some use for you. So long as you cooperate," his voice turned hard. "Or, if you do not, perhaps we will collect the bounty on your head, boy," he stared at Eric.

Groaning, Eric struggled to his feet. He spoke through gritted teeth. "Or perhaps you would like to let us go, before I burn all you own to ash."

Hope surged in Enala's chest. Had Eric recovered enough to save them?

Thaster only laughed. "Go ahead. Laurel here has taken care of that," he waved a hand at the woman with the bucket.

Enala's hope curdled in her stomach as Eric paled. "What have you done? Why can't I find my power?"

"Allow me to explain," Laurel stepped forward and grabbed Eric by the collar. Next second, her knife was at Eric's throat. With his arms tied behind his back, Eric could do nothing but stare into her eyes as she pressed the dagger harder. Blood began to trickle down his neck.

"I am a Magicker too," she growled. "One of very bad repute, you might say. Even if my powers come from the Light element. I sensed your magic earlier and tracked you down. Something told me it might be worth it. And now my magic will keep yours under check for as long as we care to have you as our guests. Understand?" she threw Eric to the floor.

Eric stared up, eyes boiling with hate. He gave a curt nod.

"Good," the woman shrugged. "Look on the bright side, boy. At least here you won't be burning any towns to the ground," she gave a dark cackle. "Or at least not the ones who are good to us."

Thaster folded his arms. "Then we have an understanding. The Magicker will be good. If you're lucky, I might just keep you around. A power like yours could prove very useful. If not, well, then we will enjoy the gold for your head," he turned to Enala and a dark terror filled her heart. "As for your friend, I'm sure there will be a place for another slave in our camp."

Just then, Enala would have given anything for her

sword. The pleasure of driving the sharp blade through the man's stomach would be worth the beating. She struggled to keep the hate from her face, helpless as she was.

Thaster waved a hand. "I will leave you to your prisoners, Laurel. You can remove the girl's gag. Let me know if she has anything interesting to say," he turned and left the wagon, leaving them alone with the Magicker.

Laurel moved across and untied the gag from Enala's head. "There you go, my lady," she smirked. "How is that?"

Enala spat at her face, but she ducked out of range and grinned. "Feisty, I see," she sat on a crate at the rear of the wagon, ignoring Enala's dark glare. "So, what are your names?"

Enala clenched her mouth shut. Eric did the same. Laurel only lay back and crossed her legs. After a few minutes she cleared her throat. "I'm afraid we're going to be spending quite some time together, my friends. I can't very well go around calling you 'boy' and 'girl' now, can I?"

"Do what you like," Enala growled, her fury spreading. A ringing started in her ears, growing as the pressure built.

"Why should we make your life easier?" Eric snapped.

Laurel shrugged, up ending her bucket to use as a foot rest. "My life is easy whether you cooperate or not. But it's up to me whether I untie you, or let you spend the next three weeks trussed up like pigs," her knife appeared again. She tossed it casually into the air and caught it by the blade. "Either way, don't think there'll be any hope of escape," the knife flashed across the wagon, burying itself in one of the wooden supports holding up the canvas.

"My name is Eric," Enala turned in surprise as Eric grated out the words. "this is Kathryn. We don't want any trouble."

"Okay, Eric and Kathryn, it's nice to meet you," Laurel

stood and moved across the wagon. Pulling her knife from the wood, she quickly cut their bonds. "Let it not be said I let a good deed go unrewarded. Make yourselves comfortable. We'll be travelling most of the day," as she spoke the carriage began to move again.

Enala rubbed her wrists, pain tingling the tips of her fingers as the blood returned. "Where are we going?"

"South," Laurel answered. "That's all you need to know. Thaster likes to keep his plans quiet, you understand," she spread her hands. "Where were the two of you going in such a hurry?"

Outside the rumble of the wheels told Enala they were picking up speed. "South," she answered. "That's all we can tell you, you understand."

Laurel laughed, a wheezing snort from her skinny nose. "Not like it matters now. Oh well, no doubt you'll tell us one day," she turned to Eric. "Now Eric, what about your powers? Where did you learn to use them? From what I hear, you caused quite a bit of carnage in Oaksville. But you seemed in control when I sensed you earlier."

"A friend taught me," Eric smirked. "Release my magic, and I'll show you just how well."

Laurel wagged her finger. "Now, now, we were getting along so well. Besides, you're in no condition for a fight. I can tell, remember?"

Eric shrugged and leaned back against a strut, his defiance spent. Enala refused to be deterred so easily. With Eric exhausted, it was up to her to get them out of this mess.

"So what makes a Magicker want to join a bunch of thugs like the Baronians?" she asked.

Laurel paused, her grey eyes catching Enala's gaze, searching for a motive behind the question. "A means to an end," she said at last. "I was never the priestly kind, but it was the Temple of the Light who found me when I was young and taught me to use my magic. The Baronians offered an escape, and a little more adventure."

Enala nodded, pleased with the new information. She thought she had recognised a Trolan tang to Laurel's accent. The Temples of the Light worshipped Darius, the God of Trola. Or former God, since he had vanished over a hundred years ago. "I hardly think murder and theft were your only options for adventure."

Laurel's eyes flashed. "No, but they were the most profitable. Besides, I was bonded to the temple until I turned twenty-five. I would still have a year of service left had I not escaped. Here, I am free to come and go as I please. Here, I am valued."

"Free?" Enala raised an eyebrow. "You're saying Thaster would just let you leave tomorrow if you wished? You think he would let a power like yours walk out the door?" she laughed, her voice taking on a mocking tone. "Not that you exactly have a door. Is this what you call 'home'?"

Laurel's face darkened and her eyes took on a dangerous glint. She rose, towering over Enala, dagger still in hand. Enala made no effort to move. She met Laurel's glare with a smirk of her own.

"You should watch what you say around me," Laurel growled.

"Oh should I now? And what would Thaster say if you were to damage his new prizes?" she laughed. "You don't fool me, Laurel. You're no more free than either of us. Thaster is in charge here, and whatever Thaster wants, Thaster gets," she eyed Laurel. "You all bow to his will."

Laurel lurched forward, hands reaching out to jerk Enala to her feet. She pulled Enala close, face to face, the breath hissing between her teeth. Enala forced herself to remain still, even as the stench of Laurel's breath caught in her nose. She struggled to stop herself from gagging.

Finally, Laurel growled and grabbed Enala's wrists in hands of steel. She picked up the rope and bound her even tighter than before. Then she marched to the flap at the rear of the wagon.

"Tell Thaster I would like to speak with him," Enala shouted as Laurel swung out of the moving wagon. She glimpsed the rutted trail through the gap as Laurel clambered around the side and made her way to the front of the wagon. Enala watched Laurel's silhouette through the canvas as she took a seat beside the driver.

She glanced at Eric. He raised an eyebrow. "Now what?" he asked.

Enala had no idea.

————

CAELIN STOOD AT THE BOW OF THE SHIP, WATCHING AS THEY passed beyond the last bend in the river. Ahead, the great expanse of lake Ardath lay revealed. The vast body of water stretched out before them, rolling green hills rising up on all sides. The noon day sun shone high above, vanishing occasionally behind the white clouds racing across the sky. The wind howled, rolling in off the surrounding hills. In the distance, white cliffs rose from the blue waters of the lake. At the top towered the spires of Ardath, beckoning them closer.

The rigging creaked as the wind took hold in the sails, propelling them out onto the lake. A collective sigh of relief rose from the marines below as they shipped oars. Caelin closed his eyes, a lump catching in his throat. The same scene ran through his mind, again and again. Two days had passed and still Michael's face haunted him, staring up from the pool of blood, dead eyes accusing.

A groan rattled from Caelin's throat. "*Why?*" he whispered to the wind. "Why did you do it?"

The wind offered no answer, and the thoughts continued to chase him. Why had he been so selfish? Why had he convinced the doctor to come? His foolish desire for Michael's company in this insane quest had led his friend to his death. Guilt weighed on Caelin's soul. Tears filled his eyes, not for the first time since they had escaped Chole.

The refugees of Sitton packed the deck, staring out with expressions of awe and apprehension. The ship sped through the water, rocking gently as small waves lapped at the sides. Caelin shivered as a finger of cool air reached down his neck, raising goose bumps on his skin.

He looked up as Inken joined him at the railing. "We're almost there," she looked at him, her hazel eyes showing strength. "They'll be there, waiting for us."

Caelin stared into her eyes, and nodded. "I hope so."

He tried to keep the sorrow from his voice, but Inken was not easily fooled. "No one could have stopped it, Caelin," she closed her eyes. "But I will never forget him, could never thank him enough for saving Eric."

Caelin barely heard her words. "It is my fault," he croaked. "I convinced him to come, told him we needed him."

Inken fell silent, looking out across the choppy waters. "It was his choice," she said at last. "And no one else's. You may have given him a purpose, but it was Michael who decided to come," she closed her eyes. "It was Michael who decided to give his life for Eric's."

"I don't know," Inken's words rang within, trickling against the flow of self-destructive thoughts. He took a deep breath, his frustration coming to the fore. "I just don't know anymore. What is the point of any of this now? The Sword of Light will not be enough without Jurrien and Antonia. We cannot even hope to stop the demon without them, let alone Archon himself."

A strong hand grasped his shoulder and shook him. "Get a hold of yourself, Caelin," Inken snapped. He flinched back at the fire in her eyes. "No matter what, it is up to us to go on now. Michael gave his life for this fight. Jurrien's last act in this world was to save us. So we must take strength from their faith in us, in their belief that we could win this fight."

The courage in Inken's voice bolstered Caelin. He straightened and gave her a nod, pushing his self-pity down to the depths of his mind. Inken was right; they had to continue, had to find a way to win this battle.

He looked around and saw they were almost upon the city. Onlookers packed the docks at the bottom of the cliffs, staring out at the strange ship approaching. Their war galley had outpaced the other refugee ships from Sitton; they would be the first survivors to reach the capital.

The crowd on the docks clambered for a view as the ship pulled up to its mooring. The marines were the first ashore, bellowing orders for people to make room for the passengers to disembark while others secured the ship. They waited patiently on-board as the refugees unloaded first, happy for them to distract the crowd.

At last they walked down the plank to the wharf. They allowed the marines to guide them through the milling crowds, and then Caelin took the lead as they reached the marble staircase leading up to the city. Gabriel and Inken stayed close as he waved to their escort, telling them to return to the ship. He knew the way from here. The men looked relieved to see the back of them. Caelin could not blame them after all they had witnessed in Sitton.

Together the three of them began the long climb to the top. Caelin knew from experience there were over five hundred steps to the stairwell. It was an impressive feat of engineering; some of the steps had been cut from the cliffs themselves, while other parts led them through caves deep in the stone. It was a long climb, but the view from the top would reveal the wide expanse of water stretching out all around them.

The refugees of Sitton had left some time ahead of them, but they still found themselves caught behind some of the slower climbers. Caelin did not mind the delay; when they reached the citadel it would be his duty to inform the king of the current state of affairs. He struggled to put the story together in his mind, but could not even begin to explain the deaths of Alastair and Balistor, never mind the murder of both Antonia and Jurrien. He had even lost Enala, the very reason King Fraser had sent him from the city in the first place.

They stopped to rest halfway up in a viewpoint carved from the cliff. Looking back towards the Hall river, Caelin saw that a host of smaller vessels now spotted the lake, making their way for Ardath. More citizens of Sitton come to seek refuge. He prayed the capital had the resources to cope with the sudden influx of people. Ardath was rich, but the island was small and could not support a large population.

When they finally reached the top they found the outer gates standing open, beckoning the last stragglers of their ship into the city. Caelin wiped sweat from his brow and made for the cool shade of the wall. Despite the winter winds, the midday sun still provided ample heat.

They walked beneath the granite walls which ringed the clifftops and entered the city. As they entered the square, Caelin looked around for a welcoming party. If Eric and Enala had made it this far, the king would surely know who the ship carried. His heart sank when he saw only city guards herding refugees down a side street. He saw no sign of the scarlet embroidered jackets of the councillors or their bodyguards, nor the blue tunics of the royal family.

He caught Inken's eye and saw she shared his concern. Shrugging, he took point again, brushing off the city guards and heading up the road he knew led to the citadel.

As they made their way deeper into the city, Caelin felt his heart lighten. This had been his home since birth; he knew these streets, knew every marble mansion, every carefully crafted fountain. He knew the stories depicted in the murals decorating the walls, the tales they told of the creation of Ardath. This was the first of the cities Antonia had founded with her followers; to be a buffer between the bitter rivalry of Trola and Lonia. She had led her people into the waste that had been this no-man's land, destroyed by decades of war. Here they had watched the land flourish at her magic's touch.

Now Ardath sat on the crossroads of the main trading routes between the Three Nations, providing protection to travellers and collecting tax from the passing merchants. The city had grown rich off trade, and flourished.

Ahead the citadel loomed, the smooth marble walls glittering in the afternoon sunlight. Soldiers manned the battlements. They stared out over the lake, alert for the first sign of trouble. The Baronian raiders continued to grow bolder, especially since the fall of Oaksville. But the king would suffer no interference to the trading routes between Lonia and Trola.

The gates to the citadel stood barred when they arrived, the soldiers on guard moving to block their passage. They wore steel plated armour and helmets with the visors down, prepared for any attack. They each carried a steel-tipped spear and short swords strapped to their sides.

Caelin marched up and offered a salute. "Good morning, men. I am Caelin, sergeant of the Plorsean army. We have just arrived from Lonia, and have urgent news for the king."

At Caelin's words the foremost soldier raised his visor, revealing a well-trimmed beard and brown eyes. His face lit up with recognition. "Caelin? It's been weeks since anyone heard from you, where have you been?"

Caelin gave a quick smile. "Elton, my old friend. I have been away on the king's business, business which I am afraid still continues. I must speak to King Fraser."

Elton nodded, hesitating a moment. "The king...has not been the most receptive to guests lately. You may find your presence is not so well received in the throne room," he paused, and then continued in a whisper. "The men say the stress has gotten to the king. He speaks to us less and less, and when he does it seems as though his mind carries a great burden."

Caelin rubbed his forehead. "I am afraid my news will only make matters worse then, but it must be given. May we pass?"

"Of course. But as I said, tread carefully, Caelin," he glanced at the other guards. "I won't be long. Do not let anyone else enter while I am gone," he turned to Caelin. "Sergeant, you and your friends can follow me. I will take you to the king."

The wheels of the gatehouse groaned as the portcullis

rose ponderously into the air. The wooden gates swung open behind it.

Caelin felt a tingling run down his neck as Elton beckoned for them to follow. He shook his head, forcing down his nerves, and nodded to his friend.

"Lead on."

12

Eric swallowed hard. The chief towered above them, arms crossed, his giant two-handed blade sticking up over one shoulder. His eyes burned with rage or amusement, there was no telling which with this man.

They stood before him, tiny but defiant. The wagons had stopped for the night an hour ago, but Laurel had only just appeared with the chief. Eric could see the amusement on her face, and he did not like the wicked twist to her grin. The man standing before them was not someone to trifle with—especially with Laurel suppressing his magic.

To make matters worse, he still had no idea what Enala was planning.

If she even had a plan.

"Well," Thaster growled. "Laurel said you wanted to speak, girl. So speak."

Enala lifted her head and looked him in the eye. "I do," she smiled, adding a sweet curl to her lips Eric had not once seen her wear.

He held his tongue, deciding it would be best to remain silent.

Thaster stepped closer. "And?"

Enala tilted her head and leaned in, the copper lock hanging across her eyes. "We have decided we will be good. It would be an honour to serve a man of your power."

The chief squinted down at her. Eric swallowed again. What was Enala playing at? This man would not be fooled so easily.

Eric jumped as the chief threw back his head and unleashed a booming laugh. The sounds sent a shiver of dread through Eric and he shrank back, reaching unconsciously for his magic but finding only a black wall stretching across his mind.

Thaster's mirth drew the attention of the Baronians nearby. He waved a hand for them to listen. "You hear that?" he cackled. "This lovely young girl would like to *cooperate* with me," he laughed again. "Says it would be an *honour.*"

The other Baronians joined in with Thaster's laughter, and a crowd gathered round to watch them.

Beside him, Enala's face reddened. Her shoulders shook as she clenched her fists. Before anyone could react, she stepped across the space separating them from the chief. Her knee flashed up, striking Thaster squarely between the legs. As the giant of a man doubled over, she brought her elbow down on the back of his head. He went down like a log.

A second later Laurel had her arm around Enala's throat and a dagger at her side. "Don't move," she hissed.

It took a long minute for Thaster to regain his feet. When he stood his face had turned a beet red and purple veins bulged in his forehead. He looked down at Enala, the rage in his eyes terrifying to behold. He raised a fist above her head, ready to strike her down.

Enala made no move to avoid the blow. Instead, she laughed. "What a man! A girl knocks you low, and the best you can do is beat her while your lackey holds her still. What a leader!"

Thaster hesitated, eyes glancing at the crowd of Baronians. These were his people, his followers, but Eric guessed there must be those within these ranks who aspired to replace him. Enala had just shown them all Thaster's mortality, showed them he could be laid low by a mere girl. If he let things stand, the vultures would soon be circling.

"Why don't you show your people just how much of a man you *really* are, Thaster. I challenge you to a fight to the death. Give me my sword, and I'll show everyone here just how much of a man you are," she laughed again. "Unless you're afraid to fight a girl."

Thaster's face had progressed from red to a dark purple. His whole body trembled, his fist still hovering over Enala's head. It looked as though it was taking all his will not to beat her to death right there. The crowd held their breath, eyes fixed on their leader, waiting for him to react.

A long moment passed before he lowered his fist. He began to laugh again, softly at first, but it quickly grew to a roar. The other Baronians joined him, though some turned away, disappearing back into the crowd. Eric guessed they had much to ponder.

The noise buffeted them, and made Eric want to shrink away and hide, but beside him Enala stood strong, staring hard into Thaster's eyes.

Finally Thaster raised an arm and the laughter died. He met Enala's gaze. "Tomorrow, at midnight. That should give you some time to contemplate your fate. Laurel!" he snapped. "Take them to their wagon. Make sure they're well fed tomorrow, the girl will need all her strength," at that he began to cackle. With a wave of his hand he dismissed them, turning his back and disappearing into the crowd.

Laurel grasped them by the scruff of their shirts and pushed them away from the crowd.

"You just couldn't play nice, could you?" she growled in their ears.

Enala pursed her lips but did not reply. When they reached the wagon, Laurel all but threw them through the flap. Eric stumbled to the back and slumped against one of the struts. His heart thumped at a hundred miles an hour.

"What the hell were you thinking?" Laurel and Eric asked in unison.

Eric glanced at the older woman, then waved a hand.

Enala answered before either of them could repeat the question. "I acted. You may be happy trapped here, Laurel, but I won't be. I won't live a day longer than I have too with the likes of men like Thaster."

Laurel grabbed Enala's tunic and thrust her against the canvas wall. "Listen here, you little *fool*. That man is going to kill you tomorrow. You have no idea what you are up against. In battle he is more a force of nature than mortal man," she paused. "And he uses black magic."

"*What?*" Eric made to stand.

"Stop!" Laurel fixed him with a glare. "Don't say a word. I should not have told you that, but perhaps now you might be convinced to give up this folly," she shook her head and released Enala.

Enala glared up at her. "*Coward*. How could you serve such a man? Your magic comes from the *Light*. How could you allow it to be corrupted by the twisted wants of one who works with that perverted force?"

Laurel's hand snapped out. The slap of her hand striking Enala's cheek rang through the wagon. Eric winced. "Shut your mouth, girl. You'd better write a letter to your family, since you're never going to see them again," she glanced at Eric. "And good luck avoiding the hangman's noose now. Thaster will deliver you straight to the authorities when we arrive in Chole. Gold is a much better investment than a troublesome Magicker," she shook her head. "Enjoy your sleep. Tomorrow will be a bumpy day, and likely your final one on earth. I'll be sure to bring you a fine last meal," with that she turned and left the wagon.

When she was gone, Eric looked at Enala. "Well? Care to elaborate?"

Enala stared at the canvas wall. She looked up at Eric's words, a blank look in her eyes, her mind clearly someplace else. She shook her head, slowly returning to reality.

"Actually, I was just trying to figure out the date. It's my birthday the day after tomorrow," she smiled. "So whatever happens, at least I'll get to see eighteen," then she laughed. "Maybe that will bring me some luck."

A chill swept through Eric at her words. A memory pricked at the back of his mind, something Alastair had once said to him. He stared into space, struggling to recall the words, but it lingered just out of reach.

Finally, he groaned and leaned his head back against the canvas wall. His thoughts turned to Inken, whether she still lived, where she might be. Her smile flickered in his mind, warming him. With a sigh, he closed his eyes.

It was a long time before either slept that night.

———

INKEN STOOD BEFORE THE GOLD EMBOSSED DOORS OF THE throne room, arms folded, foot tapping with impatience. Half an hour had already gone, and she was tired of waiting. Her nerves grew with the passage of each minute. She struggled to maintain a calm outward appearance. All she wanted to do was scream the question bouncing around in her head.

Where is Eric?

Caelin stood to her right, shoulders staunch and a blank expression on his face. She smiled, proud of the sergeant's strength. Despite his doubt and guilt, she knew he would not falter now. Whatever ghosts haunted him, they could rely on his courage to get them through.

To her left Gabriel stood with his hands in his pockets, looking uncomfortable amidst the riches of the citadel. He had said little since the events in Sitton and Inken was not sure what to make of him. Though his desire to find Enala was clear, there was a darkness in him, a haunted look to his face. And she still did not trust him after his attack on Eric.

Inken shook her head, her attention caught by a creak from the great doors. A crack appeared between them as the golden metal swung outward, revealing a manservant on the other side. He surveyed the waiting room before his gaze settled on the guard who had escorted them from the gates.

"The king will see your guests now, Elton. I hope it is important, the council is not in the best of moods," the man spoke in a haughty tone.

Elton nodded and turned to the three of them. "Time to tell your tale, Caelin," he waved for them to enter.

Inken followed Caelin through the doors into the chamber beyond. Guards stood to either side of the entrance, spears held at the vertical position. Inken took a deep breath as they made their way down the red carpet, trying to keep the strain from her face.

The walls of the throne room were made of wood rather than marble, and the rich red of the timber glowed against the flickering torches. Tapestries hung from the tall ceilings, each depicting a different time period from Plorsea's history. White glass windows ringed the room, their crystal panels looking out over the lake encircling the city.

A table stood on a raised platform at the end of the chamber, and a granite throne loomed behind it. Several men and women sat around the table, their quiet conversation buzzing about the room. Guards stood to attention in front of them, forming a human shield. Those at the table looked up as the company entered, and Inken got her first glance of the Plorsean King.

King Fraser wore a platinum crown and sat at the head of the table, but otherwise there was little to identify him as the most powerful man in Plorsea. His navy blue tunic with gold embossed buttons marked him as a member of the royal family, but others at the table wore the same blue— brothers and uncles who sat on the council. Grey streaked his hair and beard, both of which had been cropped short like the soldiers outside. She'd heard King Fraser served in the army when he was younger; apparently some of their customs had stuck. His dark brown eyes caught hers as they followed their approach.

"What is this we have here?" the king stood, his voice ringing out across the room. "Caelin, my champion, returned at last," open scorn laced his voice.

Caelin faltered midstride and Inken caught panic in his eyes. Then his face closed over and he continued his march towards the king. When he reached the ring of guards he sank to one knee.

"Aye, I have returned, my king, though my quest is not yet done," he tried to keep his tone neutral, but Inken caught the hint of defiance in his voice.

Inken grasped Gabriel's arm and led him to stand with Caelin. Together they knelt beside the sergeant.

"Ah, so you have not found the family I sent you to protect? Why, then, are you here? Where is Alastair?"

Caelin swallowed. "I am sorry, your majesty. The family are dead but for one girl. As is Alastair. He died protecting their last child, at the hand of one of our own, the traitor Balistor."

Whispers rushed around the room at Balistor's name. The king raised a hand, and silence fell. He walked around the table until he stood at the edge of the dais.

"Balistor was a traitor? Who are you to make such an accusation?"

Rage flashed across Caelin's face and then vanished. He continued in a calm tone. "I saw it with my own eyes, heard it from his own mouth. He slew Alastair, Antonia's champion, and then tried to kill the last descendent of Aria. If I had not stopped him, he would have succeeded."

The whispers grew to shouts. Some of the council stood, their chairs grating on the stone floor and banging to the ground. Glasses spilt across the wide table, and others cursed as wine dribbled onto their scarlet jackets. Though he had been a battle Magicker, Balistor had clearly been popular amongst the king's council.

King Fraser raised his hand again. This time silence did not fall until the guards thumped the butts of their spears on the stone floor.

"It sounds like you have quite the tale to tell, Caelin.

Perhaps you could start at the beginning," his tone was calm, but Inken could not miss the warning in his voice. They were on thin ice; if the king did not like Caelin's story, who knew where they would end up.

Inken licked her lips, and kept quiet.

Caelin had paled, obviously surprised by the councillors' reaction. Nevertheless, he looked to the king and began to recite their story from the beginning, when he had met Alastair in Chole.

Ten minutes later, the room was silent as Caelin told of how Balistor had betrayed them. His voice shook with emotion when he described how he had confronted the traitor, and faced him with Alastair's blade.

When Caelin finished, no one spoke. They stared at him with awe, a collection of fear and anger on the faces at the table. Inken could see some believed the story, but others were not so easily convinced. She looked to the king, trying to read the blank expression on the man's face. He alone held their fate in his hands.

"And where is Enala now?" the king asked, giving no hint of his verdict.

Caelin swallowed. "I am sorry, your majesty. My news grows worse. We were ambushed by the same demon in Sitton, where we had come ashore for supplies. We were separated from Enala, who was able to flee with Alastair's apprentice. We had hoped they might have arrived before us…" he looked around and found only blank expressions in response. "And…and worse still, the demon slew Jurrien in Sitton. We are alone in this fight now."

The room exploded, swallowing Caelin's final words in a cacophony of sound. Panic swept through the chamber and even the guards were caught up in its current. For a moment, it looked as though total chaos might break loose.

The king turned and walked to the meeting table. Drawing his greatsword, he raised it above his head and brought it down. A great crack ran through the throne room. He swung again, the metal blade slicing through the thick wood. On the third strike, the table folded in two, collapsing to the ground with a boom. The sound reverberated around the room, silencing the councillors.

"Silence!" Fraser roared, tossing his sword to the ground. He walked to the edge of the dais and sprang down to the red carpet. Caelin bowed his head as the king approached, and Inken quickly followed suit. Glancing at Gabriel, she nudged him to do the same.

"So what you are telling me, my champion, is that the last wielder of the Sword of Light is missing. That you yourself have witnessed the deaths of our beloved Goddess Antonia, and the Storm God Jurrien? These are evil tidings indeed you bring, ones so dark one might question the truth of your tale. Or the allegiance of the messenger."

Inken looked up, anger pushing her beyond caution. "He speaks the truth, your majesty. I witnessed all of it. As have others. The priests in Lon will verify everything we have said; they worked with Jurrien to send us here."

She glared at the king, refusing to drop her gaze. Their eyes locked, the silence stretching out, until at last Fraser waved a hand. "Well, we shall see then. I will send messengers to Lon, of course. And to whatever remains of Sitton We will have the truth."

"You cannot allow our men to engage with that demon," Caelin spoke up. "It is beyond mortal might now, not unless we mount a host of Magickers against it," anger was written on Caelin's face now, masking the fear hidden just below the surface.

The king stared at Caelin. "You forget yourself,

sergeant. Do not interrupt me. As for your advice, I do not need lecturing by a foot soldier in the business of magic. Now, what of the girl? Where has this companion of yours taken her, if not here?"

Caelin shrugged. "I do not know. We thought they would have arrived by now. I can only pray the demon has not found them. Either way, they fled using Sky magic, leaving no way to track them. But I believe if anyone can get Enala to the Sword, it is Eric."

The king nodded. "Very well. You have given us much to think about. Jurrien was here only a week ago, telling us of the peril faced by the Three Nations. We recalled our armies at his request; even now they are mustering at stationing points around the lake."

Caelin bowed his head. "That is welcome news, your majesty. Only the might of men is left now to protect us from Archon. We must march immediately for Fort Fall to reinforce the garrison, or the war will be lost before it begins."

Silence fell as Caelin's words echoed off the high ceilings. The councillors looked from one to another, open fear on their faces.

At last a woman stood. "There is wisdom in your words, Caelin, but we cannot act rashly. To do so would only be to play into Archon's hands. Marching north is but one option we have to discuss."

"*What?*" Gabriel snapped, raising his voice in protest. "That is the *only* option," he made to step forward, but Inken grasped his shoulder and pulled him back.

The king's guards advanced a step, hands on the pommels of their swords.

"Careful how you speak, boy," the king's voice was hard. "That is Katya, one of my most trusted councillors," he paused. "That was done once before, was it not? The armies of the Three Nations marched north to stand united at Fort Fall, to defend our people against Archon. And they were decimated. I will not so recklessly march my armies to the same fate," he looked to Caelin. "Thank you for bringing this news. I have not yet decided whether to believe your tale, but the priests in Lon will have the truth of it. For now, you may have your free run of the city, but the guards will not allow you to leave the outer walls," he waved a hand to dismiss them. "Elton will find room for you and your companions. You are dismissed."

❧ 13 ❧

E nala tried to conceal the trembling in her legs as they walked through the Baronian camp. Around her the men and women stared, fear and pity in their eyes. A few might have shown a hint of awe, but it was quickly hidden when she turned their way, and left her wondering if it was just her imagination.

She gave a mental shake of her head. It didn't matter. These people were slaves to this life, trapped by the black garments they wore to represent their 'freedom.' They were blind to the poverty in which they lived, the pitiful state of their holy tents and wretched wagon village. Their tattered clothes would be useless in the winter, and she guessed many would not live to see the spring.

Enala refused to be trapped in their cycle of suffering. She would fight and win, or die.

Ahead the crowds parted, revealing a circle of brown grass lit by bonfires. The moon and stars hid behind dark clouds, the sky a blank canvas. They would fight by the light of the flames. Enala made a mental note to be wary; she could easily be blinded by their light.

Eric walked beside her, his face blank, unreadable. Enala rubbed her hands together to ward off the chill, still trying to hide her nerves. She could show no fear here. Thaster would feed on it, and he needed no extra advantage. Although in truth, her fear was more for Eric than herself. She held his life in her hands as well as her own. One stumble, and it would cost them both.

Laurel came behind, her boots scuffing on the hard ground. Enala could almost feel her anger, prickling at her back like needles. It hung over them like a blanket, suffocating. That at least she could shrug off. The Magicker meant nothing to her.

As they entered the ring, Enala turned to Eric and hugged him. She felt the trembling in his body, and knew hers must be shaking too. She hoped no one else could see it.

"Don't go dying on me," Eric whispered.

Enala struggled to hold back tears. "I won't," the words caught in her throat. She gave a quick nod and turned away. She had to focus. From behind her she heard the thud of Eric and Laurel's footsteps as they moved away.

She walked into the circle, eyes flicking around in search of her opponent. She did not have to look far.

Thaster came marching into the light, dust rising up behind him as his boots thumped the dry grass. The dust glistened in the firelight, casting it in red and orange, and it seemed a cloud of embers trailed in his wake. He held his greatsword in one hand, its five-foot blade reaching for her. The other hand he raised above his head, as though this fight had already been won. Which, Enala had to admit as she stared up at him, might be as good as true.

But she refused to be cowed. She flashed the brute a toothy grin, knowing she must look a madwoman. Reaching down, she drew the blade Laurel had given her earlier. She looked at the short sword in her hand, and couldn't help but feel foolish wielding such a tiny weapon against the monstrous blade held by Thaster. It was not her sword, but Eric's, the one that had passed to him from Alastair. But its weight felt good in her hand, its balance similar to her own weapon.

When Thaster saw her weapon, his laughter shook the circle, silencing the crowd. "Would you like a bigger tooth-pick, girl?" he mocked. "I will break that toy with my first swing."

Enala bit her tongue and gave a curt shake of her head. A bigger sword would take time to adjust to, time she did not have. She knew the quality of the blade she held, had heard the others speak of the man who once wielded it. Alastair was a legend, and she felt honoured to hold his sword. It would be foolish to switch now.

The chief looked down at her. "Very well then," he grinned and passed his blade to his left hand. "Just for you, I shall use my left hand tonight. Perhaps that will make a fair fight of this contest."

The crowd's laughter began again, but Enala blocked them out. She stared up at the giant, taking in the massive shoulders, the legs like tree trunks, the muscles bulging in his arms. He held the greatsword in one arm as though it weighed no more than a feather.

Then she began to chuckle herself, a memory of her father emerging through the fear. He had always been fond of the old proverb—*the bigger they are, the harder they fall*. Grinning, she looked up at Thaster, the thought giving her strength.

Gods, I hope you were right, dad, she grinned, crouching in a fighting stance, sword out before her. *Otherwise this will be my last birthday.*

Around them, the laughter of the crowd ceased. Even the chief looked unsettled by her sudden change. He stared at her, the surprise in his eyes turning to suspicion. He glanced at the blade in his left hand, and then shook his head.

Enala raised an eyebrow. "You can use your right if you like," if he was debating whether to switch hands again, she had definitely succeeded in unsettling him. But she knew with all those watching, such an act would be viewed as cowardly. Changing back now would undermine his position in the tribe, and worse, dent his own confidence.

"I don't need it," he growled, forcing a grin. "Let the fight begin!"

Roaring, he started towards her, feet thumping as he moved at an almost casual stroll. Yet his pace was deceptive, his long legs narrowing the gap between them in two steps. His blade lanced out, seeking her head.

Enala was faster. She only had one hope of prevailing—keep out of reach of Thaster's blade until its weight began to wear on him. With such a large weapon, Enala hoped it would not take long. Exhaustion would flood his muscles with acid and his arms would start to ache. Then she would strike.

But first she had to survive.

The greatsword swept through empty air as she darted towards the nearest bonfire. Placing it at her back, she spun in time to deflect a second blow. As their blades met sparks flew and a shock from the impact ran down her arm. Enala cried out, stumbling back a step, grasping desperately at the pommel of her sword to keep from dropping it.

Fortunately, the fire caught in Thaster's eyes as he moved in for the kill. He hesitated, squinting against the burning light, giving Enala time to dodge to the side. Again his blade descended on empty space.

Spinning, Enala saw Thaster struggling to find her, blinking as he tried to recover his night vision. Seeing an opportunity, she leapt forward, short sword stabbing for his side. Enala almost dropped the blade in surprise when it connected, tearing through his thick leather armour and piercing flesh. She had not really expected the blow to find its mark.

Thaster bellowed in pain and the crowd gasped. His right arm lashed out, his iron fist catching her on the shoulder and flinging her from her feet. Somehow she kept hold of her blade as it tore from his side.

Enala rolled as she landed, holding the bloody weapon out at a safe distance. Shaking off the blow, she stumbled to her feet, sword at the ready as she looked for her opponent.

Thaster charged across the ring, silent now, rage burning in his eyes and the greatsword held overhead. The wound did not seem to have slowed him at all, and Enala found herself shrinking before the strength of his anger. His blade whistled as he swung it with enough force to split her in two.

Enala side stepped the blow, and the blade thudded deep into the hard earth. As Thaster wrenched at the blade, Enala kicked out, catching him in the groin for the second time in two days.

The chief roared again, half-doubling over while still clutching his blade in one hand. Enala swung her short sword, and cursed as Thaster managed to wrench his greatsword up in time to block it. A bloody fist lashed out as she retreated from range. As it sliced past she hacked out with her sword. Her blade bit into his wrist, and the scent of blood quickly followed.

The chief cursed. She retreated a few steps, expecting him to lash out, but this time Thaster did not pursue her. He held his ground, glancing down to inspect the cut in his arm. When he looked up again, the anger in his eyes had cooled to a simmer, but she sensed the berserker rage still lurked just below the surface. He studied her, taking her in, reassessing his foe.

Enala swallowed. She did not like this change of events. Thaster had finally decided to take her seriously, that she might actually pose a threat to him. There would be no more reckless charges now.

"So you know how to fight," Thaster smiled. "Well, isn't that something."

Enala scowled back, showing a courage she did not feel. As least she had injured his right arm; there would be no switching sword hands now. She raised her blade and offered him a mock salute, hoping to reignite his reckless rage. Blood dripped from her sword to her arm, but she did not waste a second to wipe it off. She kept her eyes fixed on Thaster, daring him to attack.

Instead, Thaster dropped into a fighting crouch of his own and edged his way towards her. Enala shuffled sideways, searching for a better position, or at least to get her back to the flames again.

Thaster smiled and shifted direction to head her off, trapping her near the centre of the circle. Enala glared, catching the hint of a smile at the corner of his mouth.

Realising she could no longer wait for him to make a mistake, Enala swallowed caution and drove herself forward. Her sword flicked for Thaster's face. The chief leaned back, his own blade raised to deflect the blow. Enala did not pull back, allowing her momentum to carry her forward. She attacked again, knowing her proximity would make it difficult for Thaster to bring his long blade around. Her short sword had no such limitations.

The chief grunted as her blade stung his shoulder, but his sword came down to knock hers away before she could drive it deeper. Then his fist crashed into her face, driving Enala to her knees. Stars streaked across her vision, but she knew Thaster would not allow her time to regain her sight. Half-blind, Enala flung herself forward.

Her shoulder crashed into Thaster's knees. With her small size she almost bounced off, but so far below his centre of mass the blow still managed to knock him off balance. Thaster stumbled backwards, arms wind-milling. His blade came within an inch of her head as it swung wildly through the air.

Enala rolled backwards out of range and regained her feet. She held her blade out before her, wishing for just one opening to drive it through the chief's black heart.

They circled one another, wary now, each suffering from the blows they'd exchanged. Enala's head ached from the punches she'd taken. She prayed the blood trickling from Thaster's wounds would soon leave him too weak to fight. She looked him up and down, searching for sign of exhaustion, sure no man could lose so much blood and continue to fight.

Yet the chief still towered over her, showing no sign of his slowing.

His legs, Enala decided. *That should stop him.*

She danced sideways and then darted at him, sword lancing for his face. As he raised his blade to defend himself, Enala withdrew her feint and swung at his legs. To her shock, Thaster leapt and her sword sliced beneath his boots.

Leaping sideways, Enala struck again. This time Thaster caught the blow easily with his own blade.

"Nice try, *Kathryn*. Would you like to try that one last time?" Thaster laughed.

Enala gritted her teeth. "My name is Enala, you moron," remembering too late Eric had given her a false name.

Ignoring her slip, Enala launched herself at Thaster, blade slashing out like a viper, seeking the taste of flesh. Thaster skipped backwards, his great blade keeping her at bay with surprising ease. She struck high then low, stabbed straight, dodged to the side before launching an attack. Each time his steel rose to meet her.

At last she stepped back, panting hard, cursing herself a fool for using so much energy.

Thaster's eyes flashed. "My turn."

Enala looked up at his words, and barely managed to sidestep the first blow. Even then, his sword sliced through the fabric of her coat, the steel coming within inches of her skin. Thaster left her no room to counter. He reversed his sword as it swept past, raising it high to strike her down.

Throwing herself to the side, Enala heard the thunk as the greatsword bit the hard earth. Spinning, she raised her short sword to attack, and instead found herself deflecting the behemoth's next blow. Steel shrieked and a jolt ran through her arm. The force of the blow drove her back a step, but Thaster followed, the blows coming one after another now, leaving her no time to think. Instinct alone kept her alive.

With no chance to counter, Enala fought to defend herself, and barely managed that. Thaster had found another level of skill, as though he were pulling energy from thin air to use against her. He showed no sign of pain or exhaustion from wielding the greatsword, only strength, power.

How is this possible?

Enala remember Laurel's warning—that Thaster used black magic—and knew the answer.

Anger flared in her then; that this man would resort to using such a vile force against her. Rage fed energy to her tiring limbs, giving her the strength to turn aside his next blow. Then with a scream she kicked out the way Inken had taught her, seeking to drive him backwards.

With supernatural speed, Thaster's hand shot out and caught her boot. He grinned down at her, contempt in his eyes. Grunting, he lifted her above his head and hurled her across the circle.

Enala spun through the air, the sword slipping from her grasp. With a sudden thud she crashed to the ground. Air whooshed from her lungs, leaving her winded, gasping as dust billowed out around her. Pain shot through her body and she struggled to take a breath. She lay there for a minute, sure she must be dying, choking, waiting for Thaster's blade.

At last she managed to inhale. Oxygen flooded her lungs, feeding strength to her burning muscles. Tears of pain ran down her cheeks, but she wiped them away, angry at her weakness. She managed to get her knees beneath her before she looked up.

Thaster stood over her, a mocking grin on his lips. He held her sword in one hand, his greatsword in the other.

"Would you like your toothpick back, little girl?" he laughed.

Enala closed her eyes as the rage took light, boiling through her like wildfire. Hate rose to overwhelm her, a red hot energy that left no room for sanity. Her chest burned and power surged through her veins, rising up from somewhere deep within, until her whole body shook with it. A buzzing began in her ears as the pressure built, pressing against her skull, unrelenting.

A scream rose within her, beginning in her chest and shrieking up from her throat. As it split the air, Enala felt some barrier in her mind shatter.

She opened her eyes. A brilliant red light lit the circle, and for a second she thought someone had added fuel to the bonfires. Then she saw the sudden fear in Thaster's face, his panic as he looked around the circle, his mouth opening to cry out. Screams of terror came from around them. The Baronians started to edge away, some already turning to flee.

Finally Enala looked down and saw the flames. Fire covered her body, leaping from her clothes, her arms, *everything*. It roared from her, tongues of flame taking light in the dry grass and racing out towards Thaster and the crowd. The chief did not even have the chance to run before they reached him.

His scream sent a shiver down Enala's spine. She watched as flames caught on his leggings, burning as they went. He turned and tried to run, but the fire danced all around him now. He had nowhere to go. In seconds it covered him, the inferno scorching through cloth, burning deep into his flesh.

Thaster screamed again, beating at the hungry flames, his movements already growing feeble. Enala tried to cover her ears, but flinched back from the fire dancing along her arms.

Panic took her, and she struggled backwards, fighting to escape the blaze, unable to understand where it had come from. Had Eric broken Laurel's hold on his magic? But she had heard no thunder, seen no lightning.

And why was she not burning with Thaster?

Then she heard the shrieks from the crowd. She looked up and saw the Baronians fleeing in panic. The blaze leapt among them, uncontrolled, wild, burning wherever it touched. Wagons turned to bonfires in the night as people stumbled amidst the ruin, desperate to escape. Thaster's struggles had already ceased; all that remained of the chief was a pile of ash amidst the flames.

Enala gaped, a slow dread spreading through her. She could think of only one impossible explanation—magic. Her own magic.

But how? She had never had power before, never even considered the possibility. How could this have happened?

Chaos swept through the Baronians. They fled, leaderless, defenceless against her wild magic. Ice ran down Enala's spine as she realised Eric was somewhere amongst them. She looked at her hands, searching within for a way to make it stop, to halt the destruction. Staring at the flames, she willed them to die, but she could not begin to contemplate how to control such a force.

Enala spun in a circle, but all she could see now was fire, racing out in all directions.

What have I done?

———

THE GLINT OF RED ON THE HORIZON ALERTED ERIC TO THE arrival of dawn. He released a sigh of relief, looking down from his perch on the hill. Soon it would be safe to return, to search for Enala amidst the wreckage of the camp. Until now the dying flames had been the only light to see by.

He was still struggling to comprehend what he had witnessed. One moment Enala had knelt on the ground, at the mercy of the chief. The next she was alight, flames racing out to engulf her foe.

There had been no time to think, only run. Eric had sensed the surge of energy the second Enala's magic was released. Her magic crackled on the air, wild and out of control. He knew then what was about to happen. He remembered it all too well from his own past.

Magic always awakens on the anniversary of our births, Alastair's words rose from his memory.

Eric was already running by the time the flames reached the chief.

Knowing Laurel must also sense the magic, Eric wondered why she had not stopped Enala. But there was no time to ask questions. From behind he heard the first screams of the crowd. Their fear drove him on.

As one, the crowd turned and fled in his direction. Watching them, Eric reached for his own magic, sure Laurel would be too distracted to keep it suppressed now. His power rose within him, still weak, but enough for what he needed. He launched himself into the sky, beyond the reach of the firestorm below.

Now as the sun cleared the horizon, Eric saw the scorched patch of earth marking the Baronian campsite. He swallowed hard. Nothing remained of the wagons and tents. There was not a soul in sight; the Baronians either long gone or dead. No one, except for the pale figure of a girl lying at the centre of the conflagration.

Eric stood, eyes fixed on the girl. The winds whipped at his clothing, lifting him into the sky. It could only be Enala. He shot towards her, straining to make out details, searching for sign of movement, of life.

The earth cracked as he landed, his foot breaking through the hard crust of ash which had formed on the surface. He stumbled before righting himself, then made his way closer to Enala. As he approached, he glimpsed a sheen of metal and saw Alastair's sword still lying where Thaster had dropped it. Detouring, he retrieved the blade. Its weight felt reassuring in his hand.

When he turned back to Enala, he saw her chest rise and let out a long sigh.

"You're alive," he whispered.

Enala lifted her head from where she lay. Relief flooded her eyes as she saw him. Tears cut through the ash covering her face. She struggled to her feet, kicking at the ash piled up around her.

"Eric, you're alive!" she made as if to run to him, then froze.

Eric frowned. "What's wrong, are you okay?"

Enala's face went white and her eyes rolled in her head, as though searching for someone behind her. She opened her mouth, but no words came out.

"Enala?" Eric made to step towards her.

"That's quite close enough, Eric," Laurel's voice hissed from somewhere behind Enala. "One more step, and your little friend dies."

Eric froze, frantically searching the ashes for sign of the Magicker.

He heard Laurel laugh. "Does this help?"

Eric lurched back as Laurel materialised behind Enala. She held her dagger to Enala's throat, her other arm holding the younger girl tight. A sly grin spread across her face.

"Hello again, Eric, Enala. Did you miss me?"

❧ 14 ❧

G abriel raised his mug of ale. "To Michael," he said, his voice solemn.

Glass clinked as Inken and Caelin's joined him in the toast. "To Michael," they repeated.

Gabriel took a long swig, the cool liquid refreshing after the day they'd had. And truth be told, his nerves could use calming. If the ale could wash away the anxiety he'd experienced as Caelin spoke to the king, it would be no small miracle. He was surprised they'd avoided the execution block, let alone the dungeons.

It was mid-afternoon and the bar was almost empty, but when Inken suggested a drink after their appearance before the king, none of them had argued. A few other patrons sat at the bar while they huddled together at a table in the corner. A chandelier lit the room, the flickering light of the candles casting shadows across the walls.

"He was a good man," Inken added. "Braver than any of us, to come on such a journey without even a dagger to protect himself. But that was Michael: a healer, even if he did not have magic."

Caelin nodded, taking another swig. "Agreed. Sometimes I wish I had his courage. The world needs more men like him."

Gabriel raised an eyebrow. "Really? Right now I think what we need are fighters. How many men and women will it take to hold back Archon's armies?"

"Thousands," Caelin grunted. "But what happens afterwards; if we reduce our people to numbers and swords, if we praise a man's fighting ability above all else? Or a woman's," he added at a look from Inken. "Whatever happens, we need men like Michael: doctors and builders, farmers and fishermen. Men who do not rely on violence to make their way in the world. Men like me, we do not build. We can only give our lives to protect what we already have."

"Or we can change," Inken added.

Gabriel looked at his glass, remembering his days in the forge with his father. "What if we have already changed? Picked up a sword and turned our back on peace?" he paused. "I don't know if I could go back."

Caelin shrugged. "A worry for another day. As you say, the Three Nations need warriors now more than ever. But believe me, war will make you sick to your stomach. It is the worst of man's demons."

"That may be so," Gabriel looked up. "But it is necessary, for now at least. Plorsea cannot just stand by and wait for Archon to come."

"No, we can't," Inken agreed. "Whatever alternative the councillors are considering, it won't work. Only the magic of the God's was able to banish Archon last time. Now we only have the Sword of Light, if we are lucky. It will take every ounce of might the Three Nations can muster to fight him to a standstill."

"More," Caelin added grimly.

"No," Inken shook her head. "I have to believe it's possible, that if we all stand together we can match him. The Sword is powerful, and there are hundreds of Magickers in our lands to help combat Archon's magic. There has to be a chance."

"I wish I had your optimism, Inken," Gabriel gave a short smile. "What's your secret?"

Inken met his eyes. "I think I got it from Eric."

Gabriel scowled, fighting down the anger Eric's name still brought. He may have decided to let go of his hate and join them, but the act was easier said than done. He shook his head, forcing a smile. "I'm glad Enala has him then. They're going to need all the courage they can get."

Silence fell around the table as they nursed their drinks. When Caelin finally spoke again, there was frustration in his voice. "Elton did not lie; the king has changed," he shook his head. "How could he just dismiss us like that, after all we've done...after all *I've* done for him?"

Gabriel stared at the sergeant, surprised by the venom in the words. "What do you mean?"

Caelin rubbed his eyes. "I have served Fraser for years, long before I won the king's tournament. This is not the first quest I have undertaken for him," his eyes took on a haunted look. "He has always trusted me. Though I can't say an assignment has ever unravelled this badly."

"I do not know the man," Inken offered. "But his manner did not seem to match the tales told of him."

"No," Gabriel added. "From what we heard of the king in Oaksville, he was a kind man, not quick to anger."

"He's different, there's no doubting that," Caelin

accepted. "But to all but accuse *me* of treachery? To suggest I could have killed one of our own?" his words drifted off into a growl.

Inken leaned across the table, eyes flashing a warning. "Careful, Caelin," she warned. "We are being watched," she sat back in her seat and took another swallow of ale.

Caelin's eyes widened and Gabriel would have turned to look around the bar, had Inken's foot not connected with his shin.

"Don't, you'll give us away," the hunter fixed him with a glare. "The man at the bar, the one nearest to the bartender, he's been following us since the citadel. Someone is keeping tabs on us."

From the corner of his eye, Gabriel glanced a man in an indistinct green tunic and black leggings, with a sword strapped to his side. His eyes were in his drink, ignoring the other men at the bar. There was nothing to the way he sat suggesting he might be interested in the three patrons in the corner.

Caelin swore softly beneath his breath. "Damnit. If that's true, things are worse than I thought."

Inken shrugged, but Gabriel glimpsed the same concern reflected in her eyes. "It's what I expected, after our reception. They don't want us going anywhere…" she paused. "Or, perhaps they do not want us looking around too much."

"What do you mean?"

"What do I mean?" she looked around the table. "I mean things may not be all as they appear here in Ardath. Balistor was a trusted Magicker here, and he obviously had many friends on the council. Maybe they weren't all as shocked as they seemed when you told them of Balistor's betrayal. Maybe there are other traitors amidst the king's advisors," she took a breath. "Maybe they've turned the king."

The hairs on Gabriel's arms stood up. He watched as a tremor swept through Caelin. "No, that's not possible," the sergeant growled. "I know the man; he would never betray Plorsea. He loves his people."

"Even so, how else can we explain the way he greeted you, one of his most loyal soldiers?"

Caelin fell silent, his eyes haunted. Gabriel stared at him, struggling to find some words of comfort. "What about Katya?" he said at last. Caelin and Inken turned to stare. "She seemed pretty determined to prevent the army marching north. Could she be the traitor? From what the king said, she is one of his most trusted advisors. She could be steering him down the wrong path."

Inken frowned. "It's possible. No one is beyond suspicion; they could all be traitors for all we know."

"If they were, it would certainly explain the king's despair, listening to their dark whispers all day," Gabriel said in a hollow voice.

Caelin still had not looked up from his drink. "How do we figure out who is friend and who is foe?" his voice cracked. "You say Katya could be the traitor, but how do we know if she's not just incompetent? That she truly believes holding back from the Gap is the best strategy?"

"We don't," Inken replied. "We can't. All we can do is hope to convince them otherwise. If the king is truly uncorrupted, we at least have a chance of persuading him. Same with the other councillors, if they truly serve the interests of Plorsea."

"You want to go to the king again? To the councillors?" Gabriel shuddered, remembering the detached eyes of the council staring down at him. "Who are they anyway, the councillors? How did Katya become so close to the king?"

"They are the king's advisors, elected by the people of Ardath and other provinces. They are meant to offer innovation and differing opinions to the rulers of Plorsea. They also help to govern different parts of the nation: trade, agriculture, mining, even parts of the army. Katya has been a councillor for years, and is one of the few Fraser trusts absolutely. She commands the city's defence."

"Maybe that's why she wanted the army here, to bolster Ardath's protection against Archon?" Inken asked.

"It's possible," Caelin answered. "But it wouldn't make sense. The Plorsean army cannot stand against the armies Archon will muster. Alone, we would be overwhelmed."

"And if Trola and Lonia stand alone at Fort Fall, the battle there won't last long either," Inken added.

"Agreed," Caelin replied, sitting straighter in his seat. "So we had better hope your plan works, Inken. Our only chance is to get the council to see reason. I just pray there are more loyalists than traitors in their midst."

A silence fell around the table, as each realised there was no one left to pray too. "They might be gone, but we're still here," Gabriel swallowed. "Michael believed in us, believed we could win; it's up to us to prove his words true."

"Agreed," Inken and Caelin added in unison.

They raised their mugs again, offering one last toast to their fallen comrade.

"What about Enala and Eric?" Gabriel whispered after a moment's silence. "Where are they?"

Sadness crept into Inken's face with the mention of Eric, though she tried to hide it. Gabriel watched her swallow the lump in her throat. "We must have faith. I believe they're still alive. For whatever reason, they must have decided to carry on their quest alone. Eric will get Enala to the Sword. It's up to us to keep the Three Nations together long enough for it to matter."

"Agreed," Caelin whispered.

"Agreed," Gabriel repeated.

———

"DON'T WORRY ABOUT YOUR MAGIC, EITHER OF YOU," Laurel growled. "This time I've got you *both* nicely under wraps," she bared her teeth, pressing the dagger hard against Enala's throat. "Who knew this one was a latent Magicker? Certainly not Thaster!" she laughed.

Eric wiped ash from his tunic, fighting to remain calm. "What do you want from us, Laurel?"

"Not much," she shrugged. "Just the bounty on your head, Eric."

Ice wrapped around Eric's heart and he struggled to keep the fear from his face. "You don't ask for much, do you?"

Laurel grasped Enala's hair and pulled back her head. The dagger sliced a shallow cut across Enala's throat. Blood trickled down her neck. "I don't really need her alive, you know. Now throw down your sword, Eric."

Hands shaking, Eric tossed Alastair's sword to the ground. Quick as a Raptor, Laurel threw Enala aside and scooped up the blade. She held it out before her, warning Eric to come no closer. He held his hands up in surrender.

"Excellent, there you go. I knew you could listen," she waved Alastair's sword at them. "Well, Chole is about one day in that direction. I suggest you start walking," she swiped the sword for emphasis.

Enala fell in beside Eric as they began to march in the

direction Laurel indicated. The Baronian's footsteps followed close behind them.

"Be good, and maybe I'll let Enala live when we reach Chole," Laurel laughed.

Eric's mind raced, searching for a solution. They had come so far; he could not believe their escape could fail at this last hurdle. Yet now they found themselves unarmed and powerless against the Magicker; with the sword at her side and Eric's own blade, Laurel held all the cards.

He shot a glance sideways and saw Enala looking back at him. Blood still seeped from the wound at her throat, turning her shirt to a red mess, but there was defiance in her eyes. He smiled back. After what Enala had accomplished last night, he would not want to be the one left standing between the girl and freedom.

They just needed the right opportunity.

———

ERIC SLUMPED TO THE GRASS WITH A GROAN. THE VOLCANIC peaks of Chole were just peaking above the rolling hills, towering on the distant horizon. But with night setting they could go no further. So close to the desert, who knew what lurked in the darkness. Especially now, with Antonia gone.

Beside him Enala sat with slightly more grace. Laurel had pushed them hard and with no food, they were close to breaking. Eric's legs trembled and a sharp pain pricked his spine. He lay back, inhaling a deep breath to fight the ache.

"Anyone would think you two weren't used to walking," Laurel smirked, crouching down beside them.

"Maybe it's the lack of food and water," Enala snapped back.

Laurel laughed and pulled a water skin from her belt.

She tossed it down between them. "There you are, drink up," she sat nearby, casting her eye over them. "I'll admit, the two of you interest me. For starters, why give Enala a fake name?"

Enala glared back, lips shut tight. Eric answered in her stead. "Why do you care? You'll be done with us come tomorrow."

"True, true," Laurel grinned, "but still I've been wondering. Maybe there's a bounty on your head too, Enala?"

"Wouldn't you like to know," Enala grated.

Laurel sighed. "I thought we'd gotten past this. After all, we don't want to take the hard route, do we?" her dagger slid from its sheath, glittering in the last rays of the dying sun.

Eric gritted his teeth. Then an idea came to him. "That depends on whose side you're on now, Laurel."

"What do you mean?"

Eric leaned forward, staring deep into her grey eyes. "Are you still Baronian? Is that your plan, once you dispose of us? To find another tribe and volunteer yourself back into slavery?"

Laurel scowled, waving the dagger. "Watch what you say, Eric. I don't need you alive. What do my plans matter to you?"

"He's just wondering where your allegiances lie," Enala joined in. "Are you still tied up with the trappings of that cult, or do you want to be your own person again?"

"You're still chirping on about that rubbish," Laurel cackled. "Of course I'm free, I always was, I told you," even to Eric her words sounded weak, lacking belief. After a moment's silence she stood and started to pace. Finally she spun. "I don't know what I'll do now, but it's nothing to you!"

Eric laughed. "Coward."

He reeled back as Laurel's fist smashed him in the face. His teeth rattled and his nose went *crunch* before her weight slammed him into the ground. She crashed down on top of him, hands grasping for his throat, eyes just an inch from his own. He choked for breath as she began to squeeze.

Laurel smiled at him. "As I said, the bounty for you is dead or alive, Eric. The only reason you're alive is to make my life easier. Better you walk yourself to the noose, rather than me carrying you. So let this be your final warning," the pressure on his throat eased. "Do not test me."

Eric coughed as she released him and stood up. "Now," she walked towards Enala, her sword sliding from its sheath. "Why, Enala, did you give a fake name?"

Enala stood her ground, glaring up at the taller woman, fists clenched at her side. She would die before she gave the secret away.

Closing his eyes in defeat, Eric croaked out an answer. "Because she is being hunted."

Laurel looked back. "By who?" greed flickered in her eyes.

Eric shook his head, pausing for a heartbeat to weigh the wisdom of his next decision. Laurel might be out for herself, but he had not mistaken the disgust in her eyes when she spoke of Thaster's dark magic. "She is not hunted by any mortal force. She is pursued by the servants of Archon himself."

Laurel's face paled in the twilight. "What?" she looked from Eric to Enala. "What the hell are you talking about?"

"You heard him," Enala glared back.

"You're joking?" fear shook Laurel's voice.

Eric regained his feet. "It's no joke. Enala happens to be the last person alive who can wield the Sword of Light. She is the only one left who can stop Archon. So unless you enjoy the thought of a world ruled by dark magic, I suggest hers is one bounty you don't collect."

Silence fell. At last Laurel spoke again. "This is some trick…"

"It's not," they replied in unison.

Laurel glanced between them again, uncertainty written on her face. Then she shook her head. "You're both delusional."

"It's the truth," Eric replied, resolute. "Antonia and Jurrien have already fallen. It won't be long before Archon comes. Then everyone will have a decision to make. The dark or the light. Sooner or later, you will have to pick a side, Laurel."

Laurel waved a hand, as though trying to dismiss his words. "Be quiet, the both of you. I've heard enough of your nonsense for one night. Sleep, or don't. I'm going to rest. And don't bother trying anything, I don't need to be awake to keep a couple of unruly Magicker's under control," with that Laurel turned and walked a few paces down the hill and slumped to the grass.

Despite what she'd said about sleep, she sat with her legs pulled up to her chest and her head on her knees, staring out into the darkness.

Eric looked at Enala. This was the closest they'd come to privacy in days, and there were things they needed to discuss.

She answered his first question before he could ask it. "Where did it come from, the magic? How…?"

So he'd been right, Enala had no idea. "It came from you. Just like your ancestors, you have powerful magic within you. As for why it chose last night to appear, well, we were lucky. Alastair once told me magic only emerges on a Magicker's birthday. The age varies, depending on the person and what they experience growing up. Happy coincidence that Thaster chose today to fight you," he paused and smiled. "Happy birthday, by the way."

Enala nodded. "The last few days I kept feeling this pressure within me, whenever I was angry. Last night, it just snapped, like something within had shattered. And for the first time, that pressure was released."

"I'm just glad it happened," he smiled. "Whatever dark magic Thaster was using, it was no longer a fair fight. I think we'd both be dead by now if you hadn't taken them by surprise."

To his shock, Enala began to sob. "But there were so many people, so many that had nothing to do with the fight. How many died because of me?"

"Enala, it was not your fault," he reached out and gripped her wrist. "You could not have controlled your power without training. I can barely restrain mine, even with everything Alastair taught me. And besides," his face hardened. "It's not like they were innocent. They knew what was happening, that we were slaves fighting for our very lives. They made their decision when they joined that man."

Enala's sobs started to subside. When she finally looked up her eyes still watered, but her voice was strong. "Will you teach me, Eric?"

Eric smiled. "I can try. Now?"

Enala shrugged. "At least it might take our minds off our stomachs."

Eric nodded. "Okay. Well, the first thing a Magicker must learn is meditation…"

———

LAUREL SAT IN THE DARKNESS, LISTENING TO THE RHYTHMIC breathing of the two young Magickers. She could feel their magic; powerful, bubbling below the surface, seeking its freedom as they sank deeper into their minds. Even so, it took little effort to keep the blue and red glows in check.

It left her mind free to wander.

Who are these two? The question bounced around her head. Had they actually spoken the truth? Could Enala wield the infamous Sword of Light? Was Archon really hunting her?

An icy breeze swept across the hilltop. She shivered, pulling the cloak tighter around her and burying her head into her knees. It could not be true: the tribe had heard nothing of their tale, and as nomads the Baronians picked up most of the gossip in the Three Nations.

She shook her head, her thoughts changing direction. In less than twenty-four hours, her world had collapsed. The girl's latent magic had been undetectable until the moment she released it—and by then it was far too late to stop. Laurel's magic only prevented a Magicker from tapping into their powers; once unleashed, there was nothing she could do but flee.

It had taken all she had to outrun the flames. Only the head start provided by her magic's warning allowed her to get clear. The other Baronians had not been so lucky. She guessed less than half their number had escaped the firestorm which followed.

Still though, more than enough to carry word to the other tribes. To carry word of Laurel's failure.

The other chiefs would not take Thaster's death lightly. They would be out for blood, out to show the world they were not to be trifled with. The word would go out, a list of those responsible made. The heads of Eric and Enala would be at the top of that list. For her failure, Laurel would come a close second.

Regardless of her own desires, Laurel would not be welcomed back into the fold. Yet who else would want a disgraced Magicker such as herself? Who would be powerful enough to protect her from the wrath of the Baronian chiefs?

No, she would have to disappear.

Thankfully, the bounty on Eric's head would go a long way towards accomplishing that task.

❧ 15 ❧

Eric hesitated before the gates of Chole, shrinking back from the great stone walls. The giant blocks of granite stood stark and forbidding, a grim reminder of the fate waiting for him within. Behind him, Laurel gave him a shove, propelling him through the open gates. Enala walked beside him, head held high as she returned to the city of her birth.

Inhaling, Eric struggled for calm and forced himself to continue. Tears leapt unbidden as memories of Inken rose in his mind. It was here they had met, here where he'd first discovered his love for the feisty bounty hunter. Their first kiss had not been far from this very gate. Now five hundred miles separated them and for all he knew, Inken was already dead.

He rubbed his eyes to wipe away the hot tears, determined to hide his weakness from Laurel. Sniffing back his sorrow, he forced down the memories. They had other things to worry about now.

Even so, Eric could not help but pause again as they

emerged from the shadow of the gate, overwhelmed by the change a few weeks had brought to Chole. This was a different city from the one they'd left behind. Everywhere he looked shoots of green now sprang from the earth, where before there had been only dust. Grass grew between the street tiles and vines dangled from drainage pipes, swaying in the breeze. A drizzle of rain swept through the streets, sending people scrambling for shelter.

Eric blinked, seeing then the other change to the city. Before Chole had been empty—the Dying City people called it—and all but the hardiest of men stayed clear. The city was left to the desperate and the criminal.

Now, everywhere Eric looked people moved through the streets, hurrying about their business. Even here by the gates, in what had been the poorest districts, civilisation had returned. It seemed news of the rain's return had spread fast, and many a brave soul had decided to gamble on the city's resurrection.

"So it's true," Eric turned at Laurel's words. "I could hardly believe the stories, but the rain has returned."

"It has," Enala's voice cracked with emotion and Eric saw the tears in her eyes. "It has changed so much, in such a little time. I only wish my parents had lived to see it. Thank you, Eric," she smiled at him.

Eric nodded and flashed a smile back.

"This was you?" Laurel asked, raising an eyebrow.

"A first step in a long journey," Eric shrugged.

Laurel shook her head and Eric thought he glimpsed a flash of compassion in her eyes. Then she turned away. "Come, we need to move. With all these people you might be recognised. I wouldn't want someone else trying to claim your bounty."

Eric sighed, glancing at Enala. They were running out

of time, but an opportunity to flee had yet to come. He reached within, but his magic remained tantalisingly out of reach. They were powerless against Laurel.

Laurel led them through the bustling streets, her eagerness to leave behind the crowds betrayed by the pace she set. Eric searched for familiar landmarks as they moved, but the maze of Chole's streets seemed to have only grown worse with the newcomers. At least he could see from Enala's smile she at least knew where they were.

Laurel, however, was struggling. Baronians were not welcome in most cities, even one with a reputation like Chole's. But Laurel must have been here at least a few times, as she finally led them into the more prosperous streets around the central square. The crowds grew larger and the streets bristled with street venders plying their food and wares.

"Don't suppose you could spare me a last meal?" Eric asked, nodding towards a stand with chicken on the grill. His stomach rumbled; they had not eaten in days.

"No!" Eric looked up in surprise at the anger in her voice. He had missed the growing frustration in Laurel's movements. "There's no time. We need to get off the streets."

Eric frowned as Laurel gave him a hard shove. What was she so nervous about? Surely she did not really think someone would recognise him. Unless he used his magic, there was nothing to mark him as the so called 'demon boy' of Oaksville.

No, it had to be something else.

"What are you running from, Laurel?" Enala asked from beside him.

"Quiet!" Laurel snapped. "I told you, I won't have my prize stolen from me."

"You don't really expect us to believe that, do you?" Enala persisted.

Laurel spun, her hand drifting towards her dagger. "I warned you –"

"Laurel!" a shout from nearby cut her off.

Their captor spun at the sound of her name, hand switching from the dagger to the hilt of her short sword.

Eric looked across and saw three men muscling their way through the crowd towards them. Straggled beards covered their faces and scars crisscrossed their arms. Each sported a black arm band and held greatswords in their meaty hands. The thugs wore plain clothes, but Eric guessed their usual attire was the black armour of the Baronians.

"The Hawk would like a word with you, Laurel. About Thaster's untimely demise," the first of the men growled.

The blood fled from Laurel's face. Whoever Hawk was, he clearly terrified her. Drawing her sword, she held it tight in front of her, hands trembling. She glanced at Eric and Enala, regret flashing in her eyes.

Then she vanished.

The men paused, and then started to laugh. "Well, well, look lads, I told you so. See the coward run?" they looked around the street, searching for the Magicker. "Or perhaps she just likes to fight dirty," they laughed again.

Goosebumps rose on Eric's neck as a dark light seeped from the man who led. "Come on then, Laurel. Come and get us. We shall see which magic is greater—the dark or the light."

The men edged into a circle, blades out, the darkness encircling them. Their eyes roamed the street, searching for Laurel. Eric had no idea what dark magic they were employing, but he guessed its touch would leave a mark.

Either way, the men had not yet taken notice of Eric or

Enala. They backed away together, trying to put the crowd between themselves and the Baronian thugs. They moved slowly, doing their best not to draw attention to themselves. When they reached a nearby alley, they turned and sprinted between the buildings.

Enala took the lead, Eric struggling to keep up as she raced through the twisting nooks and alleyways of Chole. Her knowledge of the city was priceless now—within minutes they had left the Baronians far behind. Eric glanced back as they ran, searching for sign of pursuit, but all looked quiet.

They raced on all the same, eager to extend their lead and lose any invisible followers.

Half an hour later they drew to a stop in the shadow of a library.

"Who were those men?" Enala asked.

"Baronians, I'm guessing. Laurel must have made a few enemies when she didn't protect the Baronian camp from your magic. We're just lucky they didn't recognise us," he paused and turned his mind inwards. His magic surged at his touch, free at last. "Speaking of which, I think we've lost her as well. My magic is back," he felt a pang of sadness at the thought of leaving Alastair's blade in Laurel's hands, but he could do little about it now.

Enala grinned. "Well that's something, because we're now unarmed and alone in a city of thieves. A few weeks can't have changed it *that* much. Where are we going?"

Eric quickly described what he remembered from Antonia's vision: the steps down from the ramparts, the narrow path which separated the buildings from the city walls, and the vines that had covered the granite blocks, hiding a dark secret beneath them.

At the end Enala nodded. "I think I know the place, but

last I heard the vines had withered and died. Although now that I think of it, they've been there as long as anyone can remember."

"Hopefully there is still a way past them," Eric whispered.

They started off again, moving at a slower place this time, neither eager to reach the gateway and the cursed world waiting for them. Eric remembered all too well the deadly land beyond, and the creature lurking there. They still had no idea how to defeat it; he just hoped his magic would be enough.

It took half an hour to cross the city, but they managed it without incident. The streets grew quiet as they approached their destination, the citizens retreating into their homes to wait out the night. Whatever changes had enveloped Chole, the growing fear on the faces of passers-by suggested the night still belonged to the unsavoury.

They stood together beneath the wall, staring up at the ancient granite blocks. Vines hung from the battlements high above, but Enala had been right—they were long dead. Whatever magic had sustained them through the centuries, it had not been enough to save them from the drought. Yet somehow, their death did not seem to have been permanent. Fresh green shoots now sprang from the dry husks of the old vines, and white flowers sprinkled the wall. Their aroma drifted down, their rich honey-like scent lingering in their noses.

"What do we do?" Enala asked.

Eric leaned back, trying to see how high the vines went. "I'm not sure. Alastair said only those with Earth magic could control the vines. But maybe there is another way through."

Enala gave a wry grin. "Like burning them?"

Chuckling, Eric shrugged. "Maybe, but we'll use my magic for now. There is a lot you need to learn before you try to use your magic consciously. But we'll save that lesson for another day."

Lightning crackled as Eric drew a bolt of energy from the sky. It struck the vines with a crash and a roar. Blue fire raced along the half-dead tendrils, burning up browned leaves and new growth alike.

As the flames died out, the remains of the vines fell to ash around them. Beneath, the empty abyss of the portal beckoned. They bathed in its flickering glow, its light swirling away into infinity. The dark energy danced in their eyes, drawing them into its embrace. The power tugged at Eric's soul, but remembering Antonia's warning, he resisted.

Beside him, Enala leaned towards the portal. He grasped her hand and pulled her back.

"Careful, Enala. Archon cursed this place a long time ago. His taint is everywhere, do not let it tempt you, or you risk being corrupted."

She gave a wan smile, her face pale. "Okay," she looked up. "At least that was easy."

Eric closed his eyes, summoning his courage. "No, this is just the beginning. Beyond, the real battle begins. Brace yourself."

They leapt together into the abyss.

———

LAUREL WATCHED AS THE TWO STEPPED INTO THE PORTAL, heart thudding hard in her chest. It had been no easy task following them through the city—in fact, she had lost them a few blocks back. Only the surge of Eric's magic allowed her to find them again.

Now she wished she hadn't. She could not believe what she was witnessing. The power emanating from the abyss reached her even in the shadows of the nearby alley. Its dark taint spoke to her, called to her. But she had overheard Eric's words, and struggled to close herself to its power.

So they told the truth, Laurel could deny it no longer.

The truth of their tale stood before her—an ancient magic leading to the Gods only knew where. It changed everything. Perhaps she could find more than just gold on the other side of that portal. Whoever Eric and Enala answered too, they were obviously powerful. Powerful enough to resist the forces commanded by Hawk.

She needed protection now more than ever.

Unsure quite what she planned, but knowing she could not stay in Chole, Laurel slipped from the shadows. Moving towards the portal, Laurel saw the vines stirring, fresh shoots regenerating from the ashes. They crawled across the stony surface, covering the portal. In seconds it would shut, closing her off from the two young Magickers.

Taking a breath, Laurel dove for the portal

And the world began to spin.

———

CAELIN STRODE DOWN THE STREETS OF ARDATH, IGNORANT to the bustle of the city around him. Frustration bubbled in his chest. It had been two days since they had seen the king, two days spent petitioning to see the council again. But their every effort had been met by blank stares and stony silence. It was becoming increasingly clear the king and council did not wish to see them.

Swinging around a corner, Caelin picked up speed. Looking back, he caught a glimpse of the man following him. Today they had separated after leaving the inn, knowing their ghost could only tail one of them. There were people Caelin wanted to speak too, and he did not want anyone interrupting their conversation.

Outside the city the army continued to muster, but they showed no sign of being ready to march. The king had not even sent an advanced party out to reinforce Fort Fall. The standing garrison at the fortress was meant to keep out the banished and odd raiding party—it would stand no chance against an army. If something did not change soon, the Plorseans would arrive too late to make a difference.

Likewise, the situation in Ardath grew worse with each passing day. Fear spread through the city, infecting its citizens with a terror not seen since Archon's war. All knew of the attack on Sitton, and many said in whispers it could only be a matter of time before the same fate befell Ardath. Even the city guards were affected, and whispers of the king's isolation only made matters worse.

Caelin still could not bring himself to believe his king had been swayed to Archon's cause. He had always been a good man, loyal to the Gods and his people. But there was no doubting it—something had changed in the man. Caelin's homecoming still rankled him. He had expected disappointment from the king, not open scorn.

He broke into a run as he rounded the next corner, sprinting for the alleyway halfway down the street. Water splashed beneath his feet, the remains of last night's rain. The wind whistled in his ears as he picked up speed, his boots thumping the bricked street. Leaning low, he ducked into the alleyway and out of sight.

Once hidden, he did not stop to check if the tracker had seen him. He picked his way through the alley, jumping over discarded garbage and a dead rat, before swinging round the next corner. Quickly, he made his way through the network of alleyways connecting the streets of Ardath, heading for a nondescript building where the others waited.

The owner of the building did not know he was coming.

When he emerged back into the open streets, Gabriel and Inken stood across the street waiting for him. The street was quiet, cast in the shadow of the city walls looming behind the houses.

Inken smiled when she saw Caelin and moved across to join him. "Looks like you drew the short straw."

"I thought he might choose me. I'm the one they know. A good thing, since I know these streets better than either of you."

"That's a bold statement," Inken laughed. "You'd be surprised where my hunts have taken me."

"If you two are done competing with one another, shouldn't we get this over with—before someone figures us out?" Gabriel suggested.

Caelin nodded and they moved towards one of the houses. At first glance the building looked non-descript, with plain stone walls and a tile roof. But as they approached, Caelin saw small hints of the owner's wealth. Well-kept gardens suggested the house had full-time help, and the trimmings of the eaves were edged with marble. The door stood closed, the thick oak shining in the cool sun. An intricate mural dedicated to the earth had been carved into the wood, another sign of the occupant's wealth.

Inside was the one councillor they knew more about than any other. Unfortunately, she was also the councillor whose loyalty they doubted more than any other.

The house belonged to Katya.

Raising his hand, Caelin banged on the door, and waited.

Silence came from within, followed by the creak of wooden floorboards and the faint shuffle of somebody moving inside. The sounds ceased when they reached the door, as the person inside placed their eye to the spyhole.

Caelin smiled and waved.

After several long seconds, there came a clack as the bolt was unlocked and the door swung open.

Katya stood in the door way, arms folded across her chest. She scowled at Caelin, eyebrow raised. She wore tight fitting clothing that hugged her supple frame and long black boots stretching up to her knees.

"Caelin, I wasn't expecting you," Katya growled. "How can I help you?" she stood stiff, clearly angry at the unexpected intrusion.

Swallowing his doubts, Caelin answered. "Katya, I know things went poorly with you and the king in the throne room. But I am here to ask you for another chance. Please, help us to see King Fraser, help me explain."

"And why would I do that?" she snapped, one hand clenched on the door, prepared to slam it in their faces. "If you wish to go before the council again, you will have to book an appointment with the clerks."

Caelin raised his hands, heart pounding in his chest. "Wait, don't, please. Look, I know you don't want to listen. I know you have a different plan. But at least hear us out first. Let us sit down like adults and weigh up the options. If yours is truly the better approach, then let the king see that for himself."

Katya stepped from the house, anger flashing in her eyes. "You have no idea what the king is planning. Who are you, a mere sergeant, to advise him on the most sensitive of military matters?

Caelin stared her down. "I may be young, and only a

sergeant. But I am no green kid enlisted in the army. This is my life. And I have seen the enemy, I have seen the power of just one of his servants. It is beyond anything I have ever witnessed from the Magickers at your command. Greater even than Alastair. And the demon grows stronger by the day."

Katya paused, uncertainty flashing across her face. Then she bared her teeth, the steel returning to her eyes. "Even so, if you wish to see the king, this is not the way –"

"They have locked us out," Caelin interrupted. "The clerks ignore our petitions and we are followed day and night. Someone does not wish us to see the king," he paused, studying the woman before him, weighing her up. Could she be trusted, or was there more behind her anger. Taking a breath, he risked a gamble. "We believe there are traitors in the council; others like Balistor who have been turned by Archon."

Katya stared him down. "And do you think I am one of these traitors."

"I don't know," Caelin replied.

The silence stretched out, their gazes locked in a mental war. Caelin stared deep into her hazel eyes, searching for a hint of doubt. But he could see no sign of treachery there.

At last Katya blinked and looked away. She opened her mouth to speak.

A shout came from above, drowning out her words. Caelin looked up and saw guardsmen racing across the battlements atop the wall.

Even from this distance, he could see the panic in their eyes.

❧ 16 ❧

Enala's stomach swirled as solid ground materialised beneath her feet and her body lurched to a sudden stop. Red hot pain streaked through her head. Her knees crumpled, the strength fleeing from her trembling muscles. Another heave of her stomach, and Enala threw up the measly remainders of her last meal.

A few minutes later, Enala finally took a great shuddering breath and sat back. Groaning, she wiped her mouth and stood on shaky legs. Looking around, she very nearly threw up again.

Piles of human bones littered the barren earth. The empty eye sockets of broken skulls glared up at them. Rusty blades and broken bows lay scattered amidst the piles, but not a shred of cloth or flesh remained. A blood red sky stretched overhead and the air smelt of baked dirt and death.

Enala stumbled backwards, a shiver running through her, fear screaming for her to flee this defiled place. She sucked in a breath, the air stifling, not a trace of wind to be felt. Stark white cliffs rose on either side of them, hedging them in. A single path cut through the bones, leading deeper into the narrow valley.

A rattle came from nearby as Eric stood. Enala's heart sank when she saw the fear on his face.

"What's wrong?" she whispered, unwilling to disturb the slumber of the dead surrounding them.

"My magic, it's not going to help us here."

"*What?*" Enala tried to control the tremor in her voice, but failed. "What do you mean? Laurel couldn't be…"

"No, not Laurel. It's this place. I can't sense anything of the Sky here—no rain or wind or *anything*. It's empty. I'm powerless in this place."

Enala stared. "What do we do?"

Eric hesitated, and then a hardness replaced the fear in his eyes. "Whatever we have to. There's no going back. We have no weapons, so our only chance is to evade the creature that lurks here. If it comes to it though, I will distract it while you run. There is a granite arch at the end of the valley. It leads to Kalgan. No matter what happens, you have to reach it," Enala opened her mouth to argue, but Eric raised his hand. "There's no time to fight about this. Come on, time passes strangely here and the longer we hesitate the more likely it is the fiend will find us."

He walked past her and started down the track into the valley. Bone fragments and gravel crunched beneath his feet, raising the hackles on Enala's neck. Shivering, she pushed down her fear and followed after him.

It took them ten long minutes to escape the boneyard. Enala winced with every step, disgust at their trespass rising up from the depths of her soul. A cold sweat stuck to her skin, useless in the stifling heat. She walked carefully, shuddering at the grinding of bones beneath her boots.

When they finally made it clear the going became easier, although gravel still slid beneath their feet on the treacherous slope. The cliffs closed in on either side, the valley narrowing to a thin canyon. Boulders dotted the hillslope, as though dropped there by giants. In places they clumped together to block the canyon, forcing them to clamber over the colossal rocks. Elsewhere they had to hold their breath to squeeze between them.

Enala soon realised the path had once been a stream bed, its waters long vanished with whatever magic had cursed this world. She saw then where the racing waters had sliced into the cliffs, leaving deep underhangs in the white rock.

She shivered. *What happened to this place?*

They continued on. Without the sun there was no knowing what bearing they travelled on, but it made no difference here. There was only one direction for them to go. They must have walked for hours, but the empty sky gave no indication of the passage of time. Enala's lungs burned, the air suffocating, the heat overwhelming. The little water in their skins was all but gone.

Ahead, Eric came to a sudden halt. Enala joined him, a grim dread settling in her stomach. Before them the path fell away, as though someone had taken a knife to the earth itself. A near sheer drop plummeted to the valley floor more than a hundred feet below. Loose gravel covered the slope all the way to the bottom.

As Enala stepped back from the edge a chunk of stones broke loose. They tumbled down the slope, picking up speed and disturbing more as they went. Their clatter echoed from the canyon walls, the rumble quickly growing to a roar. Enala winced as the landslide reached the bottom and spread out across the valley floor.

"This wasn't here when Alastair and Thomas passed this way," Eric whispered. "What do we do?"

Enala grimaced. "There's only one way to traverse a gravel slope. We have them in the mountains of Chole, though I've never seen one so steep. We have to run."

"*What?*"

"It's the only way to take them. If you try to walk down, the gravel will give way and you'll fall. If you're lucky, you'll only hurt your backside. If not, you might fall all the way to the bottom or be buried by the gravel. When you run, you're less likely to slip backwards. And even if you trip, your other foot can still catch you before you fall."

Eric eyed her, disbelief written across his face. "You cannot be serious?"

"Trust me, it's the only way," she smiled. "I'll go first."

Eric inhaled. "Just looking at it from here, the height has my head spinning. I hope you're right."

"Me too," she grinned. "Wait until I reach the bottom before you follow. Otherwise the rocks you dislodge might catch up to me," she glanced at him. "See you on the other side."

Without another word, she leapt from the edge.

The air whipped through her hair and her stomach twisted as she dropped several feet. When she struck the gravel slope, her legs almost crumpled under the shock of the impact. Stones erupted around her, slipping beneath her boots, and she began to slide. She waved her arms outwards, struggling for balance as stones scattered in every direction.

When she began to slow, Enala leapt again. Twisting in the air, she turned her hips to land with one foot stretched out in front. Dust billowed up with the impact, but an instant later she was airborne again, propelling herself back into clear air. Sweat beaded her forehead and dripped into her eyes, but she could not afford a second to wipe it away.

Squinting through the dust and tears, she continued down.

Gravel filled her boots, but with no time to dislodge it, she gritted her teeth and ignored its sharp bite. Every bound sent her flying, plummeting in free fall for long seconds before she crashed back down. She fought to keep her balance, instinct spinning her to absorb the shock of each landing. A single mistake and she would be done.

When she finally reached the bottom, Enala sank to her knees and sucked in a long breath. Dust rushed down her throat, sending her into a coughing fit. Stumbling to her feet she retreated down the valley, away from the dust. Once clear she turned and looked back up the slope.

Eric still stood at the top, his expression unreadable from such a distance. She waved a hand and he gave a short nod. After a moment's hesitation, he jumped from the edge. His first bound did not carry him far, but stones still exploded outward as his boots struck the slope. His arms windmilled as he slid, struggling to keep his balance.

Just as Enala thought he would stop, Eric leapt again, further this time. The dust rose up, concealing him in a cloud before he whipped back into view, picking up speed as he raced towards her. With each leap and bound he drew closer, his feet barely touching the gravel before sending him soaring again. A grin flashed on his face.

Enala couldn't believe it; Eric was enjoying his headlong race down the slope.

Then as Eric drew close to halfway, his smile turned to sudden terror. As he landed, Eric shrieked and his feet collapsed beneath him. He toppled forwards, his foot caught on some hidden obstruction. His face struck the gravel and he started to slide, arms thrust out in a hopeless attempt to regain his feet.

"No!" Enala shouted. "Get up, Eric!"

But it was too late. Even as he tumbled down the jagged stones, the hillside above him gave way. The landslide began as a dim rumble, a rattle of stones, but it quickly grew to a roar as the tonne of rocks rushed towards Eric.

Eric looked up and raised an arm in a vain attempt to protect himself.

Then the landslide struck.

Enala screamed as the tumbling mountain of rocks and stones swallowed Eric. She caught one last panicked look from him, then he was gone.

She took a trembling step towards the slope, arm stretched out in desperation, then stopped. Her eyes locked on the avalanche now rushing towards her. If she tried to reach Eric now, she would be buried along with him. Stealing herself, Enala backed away. Closing her eyes, fighting back tears, she waited for the rumbling to cease.

When she finally looked up again, the slope was empty. Not a sign remained of their passage—no hint of their footsteps or of Eric. A mound of gravel lay at the bottom of the slope, the only sign remaining of the landslide.

Swallowing her fear, Enala picked her way through the gravel and began to climb. She moved slowly, taking care not to disturb the loose stones. That quickly proved impossible. With every step she took, her boot sank deep into the shifting surface. Her heart pounded painfully in her chest as hooks of despair tore into her soul. Gritting her teeth, she struggled higher, sliding back a step for every two she took.

Eric had to be here somewhere, buried beneath the gravel. But the landslide had wiped away all sign of his passage. There was no telling where he had disappeared, or whether the landslide had carried him further down the slope.

Even so, Enala refused to surrender. She toiled her way up, her panic growing with each step.

"This cannot be happening," Enala whispered to herself, her breath coming in ragged gasps.

Dread clutched her heart in its icy hands, turning her muscles to dust. Eric had to be alive. He would not abandon her. She could not go on alone, could not bear to lose another friend. Cracks raced through her consciousness, the madness rearing up within her.

She stumbled across the slope, searching in a mindless panic for her fallen friend.

Finally, Enala collapsed to the ground, defeated. A scream rumbled up from her chest, coming out as a choked squeak as she wrapped her arms around her knees and began to rock.

"*No, no, no, no,*" she whispered to herself. Tears spilt down her cheeks.

He can't be gone! Enala screamed to herself, muscles burning with exertion

She glanced up the slope, seeking movement, desperate for a sign.

There was nothing but empty stones.

Eric was gone.

She was alone.

Enala looked down the slope, breath quivering in her throat. The madness rose again, threatening to overwhelm her, but she clung to Eric's words. She knew what he would want her to do. He would tell her to go on, that it was up to her now. The fate of the Three Nations rested on her shoulders. She could not let them down now, not after so many had given their lives to protect her.

Summoning her courage, Enala made her way back down the treacherous slope.

She did not look back.

———

"WELL, THIS WAS A TERRIBLE MISTAKE," LAUREL MUTTERED to herself, watching Enala from the edge of the cliff.

From the moment she had stepped from the portal, it had been the only thought on her mind. The boneyard marking the entrance to this nightmare realm was enough to send any intruder fleeing for their lives.

As soon as she appeared, Laurel had reached within to ensure her magic still concealed her. While her power felt thin and weak, she was pleased to find it still worked. Creeping closer, she had overheard Eric's grim pronouncement about his own magic.

At least that was something going for her. That, and the two swords she still wore at her side.

As the two made their way down the canyon, Laurel followed close behind. She fought to keep her movements silent—there was little point in revealing herself just yet. A plan had begun to take shape in her mind, but it could wait until they escaped this wasteland.

Then Eric had gone and gotten himself killed.

It had happened so quickly, Laurel almost missed it. One second the boy was picking up speed, his confidence growing with each bound. Then before anyone could so much as cry out, he was gone, buried beneath the landslide.

Now Laurel stood and watched Enala making her way back up the slope. The futility of the search was already obvious; she was risking her life for nothing. Eric was gone. Laurel almost revealed herself, if only to spare Enala the same fate as Eric.

But Enala would flee if she saw Laurel and in her precarious position that would be disastrous. Whatever happened, the girl could not die. At least not until Laurel had the chance to complete her plan.

Finally, crying in despair, Enala surrendered to the impossible task and made her way down. Laurel waited until she disappeared around a bend in the canyon before attempting to follow. Her invisibility would not hide the disturbance caused by her descent. Just as the two had done before her, she made her way down in leaps and bounds. Unlike Eric, she did not have any problems.

When she reached the bottom, Laurel spared a glance back up the slope, surprised to feel a touch of sadness for the boy's death. She had planned to see him hang, but it had never been personal. In truth, she felt a touch of respect for Eric and Enala's feisty resistance, for their courage in the face of death. But despite their youthful audacity, they were not immortal.

Laurel glanced down the canyon after Enala. The girl was made from the same cloth as Eric—her courage bordering on the edge of stupidity. Challenging Thaster to single combat had been pure insanity, and only her innate magic had saved Enala from death. Magic she had not even been aware of.

Laurel shook her head, still unable to believe the luck.

Taking one final glance up the slope, Laurel sent an old

prayer to Darius for the boy's soul. She may not have been a very good apprentice of the Light, but she still remembered a few things. It was the least she could offer Eric.

Then she turned her back on the graveyard, and broke into a jog.

Somewhere ahead, Enala waited.

E nala stood alone in the centre of the valley, the heat of the baked earth seeping through her boots. Cracks crisscrossed the valley floor and the white cliffs still towered overhead. The air was still and sweat soaked her clothes, leaving them sticking to her skin. She stared at the granite arch stretching across the end of the canyon. The flowers etched into the grey stone were exactly as Eric had described.

A thin mist swirled beyond the arch, beckoning her, promising freedom.

But before her stood the cursed creature that haunted this realm. It, too, was exactly as Eric described. Its yellowed bones gleamed in the light of the blood red sky. Joints clacked as it moved, a bony arm reaching down to wrap bare knuckles around the hilt of its scimitar. Metal shrieked as it drew the rusted blade. The skull's empty eye sockets bored into her, jaws set in a toothy grin.

"Ahhh, a visitor," its head tilted to the side. "And one

who is familiar. I know your scent—you are the descendent of one who escaped me…" it took a step towards her.

Enala reached for a blade that was not there. Panic rose in her chest but she forced it down. "What do you want, monster?" she asked, trying to stall, searching for a plan.

The skeleton laughed, the dull whisper echoing from the cliffs. "To hear you scream. Your death will be slow, for your ancestor's defiance," it took another step.

Enala bent down and swept up a rock. Bracing herself, she pulled back her fist to hurl the missile. Before she could swing, the skeleton froze. It stood deathly still, one bony toe clacking on the sunburnt ground. Then the skull turned on its naked spine, staring into space a few feet to Enala's right.

"I see you," it laughed. "Come out, Magicker, or I will make your death as long as hers."

A tremor of intuition ran down Enala's neck an instant before Laurel materialised.

She followed us!

Laurel puffed out her cheeks and exhaled, as though she had just run a long distance. Grimacing at the skeleton, she spared Enala a glance. "I think we might have a common enemy," she held a sword in each hand and without further word, tossed one to Enala.

Enala reached up and caught the blade by the hilt, smiling when she realised it was Alastair's. Still shaking with the shock of Laurel's reappearance, she turned to face the skeleton. Questions would have to wait.

It felt good to have a sword back in her hands. She switched to a two-handed grip and smiled. At least now she stood a fighting chance.

The skeleton laughed, and surged towards them.

―――――

THE FIRST THING ERIC BECAME AWARE OF WAS THE pressure. It pressed in from all around, steady, unrelenting, reducing each breath to short, quick gasps. An ache came from his spine, and as awareness returned he found himself curled into a ball, legs crushed up against his chest.

A dull grinding came from all around, as though the darkness itself was moving. Eric listened to the sound, struggling to recall its source. Memory came slowly, trickling back from the depths of his mind. The boneyard, the scree slope, *the landslide!*

Had he been able to move, Eric would have thrashed about in panic then. But the weight of a mountain had settled on him, trapping him in place. Coarse stones dug into his skin and a dusty darkness met him when he opened his eyes. Already the air tasted stale, his panicked gasps quickly using up what little remained.

How deep am I buried? A suffocating fear swelled within him. He held it down, struggling for calm. Panic would serve no use now. He had to think.

Gritting his teeth, Eric tried moving different parts of his body. Another bout of terror threatened to overwhelm him as he realised the pressure had locked his legs in place. He clenched a fist and found he could at least move an arm. Stones rattled and he realised where the sound came from— the slow, unrelenting crawl of gravel down towards the valley floor.

Still on the verge of panic, Eric tried to move again. A shiver ran up his arm as stones tore through his skin. Curled into a ball, he attempted to lift his arms, trying to dislodge the stones either side of his body.

Time passed and his efforts grew weaker, but he knew he was making progress. The stones pressed down on his back, the pressure growing with every strained breath.

Finally, he managed to create enough space to move his arms with relative freedom. Reaching out, he began to clear space beneath him so he could straighten his legs.

Sharp points stabbed him, slicing through his clothes and grinding against raw flesh. Fear dulled the pain and drove him on. Exhaustion slowed him, but there in the darkness he had only one goal: to escape. As the stones slid away, he twisted, levering himself into a better position. Taking another breath of stale air, he started digging in the direction he prayed was up.

Suddenly the stones to his right gave way, his movement undermining the slope's fragile balance. He shrank back as earth roared and the slope collapsed. Light flooded the darkness. Eric sucked in a breath of fresh air and levered his arms beneath him. Using every ounce of his strength, he pulled himself from the scree and back to his feet.

His boots sank to his ankles and stones rattled away from him, another landslide already threatening. Eric did not stop to think. He leapt, fear propelling him downwards. Each bound carried him closer to safety. Stones slipped beneath him with each crash landing, the force of impact flinging them up at his face.

When he reached the bottom, Eric almost dropped to his knees to kiss the ground. Puffing, he resisted and continued into the valley until sure he was beyond range of stray rocks. Then he collapsed to the ground and looked back at the slope. It towered over him, giving no hint anyone had ever passed that way.

How long was I buried? He wondered, looking for sign of Enala.

The hairs on his neck prickled when he saw no sign of her.

Turning to face the valley, he climbed to his feet and began to run.

———

ENALA DUCKED BENEATH A DECAPITATING BLOW AND THREW herself backwards. To her left Laurel darted in and swung at the skeleton. It spun with almost casual speed, its rusted scimitar turning aside the blow. A contemptuous backhand sent Laurel reeling.

Driving herself forwards, Enala stabbed at the yellowed skull. The skeleton leaned back and her sword fell short. Instinct kicked in, sending Enala sideways as the scimitar sliced through the air she had just occupied.

Laurel regained her feet and threw herself back into the fight. They shared a glance, then attacked together, blades slashing out like vipers. Using every scrap of strength they could muster, they forced the demonic creature back—one step, then two. Yet still the ancient blade blocked their every attack, the dull ring of its steel mocking them.

Enala could not help but think it was toying with them.

Then as Enala launched herself forward, slicing low at its legs, the skeleton stepped up to meet her. It turned her blow away with ease, then the rusted scimitar flashed out, driving into her side.

Enala screamed and lurched backwards. Laurel charged in to halt the creature's next attack, her frantic blows keeping it at bay.

Enala's hand groped to her side and felt hot blood. Pain throbbed from the wound, sending tremors down to her knees. She clenched her teeth and pressed hard against the gash. She risked a glance at their foe and quickly looked away.

Two steps away, Laurel was fighting for her life. It was clear the creature had her hopelessly outmatched. The skeleton cackled each time she swung her sword, batting away her attacks like a cat playing with a mouse. Without aid, Laurel would not last thirty seconds.

Swallowing her pain, Enala released her side and gripped Alastair's sword in both hands. Blood rushed from the wound and ran down her leg, but she drew on her courage and dove back into the fight.

The skeleton's grin widened as it watched her approach.

"I see you enjoy pain, young one," it's laughter sent shivers down her spine.

Enala ignored the taunt. She gritted her teeth, fighting to keep her feet as agony swept through her body.

The skeleton cackled and spun towards her. Enala brought up her sword and swung it at the deathly skull with all her strength.

The creature reached up and caught it in one skeletal hand.

Enala gasped as ice swept the blood from her face.

Before either of them could react, the skeleton drove its rusted blade up into her unprotected body.

Whatever pain Enala had felt before, it now fled before the white hot agony sweeping from her stomach. It spread down her legs and along her arms, overwhelming all other sensation. She heard a distant ring of metal on stone, and wondered if she had dropped her sword. She tried to clench her fist, and realised she could not feel her hands.

Enala stumbled backwards, collapsing to her knees. A strange ringing started in her ears, a bell tolling with each thump of her heart.

The skeleton stepped towards her.

Laurel looked between them, eyes wide with shock and terror, and vanished.

Head bobbing, Enala watched her foe approach. Tears sprang to her eyes as she struggled to control her body, determined at least to defy this creature to her last dying breath. A gurgle rose in her chest and she tasted blood, but she looked at her foe in defiance.

Pain radiated through every fibre of her being. She felt something else rising with it.

The creature looked down at her, skeletal fingers clenched around the hilt of its ancient weapon. From so close, she could see the blood of long dead foes congealed on the rust-flecked metal. It held the weapon poised over her, ready to slash the head from her shoulders.

Then it withdrew the blade, and a whispering cackle echoed up from somewhere in its yellowed skull. "Not so easy for you, young one. Did I not say your death would take an eon?"

Slowly, the creature's words sank in, seeping through the agony of her fractured mind. Fear chilled the pain spreading through her body. Looking up at the creature, hands clenched to her gut, Enala felt her terror take light. She glared at the creature, allowing the power within her to grow, letting its mocking grin feed the flames within. Energy pulsed through her veins, throwing back the shackles of her pain.

Enala felt heat in the palms of her hands.

With a scream of defiance, she threw her arms out at the creature.

Flames roared and raced towards the monster.

———

ERIC SPRINTED DOWN THE ANCIENT STREAM BED, ROCKS slipping beneath his booted feet. Several times he came close to twisting his ankle as he leapt between boulders, the broken surface threatening to send him tumbling. He paid little heed. His lungs burned and his heart pumped hard in his chest.

Please don't be too late!

The ring of blades carried to his ears, echoing off the white-washed cliffs. There was no way of telling how far off they were, but he pushed himself harder, picking up speed. He did not stop to question how Enala had gotten a weapon.

The empty sky stretched out, unbroken, giving no hint to the passage of time. Hours could have passed since the landslide buried him. Eric recalled the power of the creature they faced all too well. Not even Alastair could stand against it; Enala would not stand a chance.

His foot landed awkwardly on a loose rock and sent him spinning across the ground. Gravel sliced at his skin, but he rolled and came up running again. He dodged around a bend in the canyon, his foot striking the opposite cliff to make the turn without slowing.

Ahead the canyon straightened. At its end he caught a glimpse of Enala, on her knees and staring up at the dark skeleton he remembered all too well from Antonia's vision.

As he watched, flames erupted from the girl to engulf the skeleton.

Putting down his head, Eric sprinted for the conflagration. His spirit soared as he sensed the swelling of magic. Enala's magic had responded again to her need, summoning heat from the scorching wasteland to burn the skeleton from their path. Perhaps her power could do what Alastair's could not.

Or perhaps not.

Eric ran harder, determined to reach Enala and do what he could to help. He just hoped her magic did not spread as it had in the Baronian camp; there was no wind here to carry him from harms reach.

With a gasp of relief, he drew to a stop behind Enala. He raised a hand to shield his face from the heat, taking in the scene in a single glance. Enala knelt on the ground, flames pouring from her small frame to envelop their foe.

But now Eric saw the blood staining the ground beneath her, saw Enala swaying and the tremble in her arms. A gasp gurgled from her throat and she dropped one hand, halving the flow of fire. A chill swept through him as he realised Enala could lose consciousness at any moment.

Laughter came from the conflagration enveloping the skeleton. Its dark shadow appeared against the flames. The pop of stones shattering beneath its feet sounded unbelievably loud to Eric's ears. He heard Enala sob in frustration, saw her other arm begin to dip.

Eric stood behind her, fists clenched in rage. He had no weapon to fight with, but he could not just stand by and watch the cursed skeleton prevail. In desperation, he reached for his magic, for any power that might offer them salvation.

His magic rose at his touch, his fear feeding it strength. Before he could pull back he saw it changing, morphing into the wolf that still haunted his dreams. It stood before his inner mind, teeth bared, fur flickering with the blue light of his magic. It growled, towering over his feeble mind.

But Eric was stronger now, and he knew he could best this beast. He stared back, pushing down his fear, seeking to drive the wolf back into its cage.

It stepped towards him, already shrinking before his

courage. Grinning, he approached it, confident in his strength.

It leapt, teeth bared, and struck his spirit form. Its teeth tore into him, sending pain lancing through his soul. The fear returned, stealing away his strength and feeding the wolf's. He fought back, pressing out with his mind, struggling to force the beast from him.

A voice whispered in his mind then, cold and devoid of life. *Stop, you fool. This is the only chance we have.*

Eric froze at the urgency in the voice, his defences slipping. The speaker seemed familiar, though he was sure he had never heard it before. Too late, he realised it came from the wolf. Its jaws ripped out, enveloping his conscious.

Eric's eyes opened and the magic stared out, taking in the skeleton emerging from the flames. It stalked towards Enala, scimitar in one hand, the other stretched out to fend off her attack. A tremor ran through Eric's body as energy surged into his veins

Eric smiled—or rather the magic forced a twisted grin to his lips. It knew how to handle this foe. The answers lay not in the wasteland without, devoid of any force capable of harming it, but with the power hidden within. Reaching into the pool of magic at their core, it searched for the power Eric had buried there so long ago.

Lightning flickered in Eric's inner eye, rising from deep within. The same lightning he had pulled inside all that time ago, in the desert of Chole. The lightning Alastair had once told him might one day save his life.

With a roar of thunder, it returned to the mortal world. The hairs on Eric's arms rose as it crept along his skin, crackling as it went, eager to finally be spent. Blue light flickered in Eric's eyes. A surge of greed overtook him as he looked on the raw energy. He shivered at the raw thirst of the magic, its demand for more.

The skeleton turned to stare at him. Somehow, he could see now the fear in its empty eyes. The skull's grin faded against the lightning's glare.

Eric laughed, the sound a dull imitation of his usual baritone. He pointed a finger. Lightning flickered along its tip, and leapt for the skeleton. The blue energy merged with the flames still streaming from Enala, and struck the skeleton. A roar echoed from the cliffs, followed by a dull boom.

The skeleton screamed, stumbling back before the combined force of their magic. It screamed again, jaw hanging wide as the heat took hold. As they watched, the bones of its face started to melt, the yellowed bone blackening before their eyes. Energy crackled in the air.

Scimitar raised, the skeleton stepped towards them, but its leg gave way, snapping beneath its weight. The creature fell to the ground, blue and red flames still flickering over its body. It clawed at the stones, reaching for them.

They watched as its yellowed bones melted away to nothing.

The magic within Eric looked around in triumph, its power swelling, spreading through his body. Eric shrank before it, feeling himself being thrust back from the world. Sight and sound retreated against the roar of its might.

"Eric," Enala croaked, "help me!"

Enala's words pierced the fog, slicing through the magic's spell. His conscious rose, fighting back against the power that controlled him. The pressure in his skull grew, soul and magic vying for supremacy. But its desperation shone through, feeding him strength, even as its claws dragged through his mind.

"Help…" Enala's voice was growing weaker.

The magic's hold snapped and Eric found himself returned to his body. Turning the hooks on the magic which bore them, he hurled it back into the depths of his mind.

He stumbled towards Enala. Her torn shirt hid the full extent of her injuries, but the pool of blood told the story for him. She needed help, and quickly. Alastair's sword lay beside her, and he quickly slipped it into his belt. Then Eric crouched beside her and swept her into his arms.

He stumbled towards the arch, strength fading, and prayed salvation waited for them on the other side.

❧ 18 ❧

Gabriel's footsteps pounded down the bricked road, fear sending strength to his limbs. Somewhere in the city a bell tolled, calling the soldiers to war. Terrified citizens leapt from their path, hurrying back into the scant shelter of their houses. He was closing on Caelin now, though Inken and Katya were only a few steps behind.

A single question tumbled through Gabriel's mind as he chased after Caelin.

Is it the demon?

The wall loomed ahead, the pale figures of the city guard scurrying across the ramparts. Their movements seemed panicked, chaotic.

"What's happening up there?" Gabriel shouted over the clang of bells.

"Nothing good," Inken hissed as she drew level with him.

"If it's the demon, we don't stand a chance," Gabriel whispered, half to himself.

A chill dread crept into his stomach as they reached the

walls. Caelin bounded up the steps, Inken not far behind. Gabriel followed, heart pounding, waking nightmares of the demon sending terror through his very soul. Never before had he felt so helpless; to stand before the dark magic wielded by the creature, and know he could do nothing to save Enala from its wrath.

Even so, he would not bend now. As long as he lived, he would fight.

Their boots thumped on the stone stairs, tiny pebbles scattering beneath their feet. The cries from the guards grew more frantic as they approached. Gabriel struggled to stop the shaking in his legs, pushing down his fear.

At the top they did not pause, the three of them and Katya spilling out onto the battlements. Men milled about them, staring out over the dark waters of the lake. Gabriel held a hand over his eyes to shield them from the autumn sun, squinting at the distant hills. The sun's warmth returned some of the feeling to his hands, frozen by the cool air.

Together they looked out over the lake, expecting to see the dark silhouette of the demon soaring towards them.

Instead, Gabriel found his fear turning to awe. Across the lake, a dozen golden specks marred the horizon, miles away still, but coming closer with each passing second. Gabriel stared, not quite believing what his eyes told him.

He had never seen the Gold Dragons before, only the vicious Red which had almost killed him. His heart soared all the same, his thoughts turning to Enala, and the sudden hope she might be with the creatures.

The specks continued to grow, until soon Gabriel could make out each beat of their golden wings, see the flick of their tails and the rows of teeth glinting in the sun. Reptilian tongues flicked out as they approached, flames licking the air before them.

Gabriel held his breath. Not one of them could believe it. They could only stand there and stare in wonder, unable to comprehend this miracle, but thankful beyond measure. The Gold Dragons could only be here to help in the fight against Archon, to fulfil their part in the ancient treaty.

Beside him, Caelin thrust his fist into the air in silent joy.

Gabriel grinned. Now, surely, they might just stand a chance.

"Men, stand to!" Gabriel felt his hopes curdling as Katya's voice bellowed across the wall.

———

AN ICY BREEZE SWEPT OVER ERIC AS HE STEPPED FROM THE portal onto the neatly manicured lawns of the citadel. He shivered in the frigid air, turning to stare at the stone walls rising up about him. Torches burned in brackets around the courtyard, their light casting an orange glow across the snowy grass. Stars lit the sky and somewhere in the darkness an owl called.

Eric stumbled as he shifted Enala's weight to his other shoulder. He squinted against the torchlight, searching for an exit.

Shouts came from around them and the steel doors at the end of the yard burst open. Guards appeared, spears held at the ready. They charged across the slippery grass, voices raised against the intruders. Steel armour rattled beneath their woollen cloaks.

Eric made no move to run. He would not get two steps carrying Enala's dead weight. Even so, only their obvious distress stopped the guards from killing them on the spot.

Eric stood helpless with Enala in his arms and waited as the guards surrounded them, spear points bristling.

A man barked orders and the guards closed ranks, cutting off any chance of escape. Then the man stepped towards them.

"Who are you? How did you get into the citadel?" he demanded.

"We're friends," Eric's voice shook with the cold. "I can explain everything, but you have to help her. She's been stabbed. If she doesn't get to a healer soon, she'll die."

The man hesitated, his eyes taking in the blood seeping from Enala's cloak, already staining the snow beneath them. The truth of Eric's words was clear for all to see.

"Please," Eric whispered. "She's important. You cannot let her die."

The leader took a deep breath, then nodded. He barked out a string of orders. Two men lowered their spears and approached Eric. Two others joined them, their spears aimed in his direction. Eric reluctantly allowed them to take Enala's weight. Carrying her between them, the men retreated from the circle and disappeared through the steel doors.

"Thank you," Eric croaked to the leader.

The man nodded. "Explain yourself."

Rubbing his arms to ward off the cold, Eric gave a quick summary of who they were and how they had come to be there. The soldiers stared back, eyes hard and unforgiving. With their woollen cloaks, the cold did not seem to affect them. Eric could read the scepticism in their eyes, and doubted they believed a word of his tale.

When he finished he spread his hands. "Do what you want with me, just make sure Enala survives."

The leader stared at him, eyes unreadable. At last he

nodded. "The council did receive word from Jurrien some time ago about a company who would bring a girl to us. No doubt the council would like to be the ones to judge the truth of your tale. They do not convene until morning."

Eric nodded. His teeth began to chatter and to his surprise the man laughed. "Until your story is verified, we cannot trust you. But let it not be said we Trolan's do not know how to treat a guest."

He retrieved a pair of iron cuffs from his cloak and tossed them to Eric. "Put those on, and we will show you to someplace warmer where you can wait out the morning."

The cuffs must have been deep within his cloak, because the metal still felt warm. Shivering, Eric locked them about his wrists and nodded to the guard.

The man gave a short smile and waved Eric towards the doors. "Follow me."

———

SHAME WELLED UP IN LAUREL'S CHEST AS SHE WATCHED Enala's healing. An hour had already passed, the air crackling with the magic of the three healers. Light flowed from their hands to wrap Enala in a blanket of power. It seeped into her skin, seeking out the injuries within. But healing did not come without cost; Laurel knew that from experience.

Enala had spent the last hour writhing in agony. Her shrieks would have sent grown men reeling, and only the strength of two guards had been able to hold her in place. Sweat beaded her pale face and her blond hair hung dull and limp. The copper lock burned a bright red, hinting at the power locked within. But Laurel kept a tight hold on Enala's magic, ensuring the Magickers could work in safety.

Laurel listened, unseen, to the whispers of the healers.

They were worried the magic might not take, that Enala would not survive the night. Laurel smiled at their concern; they did not know this girl like she did. If she could survive the horrors of that creature, she would survive this.

It took another hour before the worst had passed. Her skin slowly regained its colour, a healthy pink returning to her cheeks. The shrieks started to subside as Enala settled into sleep, a gentle frown replacing the scowl.

At last the healers declared her healthy. Laurel smiled, wishing she could thank them. It was clear the effort had cost them; exhaustion ringed their eyes and haggard lines were etched across their faces. Shoulders slumped but smiling in triumph, they left the room one by one.

Then Laurel was alone with Enala. Closing her eyes, she slumped into the chair beside the girl's bed. The skeleton's cackle rang in her mind. Shivering, she wrapped her arms around herself, the fear rising within her. The creature had unmanned her, her strength evaporating before its over-whelming power. When Enala fell, the last shred of her courage evaporated.

With the creature intent on Enala, Laurel had cloaked herself in magic and fled for the archway. Enala's screams and the skeleton's dread laughter chased after her, but she closed her ears to the girl's plight. She sensed the surge of magic as Enala unleashed her power, but knew it would not be enough to overcome the monster.

Laurel had done what she'd always done. She had taken care of herself. She had left the girl to die.

So why do I feel so guilty? She shivered, watching Enala sleep. *How did you survive? How did Eric survive? What the hell happened in there?*

Laurel shook her head, still trying to come to grips with what had unfolded. When the portal dumped her in the citadel, she'd had no idea where she had escaped to. Remaining invisible, she slid through the courtyard, listening to the guards.

When she learned she was in Kalgan, she could not help but smile. It would take a long time for the Hawk to find her here.

Then the two Magickers had stepped from the portal, and all hell had broken loose.

Now Laurel found herself conflicted. When she had followed them into the portal, she'd thought to use Enala as leverage against the Trolan's. No doubt they would pay a steep ransom for her life.

But here in the citadel, the height of Trolan power, she knew such a plan could only end in disaster. Even if the Trolan's eventually recognised Enala and were willing to pay for her life, Laurel would stand little chance of escaping with her ransom. While she possessed a few unique abilities, she was not powerful. The Battle Magickers of Trola would hunt her down within hours.

Nor could Laurel ignore the shift in position between herself and Enala. They had stood together against the cursed skeleton, fought side by side to survive its relentless attack. Enala's bravery had saved Laurel a dozen times in the short minutes of the battle.

In return, Laurel had left the girl to die.

Taking a deep breath, Laurel released her magic and reached out to touch the sleeping girl.

Enala's eyelids fluttered and a low crackle came from her throat. Then her sapphire eyes opened and looked up at Laurel. She did not miss the suspicious glint in their murky depths.

"What are you doing here?" she croaked.

Laurel bowed her head. "I followed you from Chole. I

thought it might be the best way to escape the Baronian thugs hunting me. I...I'm sorry I ran when it stabbed you."

Enala's mouth twisted in a frown. "You...yes, you vanished," she shook her head. "No, *I* should be thanking *you*. You were the one who gave me a fighting chance in the first place."

"The creature made it clear the only way either of us would survive was to work together...I should not have abandoned you."

Enala smiled. "There was nothing more you could have done. As you say, we only stood a chance if we stood together. I was finished..." she shuddered. "If not for Eric..."

"How did Eric help you? His magic should not have worked there; there was nothing of the Sky element in that world."

"I don't know, but somehow he summoned lightning. Combined with my fire magic, it was enough to destroy the creature."

Laurel stared at Enala, wondering if she had dreamt the whole thing. Eric was powerful, but he was no God. He could not have created lightning from nothing.

"So," Enala interrupted her thoughts. "What will you do now? You aren't thinking of kidnapping us again, are you?" she looked at Laurel with humour in her eyes.

Laurel laughed, but before she could answer a knock came from outside. She wrapped herself in magic once more, vanishing from sight.

The door opened and a man with greying hair entered. His face looked haggard, with wrinkles lining his forehead and he sported a patchy beard. He wore a plain brown doublet, long black pants and a scarf wrapped around his neck. He carried a jacket over one arm and a sprinkling of snow dotted his shoulders. A sword was strapped to his waist. He carried a small pack in one hand and a thin golden crown nestled on his temple.

His pale green eyes surveyed the room, passing over the hidden Laurel and settling on Enala.

"Ahh, awake I see, and healed too! I am so glad," the man smiled, moving to stand at Enala's bedside. His voice was a rich bass tone. It could have come from a man twenty years his junior.

Enala stared up at him, confusion written across her face. "Who are you?"

The man gave a booming laugh. "Why, I am the king of course. And my guards tell me that *you* are Enala."

The girl nodded, struggling to sit up in the bed. "Yes, I'm Enala," she stammered. "It's ah...an honour to meet you, your majesty?" unable to do anything else, she offered her hand.

The king laughed again and accepted the gesture. Laurel watched the exchange in silence, hardly daring to breath.

"Nice to meet you too, Enala. And you can call me Jonathan. We are family, after all."

Enala swallowed visibly. "You know?"

Jonathan grinned. "I do. Your companion told my guards an abridged version of your story, and given your rather miraculous appearance, I at least am predisposed to believe it."

"I see," Enala looked lost for words. "I...I...What happens now?"

"That depends on you," he hesitated. "How do you feel?"

Enala's hand drifted to her stomach. Surprise flashed across her face when she found the skin whole. Laurel suppressed a shudder, remembering the gaping wound left by the skeleton's scimitar.

Enala smiled at the king. "Looks like I'm fine."

"Excellent!" the king clapped his hands. "In that case, we can talk. I would not have wanted to disturb your healing," he moved across to the bedside chair and sat down. "I'm not sure whether you know much about Trola, but all is not well in my kingdom. Since my magic failed a few months ago, I have lost the faith of my council, and with them, my people."

"What do you mean?"

"Despite our many decades of peace, the Trolan people still place a great amount of value on the strength of their leaders. When my magic failed, I became the first king to rule Trola without magic. The council saw that as a sign of weakness, saw me as a failure with no right to rule. Over the last few months they have used their power to undermine me. Today, I have little power or control over my own kingdom, other than a few men who remain faithful. The council rules in Kalgan now."

Enala stared at the king. Laurel shifted on tired legs, closing her eyes as the silence stretched out.

"And I am not entirely sure the council still serves the Trolan people," Jonathan whispered.

"What do you mean?"

"I believe there are some on the council who have been corrupted, who now work in the thrall of Archon."

Laurel shivered. Ever since these two had come into her life, the whispers of Archon had been unrelenting. Even here, in the greatest city in the Three Nations, it seemed dark powers still lurked in the shadows. Not even the Trolan council was immune.

"Where are the council now?" Enala asked.

"Fortunately, you arrived late in the evening and they had already retired for the day. Word of your arrival will have spread by now, but they will not reconvene until morning. They will summon you and your friend then. Whether they will believe your story or not, I do not know."

Enala made to get out of the bed and then hesitated, the sheets drawn up around her. She blushed, realising the healers had taken her clothes, that she was naked beneath the covers. "But they have to believe us!" she insisted. "You have no idea what we've been through, the sacrifices we've made to get here."

"It might not matter. There has been no word from Jurrien or Antonia in weeks. They know there is a girl called Enala who is meant to wield the Sword of Light, but that does not mean they will believe you are that girl."

"There is an easy way to test that! Let me hold the Sword. If I survive, then they'll know they have the right girl."

"The Sword is not here though," the king replied, voice grim.

"*What?* Where is it? It's meant to be here!"

"When I lost my powers the council had it moved to Witchcliffe Island. For safekeeping, they said. No one is allowed there. A powerful magic was cast to keep people out."

"They must allow me to go there, to try it," Enala argued.

"I do not think they will," the king hesitated. "I can argue on your account, but they hold little respect for me now. It will not do much good. I think they will lock you up, at least until someone verifies your story."

Enala's eyes flickered to where Laurel hid. "What do we do?"

The king stood. "You can come with me. I can get you out of the citadel, take you to the island. My few remaining men have secured keys which will allow us to pass through the magic protecting the Sword. But we have to go now, before the council can stop us."

"Are you sure?" Enala frowned. "What if they can be convinced?"

"It's a possibility," he paused. "But is it worth the risk? Better to ask forgiveness, than permission."

Enala stared at the older man. Laurel held her breath, thinking over what had been said. It was a difficult decision, with both options fraught with risk. If they caught Enala attempting to escape, they would never let her near the Sword. But if they were going to lock her up anyway…

Enala finally nodded. "Okay," she looked around. "But I have no clothes…and we need Eric."

The king reached into his rucksack and tossed some clothing on the bed. "I hope they fit. As for your friend, I'm not sure where they are holding him. My man followed you to this room. By the time he returned to seek out your friend, guards loyal to the council had already taken him. He could be anywhere in the keep."

"We may need his magic."

"We may. But the keep is massive and we don't have the time to search for him. We would be caught for sure."

The girl took a deep breath. "Okay. I'm sure he will figure out what's happening, somehow."

Laurel smiled at the obvious message in Enala's words. She nodded her silent agreement. She wondered how Eric would react to her sudden appearance.

"Good. I'll wait outside while you get changed. Be quick!" he slipped out the door and closed it behind him.

Enala rolled out of bed and slipped into the fresh clothing. The jacket hung loosely off her small shoulders and the breaches needed a belt, but they would protect her from the icy weather outside. Laurel's own jacket was far too thin for the Trolan climate.

"Don't worry, I'll tell him," Laurel whispered. "Good luck!"

Enala grimaced in her direction. "Thank you. I think I'm going to need it."

✦ 19 ✦

Gabriel turned to see Katya moving through the crowd of soldiers. She swung her sword as she moved, laying into the fleeing men with the flat edge of the blade. Her eyes burned, her face a mask of rage.

"Any man that abandons his post will see the noose," she growled, and her words finally sank in. The men slowed, glancing back at the approaching dragons, as though weighing their chances.

Gabriel could not help but smile. Dragons had not been seen in the skies of Plorsea in decades—who could blame the men for panicking? Even so, he stifled his grin. The councillor was right, this was a time of war. Plorsea could not allow the fear of cowards to cripple its army.

Beside him, Caelin stepped forward. "Do not worry, men," his parade ground voice boomed over the clamour. He waved a hand at the approaching dragons. "Those are Gold Dragons, the last tribe allied with men. They mean us no harm; they are here to help. I spoke with them in Dragon Country, they are no threat."

Katya cut her way through the crowd of soldiers. When she reached them, Gabriel saw her anger had not abated since their unexpected visit. "Did you bring these beasts here, Caelin? Did you know they would come?"

Caelin met her frosty stare. "No, I did not bring them here."

"But you did not think to mention to the king that you had spoken with these creatures?"

"You will have to forgive me, it was a rather brief meeting and I had more pressing things to discuss. Perhaps if someone had allowed us another audience, I could have told you."

Katya shook her head. "What are they doing here, unannounced?"

"You will have to ask them that yourself," Caelin offered.

"You think we can just *talk* to those beasts?" Katya growled. "Those are *dragons*, you fool, in case you hadn't noticed. I can't just have them flying up to the city uninvited. Who knows what their true motives are."

Gabriel's stomach twisted. "What do you mean?" he interrupted. "Those are Gold Dragons—they're our allies, friends of Enala."

Katya turned her frosty eyes on him. "And where is this 'Enala' I keep hearing about? Vanished, dead for all we know. As for the alliance, there are few who even remember it exists. It is a forgotten treaty forged by a long dead king. You are both fools if you think we should allow such powerful creatures to fly right up to the city," she waved an arm to encompass the buildings behind them. "You would entrust all those lives to an outdated piece of paper?"

Gabriel made to reply, but Inken's elbow in his side cut

him off. Simmering, he pursed his lips and bit back his response. It would not do to lose his temper now, not while the situation on the wall still hung on the edge. Air hissed from his nostrils as he breathed out and looked to Caelin.

But Caelin did not reply. He stood stiff as a board, staring at Katya, panic in his eyes.

Katya shook her head. "Nothing. Unsurprising. You are a fool, Caelin, and I won't risk everything we have on the word of fool," she turned to the men and raised a fist. "Men, to arms! Prepare the catapults. Archers to the fore. You there, find me a speaking trumpet. Perhaps we can persuade these creatures to leave without bloodshed."

Gabriel gaped, unable to believe what he was hearing. He opened his mouth to scream at Caelin, to demand why the sergeant had frozen, but his tongue twisted in his throat and only a strangled squeak came out. He choked, his mouth dry, unable to form coherent words.

Gabriel stood rigid, staring at Katya, at Caelin. He made to move, to grab Caelin and shake him, but found his muscles locked in place. His whole body stood frozen. With growing horror, he realised Inken and Caelin were in a similar state.

Around them the soldiers began to move, rushing for weapon stashes and manning the great war machines mounted to the battlements.

His eyes flicked to Inken and Caelin and saw his panic reflected in their eyes. Swallowing, Gabriel glanced at Katya, watching as she strode through the men, bellowing at the top of her voice. Her eyes found them, and Gabriel thought he saw her lips twitch in the slightest smile.

Dark magic, the thought swept through Gabriel's mind.

He stared at Katya as she swept through the Plorsean

ranks. They had been wrong to trust her, to try and make her see reason. She had been Archon's agent all along. Being a senior councillor, it was not hard to see how Katya might have influenced the king. Who knew what dark magic she had worked in Ardath.

Gabriel closed his eyes and gritted his teeth, fighting against whatever magic held his body. His muscles trembled and his knees creaked, but nothing changed. He could almost feel the dark forces surrounding him, the ghostly tendrils binding his limbs in iron. Only his eyes remained untouched, leaving him free to watch, horrified, as the dragons grew ever closer.

This cannot be happening.

"Dragons!" Katya's voice boomed out. Someone had found her the speaking trumpet. "Why do you enter Plorsean lands uninvited. Turn back now, you are not welcome here."

Gabriel sucked in a breath, his muscles straining to break free. His eyes flicked to the men nearest them, praying one would realise something was amiss. But no one was watching them; all eyes were on the approaching dragons. Soldiers raced along the parapet, taking up positions at regular intervals and crouching to string their bows. A catapult groaned as it turned to face the oncoming threat.

In the distance, the dragons roared and fire criss-crossed the sky.

No! Gabriel swore to himself. This had to be stopped. He clenched his fists, eyes flicking again to his companions. It took a moment for him to realise he had moved his hand. Hope blossomed in his chest and he struggled to bring feeling back to the rest of his arm.

Katya returned to where they stood frozen, a sad look

on her face. "I have to admit, I'm disappointed you were wrong, Caelin," her eyes looked distant. "Dragon's would have been a welcome ally, but those beasts have not come to make peace."

Gabriel felt the blood flee his face. *This cannot be happening!* Plorsea was about to fire on their most powerful allies. The dragons believed they were approaching friends; the surprise attack would decimate them—along with any future chance of alliance.

And those who survived the carnage would wreak bloody revenge on Ardath.

Katya still stood close by, her grim eyes watching the dragons approach. Gabriel felt another surge of hope as a tremor ran through his arm. He strained his muscles further, seeking every inch of give he could find. Then, slowly, he lowered his hand to the pommel of his sword.

Golden scales flashed with the beating of wings. The dragons had already crossed the halfway mark of the lake and were closing fast on the city. They would be within range in seconds.

"Men, prepare to fire!" Katya called.

Gabriel stood rigid as Katya paced past, shouting orders to the men on the catapult. Her eyes glittered, studying the dragons' approach, ignorant now to the three of them. His fingers found the pommel of his sword and wrapped around the leather hilt. As he clenched it tight, a shock ran from his arm into his body, and a pressure snapped in his mind.

Shaking his head, Gabriel risked a glance at Caelin and nodded. His sword rasped from its scabbard.

In front of them, Katya raised an arm, eyes fixed on the advancing dragons. She opened her mouth to give the order.

Stepping up behind her, Gabriel drove his blade through the councillor's back. The sharp steel slid in to the hilt and lodged there. Katya stiffened on the blade, her sharp groan echoing across the battlements. Her head half-turned, staring in shock at Gabriel. Her mouth opened, but only blood came out.

Staring into Katya's eyes, Gabriel felt ice grow in his chest. In that moment, he had a terrible thought—maybe he'd been wrong, maybe Katya was not the traitor. Heart pounding hard against his ribs, he released the blade. Katya toppled to the ground.

Her dead eyes stared up at him, accusing.

Caelin stumbled as the spell broke and Inken shuddered beside him. Then she was swinging the bow off her shoulder and into her hand. She had an arrow nocked before Caelin had even drawn his sword. Together they stepped up on either side of Gabriel, weapons at the ready.

Around them the soldiers stared, unable to comprehend the sudden death of their commander. It only took another second for that to change. Almost as one, a hundred bows turned in their direction.

Yet all Gabriel could do was stand and stare at the dead woman at his feet.

———

ERIC PACED ACROSS THE BEDROOM, THE SOFT CARPET yielding beneath his sandaled feet. Incensed candles in the chandelier above cast their flicking light across the walls and left a citrus tang in his nostrils. A cushioned bed sat in the centre of the room, beckoning. But he could not sleep, not now, not while Enala's fate still hung in the balance.

He glanced towards the heavy wooden doors barring his

exit. They opened into a corridor where two guards waited, ensuring Eric did not make any unaccompanied trips into the citadel. Taking a breath, he moved towards the doors and then stopped, knowing it was useless. He had already tried that route. The guards had said in no uncertain terms he was to remain in this room until morning.

At least he could be thankful for their treatment of him. The first thing they'd done on reaching his makeshift prison was to un-cuff him and usher him into an adjoining room. There a hot bath waited. Still shivering from the cold outside, Eric had not needed any further encouragement. He pulled off his bloodstained clothing and slid into the hot water. The guards took his ruined clothes and quickly departed. To his surprise, they left Alastair's sword where he had discarded it.

He returned to the bedroom wearing only a towel, where he found a white bathrobe and thin pair of sandals waiting for him.

Now hours had passed and still there was no word of Enala. Eric moved to the bed and sat down. He ran his hands through his hair, desperate to know if she had survived. Kalgan was the richest city in the Three Nations; surely they must have healers.

She will be okay, Eric reassured himself.

A fire burned in the grate on one wall, the flames casting a warm glow to mix with the candlelight. The walls were plain and windowless, there would be no escape there. Of course, with his magic he was confident he could fight his way out if necessary. But it would not come to that. These people were their allies, it would not be prudent to start blasting through walls just yet.

He lay back on his bed, the soft cushion yielding beneath him. With a wry grin, Eric realised this was the most comfortable bed he had ever lain on. Whether they believed him or not, the guards had not joked about making him feel welcome. He just hoped Enala was receiving the same attention.

Swallowing a lump in his throat, Eric closed his eyes. Inken's face drifted through his mind, her wry grin flashing beneath her fiery red hair. How many days had it been now? How many nights since he'd left her in the ruin of Sitton. Even without the time warp of the Way, he'd lost count.

Staring up at the high ceiling, Eric prayed she still lived.

Then, exhaling, Eric began to meditate.

He wasn't sure how long he lay there before a bang on the door woke him. A guard entered carrying a steaming plate of food. He placed it on the bedside table and flicked Eric a smile.

"Sorry to wake you, but I thought you could use an early breakfast. Glad you got some sleep, you're looking better than when we found you," he waved at the door. "Sorry for the lock and key too. If what you say is true, it's a relief to have you. Without the king's magic and the Sword, things have grown…dark here in Trola."

"Is my friend okay?" Eric asked.

The guard nodded. "I heard the healers have given her the all clear. Must have taken them a bit of magic, she looked a bad way when you arrived," he turned and moved back to the door. "Enjoy your breakfast, the council will want to see you within the hour."

Eric's shoulders loosened as relief undid the knots in his stomach. *She's okay!*

As the door closed he turned to the plate of food. It held a generous portion of bacon, eggs and beans, along with sausages made from a darker meat than he'd seen in

Plorsea. He guessed it would be lamb or sheep—the mountainous countryside of Trola was good for little else.

Ignoring his cutlery, Eric picked up one of the sausages and took a bite. Red juice ran down his chin as the charred meat touched his tongue.

Somewhere in the room, a woman laughed.

Eric jumped, spilling beans across the bedsheets.

"Didn't anyone ever teach you to eat like a gentleman?" Laurel laughed again, appearing next to him on the bed.

Eric scrambled backwards, but Laurel's hand flashed out to cover his mouth.

"Ssssh ssshh, Eric. We don't want to alert the guards. Enala has a message for you."

———

THE DEMON SUCKED IN A DEEP BREATH OF AIR, TASTING THE salt on the ocean breeze. It looked down at the city of Kalgan, nestled in the curve of the Trolan coastline. Rugged beaches stretched out to either side, and in the north forest grew right to the city walls. Waves smashed against the seawalls, driving salt spray into the air to cover the city with mist. In the distance an island sat in the deep waters of the bay.

A smile twisted its lips as it looked down on its old home. Slowly the winds holding the demon aloft dissipated and it dropped lower in the sky. It had taken some time to gain control of Jurrien's magic, forcing the demon to travel much of the journey on foot. But when it finally mastered the Storm God's power, the final hundred miles had flashed by in hours.

The demon had hesitated at Ardath, reaching out to check for the presence of its prey. There was no trace of them, but still it paused to consider the city's destruction. But it had sensed the power of its comrades, other emissaries of Archon. The demon smiled. They were specks compared to the power it now wielded, but their presence meant Archon had other plans for the city.

There had been no sign of its prey elsewhere either. It listened for word from Archon's spies, but the trail had gone cold. It seemed the two had vanished.

It did not matter now though. Somewhere below, the Sword of Light waited. It would find the blade and reclaim Thomas' ancient birth right. They could not hide the Sword; it would tear the city apart brick by brick if necessary. Then, finally, the power Thomas had once wielded would be restored.

The wind roared and its cloak flapped out. Lightning flickered along the blade in its left hand. He grinned.

Before the demon could unleash the power, it felt a familiar magic stir in the city below.

The demon frowned. *Now how did you get here?*

———

"THIS IS A BAD IDEA," ERIC WHISPERED.

"A bit late to turn back now," Laurel hissed back as she relieved the unconscious guards of their swords.

"Thanks, so glad you pointed that out," he replied in a bland voice.

He hoped Enala knew what game she was playing at, trusting Laurel. But he had little choice but to go along with the plan. It had apparently taken most of the night for Laurel to discover where they were keeping him, and even longer waiting for a chance to slip into his room undetected.

Enala and King Jonathan were a long way ahead of them by now.

Eric glanced up and down the corridor, his nerves fraught. The sun was up and the council could send for him at any minute. They must know Enala was missing by now. There was no more time to waste; they needed to get out of the citadel, now.

But first, he needed proper clothes. He winced as Laurel tossed him a pair of pants. These were followed by the guard's jerkin, cloak and boots. Using the robe to shield himself and keeping a wary eye on Laurel, he began slipping into the clothing.

Laurel laughed when she saw him watching her. "Don't worry, you're not my type," she still didn't turn away.

Eric flushed but finished pulling on the clothes. They were too large for him, but at least he would have some protection from the cold air outside. Together they dragged the guards into the bedroom and locked the door behind them.

Laurel slipped past him. "This way," she whispered.

Swallowing, Eric glanced back at the doors. *Too late now*.

Taking a firmer grip of Alastair's sword, he followed after her, slipping down the silent corridors. Eric glanced through open doors as they moved, surprised by how empty the citadel seemed. They did not encounter a single soul as they made their way through the keep.

Eric shook his head, worry gnawing at him. Despite the early hour, there should have been people, servants and workers moving about to prepare the citadel for the day ahead.

"Where is everybody?"

Laurel shrugged. "The place is all but empty. I checked too many rooms to count looking for you—there's nobody here. It seems the occupants of the citadel have gone elsewhere."

Eric frowned. Something didn't add up. *Where have they gone?* The empty corridors offered no answers. Even the guards were sparse, absent.

It took ten minutes for Laurel to lead them back to the courtyard where they'd first arrived. There were no guards in sight now, and Eric guessed they had only been drawn there by the crash of their arrival. In the dawn's light he saw a few scraggly trees growing up the walls, but otherwise the lawn was empty.

"This is where your magic comes in, Eric," Laurel gave a wry smile. "Just don't drop me."

Eric shot her a glare. "Don't tempt me."

Closing his eyes, he reached for his power. It rose with intent, made bold by its conquest in the wasteland of The Way. But Eric had no patience for its mischief; Enala needed his help and he was not about to let his magic get in the way. He crushed down his doubt and brushed aside the growls of the magic's wolf.

Wrapping the magic in his command, he reached out and drew the winds to them.

Eric held out his hand to Laurel as the winds gathered. She took it, and an instant later they lifted ponderously off the snowy grass. He grinned at the pale fear on Laurel's face as the ground fell away beneath them. They soared up into the heavens, far higher than necessary.

The city of Kalgan stretched out beneath them, slate rooftops shining in the morning sun. The domed towers of two temples shone golden at either end of the city, while the citadel towered on a hill at the centre. On the coast, docks stretched out into the harbour. Ships rocked at their berths, the rare westerly wind driving waves straight in from the ocean. Witchcliffe island loomed in the distance.

As he reached again for his magic, he sensed a tremor of disturbance in the sky. Another power tingled at the back of his neck, racing closer. It felt hauntingly familiar.

God magic, Eric realised, an instant before the demon rose into view.

The scrape of the wooden keel on gravel jolted Enala from her dreams. She looked around, eyes struggling to adjust to the darkness staining the world, and glimpsed the vague outline of the king as he leapt from the stern. Stones crunched again as Jonathan dragged the dingy farther up the beach.

Enala toyed with the silver bracelets cuffed around her wrists. The emeralds embedded in the precious metal seemed to glow with a light of their own, and in the pale moonlight she caught the glint of strange symbols etched along their length. Jonathan had given them to her as protection from the magic that had been cast over the Island. Their spells would kill anyone who stepped foot there without permission.

She just hoped the bracelets worked.

"Come on, quickly," Jonathan shouted above the crashing waves.

Enala struggled over the wooden benches and leapt down to the beach. The stones sank beneath her feet as she landed, and a wave rushed up to drench her boots. She swore, stumbling farther up the dunes and away from the ocean. The bracelets burned hot for half a second and then cooled once more.

She turned to watch Jonathan tie the boat to a post in the beach. He still carried his duffle bag, clutching it close as though his life depended on it. On the journey here she had watched the king, her first impressions of him quickly changing. Jonathan was not the confident man he had appeared back in the citadel. He spent most of his time casting nervous glances behind them, and jumping as water lapped over the sides of the row boat.

Enala shook her head. She could already see why the people might have lost confidence in this king. His nervous ticks made him seem weak, but perhaps she was not giving him enough credit. He had defied the council and spirited her out of Kalgan—that had to count for something.

Swallowing her worries, Enala decided to do her best to ignore his behaviour. She just hoped he knew what he was doing.

Together they trekked up the beach, the stones giving way to soft sand. Overhead the red cliffs of Witchcliffe island loomed as shadows against the dark sky. The wind whistled through the wiry branches of the trees dangling from the sheer walls. A faint glow lit the distant horizon, signalling the approach of dawn.

Jonathan led her off the beach and up a trail through the long grass growing on the sand dunes. Without a torch they relied on the moonlight to guide them. Enala soon found herself tripping on the thin grass roots criss-crossing the trail, and cursed Jonathan's lack of foresight. Insects buzzed around her head and flew at her face, the vicious flies biting wherever they discovered flesh. Enala swore and swatted them away as best she could.

It did not take long to reach the first fork in the trail. A left turn continued along the beach, while the right led to the base of the cliffs where Enala glimpsed a narrow staircase carved into the rock. As they drew closer, Enala saw that wind and rain had worn the stairs smooth. Someone had strung a rope through hoops hammered into the cliff-face, but there was little else to prevent them plummeting to their deaths.

At least it's something, she thought, fighting down her nerves.

Jonathan paused when they reached the bottom and turned back. His face was pale and sweat beaded his forehead.

"These steps are treacherous, so be careful. Halfway up we will encounter the second protection spell. It will not be visible until we are right in front of it, but it encases the top of the island in a dome of magic. Only those who carry the correct keys can enter."

"Your bracelets are spelled to let you pass through the dome unharmed. Inside is a third protection, a maze which we must navigate together. The magic there is strange, ever changing to stop any threat powerful enough to bypass the first two traps. The bracelets may not protect you from everything," he pulled down his shirt to reveal a gold and emerald necklace. "Nor will my amulet. We will have to work together to survive. Are you ready?"

Enala ran her fingers over one of the bracelets, feeling the small indentations the emeralds made. She nodded. "Let's go."

They made their way up, step by cautious step. Loose stones littered the stairs, rattling as their stray feet kicked them from the edge. After a few minutes of climbing, they were too high to hear the thud as they struck the ground below.

They continued up, clambering over branches where the scraggly trees overgrew the path. Small thorns crisscrossed the trunks and pointy leaves sliced at their skin as they squeezed between the branches.

It did not take long for Enala's legs to start burning from the upwards march. After half an hour still the steep incline offered no pause. Enala's lungs stung, but she pressed on. She panted along behind Jonathan, surprised by the large man's stamina. The dim light offered no sign of the beach below, but by now it must be far beneath them.

It took another half hour before Jonathan finally came to a stop.

"This is it," he announced.

Enala leaned against to the cliff, panting for breath as she peered over his shoulder. Her eyes widened. Ahead a transparent bubble enveloped the path. Colours swirled across its surface, while beyond the path continued, winding its way up through the ghastly trees. The bubble stretched outwards in all directions, disappearing into the sky far above.

"How high does it go?" Enala asked.

"As I said, it forms a dome around the top of the island, to ensure none can pass unchallenged," Jonathan answered. "When we enter, you must stop on the other side. We will need to take our bearings before continuing into the maze. Even with the keys, it is designed to confuse the mind. And there are dark creatures lurking there."

Enala stared at the barrier. "What maze? I can see the path on the other side."

"You'll see," was Jonathan's only answer before he stepped into the bubble.

Enala watched, expecting him to continue walking along the path on the other side. Instead, he vanished. Staring into the barrier, Enala bit the side of her cheek, wondering where the magic led.

Taking a deep breath, she stepped after Jonathan.

The bubble bent inwards as she entered, it's cool surface pressing to her skin. Then a screech ran through her ears and the world spun. The barrier snapped closed and a strange wetness enveloped her body. Fighting down panic, Enala held her breath and took another step. The ground still felt solid, even as her eyes watched the world continue to spin.

Lungs screaming, Enala pressed on, unsure whether she could breathe in the strange material. Her stomach twisted and her chest strained with the desire for air, but her feet did not betray her. A heartbeat later the spinning ceased and she stepped from the wetness into the maze.

The air howled, tearing at her clothes and threatening to push her from the path. Sand or something like it whipped at her face as she tried to make sense of what she saw. Shadows spread out through a world tinted blue, some just beginning to form as others faded into the misty ether. Ahead the path splintered out in a dozen different directions, each trailing away into the ghostly landscape.

One path called to her, and without thinking she made to step towards it.

A firm hand grasped her by the shoulder. "Stop," Jonathan whispered in her ear. "Wait. We must stick together if we are to survive. The maze is alive, and it lies. If it draws you in, you will never see the real world again. Do not trust what your senses tell you."

Enala felt a fog enveloping her mind, slowing her thoughts. After a time, Jonathan's words seeped into her consciousness. She shook her head, trying to clear her thoughts. "Then which path do we take?"

Jonathan raised a finger to his lips. He pointed at the shadows. They continued to shift, some growing while others shrank, but bit by bit the maze grew clearer. Through the apparitions she saw ceilings and stairwells which seemed to fold back on one another, and in places the trails led straight up walls. Her stomach twisted at the impossibilities of the maze before her.

The bracelets burned at her wrists, and some of the queerness faded away. One pathway grew clearer, though the others criss-crossed it like tangled wool.

"Do you see it?" Jonathan whispered.

"I think so," Enala nodded.

"Good. We must take care. The magic of our keys might not last the trip. If it runs out, we will have to rely on our own cunning to escape," he paused. "Whatever you do, do not touch the shadows that surround us. They are death. And keep quiet, we are not alone here. Dark creatures roam these corridors. It would be best if we avoided them."

Jonathan swallowed. "Follow me," he stepped onto the path.

Enala could not miss the fear in Jonathan's eyes. Biting her lip, she braced herself against the wind and followed in his footsteps. She prayed his courage would hold. Whatever lurked in these shadows, she did not wish to face it alone. But she had a feeling Jonathan's hands were not the safest in which to place one's life.

Still, he was the only guide she had. They made their way deeper into the maze, shadows pressing in on them. Enala kept her arms close to her sides, mindful of

Jonathan's warning. Her fingers brushed across the bracelets, drawing scant comfort from the warmth of their touch.

Her thoughts turned to Eric, and whether Laurel had found him. It did not feel right to continue without him, not after they had been through so much. She had watched him die—and somehow come back to life. She thought she was dreaming as Eric stumbled towards her, his clothes brown with dust and lightning leaping from his fingers to join her flames. She would feel better with him at her side.

But he was not here. It was up to her to find the Sword, to bring it back to Kalgan.

Time stretched on as they passed through the strange realm. Bit by bit the wind died away, leaving silence in its wake. Not even their boots made a sound as they trod the dark path. The fog slowly returned to her mind, turning her thoughts to porridge. She kneaded her forehead and tried to focus on the true path. Jonathan walked ahead of her, his stride becoming hesitant.

With the maze all around, they did not stop for food or rest. The path led inexorably upwards, staircases and steep tracks carrying them further into the ghostly sky. The shadows drifted like clouds, moving across the path to slow their passage. Somewhere outside, Enala guessed they must be nearing the summit of the island. But the maze stretched on, endless.

"Almost there," Jonathan whispered after what seemed like hours.

Enala grunted, too exhausted to reply. Her body ached and she had come to the end of her strength. The Magickers may have healed her body, but they had not restored her completely. Her stamina was gone.

A chill wind blew from behind them. The hackles on

Enala's neck stood as she smelt the stench of rotting carrion. Her stomach swirled and she slowed, turning to search for the source of the deathly tang.

Behind, a beast stood on the path, its hungry red eyes following them. Saliva dripped from its gapping maw and rows of dagger-like teeth glinted in the shadow light. Long arms reached for them, claws stretched wide. It crouched, the knotted muscles taut and ready to spring. A broad tail flicked out behind it. Jet-black scales covered its body from head to foot.

Enala knew enough of the dark tales told in Chole to recognise a Raptor. She could not fathom how one had come to be here, so far from the desert, but there was no mistaking the greed in its eyes. Moving carefully, she edged her way backwards up the path.

A shout came from behind her. She glanced back in time to see the colour flee the king's face. Terror overtook him as he screamed again. He turned and bolted, leaving Enala for dead.

Enala swore and raced after him. Behind, the Raptor roared, turning her stomach to ice. Jonathan's long legs quickly outpaced her, while Enala felt her strength fading with each step. Before she could catch him, Jonathan disappeared around a corner in the maze. Another roar came, right behind her now.

Goosebumps prickled on Enala's neck and instinct shrieked for her to move. She dove, the ground rising up to meet her as a shape whistled past. Claws caught in her cloak, almost tearing it from her neck. Then the fabric ripped and the creature's momentum carried it past.

Springing to her feet, Enala searched the shadows for a weapon. Jonathan wore a sword, but that would do her little good now. The cowardly king was long gone. Her search came up empty—this world held nothing but shadows.

And the Raptor. It had regained its feet and now stalked towards her, head bent low and outstretched, teeth glistening. Its slitted nostrils widened as it scented her. A low rumble came from its throat.

Enala backed away, fear making her heart thump painfully in her chest. She could not flee this thing, that much was clear. Nor could she fight it with her bare hands. That left only one option—magic.

Staring at the beast, Enala sought to summon her fear, her rage; anything that might bring the magic forth. The fear was easy, bubbling beneath the surface, threatening to steal away the last vestiges of her strength.

The rage followed, festering at the king's cowardice. With his sword they might have stood a chance, might have overcome the beast. Instead, he had fled, leaving her there to die.

Enala growled, anger stirring as she stepped towards the beast. It burned through her body, searing away her fears. The creature stilled, staring at her, the hunger in its eyes turning to doubt. She felt the power rising within her and made no attempt to control it. She needed it now and did not care if it wreaked havoc in this phantom realm.

The power throbbed in her chest, burning as it spread through her skin.

Enala closed her eyes and willed the fire forth.

Heat encircled her arms, burning into her wrists. For a moment, she thought the flame magic had taken light but when she looked her hands were empty. Instead the bracelets shone bright on her arms, their heat scorching her skin. Pain lanced from her wrists, bringing tears to her eyes.

She gasped, concentration snapping, and the power sank back into the depths of her subconscious.

She looked up in panic and knew the Raptor could sense the change. Its jaws widened in a reptilian grin. It started forward again, unstoppable.

Enala wiped the tears from her eyes and turned to flee. She raced down a random path, mind racing as she searched for a new plan.

What happened to my magic?

But there was no time to dwell on that question. From behind came the monster's roar as it leapt after her. She could not avoid it for long, and who knew which path she now tread. Jonathan had warned her to stay on the true one —though his word suddenly held little value to her.

Ahead a shadow loomed and Jonathan's words came back to her.

To touch them is death!

An idea flashed through her thoughts and she ran on. The shadow wall loomed, a ghostly barrier blocking the way. Half her mind urged her to spring through, to test the truth of Jonathan's warning. But there would be no second chances here and out of options, she put her faith in the cowardly king.

At the last moment, Enala spun to face the creature. It bounded towards her, claws outstretched, mouth wide to tear her head from her shoulders. It roared—and sprang.

Enala only had a split second to react. She dove for the ground, as she had earlier. The beast's momentum carried it past once more, straight for the shadow wall blocking the path. But this time the Raptor was ready. Its claws lashed out, biting deep into the flesh of her arm. She screamed as the beast's weight caught her, almost tearing her arm from its socket.

Then the beast struck the shadow. The wall disintegrated at the Raptor's touch, collapsing down to envelop the creature in darkness. It thrashed, jaws gaping as the shadow engulfed its head. The red eyes rolled back in its skull and its legs kicked helplessly.

As the Raptor weakened, Enala struggled to free herself from its claws. Pain tore into her, unbearable, but the shadow was crawling over the beast towards her. She guessed if it reached her, she would soon join the Raptor in its suffocating death. Claw grated on bone as Enala fought to break away.

Steel flashed as a blade descended towards her. Enala flinched as it struck the creature's arm: once, twice, three times. On the final blow the limb snapped and Enala tore herself free.

She stumbled backwards, looking around for her saviour. She found Jonathan standing over her, his brow wet with sweat and his breath coming in heavy gasps. His eyes still shivered with panic, but somehow he had summoned the courage to return.

Enala could not decide whether to embrace the king, or punch him in the face.

Then the maze collapsed around them, and there was no time for either.

CHAPTER TWENTY ONE

An involuntary tremor ran through Eric as the demon laughed at them. Panic shook his hold on his magic and they dropped half a foot. Laurel shrieked and gripped his hand tighter. Eric grimaced and steadied the winds.

"Ah, my old benefactor, however did you come to be here?" the demon's voice crackled with power.

Eric did not bother to reply. He reached out to the swirling winds, then turned and fled for the city. His racing heart thrust him onwards—he knew this was not a fight they could win. Their only hope was to find shelter in the buildings below. He tightened his hold on Laurel's arm, dragging her with him.

Then the winds gave an abrupt *crack*, and disappeared as though sucked into a vacuum of nothingness. Eric found himself falling, tumbling towards the city below. The rooftops raced up, the spires of a nearby church beckoning.

Eric reached desperately for his magic, fighting back fear as his stomach climbed into his chest. He reached for the wind, cords of magic seeking any parcel of air. But the sky was empty—there was nothing, nothing, noth—*there!*

The wind howled as it caught them, halting their freefall. Looking down Eric hesitated, then drove them towards the pavement, eager to regain solid earth. The demon now ruled the sky. Its laughter came from behind, its magic hot on their heels.

Eric sucked in a breath of relief as they touched down, but there was no time to waste. Laurel tugged at his arm, dragging him down the street. She could not know what they faced, but nor was she a fool. There was no mistaking the power of the demon.

Before they could take five steps a roar came from behind them. Eric felt his ears pop with the release of energy. The earth in front of them split open, the bricked road tumbled into the chasm. Houses on either side of the road tore in two with a violent crack. Screams came from nearby citizens as the earth shook them from their feet.

The demon's cackle rose above the chaos. Eric spun in time to see it touch down, the black cloak billowing in the breeze. It held a sword in either hand, one dark green, the other blue. Energy rippled in the depths of those blades, a dark power which sent a chill to his very soul.

"Stick around a while, won't you," the demon smirked.

Summoning his courage, Eric took a step towards it. "Stay back," he growled.

The demon ignored him, striding forward, dark eyes locked on them. "I don't believe I will, mortal. Now, where is the girl? Where is the Sword?"

Eric answered with lightning.

The air crackled as he unleashed the bolt. Then a surge of energy struck Eric, sending him reeling back, and the lightning stopped dead a few feet from the demon. It hung there, frozen in place, and yet still sizzling with power. The demon laughed and waved a hand.

The blue fire reversed direction, slamming into Eric's chest and flinging him backwards. Air exploded from his lungs as he struck the ground and went tumbling across the ground. The chasm loomed up before him. He grasped for purchase, his body plunging over the edge.

Laurel's hand found his, halting his fall. Grunting, she managed to pull him back from the brink. Together they scrambled clear. He stood, accepting a shoulder from Laurel. They looked across at the demon, helpless fear taking hold. Eric clenched his teeth against the pain rippling through his body.

"Where is the girl? Where is the Sword?" the demon ground out.

It stalked towards them, cracks radiating from where its boots struck the road. The air shimmered, rings of heat seeping from the *Soul Blades*. The earth shook again, driving them to their knees.

Vines erupted from the ground around them. Laurel lashed out with her blade, struggling to hold them back, but to no avail. In seconds they held her immobile. Eric did not even have time to draw Alastair's sword before he found himself trapped in their iron grasp. Thorns stabbed deep into his skin and his chest ached as they began to squeeze.

"*Where?*"

Air exploded between Eric's teeth as the breath was crushed from him. Hot blood ran from his wrists and he shuddered as the thorns scraped against bone. He opened his mouth to scream, but his lungs were already empty.

"Please," he croaked.

The demon stood just two feet away now. It sheathed the blue sword and reached out with a pale hand. Cold fingers grasped Eric's chin and tilted back his face, forcing him to look into the dark depths of what had once been Thomas' eyes. The pressure on his chest eased a little. He sucked in a breath of precious oxygen.

"Well?" the demon growled.

"You're too late," he rasped. "Enala has the Sword, she's gone."

The demon's fingers dug into his cheeks. "Liar."

Eric screamed as its fingernails tore his skin. The vines began to move, dragging their thorny tips through his flesh. He shrieked again as they cut long gashes down his body. Blood dripped from his chest, soaking into the earth beneath him. Agony swept through him in waves. He could almost feel his mind breaking before the onslaught.

The demon drew back its hand. Blood stained its fingertips. "Ah, how I would love to feel Antonia's pain, to see her magic used against one of hers. She has been quiet for so long now, subdued by the blade's magic. But perhaps she can still taste your blood," it ran one bloody finger down the green *Soul Blade*.

Light erupted from the sword at the demon's touch. Eric closed his eyes, but even so a bright track blazed across his vision. The light burned through his eyelids, but trapped in the vines he could not turn away. The demon cursed and stumbled back, shaking the sword as though it had scorched him. But its fist remained locked around the pommel, the demon either unable or unwilling to release it.

As the light blazed stronger, a voice whispered in Eric's mind.

Eric, can you hear me?

Eric's spirit soared at Antonia's voice. "Yes!"

Then listen, I cannot hold him long. I have been saving my strength for this moment, but even so, it is not much. I cannot escape.

Eric's hope shrivelled away, but he remained silent.

There is much you don't know, much Alastair and I were meant to tell you before things went so wrong. Secrets we kept for the safety of all, to ensure Archon did not discover the truth. Enala is not the only ancestor of Thomas' sister, Aria. Watch, and you shall see.

Eric's vision faded to black, before a new image took shape in his mind's eye. A cross-roads materialised, the streets obscured by the darkness of night. Buildings ringed the intersection. A single lantern burned on the corner, illuminating a pale circle of light. A man stood beneath the lantern, his hands deep in the pockets of his trench coat. He turned to look down the street, waiting.

A couple appeared from the shadows, their breath steaming in the cold. The woman held a bundle of cloth in her arms, clutching it close to her chest. The man wore a sword at his side and strode with the confidence of a fighter. Their faces were familiar, calling to Eric from the depths of his memory.

With a chill, he realised they were Enala's parents.

The man at the cross-roads turned to watch the approaching couple. They met beneath the glow of the lamp, faces huddled close to hide the whispered words.

Eric heard them anyway.

"Thank you for coming," Enala's father began. "You don't know how hard this is for us."

"Then why are you doing it? Why choose me?" the other man's voice was familiar too.

Eric struggled to place it as the woman replied. "We do this because we must. Our custom demands it," she smiled, her voice filled with warmth. "And we chose you, Allan, because we know you. You and your wife. You are the ones we want."

No, no, no, the words raced through Eric's mind as the scene faded. The last thing he glimpsed was of Enala's mother passing the bundle to the man called Allan. *It cannot be true!*

Allan was his father's name.

Yes, Eric, it is the truth. You are Enala's twin brother, you too have the royal blood, Antonia's voice returned, but it was fainter now, diminished.

"*How?*" Eric's mind reeled, unable to comprehend the vision. "*Why?*"

Aria and her children were hunted from the moment Alastair took them into hiding. Archon was desperate to see them dead, and only the most desperate of measures could keep the line safe. Over generations, it became tradition for your ancestors to separate their children at birth, to adopt one into a worthy family. You were such a child.

Eric shook. "No, no I knew my parents. This cannot be possible."

The light from the *Soul Blade* shivered. *You saw the truth, Eric. Both Enala and yourself have the blood to wield the Sword,* she paused. *But you must be strong to use it. You must have conquered your own power if you are to stand a chance of wielding the Sword.*

"Enala has only just begun to learn," Eric whispered.

Then it must be you, Eric, though you too are still learning. You must not die here.

Eric's mind still whirled, still fought against Antonia's words. "How can this be? Did Alastair know this?"

I never told him, though he may have guessed when I sent him to you.

Eric choked back tears. He struggled to concentrate, though pain still rippled from where the vines were embedded in his flesh. "None of this matters, Antonia. It's too powerful, I cannot escape."

Do not worry about that. But we are out of time; the demon will soon take control of my powers again. I give you my blessing, Eric. Good luck.

With her last words, warmth flooded into Eric's body. As it spread the vines drew back, falling to the ground where they withered and died. The warmth spread, encircling his wounds and drawing out the pain. He watched as gashes in his flesh closed over, the skin knitting itself back together.

As the last of his wounds healed, the warmth vanished.

Eric looked up to see the demon's dark eyes watching him. The emerald light of the *Soul Blade* had returned to a sickly green. Purple veins stood out on the demon's arms as it gripped the sword hard.

"What did she tell you, boy?" Rage burned in its eyes.

Eric summoned his magic, bracing himself for another round. *What is Antonia playing at? She knows I cannot win this fight.*

"Do not worry yourself about that, demon," Laurel stepped between them.

Eric stared at the ex-Baronian, shocked by her interference. She too had been freed, her wounds healed by Antonia's magic. She looked sideways at him and flashed a smile. She no longer held her sword, but she stood with a strange confidence, defying the demon.

"She spoke to me too," a shiver ran through Eric as she faced the demon. "I know what I have to do," she raised an arm. It flared bright white as she summoned her own power.

The demon laughed. "You think you have the strength to challenge God magic?" the other *Soul Blade* scraped from its sheath.

Laurel shook her head. "No, I do not have the power to challenge your stolen magic. But you cannot wield them without your own dark magic, *demon!*" she spat.

The demon froze, the light from the *Soul Blades* dying away. Its face twisted with hatred. The dark eyes bored into Laurel, its body trembling as it fought to break the spell. The same spell the Magicker had cast over Eric and Enala.

Laurel stared back, arms outstretched, concentration etched into the lines of her mouth. Light flashed again and her eyes glowed with power.

Eric stared, frozen with indecision. What had Antonia told Laurel? What had she done?

Teeth gritted, Laurel turned to him. "What are you waiting for?" she ground out. "I cannot hold it for long. *Go!*"

Still Eric hesitated, tears springing to his eyes. There was no denying the truth behind Laurel's words. "Why are you doing this?" he whispered.

Laurel gave a sad smile. "That's between me and Antonia," her face softened. "Go, Eric. Find Enala, get the Sword, save the world. *Go!*"

Eric leapt for the sky.

———

Laurel stared at the demon, arms trembling. She blinked back tears, unable to take her eyes from its hateful glare. Only Antonia's warmth kept her strong, unwavering before its fury.

"You cannot hold me, mortal," the demon grated.

Laurel bowed her head, tearing her eyes from the deathly face. It was, she knew, the face of her death. She could feel her pool of magic withering; the energy it took to hold the demon was sucking it dry at an alarming rate. She did not have much longer.

She prayed to the Goddess it would be long enough.

She had told Eric the Goddess' words were between herself and Antonia, but in truth the decision had been a simple one. They could not hope to destroy this demon, not without aid. But bolstered by Antonia's final gift, she had the strength to hold it, at least for a time. Her Light magic, against the darkness swirling at its core.

If not for Antonia, Laurel would never have had the strength to hold it back. Even without the *Soul Blades*, the demon was unbearably strong. Its magic surged against her, fighting to pierce the Light magic smothering it. One second's lapse, and it would be free.

But for now it remained trapped in the blanket of Laurel's magic. Without its dark magic, the demon could not access the power of the *Soul Blades*, could not even move the body it possessed. It was helpless, for so long as Laurel could hold it.

Or almost helpless. Antonia had warned her that the *Soul Blades* had power of their own—power to defend their wielder. If Laurel or Eric attacked the demon directly, their power would be unleashed and the demon freed.

Antonia had given her the strength to stop the demon, but they still had no way to kill it. Their only hope to stop it was the Sword of Light, but the Sword was far beyond reach. That left only one option. Laurel had to hold the demon, to give Eric the chance to escape.

There was no other alternative; if she did not hold it, it would kill them all.

"I can feel you weakening, girl. You're dying. Release me and I will let you live," the demon whispered, its voice seductive.

Laurel looked up and laughed. Darkness radiated from the demon's soul, the falsehood of its words clear in her mind's eye. There would be no mercy from this creature, not once its magic was free of her binding.

Closing her eyes, Laurel took a deep breath to calm her racing heart.

Standing amidst the ruin, she waited for death.

CHAPTER TWENTY TWO

Inken held the bowstring tight against her cheek, arrow nocked and sighted at the nearest soldier. She glimpsed Caelin taking up position on the other side of Gabriel, sword in hand. Gabriel himself stood motionless, staring down at Katya, his sword still embedded in her back. The councillor lay dead at their feet, her empty eyes staring up at them.

A heavy tension hung in the air as the men edged closer, weapons held at the ready. One false move and the three of them would be peppered by arrows. Indecision held them back for now, but it would only take one raised voice to break the spell.

Inken swallowed hard, her eyes sweeping the battlements, reading the odds. They faced at least two dozen archers. There could be no resistance here, only a pointless death. Taking a breath, Inken slowly released the tension on her bowstring and removed the arrow. Crouching, she laid her bow on the ground and raised her hands. Caelin followed suit.

A man forced his way through the gathered soldiers. She recognised him as Elton, the man who had greeted them at the gate and seen them to the king. His face held no cheer now, only anger and fear. As he approached, she saw his eyes flick back towards the oncoming dragons.

"How could you do this, Caelin?" he hissed. His voice shook with anger.

Caelin let out a long sigh. "She was working for Archon, was about to fire on our allies. We couldn't let that happen."

"How can you say that?" Elton shook his head. "She has served our king and nation faithfully for years! I know her, *knew her!*"

"And do you not know me?" Caelin stared hard at his brother soldier. "Was it not you who said the king had been acting strangely, that he had not been himself? He was under Katya's influence, under the spell of her black magic. Even now she was using it, freezing us helpless. Only Gabriel managed to break free of the spell, to stop her."

Inken glanced at Gabriel, seeing the uncertainty in his eyes. She could read the guilt there. He was second guessing his actions, questioning whether Katya had really been the traitor they believed. Yet the proof was before them; the councillor had been about to fire on their allies, and the spell had broken with her death.

Yet one question still rang in her head.

How did Gabriel break the spell?

Before she could contemplate the matter further, the soldiers around them began to scream, drowning out her thoughts. Inken swung around, and found herself taking a step back in sudden fear.

A dragon alighted on the battlements, its great wings spread wide to cast the wall in shadow. It towered over the trembling soldiers, golden scales glittering in the midday sun. The giant head leaned down towards them, the intelligent eyes inspecting them in detached curiosity. The long tail rose up behind it, poised as though to strike.

Where is the one who addressed us with such uncouth language? the dragon's voice echoed in her mind as it bared its teeth.

Inken covered a smile, watching Elton's face pale. He gaped like a fish caught out of water, staring in terror at the beast perched above him. A sudden sweat beaded his forehead.

Across the wall, weapons bristled as the soldiers pointed arrows and crossbows at the dragon. Arms shook and eyes widened with fear. The men stood in terrified silence, waiting for an order.

Realising they were seconds from disaster, Inken nudged Caelin. "Speak, sergeant, before these men get us all killed."

Caelin's lips tightened. "Hold your fire," he bellowed. "These are our *allies!* See how they have not rained fire down upon us?" he swept his arm out at the dragons hovering overhead.

He glanced then at Elton. Inken caught the unspoken question in the look. When no answer was forthcoming, Caelin turned to address the dragon.

"Greetings, Enduran. It is good to see you again," he bowed. "Welcome to Ardath. What brings you here?"

Surprised, Inken looked closer and realised Caelin was right. This was the same dragon they had spoken to in Malevolent Cove.

Jurrien came to us, asked my tribe to stand again with the humans. We have spent many days debating his request. At first, some refused to come, but when we discovered what Archon's demon had wrought in our land, even they joined us. There is no more neutral ground now. All must fight, or die.

Caelin nodded. "We are glad to have you. I must apologise for the greeting," Caelin continued. "It seems Archon's servants are a plague in our nation. This woman," he waved a hand at Katya, "was his agent. She is the one who offered you insult. I am glad you still wished to talk with us."

Enduran's head twisted to stare at the dead woman. *You are a strange people, to allow traitors to grow so easily in your midst.*

Inken suppressed a laugh as Caelin bowed his head. "Agreed. It is our great shame to admit it. I am sure my king will be more diligent in who he seeks council from in the future."

A crackling rose from Enduran's chest which Inken interpreted as laughter. *I should hope so,* the great head turned to survey the soldiers. *Such fragile creatures, you should not be wasting your energy fighting one another,* the dragon yawned, flashing its giant teeth at the men.

As one, the Plorsean guards took a trembling step backwards.

Caelin smiled. "Try not to terrify them too much, Enduran. Most have never seen a dragon before," he paused before moving on. "Your aid is sorely needed in this fight. I am sure the king will welcome your arrival. We will speak to him presently. Elton here will see about making arrangements for your people's comfort."

Inken looked up at the circling dragons and gave a quiet chuckle. Enduran's head turned at the sound. *I agree, little one,* she jumped as the dragon addressed her. *We are too large for this city. But there is plenty of space in the hills. We will camp at the lake's edge. Please send our regards to the king, Caelin, and offer him our invitation to speak further of the coming war,* at that Enduran's wings beat downwards and he lifted from the battlements. He soared up to re-join his tribe.

Inken turned to Elton. "You can thank me later for getting you out of that one."

Elton looked from her to Caelin, his eyes wide, his mouth twisted with indecision. Inken almost laughed again, unable to decide herself how the change of positions had come about.

Caelin took pity on him. "Elton, there is no need for you to make a decision on our guilt. We surrender ourselves freely to you. Take us to the king, and allow him to decide our fate. We will bring the dragon's words with us."

Elton breathed a sigh of relief. "You're right, Caelin. I don't know what's going on, but the king will know the right of it," he gestured to a couple of nearby soldiers. "Bring their weapons, and keep a close eye on them," raising his voice he called to the other guards. "Stand down, the threat has passed, for now."

Inken smiled to herself as Elton led them down the stairs.

Well, that's one way to get an audience with the king.

————

The dawn had broken. That was the first thing Enala noticed as the shadow maze dissolved. The golden globe of the sun hung low on the horizon, its light banishing the chill in her bones. She held her arm as it throbbed with the beat of her heart, fighting to stem the bleeding.

She stood and looked around as the last shadows faded into the ground. Somewhere in her reckless sprint through the maze, she had finally reached the top of the cliffs. Soft, short cropped grass grew out around them, covering the peak. A flock of sheep grazed nearby, a few looking up to study the intruders on their private mountaintop. In the distance, the pasture gave way to small trees. The forest led down a gentle slope, where the rest of the island spread out beneath them.

Enala found her gaze drawn across the pasture to where a rundown building overlooked the harbour. Fragile sandstone walls stood against the mountain breeze, decorated with faded murals of the sun and stars. In each painting a figure stood in the light, a silent guide against the darkness. Cracks riddled the walls and the roof had long since collapsed.

Granite pillars lay strewn amongst the grass and across the steps leading up to the temple. Broken stone marked where they had once stood, bordering the temple stairs. Moss grew on the leeward surfaces of the stone, rusted braziers still attached to the top of each.

"This was a Temple of the Light," Enala whispered. She looked round again. "But what happened to the maze?"

Jonathan shrugged. "I do not believe the creatures and the shadows were ever meant to come into contact. They were polar opposites of the same spell. When you tricked the Raptor into charging the shadows, it triggered a chain reaction which twisted the protection back in on itself. Either way, we are here."

Enala scowled. "No thanks to you," she snapped, her anger flaring to life. "You ran."

Jonathan hung his head. "I know," he clenched the sword tight in his hand. "I am sorry, I allowed my terror to overwhelm me. That place...it unmanned me," he took a breath. "Can you forgive me?"

Enala looked away, tempted to tell the cowardly king to leave. *At least he came back*, she reasoned.

At last she nodded. "The Sword is in there?" she asked.

"Yes, I believe so. We have passed the last of the protections. All that is left is for you to claim the Sword," he held out an arm, indicating she should lead.

Enala drew in a breath of mountain air, setting aside her doubts. She was here for a reason; she could not afford to be side-tracked. The soft ground sank beneath her feet as she crossed the field, mud sticking to her boots. The sheep cast jumpy glances at them as they weaved between them, their nervous *baas* coming from all directions.

Stepping over the fallen columns, Enala climbed the staircase to where the open doorway beckoned. She walked through the musty shade of the anteroom and continued into what must once have been a great chamber filled with priests and worshipers. Now though, the place was a ruin.

Stone tiles from the fallen roof lay in disordered piles and rotted wooden beams littered the floor. The chamber now appeared as an open air courtyard, although signs of the temple remained. Four stone pillars stood untouched near the centre. Images representing the Light were carved into each: flames and stars, the sun and moon. Furtive eyes watched from the top of the pillars, looking inwards to a stone altar in the centre of the room.

It was to the altar Enala's eyes were drawn. There, hovering point down, was the Sword of Light. The steel blade glowed like the noonday sun, its light streaming across the broken courtyard to cast off the shadows of dawn. The great blade extended at least three feet. Above the two-handed grip a diamond sat in the pommel, shining with a golden light.

Enala swallowed, frozen with awe.

She glanced back at Jonathan, a sudden fear giving her pause. She had heard tales of the Sword's power, how it was deadly to all but a chosen few.

What if they had been wrong?

"What now?" she asked.

Jonathan attempted a smile, but could not keep the nerves from his face. His eyes flickered to the Sword and he shook his head. Enala followed his gaze. For a moment, she allowed its light to wash over her, feasting on the sight of it, feeling its power tugging at her soul.

Then doubt snapped her back to reality and she retreated a step. She shuddered and would have turned back then, if not for the sacrifices her friends had made to get her there. This was not what she wanted, what she dreamed of.

But she had no choice. Seeing there would be no more aid from Jonathan, Enala glanced down and realised she still stood within the anteroom, on the threshold of the inner chamber. Closing her eyes, she summoned her courage, and stepped forward.

As her foot crossed the wooden level marking the perimeter of the chamber, a dread swept over her. Hairs prickled on the back of her neck and ice fed her veins. In that instant she knew she'd made a mistake, that something had just gone terribly wrong. Something lurked in the shadows of this place, some other magic.

The bracelets on her wrists blazed to life. Their angry red glow bathed the sandstone walls, battling with the light of the Sword. She gasped as the bands contracted, shrinking until the hot silver cut into her skin. Their heat seared at her wrists, wrapping them in cuffs of flame.

With a scream she dove backwards, desperate to escape the courtyard. But an invisible force took hold of the bracelets, trapping her in place. They held fast against her, oblivious to her shrieks.

Then she felt the first tug, as they began to draw her inexorably into the temple.

Enala fought to free her wrists from the fiery grasp, crying out for help, twisting to look for Jonathan. Her boots slid beneath her, scrambling for purchase on the broken floor.

Bit by bit, the cuffs dragged her towards the centre of the broken chamber.

"Help!" she yelled, trying to jolt Jonathan into action. "Jonathan, *do something!*"

An icy hand crawled inside her chest as she heard Jonathan's laughter. He strode past her to stand beside the stone altar, eyes fixed on her now, an eager hunger on his face.

Enala shook her head, mouthed the word 'no,' but could not find her voice. She kicked at the wooden beams, pushing back against the steady pull of the bracelets. Tears burned her eyes as she fought, determined to resist. The pain of the Raptor injury felt dull compared to the agony of her wrists.

The cuffs drew her to one of the stone pillars. Her back thudded against the cool marble as the bracelets struck. Then they continued their relentless crawl upwards, lifting her from the ground as the metal welded to stone. She dangled in the air, boots scrambling for a foothold against the smooth stone at her back. The cuffs bit deeper as the burning metal took all her weight. Blood ran down her arm from the gash left by the Raptor.

Enala kicked out, furious, desperate to free herself from the entrapment. The stench of burning flesh reached her nose as she bit back a sob. Her chest contracted and she struggled for breath, her weight pushing down on her lungs.

Jonathan walked forwards, raising a hand in mock solute. "We arrive at last, kinswoman!"

———

Eric flashed across the sky, the white caps of the raging ocean far below. Ahead Witchcliffe Island grew steadily larger, its peaks obscured by a dome of shimmering air. His heart beat hard in his chest, Laurel's final words still ringing in his ears.

What had Antonia told her? What could the Goddess have said to convince Laurel to take on the demon alone? She had no hope of winning, of that Eric had no doubt.

She was giving her life for his.

The wind whipped away his tears. They had been enemies since the day they'd met, yet she had made the ultimate sacrifice for him. The woman had changed, or perhaps he had simply missed the good within her. He had seen it when she stood alone against the demon though, when she had told him to flee.

Pulling more energy from within, he pushed the winds faster. He would not allow her sacrifice to be in vain.

Light flashed as an explosion tore the sky over the island. Eric dropped like a stone as the shock wave struck him, disrupting his magic and ripping the wind from his grasp. A brilliant light rushed from the top of Witchcliffe Island, casting the ocean below in a patchwork of angry shadows.

Eric shielded his eyes against the glare. Pushing down his fear, he took a firmer grasp of the wind and halted his free fall.

What just happened?

Slowly the light faded to a dim glimmer, then died away. He stared ahead at the island. The veil of haze had lifted, revealing red cliffs stretching up into the sky. Above the peaks he made out a distant building, sun glinting off the brown walls. Another light seemed to come from within, seeping out through the broken roof. Blinking his eyes, he tried to make out the source.

He was still some distance away, but his gut told him it was the place.

Eric just prayed the explosion had not come from Enala attempting to wield the Sword.

My sister, he was still struggling with Antonia's revelation. But however he felt about Antonia and her secrets, he was not going to let Enala throw her life away. Not after all she had sacrificed for the Three Nations.

And certainly not before he broke the news to her.

I'm coming, sis.

CHAPTER TWENTY THREE

"What are you doing?" Enala spat, writhing against the pillar. Anger helped to dull the pain, but there was no breaking the hold of the silver bracelets.

"What I have been planning for months, my dear. You see, this place does not belong to the council, the magic protecting it was not theirs. I created all this long ago, before my magic was lost. I designed it to protect the Sword from everyone but me."

"Why?" Enala grated. "The Sword is the only thing left to protect us from Archon. And you cannot even use it without your magic."

"Yes, yes, you are right, of course. Try not to rub it in," he wagged a finger. "But I could not simply pass its power to another. The Sword is *mine!*"

Enala struggled to breathe as her weight pulled down on her arms, constricting her chest. She tried to calm herself, but her heart refused to slow and the lack of air made her head swim. Her feet beat at the pillar, trying to take some weight from her arms.

"This doesn't make any sense, Jonathan," she gasped. "Why are you doing this?"

"All will be clear soon, my dear," he walked round the alter, pulling materials from his pack as he went. "I suppose you deserve some explanation before you die though. You don't mind if I work while we talk, do you? I imagine the council will have noticed your absence by now. I must be ready for when they arrive," he flashed her a grin.

His words froze Enala in place. "You're going to kill me? *Why?*" her shout came out as a weak cough.

She stared at the objects as he arranged them on the alter. A pestle and mortar lay alongside a small velvet bag. Vials of strange liquids joined them, the dark red of one looking suspiciously like blood.

"You have no idea what it is like," Jonathan's voice had a bitter tang, "to be born with such a gift as magic, only to feel it slowly shrivel and die in your hands," he took up the mortar and began pouring in measurements of the different liquids.

"My greatest fear was that one day it would vanish completely. I may have never been as powerful as the likes of *Alastair*," he spat the name. "Who never once tried to save the magic of my line. But it was mine, and gave me happiness in an otherwise joyless life."

"So, coward that you are, you hid the Sword away, so no one could use it?" Enala growled.

"Yes, yes, yes, but that is not the end of it," Jonathan snapped back. "I made plans, you see. Plans that required the Sword, plans for which you are the final piece of the puzzle."

Enala struggled to think through the pain, battled against her own weight to breathe. She locked her eyes to Jonathan, willing him to die. Her magic bubbled up within, straining just below the surface, until she was gasping from the pressure of its unspent force. Then the cuffs flashed brighter and the power sank back into the depths of her mind. She shrank back against the stone, tears streaming down her face.

"Good girl, Enala. Don't worry, this will all be over soon," he moved back to the alter.

Enala spat, wanting nothing more than to tear his head from his shoulders.

"For years I searched for a cure, for a way to break Archon's curse. But his magic was too great and my own too weak for such a task. So I turned my studies to other matters. Like how to restore lost powers."

"You are trying to bring back your own magic?"

Jonathan pursed his lips. "Would that I could, but unfortunately such a feat also proved impossible. However, through my studies I did discover that Magickers can link their power, though it is very dangerous. One might accidently suck the very life force from another, or be overcome by the influx of power. It was not much good to me, but the discovery put me on the right track."

"Finally, I found the spells which would allow me to use that connection to rob another Magicker of their power, and transfer it to me. Of course, it does require the donation of the other Magicker's life to complete the process."

Enala stared at the mad king, unable to believe what she was hearing. "But why me? Surely you could have taken any Magicker?"

"Yes, yes, yes, I know. But what would be the *point*? It is our *family's* magic that allows us to wield the Sword. So I had to be patient, had to bide my time and wait for you to arrive," he grinned, "but I did not lie idle. As I said, I had this place created, protected so that I could work unhindered. And I moved the Sword here, so when you arrived you would be forced to enter my rabbit warren."

"You're insane. Eric, the council, they'll kill you for this!" Enala pulled against her bonds, hot tears in her eyes. Her arms ached, blood still running from the wound left by the Raptor. She watched as Jonathan continued preparing whatever mad potion his spell required.

Her head pounded, her thoughts growing foggy from blood loss. Straining her arms, Enala hauled herself up to relieve the pressure on her lungs and sucked in a breath. The cool tang of salt carried strength back to her muscles, but she could not hold herself up for long. She collapsed back against the restraints and the pressure returned.

Jonathan finished grinding up his concoction and moved across to her, mortar in hand.

"I need you to drink this."

No way am I drinking that, Enala glared back, turning her head and clamping her jaw shut.

Jonathan reached out and grabbed her by the neck. As he squeezed Enala kicked out, aiming for his groin. The king twisted away, raising a knee to protect himself. Then he pressed up against her, his weight holding her tight against the rock. With his spare hand he grabbed her jaw and tilted her head back.

Enala stared into his eyes, mustering every ounce of hate she possessed, and clenched her jaw tighter. Grunting, he pinched her nose, cutting off her meagre supply of air.

Lungs shrieking, Enala squirmed against Jonathan's hold. Her head spun but she held on, determined to defy him to the last. Jonathan's grin widened as the seconds ticked away. Her lungs cried out for air, her brain demanded it.

She fought against the urge, but it was unconscious,

instinctive. She gasped a lungful of air, and screamed in pain and hatred. Her cry was cut off as Jonathan poured the noxious contents of the bowl down her throat. She choked and coughed, trying to spit it out, but he clamped a hand over her mouth until she was force to swallow. It burned right down to her stomach, leaving a bitter, furry taste in her mouth. Tears ran down her face.

"Good girl. Don't worry, it will be over soon," Jonathan said at last, moving back to the altar.

"Coward," she spat, coughing in a feeble attempt to throw up the awful concoction. She felt half-suffocated. A numb tingling spread through her muscles and she almost wished herself dead, just to end the suffering. "Why don't you remove these cuffs and we'll see how brave you are," she growled. "You couldn't even stand against your own creature in that maze."

Jonathan glared at her. "Yes, well, sometimes magic takes on a life of its own. Especially when mine was no longer there to hold its form."

An uncontrollable tremor ran through Enala. How she wished she'd pushed Jonathan into the shadows of the maze when there'd been a chance. Or off the side of the cliff. But it was too late now. Jonathan had won. Despair grew in her chest, mixing with the burning strain from her lungs.

To her shame, Enala started to sob. "Please, don't do this. I never wanted any of this!"

Jonathan turned his back and continued his work. "Sorry, my dear. Really, neither of us have any choice in this matter. I must regain my magic and my Sword, and you are the only one who can help me with that," he shrugged. "Such is life."

Silence fell, broken only by Enala's laboured breathing and the grinding of the pestle. The sun crept above the lip of the walls, casting its warmth across the Temple of Light. As it struck the Sword, the blade's light grew to match it, blazing across the courtyard.

What can I do? Enala felt her courage breaking, the insanity rising from within. She prayed Laurel had found Eric—he was her only hope now. Yet there was no sign of him, no hint of his approach. A steady pain wracked her body, feeding the madness within.

"Please, let me breathe! I'm dying!" Enala choked.

Jonathan chuckled. "Sorry about that. When I made them, I had no idea who I would be using them on. They were designed for a larger person. I'm afraid I cannot control them without my magic. But not to worry, I'll be sure to fix that right up when I have it back."

Jonathan's laughter fed fuel to her fury. Enala gave herself to it, thrashing against the pillar, kicking and screaming her hatred at the king's back. She strained against the bracelets until it felt like they would cut right to the bone. Still they remained fixed, immovable, and her rage soon succumbed to exhaustion. Collapsing against the cold stone, Enala fell silent, staring at the mad king.

Tears blurred her eyes and her mouth was dry. She could feel the desperate thud of her heart against her chest, the throb of blood in the numbness of her fingers.

Jonathan turned and raised the mortar to his mouth. He drank quickly, a scowl fixed to his face. Apparently his brew tasted no better. Its horrid smell wafted to Enala's nostrils and her stomach wrenched, but nothing came up. The last of her strength faded away. She began to sob again, knowing each choked breath brought her closer to death.

Then he stood straight and stretched out an arm across the alter. His meaty fingers wrapped around the leather hilt of the Sword of Light. He pulled it to him, smiling as he looked into the glimmering metal. The light of the diamond glowed in his eyes. There was open greed on his face when he looked from the Sword to Enala.

"Almost there," he walked towards her, blade in hand. "Soon I will be whole again."

Enala watched him come, limp against the pillar, hanging helpless from her cuffs. There was no more fight left in her.

"Thank you, Enala, for your sacrifice."

Enala thought he almost sounded sincere. She would have laughed, if she could breathe.

He raised the weapon, the deadly point poised to strike. Enala stared into the glimmering light of the Sword. Time seemed to hang still as dread clutched at her soul. She could find no hope in that fabled light, no power to conquer this darkness. This was the magic meant to save the Three Nations, to save them all from Archon.

Instead, it was about to end her life.

Enala clamped her eyes shut, and waited for death.

―――――

Eric raced across the sky, desperate to reach the building sitting atop the cliffs. He squinted against the sun's glare, unable to make out more than the broken roof. A sick feeling in his gut drove him faster. Enala had only to touch the Sword for its magic to overwhelm her; he prayed he was not too late.

What was that explosion? He asked again, his instincts screaming.

The beach flashed past far below as he reached the island and dropped towards the clifftops. From above he could make out little detail of the building, but as he approached he realised it could only be a temple. The broken roof revealed the ruined interior, where a stone altar lay amidst the rubble. A man stood beside the alter, leaning out to grasp the source of light in the makeshift courtyard.

The Sword! Eric realised as the blade came into focus. *But where is Enala?*

Eric dropped lower, watching as the man grasped the Sword and pulled it to him. The man paused for a heartbeat to stare at the fabled blade, then turned and approached one of the standing stones. Eric stared, trying to understand what was happening. The man could only be King Jonathan, but he could not see Enala anywhere.

Drawing closer, he noticed something different about the pillar Jonathan was making for. He squinted, trying to identify the difference, and with a jolt he realised someone had been tied to the pillar.

"*Enala!*" he screamed, but the wind caught the word and stole it away.

Confusion gave way to panic. Discarding caution, Eric plummeted from the sky, racing towards the temple. Jonathan stood poised before Enala now, the Sword of Light extended towards the girl's prone form. She did not move as the blade drew closer. Light shone from the Sword, its glow casting shadows across courtyard.

"Enala!" Eric called again, closer now.

Jonathan looked up, his face pale in the Sword's light. His eyes widened at the sight of Eric hurtling towards him and panic twisted his face. His head whipped around and for a second Eric thought the king would flee.

Then Jonathan looked back at Enala, and raised the Sword to strike.

"*No!*" Eric yelled.

With no time to think, Eric grabbed for the closest

weapon at hand—the winds holding him aloft—and hurled them at Jonathan. His stomach lurched as the power of flight abandoned him, while the winds shrieked towards the king. Eric barely noticed his body go into freefall; his mind flew with the winds, driving them onwards, directing them with all his strength at the traitor.

The Sword shone as it plunged towards Enala, the deadly tip aimed straight for her heart. The wind howled and there came a muffled thump as the gale smashed Jonathan from his feet. He tumbled across the rubble strewn ground, skimming like a pebble across water.

But the force of the blow had knocked the Sword from his grasp. The blade spun through the air, tip flashing with the magic within, and plunged into Enala's chest. As it struck a shriek of pain exploded from Enala and her eyes widened in shock.

Then she slumped against her restraints and her eyes flickered closed.

"*No!*" Eric screamed.

And the ground rushed up to meet him.

CHAPTER TWENTY FOUR

Eric woke with a groan, every muscle in his body aching. Opening his eyes, he pushed himself into a sitting position. When he moved to put weight on his leg, agony lanced from his shin and something in his leg went *crack*. He collapsed back to the ground, muffling a shriek, and looked for Enala.

"*You fool!*" Jonathan screamed. Before Eric could move rough hands grabbed him, dragging him up. The king shook him. "*What have you done?*"

Eric's leg smashed against a pillar and this time he could not bite back his scream. Struggling in the king's grasp, he struck out blindly with his fist. It connected with what felt like a chin, but did not seem to make any difference to the madman's iron grip.

The king lifted Eric above his head and tossed him like a ragdoll into a nearby wall. Eric raised his arms to protect himself as he crashed into the stone and landed in a pile of roofing tiles. Their jagged edges cut his skin as he rolled aside.

Heavy footsteps came from nearby, driving him up onto

his good leg. He managed to bring himself to a half-stand before a meaty fist slammed into his stomach. Air whooshed from his mouth and he stumbled backwards, pain lancing from his broken leg as it took his weight.

Looking up, he tried to avoid the next blow.

Scarlet fury twisted the king's face as he swung again, this time aiming for his head. The air rustled in Eric's hair as he ducked and reached for his sword. His hand scrambled at the empty sheath. Dread caught in Eric's throat; Alastair's sword must have slid free when he crashed.

Jonathan did not miss the futile gesture. Stepping back, he spun to look where Eric had fallen. They both saw the blade at the same time. Eric managed one stumbling hop before Jonathan reached the weapon. Reaching down, he wrapped his thick fingers around the hilt and raised it in front of him.

"You will pay for what you've done," the king growled.

Eric mustered his strength and dove into his magic. Reaching for the sky, he searched out the nearest storm. Energy crackled and black clouds appeared overhead. Thunder roared as lightning fell. It struck Eric's outstretched hand and danced along his arm, banishing his fear.

"Give up. Don't make me do this."

The king scowled and stepped towards him. Lightning leapt from Eric's fingers.

Jonathan flinched back and raised Alastair's sword to protect himself. The lightning flashed as it struck the blade, followed by a roar and sucking sound as it disappeared into the cool metal.

The king blinked, holding the weapon out in front of him as though it were a snake about to bite him. Then he laughed and flashed Eric a wicked grin. "What an inter-esting sword. Very useful," he stalked towards Eric.

Eric stumbled backwards, trying to put a pile of rubble between himself and Jonathan. He flung another bolt at the traitor, but the king only raised the blade, and the energy vanished again into the weapon. Apparently whatever spell Alastair had cast on the sword still held, protecting its wielder from magical attack.

As Eric retreated he glanced at Enala, then quickly looked away. She still hung by her arms, silver manacles chained tight to her wrists. The Sword of Light had impaled her high in the chest, pinning her to the column. Blood stained her shirt and ran down the stone behind her. He bit back a sob, unable to believe she might still live.

Jonathan screamed and swung Alastair's blade in his direction. Eric was well out of the king's range, but he still ducked behind another of the stone columns, eager to put as many obstacles between them as possible. His mind raced, searching desperately for a way to overcome the madman.

"Come out, come out, little Magicker," the king hissed. "Don't you want to help your friend? She's bleeding to death over there, you know," he chuckled, leaping out from behind the column.

Eric swallowed hard, still staggering backwards, broken leg dragging on the ground.

What do I do?

Changing tactics, Eric reached for a gust of wind and threw it at the king. It rushed through the broken ceiling and struck Alastair's blade, whistling as the protection sucked it into the abyss. But the blade could not completely block the more dispersed attack, and the king staggered backwards. Eric took advantage of the extra moments to place the altar between himself and Jonathan.

"Come here!" the king shouted, swinging the sword through the gusts. He staggered around the altar towards Eric.

Eric watched him come, realising the king was limping as well. His earlier attack must have caused more damage than he'd realised. A spark of hope returned as he considered how to take advantage.

"Who are you, imposter?" Eric shouted, trying to stall. "What do you want with Enala?"

Jonathan smiled. "I am no imposter, you fool. I am King Jonathan, and I want her *magic*," he slashed at Eric, but another gust forced him back.

They stood facing each other, locked in a desperate stalemate. Jonathan was panting heavily and sweat ran down his face. Eric fought down his own pain, struggling just to keep his feet. He had to fight on, had to end this now if there was to be any possibility of saving Enala.

"Then I'll give you one last chance to surrender, Jonathan. Put down the sword, and I'll spare your life," Eric warned.

Jonathan's laughter rang from the stone walls. "And how do you plan on killing me, young Eric? With your broken leg and worthless powers?" he raised Alastair's sword. "Why don't *you* give up, and maybe I'll give you a quick death," he glanced at Enala. "If she is still alive, I believe it's in both our interests to finish this quickly," he observed.

Thunder rumbled as Eric summoned the power of the storm. He was thinking back to what Alastair had taught him about magic, about how his own magic worked. Alastair had once said magic was finite—that if he drew on too much of his own, he would eventually expend his own life force. Staring at the sword in Jonathan's hands, a plan had come to him.

He did not know how the spell had been cast on Alastair's sword, but surely it could not absorb an infinite amount of power, especially without someone to refresh it's magic. Perhaps if he threw enough energy into the blade, the spell would shatter.

Jonathan strode towards him, sword at the ready. There was no way of knowing if his theory would work, but Eric had run out of options. Throwing out his arms, he released the lightning.

Blue fire surged through the Temple of Light, casting shadows across the room. The roar as it came was deafening. Jonathan flinched back from its might, face lit with fear. Despite his words, he too was unsure of the blade's power.

As the lightning struck Alastair's sword, Eric gritted his teeth and pressed on, unleashing a continuous stream at the weapon. Blue light burned across his vision, all but blinding him. Jonathan disappeared behind the fury of the lightning's dance, until all he could feel was the strange vacuum where his power vanished into the sword.

Blinded by his own attack, Eric did not see the first blow coming as Jonathan's fist lashed at him. Eric reeled back, losing his grip on the magic. The lightning flashed and died away, abandoning him to the king's fury.

Jonathan struck again, knocking Eric from his feet. He stared up at the hateful monarch, unable to believe the king had fought his way through the onslaught. Before he could move the king's foot crashed down on his chest, pinning him to the ground. Alastair's blade hovered overhead, poised to strike.

"Goodbye, Eric."

Eric rolled as the blade flashed towards him, sending the

king tumbling. He bit back a cry as rubble struck his broken leg. Coming to a rest against one of the pillars, he used it to stagger to his feet.

Well that didn't work, Eric cursed.

Returning to the wind, he hauled it down from far above. At least that would slow the coward.

Gusts whipped about him, carrying cool air from high above. Goosebumps pricked Eric's skin. He tucked his hands into his cloak to ward off the cold. Then an idea, a memory, came to him.

Drawing on more power, he sent his magic further afield, reaching higher than ever before. There he grasped at every whisper, every gust he could find and drew it down. Taking a breath, he directed the swirling mass at the approaching king.

Jonathan paused as the gale struck. It tugged at his cloak and whipped around him, shrieking in his ears. Eric could sense Alastair's sword working its magic, but drawing on his own power, he redoubled his efforts.

Even from ten feet away, Eric could feel it working.

Jonathan stared at him. "Wha– what are you doing?" he stammered, the cold winds sucking the words from his chest.

A shiver ran through the king. Ice began to gather in his beard and settle on his shoulders. His face took on a blue tint and his jaw clenched. He waved Alastair's sword around his head, as though it's magic could ward off the air itself. Beneath him, a frost formed on the broken tiles.

When the sword finally slipped from the king's numb fingers, Eric was ready.

Throwing out his hand, he released one final bolt of energy. Lightning flashed across the space between them, taking Jonathan full in the chest. The air crackled as the blast knocked the king from his feet. He did not get back up.

Alastair's blade struck the ground, and shattered.

Eric turned and staggered towards Enala. His heart twisted in agony as he drew closer, unable to bare the horrifying sight of his sister.

The Sword had sliced clean through Enala's chest and struck the pillar behind her. Blood still seeped from the wound and had begun to congeal around the blade. It's light bathed her face, her jaw locked in a painful grimace. Her eyes were closed.

Eric reached her, struggling for breath. When he had last seen her, she had just been stabbed by the cursed skeleton, barely able to stand. This was much, much worse. He closed his eyes, hope fading.

A half-choked sob rattled from his chest. He reached for her hand, trying to prize the cool metal from the rock. The silver bracelets refused to budge, the metal so tight around her wrists they seemed almost fused to her skin. Blood trickled from where they bit into her flesh.

"Eric," Enala croaked.

He jumped, so shocked by her voice he thought for a second Jonathan had recovered. He looked around, but the king still lay where he had fallen.

"Eric," Enala whispered again.

Eric allowed a wild hope to take hold as he turned to her.

"Yes, I'm here."

"Eric," he leaned close to catch her words. "Get me off this damned pillar," Enala coughed, and blood bubbled from her mouth. She groaned, head leaning back against the cold stone.

Eric nodded. He ran to where Jonathan had fallen and swept up the hilt of Alastair's sword. Part of the shattered blade still remained in place. He returned to Enala and held the weapon at the ready.

"Let's hope this works."

With cautious movements, Eric wrapped an arm around Enala's waist and took her weight from the cuffs. A rattle came from her chest as she sucked in a breath. Hot blood stained his hands but he ignored it, aiming the ruined sword at her right cuff. Silently he prayed Alastair's sword still contained enough magic to counteract whatever spell Jonathan had cast. He stabbed the jagged edge of the blade against the silver band.

The silver gave way almost instantly, the soft metal crumbling beneath Alastair's sword. He repeated the procedure with her other arm and took her weight as she slumped against him. Clutching the broken sword under his arm, he carried her to the altar and gently laid her on the stone. Alastair's blade clattered down beside her, but he did his best not to disturb the Sword of Light still lodged in her chest. He distantly remembered Caelin's advice from so long ago—*leave it in, or you'll bleed to death.*

"Thank you," Enala croaked.

"Just stay still, Enala. You're going to be okay."

A dry laugh wracked her body, followed by a groan. "You don't give up, do you?" she gasped.

Eric shook his head. "Neither do you, remember?" tears spilt from his eyes. Thoughts raced through his head as he searched for a way out. "I guess it must run in the family," he whispered.

Enala's eyes opened to stare at him. "What?"

Eric smiled through his tears. "Turns out I'm adopted. I'm your long lost brother, Enala."

Enala groaned and gave a weak smile. She opened her mouth to respond, but dark laughter cut her off. It echoed around them as a shadow fell across the alter. A shudder ran through Enala, her pupils dilating with fear. The hairs on Eric's neck rose in warning. Dread filled his veins as he spun.

The demon hung overhead, a dark grin spreading across its face.

"So you are the other one. My master has been looking for you, Eric."

CHAPTER TWENTY FIVE

King Fraser sat on his throne and stared down at them. A sword lay across his lap, his hands resting lightly on the hilt. His lips pursed in a tight scowl, jaw jutting as he clenched his teeth. The other council members sat around the table on the dais, but silence filled the king's court—no one dared so much as breath.

Caelin licked his lips, trying to ignore the vein throbbing on the king's forehead. He was more than aware of their perilous position; justified or not, they had killed a councillor in cold blood. If they could not talk their way out of this, their heads would not be far from the chopping block.

So far he had explained their suspicions, and their meeting with councillor before disaster had struck on the wall. The king had made no attempt to interrupt, his face remaining stony and impassive.

Beside him Gabriel shifted from foot to foot, his nervous fear betrayed by the way his eyes flicked from the councillors to the king. Inken stood on his other side, her casual stance in stark contrast to the blacksmith. Her eyes flicked to him and he caught the briefest of smiles. He found her confidence reassuring.

When he finally reached the magical paralysis that had frozen the three of them, the king broke him off mid-sentence.

"Enough!" he saw Gabriel jump at the king's shout. "I have heard enough of these stories, Caelin. I can assure you I have been under no spell. No dark magic has been worked on me. But this is the second 'agent' of Archon you claim to have killed—who until this moment I had regarded as a trusted member of my council. I shall need proof if you expect me to believe Katya was a traitor."

Caelin's heart sank as he stared down the king. From the corner of his eye he caught a moment's panic come over Inken's face, quickly hidden. His response caught in his mouth, his words retreating before King Fraser's rage.

"We will search Katya's apartment and belongings for sign of this alleged betrayal. And I would speak with these dragons, who claim to have come to aid us," he hesitated, eyes looking around the court. "I do not know what happened on that wall. But from what I have heard, the men were panicked and close to breaking before Katya arrived. I do not know why she decided to fire on the beasts, but at this point my belief is she thought the action justified. For her courage alone in holding the walls, I would praise her," he shook his head, glaring down at them. "But she is dead."

Caelin shrank as the king's eyes found him. He stared into his monarch's face, willing him to retract the words, searching for the man Fraser had once been. Surely with Katya dead, reason should have returned to the king. But there was only rage in those dark eyes.

Then the king let out a long breath and some of the

anger went out of him. "I do not know what to do with you. I find myself doubting your story more and more, Caelin. Up to this moment, there is still no proof of anything you have claimed, either with Balistor or Katya. I gave you the benefit of the doubt, gave you free rein of the castle. In payment, you stained the city walls with the blood of my most trusted councillor. You have left me no choice."

"Your majesty," Caelin interrupted.

King Fraser raised a hand. "*Silence!*" his gaze swept the room, taking in each of them. "You have said enough. You and your two companions cannot be trusted to have free rein of the city, or the citadel. You leave me no choice but to lock you away until the truth of this matter becomes clear."

Before Caelin could raise his voice in argument, the king waved a hand. Iron hands grasped him by the shoulder, holding him tight. He glanced back at the two guards behind him, taking in the grim determination in their eyes. The sick dread of treachery swept through him, washing away all thought of resistance.

For all his years of service, King Fraser had repaid him with betrayal.

Caelin went limp, eyes falling to the ground. There would be no fighting their way out of this. Guardsmen ringed the throne room, spears at the ready.

Inken did not see things the same way. Her calm had vanished, swept away by a red hot rage. Growling, she pushed the first guard away and spun to face the king.

"*Your majesty!*" she shouted. "We have come a long way to help you, have given everything for Plorsea, for the Three Nations. Who are you to judge us, sitting safe up there on your throne. How *dare* you try to lock us away."

The king scowled. "Silence, woman. Men, get them out of my sight."

Inken screamed and leapt for the dais. Before she could take two steps a guard tackled her to the ground. She went down, kicking and screaming as another man joined the fray. It took a third before she finally subsided, going limp on the tiled floor. Together the men dragged Inken to her feet. Blood ran from her nose, staining her white top, but she glared around the throne room in defiance.

"This is a mistake, Fraser!" she shouted.

The king waved a hand and turned back to the table of councillors. As the guards led him from the room, Caelin saw the king take his seat at the head of the table.

Outside, the guards pushed them together and took up positions ahead and behind them. A jab in the back told Caelin to move. They marched down the wide corridors of the citadel, footsteps dragging on the soft carpets. The hallways were empty now—everyone who could be spared had been called to man the walls. Allies or not, dragons were fearful beasts, and the citizens would rest easier seeing the soldiers manning the walls.

A few minutes later they turned from the well-lit passageways down a stairwell leading into the depths of the keep. A cold sweat broke out on Caelin's forehead as his mind began to work again. A cool wind blew up from the dark depths below. He knew this staircase—they were not being taken to a tower keep or warded room. They were being led to the dungeons.

One of the guards took a torch from a wall bracket, providing a thin circle of light in against the darkness. They continued down the staircase, the light of the flames only carrying a few steps ahead. Caelin moved slowly, taking care on the slick steps. He thought of all those who had come before, the centuries of men and women who had disappeared into this darkness.

Caelin shuddered, suffocating in the pitch black. He could feel it pressing in on him, drawing away the light, smothering hope. The warmth fled from his face and his fingertips grew numb with the cold. He glanced back at the guards, but they stared straight ahead, all but ignoring their prisoners but for the odd shove to keep them moving.

The cold seeped deeper, creeping into Caelin's skin and sending shivers down his spine. He looked across at his companions in the darkness, and saw his own fear reflected in their pale faces. They could sense it too—the wrongness about this place. But the guards still held them fast, ushering them downwards, leaving no opportunity to flee.

Four or five stories beneath the keep, the staircase came to a sudden end.

At the bottom was a single corridor lined by thick wooden doors, disappearing beyond the reach of their torch. There was nothing else to light the space. Caelin shuddered as he realised they would be left alone in the darkness. The empty black beckoned and he felt his courage melting. He turned back to the guards, ready to beg for them to leave the torch.

Beside him, Gabriel jumped as a rat skittered past. The guards chuckled and pushed him forwards. He stumbled into Caelin, knocking them both to the ground. From the floor he watched the panic catch in Inken's eyes, saw her turn to flee, but a steel gauntlet struck her in the face and sent her stumbling backwards. Caelin reached out to catch her as she fell.

They lay together on the icy stone, looking up at the grim faces of the guards. Chainmail rattled as their captors drew their swords.

"Stop, please, we won't struggle," Caelin raised his hands. "There's no need for that."

The lead guard stepped forward. He held an iron key in his gauntleted fist. "Here," he tossed it to Caelin. "There is a cell at the end of the corridor. You will unlock it. You will leave the key in the door and enter the cell. Do not try anything."

Caelin caught the key and nodded. "Okay."

Together they backed down the corridor. The guards pressed forward, swords extended to block their escape, leaving nothing to chance. To either side of the corridor the doors stood barred, but there was no escape there anyway. The only exit from the dungeons was through the men facing them. Caelin shivered as the dark swarmed him.

Caelin froze as his back brushed against the door at the end of the corridor. Heart pounding, he turned slowly and felt for the lock. His back felt exposed, unprotected from the approaching guards. He fumbled for the keyhole, struggling to place the key in the dim light of the torch, then a click came as the mechanism within the door drew back the bolt. The hinges creaked as it opened.

"Get in," the guard ordered, his sword glinting in the torchlight.

Caelin swallowed, biting back a response. The full truth of the king's betrayal crashed down around him, as he realised with sick certainty they would never leave this hole in the ground. The absolute darkness of the cell beckoned, but his feet refused to obey. Beside him, Gabriel and Inken were also frozen, unable to take that final step into captivity. He could almost sense the pain radiating from the cell, the waves of despair crashing down upon him.

He yelled as the sharp tip of a sword prodded his back. Biting his tongue, Caelin strode into the cell. In the pitch-black he did not look back, but heard movement as Inken and Gabriel joined him. With another groan of rusty hinges, the door slammed shut behind them, leaving them alone in the darkness.

Panic rose in Caelin's chest as the empty black crowded him. He fought for control, for a moment's sanity. Every instinct shrieked for him to turn and pound on the door, to beg for release, for light. The darkness hung over them, absolute, overwhelming, pressing down on his very soul. He struggled for breath, the black almost like liquid, suffocating him. A scream rose up within him, tearing at his chest as he fought to stifle it.

"This seems like a place you go to be forgotten," Inken's words echoed in the small space.

"Or a place where no one will ever find you," a voice replied from the darkness.

———

Eric stared up at the demon. He felt strangely detached, without fear or panic. He crouched beside Enala, a defiant anger bubbling in his chest. Its heat crawled through his veins, pushing away the pain, feeding strength to his desperate body. Enala's hand was warm in his. He gave it a squeeze and stood. They had gone through too much, beaten the odds too many times to fail now.

The demon dropped from the sky. Dust billowed out as it crashed to the tiled floor. It straightened and looked around the ruined temple, a strange look in its demonic eyes.

"Curious. When I ruled, *his* temple was a place of pilgrimage. People would travel here from all over Trola, to beg for *his* return," he laughed. "No longer, it seems! The people have all but forgotten Darius."

Eric faced the demon. "You heard what I said, demon,"

he growled. "I am Enala's brother, descended from Aria herself, sister to the man whose body you possess. I wield the Sword of Light. You had better run, if you wish to live."

The demon grinned. It raised its hands and gave a slow clap. Then it drew back its cloak to reveal the green and blue stained crystals set in the pommels of its *Soul Blades*. "I have mastered the God powers of Earth and Sky. I am not afraid of the Sword of Light. No, I will prise it from your cold dead fingers."

Eric looked down at Enala, watching her laboured breathing. Indecision gripped him. The Sword was the only thing stopping her from bleeding to death. If he pulled it free, she would die in minutes. There would be no chance of returning her to the healers in Kalgan. He would be condemning her to death.

Yet he did not stand a chance without it.

"Eric," Enala croaked. "Take the Sword and finish the damn thing."

Eric shook his head. "No, I can't!"

Enala gritted her teeth, eyes clenched closed. "Eric, you know what's at stake. Demon or not, Thomas was the first to use the Sword. You cannot let it fall into his hands," she coughed the words. "*Take it!*"

Eric wiped tears from his eyes. "I can't lose you too, Enala," he took a steadying breath. "So just stay with me, okay?" his voice cracked, but he reached down to clasp the hilt of the Sword.

Closing his eyes, he began to pull. Enala screamed as the blade shifted. The sound tore at his soul, but he could not turn back now. Biting back tears, he drew the Sword of Light from her chest. Enala thrashed against the altar as the blade slid clear. Blood began to bubble from the naked wound.

Enala's shrieks died away and her head sank back against the alter.

Holding the Sword of Light in his hand, Eric hardly noticed. He could feel its power as it flowed down his arm, swirling within him, seeking out every dark crevice of his soul. He stood before it like a leaf in a flood, overwhelmed, helpless before its power. Light shone through his mind, a threatening edge to its touch.

Eric focused on the light, feeling out its power, fighting the lure of its pull. It wound its way deeper, curling around his soul. Within, his own magic rose in response, its blue glow mingling with the pure white—one feeding the other, or fighting for control, he could not tell.

Then, anxiety driving him, Eric reached out with steely resolve and grasped the flickering lights. The blue of his own magic succumbed easily, but the white reared back, fighting against him. The Sword's magic turned red hot, threatening to burn his mind to a crisp.

But Eric had no patience for the unruly force, no time to waste. Threads of power spun from his magic, blue ropes that wrapped their way around the white light. Twisting and turning, the Light fought against him, but he left it no place to go. With a final flash of red, the light settled, trapped in the bindings of his power.

Opening his eyes, Eric smiled. The Sword glowed in his hand, its brilliance banishing all but the deepest shadows in the temple. The power of the Light, returned to Witchcliffe Island.

"This ends now, demon," he swore.

"You are strong, to overcome the pull of the Sword. Still, it will do you no good now," reaching down, the demon drew its *Soul Blades*.

Eric leaned down and kissed Enala on the cheek. "Stay with me," he whispered.

The power of the Sword thrummed in his ears, burning away pain and feeding strength to his limbs. Even so, Eric could not move quickly on his broken leg, and the demon had two swords to his one. He could not let this become a battle of blades.

The demon's cloak cracked as it strode towards Eric, a dark grin on Thomas' worn face. It had fought this battle twice already; both times Eric had been overwhelmed in moments. Even with the Sword of Light, he knew the odds were against him.

Even so, he would fight on. This monster's terror had to end—here and now. However slim, the Sword at least gave him a chance.

Reaching down, Eric sought to draw on the Sword's power. The light fled at his touch, slipping free of his magic. Clenching his fist around the Sword's hilt, Eric followed the power as it retreated into the blade. There he wrapped it again in his magic and pulled the bindings tight.

White flames raced along the length of the blade, burning bright as the noonday sun. Heat seared at Eric's face, far fiercer than any mortal flame. He flinched away, unable to bear it, until the Sword's magic seeped back into his body. His skin cooled as it spread through his limbs.

Eric smiled across to where the demon stood watching him. A weariness lurked in its eyes now, a grim smirk on its lips. It held the *Soul Blades* stretched out towards Eric. He remembered how Thomas had required instruction from the Gods to wield the Sword of Light, and grinned.

"I'm a fast learner," he mocked. "Unlike some."

He flicked out the Sword and a column of white hot flame leapt towards his foe. Where dragon flame had once been hot enough to drive the demon from Malevolent Cove, the Sword's fire was fiercer still. It swept towards the demon, stone melting beneath its touch.

The demon hurtled sideways, a gust of wind carrying it skywards.

"Impressive," it growled. "But you are a mere novice, injured and exhausted. You will perish here, boy!"

Then it fell, hurtling towards Eric with blades extended. Energy flashed within the tainted steel, the green and blue glows reaching out to mix with the white of the Sword.

Eric raised his arm and hurled another inferno at the demon. It lurched in the air and came on, but Eric was already moving. The winds cast him into the sky. Behind him the familiar vines exploded through the pavement, engulfing the space where he'd just stood.

Smiling, Eric allowed the wind to carry him higher. He would not be caught in the same trap twice. His breath came faster as he felt the power flooding his body. It swept through his muscles, washing away all pain, all sensation, leaving him free to tackle the demon. The white of the Sword fed his magic, its unlimited energy recharging his own.

He lashed out with the fire again, eager to destroy the jungle below. The flames roared as they devoured the demon's creations. Directing the wind, Eric landed atop one of the pillars and watched as the demon settled opposite.

It hissed, teeth bared, pale fingers gripped hard around its blades. Thick smoke rose from the temple, turning the space between them black. Eric raised the Sword as the demon disappeared into the smoke. His clothes whipped in the wind as he prepared to take flight.

The crackle of lightning leant Eric precious seconds. He dove from the pillar as blue fire turned the granite to molten stone. The winds propelled him up through the acrid smoke. He coughed as black soot caught in his throat, then he rose above the burning stench.

Air whooshed as a blade flashed for his face. Eric ducked, dropping a foot, and the sword swept overhead. He lashed out at the demon's feet but Thomas shot backwards out of range.

They circled one another, air crackling with energy as they soared higher. Eric drew on the Sword's power and unleashed a wave of white fire. The demon drew back. Then the blue blade crackled. Lightning flashed and the wind howled as the Sky elements lashed out to halt the flame's advance.

A blast exploded outwards, smashing into Eric and spinning him through the air. He struggled to keep hold of the wind, drawing the gusts into a tighter spiral. Flames flashed and thunder clapped as blue lightning smashed the temple below. He prayed Enala had not been hit.

Eric looked up to see white fire licking at the demon's cloak. It beat at the flames, face twisting with pain. Shielding his eyes against the glare, Eric watched its pale flesh blacken and burn.

It still has no defence against the Light, Eric thought with a smile. If only he knew more about what the Sword could do.

The demon screamed and tore the flaming cloak from its body. It scowled at him, lightning crackling along the blue blade. A dark green glow came from the other. Beneath, the earth shook with its rage.

"Is that all you have, boy?" it growled.

Eric glared back, frustrated by his own limitations. He knew the Sword was capable of so much more than simple fire. The God magic controlled all aspects of the Light. It was capable of feats he could not begin to imagine. But there was no time to learn now. The fire would have to do.

Across from him, the demon dropped into the smoke and vanished from view. Eric swore, eyes searching the roiling clouds below. The blaze was everywhere now, flames catching at the rotten walls. He could hardly make out the building through the smoke and fire. He hoped Enala was still safe at the centre of the courtyard where the flames had not yet reached.

Reaching out with his senses, he searched for his foe, for the tell-tale whisper of magic.

A sudden gust pushed him down as the winds holding him aloft gave way. He fell, tumbling into the acrid smoke towards the distant earth. Panic gripped him, but a few feet above the ground the winds returned and he caught himself.

As he touched down, vines sprang from all around, their thorny tendrils shooting out to catch his fragile body. The demon charged through the smoke, *Soul Blade* raised to strike Eric down.

But the Sword of Light moved faster. Flames danced out from him, turning the vines to ash and flinging the demon into a nearby pillar.

Eric grinned as the demon climbed to its feet. Gripping the wind still spinning through the temple, he sent it out in a blast of fury. It caught the smoke and carried it upwards, blowing it from the building and into the sky. The temple reappeared as the wind died away.

But the demon had vanished. Eric spun, searching the ruins. Its laughter came from the shadows to his right, then left, always moving. He glared around him, chasing ghosts through the empty temple. He caught sight of Enala, still lying on the altar but conscious now, clutching her cloak to her chest. He caught the glint of metal and saw her other hand wrapped about the hilt of Alastair's shattered blade.

Stones rattled from behind. Eric spun in time to parry the demon's blow, energy crackling as the blue and white blades clashed. Then Eric slashed out with the greatsword, feeling a satisfying crunch as the blade caught flesh.

The demon stumbled, its growl echoing from the temple walls. The face of Thomas constricted, grey lines creeping through the pale skin. Burns scorched his flesh and as Eric watched, dark shadows began to creep beneath his skin.

"*Enough!*" the thing that had been Thomas hissed.

Fear caught Eric as the demon surged forward, faster than thought. Instinct screamed for him to move, but his broken leg caught beneath him and he tripped. Eric shrieked in agony as the demon's blade drove into his stomach. A deathly cold hand grasped his throat and pulled, dragging him further onto the blade. He gasped as the demonic steel tore into him.

"Goodbye, Eric," the demon's lips pressed against his ear. "Say hello to Antonia for me."

With a casual smirk, the demon shoved him to the ground. The *Soul Blade* slid free, its dark green glow flickering in the sunlight. The Sword of Light slipped from Eric's hands, scattering across the tiles. Sparks of flame burst from the blade with each bounce.

The Sword's magic fled Eric's body. Without it, the pain returned to strike him down. A chill spread from his stomach and the same dark shadows he had sensed in Malevolent Cove reached out to claw at his soul. The edges of his vision blurred and he felt hot blood pooling beneath him. He clutched at his stomach, struggling to stem the bleeding.

Rubble crunched beneath the demon's boots as it

walked towards the Sword of Light. Sheathing Jurrien's blade, it reached out to pluck the Sword from the broken ground.

"*No!*" the demon swung at Enala's cry.

As it turned, the shattered remnants of Alastair's blade took it through the eye.

Eric gaped, staring at Enala's heaving body. She collapsed back to the alter, the last of her energy spent with the effort it had taken to hurl the blade. A convulsion tore through her, lifting her body from the hard stone. Blood bubbled from her lips and spread across the altar beneath her. A gurgling groan came from her chest.

Beside him, the demon screamed. The sound tore at Eric's ears; it's shriek like a hundred nails on a chalk board. He fought through the sound, through the pain in his leg, through the chill spreading from his stomach as his lifeblood leaked away. This was his chance—if only he had the strength to take it.

Clenching his fists, Eric fought back against the shadows clinging to his soul. He gathered the last of his courage and lunged for the Sword of Light. His fingers scrambled at the hilt, pulling it to him, though he had lost the strength to lift it.

The Sword ignited at his touch, feeding new strength to his dying body. Its power burned through him, extinguishing the shadows of the *Soul Blade*. The pain faded until it became just a dull throbbing within, a distant reminder of his impending death. Drawing on the Sword's power, Eric stood.

The demon staggered across the temple floor, blindly clutching at the broken sword still piercing its skull. Dark magic flashed about it, shadows racing around its warped body to vanish into Alastair's blade. Some part of Alastair's enchantment still held. Yet Eric could already see the shadows gaining power, as more and more escaped the clutch of the sword.

Eric had no idea what the demon was trying to do, but clearly the blow had not been fatal. It was distracted though, and that was all he needed.

Stepping up behind the demon, Eric raised the Sword. Energy blazed from its depths, not flames this time but a pure white light which cast the shadows from the demon. It started to turn, must have felt the gathering power, poised to strike it down.

Eric swung the Sword with all his strength. The Sword blazed as it sliced through the creature's robes and pierced the body beneath, the body that had once belonged to the king of Trola. A blood curdling cry bellowed from the twisted mouth. Then energy erupted from the Sword, engulfing the demon and cutting off its final scream.

The light spread across the old king's body, raising red welts wherever it touched. The demon shuddered and a gasp echoed from the pale lips. The head slumped, then turned to look at Eric.

Eric stumbled backwards as he glimpsed the demon's eyes. Hazel had replaced the black, and the man from Antonia's vision stared back at him.

"*Thank you*," Thomas' words whispered through the temple.

Then light exploded from the blade, engulfing them both in its power.

EPILOGUE

Enala dragged herself across the broken floor towards Eric. She locked her eyes on the young Magicker, fighting back pain, struggling for breath. Her chest gurgled with each gasp, as though filled with liquid, as though she were drowning in her own blood. Fire burned in her heart and sleep beckoned, it's cool depths offering sweet relief.

But she could not give in. Not while Eric, not while *her brother*, lay dying.

She crawled on. Flames flickered nearby, their heat washing across her broken body. Smoke drifted overhead, but where she lay the air remained clear. A crash came from nearby as another part of the roof collapsed, the orange flames consuming the crumbling ruins of the temple.

Closing her eyes, Enala pressed on.

Rubble ground against her skin, but she hardly felt it—sensation had long since fled with the lifeblood trailing behind her. All that remained was the slowing thud of her heart, the searing in her lungs, the slow suffocation of her body.

It seemed an eternity had past when she finally reached his side. He lay amidst the ash that had been the demon, body bleeding and broken. She stretched out a hand and grasped his arm. His eyes opened at her touch. He attempted a smile, but it came out as a grimace.

"Enala," he croaked.

"I'm here. You did it, Eric, you beat it."

His eyes closed again as he groaned. "That's something at least."

Tears blurred in Enala's eyes—not for herself, but for the sight of Eric lying there dying. She remembered Inken, the kindness she had given Enala, to bring her back from the madness. She remembered the love the two shared.

Enala shut her eyes. She had nothing and nobody left in this world, but Eric had someone who loved him, a future after all this. She could not bear to watch him die.

Gritting her teeth, she squinted through the smoke, searching for something, anything. Her eyes swept the burning courtyard, catching on the Sword of Light. But the Sword was no good to them now—the Light did not encompass healing powers.

Then Enala noticed the dark sheen of the *Soul Blades*. Somehow they had survived the conflagration unleashed by the Sword of Light. They lay in the rubble, discarded. The green glow of Antonia's sword danced in her eyes, drawing her in.

Antonia was the Goddess of the Earth, and the *Soul Blade* held all the power that entailed. Enala vaguely remembered the little Goddess, from when she had retreated into a catatonic state. Earth magic could heal—Antonia had healed them all on that dark beach so long ago.

Summoning the last dredges of her strength, Enala started to crawl again. The *Soul Blades* were close, but the distance could have been miles for all it mattered to her. She was dying. She could feel the last of her life bubbling from her chest, strangling her every gasp. Agony swept through her body, but she persevered.

Reaching out, Enala wrapped her fingers around the leather pommel of the *Soul Blade*.

Antonia, help us! she screamed in the confines of her mind.

There was no answer, only the gentle ebb and flow of light from the sword.

"Please, Antonia," she whispered, fading fast. "*Help us.*"

Still nothing happened. A sob tore through Enala. She struggled for another breath, but found herself choking, drowning. Tears poured from her eyes as she strained for one last mouthful of air. Heat radiated at her back and the air shimmered, the fire coming closer. Even so, a cold was spreading through her limbs. She could no longer feel her legs.

Enala clutched the *Soul Blade* tighter, dragging it across the tiles. The Goddess was right there, so close, so powerful, yet it seemed she was helpless to aid them.

In desperation, Enala reach out with her mind, the way Eric had explained while they meditated. Darkness blurred the edges of her vision, the light fading from her eyes. With a final push, she reached outwards, seeking the Goddess.

Enala felt the last sensation of her body fall away. She drifted up into the air, floating aimlessly.

Is this death? she wondered.

Yet there was the *Soul Blade*, glowing with a brilliant green light edged with black. Trapped within was the one being who could save them. Dead or not, Enala had to try. Staring at the sword, she stretched out an arm. Her spirit fingers sank into the cool metal and she dove deeper, throwing caution aside in her desperation to reach the Goddess.

Antonia, help us! Her cry rang out across the spirit plane. *Please!*

Enala shivered as a force rose at her words, brushing against her soul. At its touch, she was flung back from the blade. Crashing into her body, sparks flew across her vision. The pain returned, and the desperate need for air.

Then a gentle warmth blossomed around Enala, spreading from the arm that still clutched the *Soul Blade*. A light grew around her, expanding to encompass Eric, until they were both surrounded by a dome of energy. Its power bathed their broken bodies, seeping deep into their skin, seeking out the wounds within.

The burning at Enala's wrists faded away. She glanced down to see the red rings vanish, disappearing without so much as a scar. Sucking in a breath, air rushed into her lungs, sending strength flooding back to her muscles. The gurgling died to a tremor as the liquid fled before the magic. The pain from her chest came last, falling away until only a dull ache remained. Slowly, that too began to fade.

Reaching up, Enala wiped tears from her eyes. She looked across at Eric, witnessing the magic's touch there too. The wound in his stomach healed before her eyes, the skin knotting itself together as though stitched by an invisible hand.

The magic was working. She could feel its power, thrumming through her blood.

Eric opened his eyes and looked at her, wonder on his face. She smiled back, then coughed in the acrid smoke. But it was nothing now, compared with the slow, creeping suffocation of a few moments ago.

"Antonia?" he asked.

Enala shook her head. "I don't know."

Then, deep inside, Enala felt something go horribly wrong.

———

ERIC COULD NOT BRING HIMSELF TO BELIEVE WHAT HE WAS feeling. Magic surged around him, powerful and healing, its touch so familiar he would have recognised it anywhere. The Goddess, Antonia, had returned.

Opening his eyes, he saw Enala staring at him. She wore a sad smile on her face, but he could see the worst of her wounds had already healed.

"Antonia?" he asked.

"I don't know."

Enala shook her head, and then her eyes widened. A tremor shook her, her body convulsing against the hard tiles. She stiffened, and he saw her fingers were wrapped tight about the *Soul Blade*. Energy crackled along the steel, flickering in sparks and bursts, shooting up into the dome surrounding them.

With a whoosh the magic went out, vanishing back into the blade, leaving them alone in the burning temple.

Eric pulled himself into a sitting position as Enala rose, Antonia's *Soul Blade* still clutched in her hands. Her wounds had healed—not a scratch remained on her—but Eric could sense a wrongness about her, a difference. She stood stiff and straight, her movements disjoined, like a puppet on strings.

Putting his arms beneath him, Eric stumbled to his feet. Standing opposite Enala, his sister, he stared hard into her sapphire eyes. Except now he saw they were no longer blue, but a deep, emerald green.

"Enala?" he whispered.

A tremor went through her as he spoke her name. Her face twisted, as though in pain, and he saw a flash of blue rise from the depths of her eyes.

"Eri–" Enala croaked, cutting herself off.

The green returned stronger than ever, glowing with some internal power. The shivering ceased. She stood straight as a pin, staring at Eric as though he were the strangest of creatures.

"Enala?" he tried again.

There was no tremor this time. Enala tipped her head to the side, watching him with detached curiosity. She did not speak. The light in her eyes brightened, the green flickering across her pale skin and mixing with the flames.

"Enala, what's happening?" he stepped towards her.

"Stop," Enala spoke, the word coming out as a crackling, metallic shriek.

She raised her arm and pointed the *Soul Blade* at Eric's chest. Green light flashed. Plants burst from the tiles between them. Saplings sprang from the earth, growing to great redwoods in the time it took Eric to retreat a step. Vines curled their way up the massive trunks and dense shrubbery spread across the temple floor, smothering the flames in a sea of green.

Enala laughed, a harsh, soulless shriek like the grinding of metal on stone. The sound rattled through the forest, sending a shiver to the depths of Eric's soul.

"Enala, please! Something's wrong, this is not you! It's the *Soul Blade*, you have to fight it, to stop it before it destroys you!"

The *Soul Blade* crackled, blinding him with its light. The laughter came again, grating in his ears. The forest trembled and groaned as the tree trunks bent towards him.

Enala stood amidst it all, bathed in the power of the Goddess, a dark look of torment cast across her face.

She stared at Eric. "Don't look for me."

Then she vanished into the forest.

———

FIND OUT WHAT HAPPENS NEXT IN SOUL BLADE AND DON'T forget to leave a review if you enjoyed the story.

NOTE FROM THE AUTHOR

Thank you for reading Firestorm, I hope you're enjoying the adventure so far! As the second instalment of the trilogy, the stakes have been upped and things are growing desperate in the Three Nations. As things now stand, Eric and his companions have had a few victories, but without the Gods, the battle is on to stop Archon's advance.

As always, reader feedback is a huge part of its continued success, and all reviews would be very much appreciated for Firestorm.

FOLLOW AARON HODGES
Join Aaron Hodges on his newsletter to r**eceive TWO FREE novels and a short story!**
https://aaronhodgesauthor.com/newsletter

ALSO BY AARON HODGES

The Sword of Light

Book 1: Stormwielder

Book 2: Firestorm

Book 3: Soul Blade

The Legend of the Gods

Book 1: Oathbreaker

Book 2: Shield of Winter

Book 3: Dawn of War

The Knights of Alana

Book 1: Daughter of Fate

Book 2: Queen of Vengeance

Book 3: Crown of Chaos

The Evolution Gene

Book 1: Reborn

Book 2: Havoc

Book 3: Carnage

Descendants of the Fall

Book 1: Warbringer

Book 2: Wrath of the Forgotten

Book 3: Age of Gods

Book 4: Dreams of Fury

The Alfurian Chronicles

Book 1: Defiant

Book 2: Guardian

Book 3: Conquest

The Swords of Heaven and Hell

Book 1: Darkstrider

The Four Circles

Book 1: Help! My Wizard Mentor Had A Heart Attack And Now
I'm Being Chased By A Horde Of Giant Spiders!

The Untamed Isles

The Path Awakens